MARK ROBERTS

KILLING TIME

HEAD
of ZEUS

First published in the UK in 2018 by Head of Zeus Ltd

9 7 5 3 1 2 4 6 8

A catalogue record for this book is available from
the British Library.

ISBN (HB): 9781786695093
ISBN (ANZTPB): 9781786695109
ISBN (E): 9781786695086

Typeset by Adrian McLaughlin

Printed and bound in Great Britain by
CPI Group (UK) Ltd, Croydon CR0 4YY

MIX
Paper from
responsible sources
FSC® C013604

Head of Zeus Ltd
First Floor East
5–8 Hardwick Street
London EC1R 4RG

WWW.HEADOFZEUS.COM

For Edna
who gave me the two greatest gifts ever

Liverpool and Merseyside

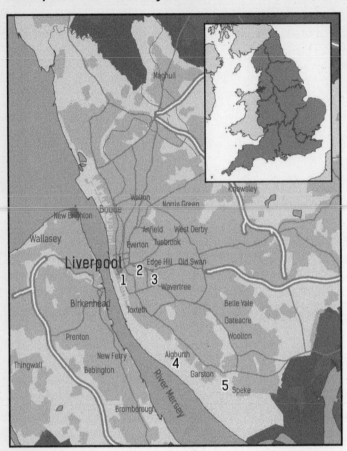

1. Merseyside Police HQ

2. University of Liverpool

3. St Michael's Care Home

4. Eve Clay's house, Mersey Road

5. Trinity Road Police Station

Liverpool City Centre

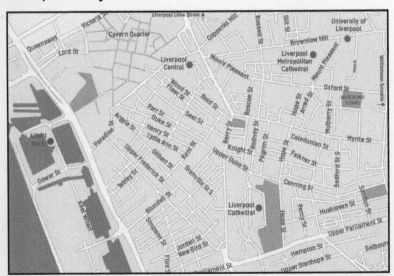

October 1987

Prologue

'What's going on, Sister Ruth?' asked Eve Clay, at the door of Mrs Tripp's office. Behind the door, unfamiliar adult voices mingled with Mrs Tripp's and there was much laughter, but it sounded forced and unreal to Eve's ears.

'You know what it's like here in St Michael's, Eve.' Sister Ruth's voice dropped to soft and confidential and she stooped to Eve's eye line. 'All kinds of rumours and stories are flying round the home, and if it's not the kids spreading them, it's the adults.'

'Who's in there with Mrs Tripp?' Eve recalled the flash BMW parked outside St Michael's Catholic Care Home for Children, and she could smell the smoke from an expensive cigar behind the door.

'People who wish to meet you.'

'Come in with me, Sister?'

'I can't go in with you. Mrs Tripp refused me point blank. But I'll be with you...' she kissed Eve on her head '... in there. Listen to me, Eve. I've known you on and off since you were three, when we were both in St Claire's. Whatever gets said in there, you must swear to me on Sister Philomena's memory you'll stick to your guns and only say *Yes* if it's what you really want. Don't say *Yes* to anything you don't want.'

'I swear on Sister Philomena's memory, I won't say *Yes* to anything I don't want.'

Sister Ruth wrapped her arms around Eve and gave her the fiercest hug she could remember.

'You're crying, Sister Ruth. Why are you crying?'

'I'm not crying, Eve. I've got a cold. Get in there and imagine me and Sister Philomena standing right beside you.'

Eve knocked on the door and the voices in Mrs Tripp's office fell silent.

'Come in!' said Mrs Tripp, her normally tart voice infused with saccharine.

Eve opened the door and, stepping inside, looked through a light haze of smoke at Mrs Tripp and three adults she had never seen before. Mrs Tripp sat on a hard-backed chair. Facing her was a woman in between two men. All eyes were on Eve.

Mrs Tripp patted the empty chair beside her. 'Eve, come and sit next to me, sweetheart.'

Bloody hell! thought Eve, walking towards the group. *Sweetheart?*

Eve picked up the chair next to Mrs Tripp and moved it away from the boss of the children's home and positioned it at an angle slightly away from the adults.

She weighed up the strangers. The elegant, well-dressed blonde in her forties sat between two men in suits: a fat bald man to her left, smoking a cigar, and a sombre bloke who looked like he had never laughed in his fifty-odd years.

'I see you support Everton, Eve,' said the blonde woman.

She looked down at her Everton top and said, '*Nil satis nisi optimum.*' A ripple of approval drifted across the visitors. 'It's Everton's motto and it happens to be totally true. Nothing but the best will do.'

The blonde woman and the fat bloke laughed, and even sober-sides cracked the briefest smile.

Eve turned her attention to Mrs Tripp. 'It seems these people know who I am, but I don't know who they are. Isn't it time you made with a few introductions?'

Mrs Tripp laughed and said, 'You're incorrigible, aren't you,

Eve?' There was a sudden gear change in her voice as she said, 'This lady is Amanda Ryan. And the gentleman to her left is Mr Dove... and to the right is Mr Mann.'

'Thank you, Mrs Tripp,' said Amanda Ryan. 'Eve, how old are you?'

'Nine. How old are you, Amanda?'

'How long have you been in St Michael's Catholic Care Home for Children?'

'I came here in October '84 when I was six.'

'And before that?'

'I lived in St Claire's with Sister Philomena. And Sister Ruth. Sister Ruth was her friend and helper.'

'So you've always lived in institutions?'

'No. Sister Philomena didn't give birth to me, but she was better than a mother to me until the day she died. It's unfair to her memory to say I was institutionalised when I was with her. I'm not having that, Amanda. Sorry.'

Fat Mr Dove puffed on his cigar, nodded and looked impressed.

'Eve,' said Amanda. 'I didn't mean to disrespect Sister Philomena's memory. I'm sorry.'

'Apology accepted, Amanda. So why are you here? And why do you want to talk to me?'

'I want to show you something.'

As Mr Mann handed Eve a brown A4 envelope, he said, 'Open it!'

Eve took out a set of colour photographs. The top picture was of the back of a large detached house with a tennis court and an outdoor swimming pool. She slid this to the bottom of the pile and looked at the next photograph, of a large girl's bedroom with a TV, Hi-Fi and a wardrobe big enough for dozens of outfits. The next picture was of a huge bathroom with a jacuzzi and a sauna room.

Eve put the three pictures back in the envelope along with the ones she didn't look at. 'Is that your house, Amanda?' She handed the envelope to Mrs Tripp.

'Yes. Let me explain who we are. Mr Mann is my lawyer and Mr Dove is a social worker who specialises in caring for families, and children in particular.'

'Why are you here?'

'Because I want to adopt you, Eve.'

Eve felt as if all the air had suddenly been sucked out of her lungs and her skeleton turned to jelly. By a huge effort of will, she caught her breath and straightened up as best she could.

'You want to adopt *me*? Why?'

Mr Mann picked up his briefcase and took out a set of papers and a fountain pen.

Amanda smiled. 'I'm heavily involved in working for children's charities across Merseyside and the northwest of England. Your name started cropping up around the time you moved from St Claire's to St Michael's. You are a very well-known and much discussed young lady. I took a huge interest in you and spent time and money finding out all about you. Your spirit and feistiness are legendary. Your spirit walked into the room ahead of you. And I like that. Mr Mann?'

He cleared his throat.

'We didn't just rely on hearsay,' said Mr Mann. 'Miss Ryan did extensive research into finding out what sort of a child you really are. She spoke to many people and they all had a variety of positive things to say about you. But one word, one word, came up in every interview. Stubborn. My client, Miss Ryan, has a lot invested emotionally in this project. We have an offer to make to you...'

Eve turned to Mrs Tripp. 'What did I say to you, when I was six, when I first came into this office in October 1984?'

'Hear them out, Eve!' She smiled but her teeth were clamped.

'The paperwork is in place and finalised,' said Mr Mann. 'Miss Ryan wants to adopt you.'

Eve looked directly at Amanda Ryan.

'But the offer comes with a condition,' continued Mr Mann.

'Amanda, it doesn't matter what people say I am. Why didn't you take me out for a day? Get to know me for yourself?'

'I have every confidence that this can be a successful adoption because…'

'Have you got kids of your own?'

'No.'

'A husband?'

'No.'

'Too much information, Amanda,' said Mr Mann.

'Are we related by blood?'

'You could have an incredible life with Amanda, Eve,' piped up Mrs Tripp.

'Are we related by blood, Amanda? Yes or no?'

'No.'

Eve got to her feet and turned to Mrs Tripp. 'I told you when I was six years old, the first time I was in your office – you bring me my birth mother or father to take me away or I'm staying in care until I'm eighteen. Amanda is not my birth mother, is she? Amanda is not my blood relative, is she?'

The air was thick with unpleasant silence and when Eve looked at Amanda she was crying silently. Eve marched to Mrs Tripp's desk, snatched up a handful of tissues from a box and gave them to Amanda. She stood facing the four adults with her arms folded.

'If you sign the contract,' said Mr Mann, 'within a matter of days, you will be living with Amanda as her daughter. When you are eighteen, you will come in to a vast amount of money. The world will be yours, Eve,' Mr Mann insisted. 'My client will make a large donation every year to St Michael's…'

Eve glowered at Mrs Tripp. 'Will she now?'

'For the benefit of all the children, all your friends, we're talking big holidays, season tickets for Everton and Liverpool…'

'You're talking nonsense, Mr Mann, or you might as well be…'

'Eve, if you sign,' said Amanda, through her tears, 'I can make you the happiest girl in the world and you can make me the happiest woman.'

'Amanda, let's clear the room and we can have a heart-to-heart, you and me, about what's going on here. It's... bizarre.'

Amanda opened her mouth to speak but Mr Mann put his hand on her arm.

'I can't... until you sign. If you refuse, Eve,' said Amanda, 'I'll walk through that door and you'll never hear from me or see me again. It's a once-in-a-lifetime offer! Do you know, I am friends with a lot of Everton players' wives and girlfriends. I can get you to meet them.'

Eve scanned the serious faces around her, all eyes pinned on her. She counted to ten and said, 'Give me the paper and pen, Mr Mann.'

'This is a good decision, Eve,' said Amanda. 'You won't regret it, I promise you, darling. I'll get a box for you at Goodison Park, take you to all the away games.'

Eve took the papers to Mrs Tripp's desk.

'I need three signatures where I've pencilled in an X,' said Mr Mann.

Eve wrote in her best handwriting against the three crosses.

'Thank you, Eve,' said Amanda. 'Thank you, you won't regret it.'

She handed the paperwork back to Mr Mann whose smiling face quickly fell to a place between puzzlement and anger as she stared him down.

'Who in the name of God,' asked Mr Fat Mann, 'is Neville Southall?'

'He's Everton's goalkeeper.'

'What's going on?' asked Amanda, as Eve walked to the door.

She stopped and turned. 'I couldn't live with you, Amanda. You might have all the tea in China but you're downright strange. You think you can buy me like I was a puppy in a pet shop. *It's a once-in-a-lifetime offer?* Well, no.' Eve opened the door. '*Nil satis nisi optimum!*'

She slammed the door shut and, seeing Sister Ruth along the corridor, felt a huge wave of relief.

'Amanda Ryan just tried to buy me.'

Behind Mrs Tripp's door, voices were rising.

'I didn't know. I've heard so many things. If I'd been certain of what was coming, I'd have warned you.'

They walked towards the stairs, away from Mrs Tripp and her visitors.

'I think I know what your answer was, Eve.'

'Mrs Tripp isn't getting rid of me that easily.'

As they walked down the stairs, Sister Ruth placed her hand on Eve's shoulder.

'I haven't got a price and I never will have.' She kissed the badge on her Everton shirt. '*Nil satis nisi optimum*. Nothing but the best will do.'

Day One

Thursday, 1st December 2020

Chapter 1

8.51 am

'Wishful thinking never turned maybe into a fact,' said Detective Inspector Eve Clay, blood banging in her ears as her car bounced over another speed bump on Queens Drive.

'The woman who found Marta said it was definitely her.' Detective Sergeant Gina Riley's voice rose from Clay's hands-free iPhone on the dashboard.

'It feels too good to be true. This is the eighth day the kid's been missing. By the usual reckoning, Marta Ondřej should be dead and buried.'

Clay accelerated towards the railway bridge on Queens Drive.

'Maybe, but the woman who put the call in to switchboard said it's Marta, said she recognised her from the picture we plastered over the media and internet.'

Driving under the bridge, a train roared above Clay's head. She pressed her foot down on the accelerator, rising from sixty to seventy miles per hour, weaving between two lines of traffic, one heading towards the schools close to Sefton Park and the other heading towards the north end of the city.

On the corner of Queens Drive and Allerton Road, she turned her siren on. In her head, Clay converted the last few minutes into a coherent sequence of events.

'Stay on the line, Gina,' said Clay. 'My mind's racing.'

The call from switchboard had come as she dropped her four-

year-old son Philip off at St Swithin's Catholic Primary School.
Marta Ondřej had been discovered in Wavertree Mystery Park.

As she passed through the red light at Penny Lane, two lines of city-bound traffic parted to the left and right to make a channel for her as she raced towards the junction of Smithdown Road and Grant Avenue. Drivers stuck at the red light there edged forward nervously and she was forced to slow down to make it through safely.

Marta's face – the image Clay had circulated from the child's passport photograph following her disappearance and abduction – filled her mind: fourteen years of age, thick dark hair, olive skin, large brown unsmiling eyes, and a distinct air of vulnerability. Clay wondered with mounting dread what had happened to her in the eight days since she had gone missing.

An oncoming bus squealed to a sudden halt as Clay turned sharply into Grant Avenue and saw the black railings of the Wavertree Mystery Park. She slowed down and examined the green space behind the black railings, vast and empty and swathed in mist.

'Jesus wept,' said Riley. 'Are you OK?'

Clay had left Philip at the doors of the infant department with his reception teacher's classroom assistant, explained it was an emergency...

'I think I can see someone, Gina, but I can't tell from here if they're male or female. Call the translator, please.'

'Translator's already on her way. Kate Nowak.'

Good, thought Clay. The translator they'd used since the day of Marta's disappearance was efficient and discreet.

'See you there,' said Riley.

Clay turned off her siren and parked on the pavement alongside a gate into the wide-open park. Out of the corner of her eye she saw a brown robe, head-dress and sandals on the back seat: the costume her son was supposed to wear for the rehearsal of the nativity play today. He was Joseph, but she'd forgotten to hand it over to him as she dropped him off.

Frosted grass crunched like breaking glass beneath Clay's feet as she sprinted in the direction of the lone figure. A gang of seagulls erupted into the air as she hurried into their space and, with each step nearer, Clay saw the figure shift from its feet to its knees.

It placed its hands in front of itself, pressed its face into the earth and appeared to be eating snow and ice.

Sirens advanced from three directions and cold air overwhelmed her senses as the figure beyond her breath became a small, thin female. The black anorak, green skirt and black ankle boots that she had been dressed in on the day of her disappearance had been replaced by a pair of pyjamas.

She lifted her face from the snow and smacked her lips.

The girl's thick black hair was gone and her head was covered with rough patches of stubble. Clay's heart sank further when she read deadness in the girl's face and a mesmerised glaze in her eyes. *You look like you've just come out of a concentration camp*, thought Clay, sickness hitting her hard at the core.

It was Marta Ondřej, a child Clay believed she would never see alive.

Clay slowed down and stopped, maintaining a distance from the child. A wave of pure relief swept through her as, double-checking the face, she confirmed to herself that she was metres away from the missing girl they'd been searching for.

'Marta,' said Clay with kindness, as she edged closer, her hands held up in semi-surrender. 'Marta Ondřej.'

Her mother had confirmed that her daughter had almost no English.

'Marta.' Clay smiled as she stooped down.

Slowly, Marta stood up and turned her back on Clay.

As she walked around Marta, Clay held out her hands and summoned up all her strength to smile. 'Marta? Marta Ondřej? It's OK, Marta. I'm a policewoman.'

Clay recalled the second statement that Marta's mother had made about her daughter. *Marta is simple, a retard, not full in the head. She is fourteen in years but four in the head. She is a child.*

She indicated herself, smiled and spoke the words of Czech she had learned for this eventuality. *'Policistka.'*

She checked Marta's features against the photograph that had been circulated within hours of her abduction. The child shivered in the morning cold and continued to look through Clay in silence. Marta turned her head slightly at the sound of footsteps heading towards her, then looked round at Clay with terror.

'Keep back!' said Clay.

Detective Sergeant Karl Stone and Detective Sergeant Gina Riley stopped at a short distance. Clay looked down at the child's fists, clenched at the sides of her body, and saw a silver foil at her feet.

'Eve?' Riley whispered through the mist. 'Central switchboard has the mobile number of the woman who found Marta and called 999. But she's switched her phone off.'

'Do we have a name for her yet?' asked Clay, reaching a hand out towards Marta, imagining her own son in a foreign country, abducted and missing for a week and approached by the police. 'Please don't be frightened, Marta. Please, Marta.'

The child held out her left hand, touched Clay's fingers.

'The caller's name is Lucy Bell. No one by that name's known to us in Merseyside. There are some on the National Police Computer. That's all we've got for now. We're tracking her down via O2, her mobile service provider.'

'What the hell was *Lucy* thinking of?' asked Clay, bottling the anger and frustration inside her, digging deep to glaze her voice with as much sweetness as she could muster. 'OK, Marta?' She smiled and covered the girl's frozen hands with her own. *She waltzes off,* thought Clay, *leaving you unattended.*

'Lucy?' Clay directed the question at Marta.

Marta didn't react. DS Stone picked up the foil and placed it into a small evidence bag.

Did Lucy give you chocolate? thought Clay, looking at the distance to the shops on Smithdown Road, and deducing that if Lucy Bell had given chocolate to Marta she'd had it on her.

An ambulance turned the corner from the Picton Sports Arena and travelled across the grass towards them, the siren stopping as it drew closer.

'Want me to go with Marta, Eve?' asked Riley.

'Please, Gina,' replied Clay. 'Call Kate and tell her to meet you at Alder Hey in the Park.'

'How long do you want me to stay with her?'

'Until she talks.'

Riley presented herself to Marta and smiled, 'It's OK, love, I'm a policewoman. Look!' She showed Marta her warrant card. 'Policewoman.'

'*Policie Žena,*' confirmed Clay.

Marta's face creased into a mask of fathomless sorrow and her eyes filled up with tears.

As the ambulance slowed to a halt, Riley placed an arm around Marta and held her closer to her side. Clay took a discreet series of pictures: shaven-headed face full on; a whole picture of her front; head to toe; her profile as she turned; the back of her head as she walked with Riley towards the ambulance; a head-to-toe view from the back.

'Come on, Marta,' said Riley. She found the girl's hand and folded her fingers around hers. 'My goodness, I can feel your ribs poking out.'

Clay noticed the way Marta walked, her feet flipping up as if she had to think through the process, step by painful step. Taking a deep breath, she composed a brief email to Detective Sergeant Barney Cole, the team's anchor man in the incident room at Trinity Road Police Station, and fired it off with a boulder-like heart.

In her hand, Clay's phone rang out; she saw it was from Detective Sergeant Bill Hendricks.

'Where are you, Bill?' asked Clay.

'It's shaping up to be one of those days, Eve. I was on my way over to the Mystery when I got a call from switchboard. I'm on my way to 682 Picton Road. It looks like an arson attack. The woman who reported it said there were two men living in the flat.'

'I'll meet you there,' said Clay, running back to her car, an invisible vice tightening around her skull as a vision formed of a child-abducting monster whose cruelty knew no bounds.

Chapter 2

9.14 am

In the incident room at Trinity Road Police Station, Detective Constable Barney Cole stood up from his desk and walked to the large plate-glass window, feeling that the muscles in his buttocks were about to spasm into cramp after long days sitting in front of his laptop and waiting for the phone to ring with some *good news*.

In spite of a massive campaign in the media for public help, there hadn't been a single sighting of Marta. A dedicated team had looked at hours of CCTV footage within a one-mile radius of Marta's house, and not one image of her had emerged. A bitter conclusion had been reached and generally accepted: the perpetrator or perpetrators were wise to the CCTV in the neighbourhood.

Cole recalled his first visit to Marta's house, accompanied by Kate Nowak, and his conversation with the girl's mother, Verka. Just over three weeks after landing in England from the Czech Republic with her mother, Marta walked out of the shared house on Smithdown Lane that she had lived in since she'd arrived in Liverpool. Of her seven Roma Czech housemates, three were women, two were men and two were children under the age of ten. All had been quickly ruled out as suspects in the abduction case, their rage and sorrow at Marta's abduction as genuine as their unshakeable alibis.

Waking up from a catnap that had turned into a two-hour sleep, Verka Ondřej had reported her fourteen-year-old daughter missing at Admiral Street police station, twenty metres away from her home at 101 Smithdown Lane.

Cole turned his back on the mocking fog and went back to his desk where he remained on his feet, and called up the slide show on his laptop of the three available images of Marta supplied by her mother.

Marta the new-born baby, wrapped in a white blanket with several holes in it, her face the only part of her body visible, brown eyes as large as saucers set in soft and perfect olive skin.

In the next image, Marta, aged three, was walking down a road in a village that looked like it had come through the fiercest battle in a medieval war of attrition.

Not for the first time, Cole did the maths, and rechecked his sums on deprivation. The picture was from 2009. The toddler-sized Manchester United top and shirt looked fifth-hand and was the Red Devils' official home kit in the 2001–2002 season, making Marta a child born at the bottom of a barrel.

As he paused on her passport photograph, Cole heard the incident room door open and looked up as Detective Constable Clive Winters entered the room.

'How was your leave in the Lakes?' asked Cole.

'Great food, shit weather. Wrong time of year to go but Mae insisted. It was her fortieth, after all, so I just said *Yeah*.' Winters fell silent, the smile on his face fading. 'What's up, Barney?'

'Marta Ondřej.'

'I just heard. Brilliant news. She was found alive.'

'That's the good news.'

'What's the bad?'

'We don't know what's happened to her in the last eight days.'

'Where is she?' asked Winters.

'She's on her way to Alder Hey with Gina Riley.'

'Gina's great with kids. She's in the best hands, Barney.'

'I know that. Eve emailed me from the Mystery. She wrote, *She's silent and traumatised. I fear the worst.* I phoned Eve and asked for clarification.'

Winters pulled up a chair and asked, 'What did she say?'

'Eve said they shaved her head and dressed her up like she's just come out of Dachau. She's pretty certain there were racial dimensions to the abduction, so she's asked all the duty superintendents to put out an instruction. Any reports of racially motivated violence on Merseyside get reported back to me.' Cole shook his head and remembered a second visit to Marta's home to show solidarity to her mother Verka, in spite of the frustrating news that there was no sign of Marta.

'Are we still searching the Williamson Tunnels?' asked Winters. 'There are loads of ways in for a nosey kid.'

'We called our subterranean search off – manpower issue. But both Williamson Societies have got volunteers down there as we speak. Shit!'

'What?'

'I have to tell them to stop searching. Marta's mother was sure she wasn't down there – she doesn't like enclosed spaces and is scared crazy of the dark, but we had to search just in case. Given the complete lack of CCTV sightings, it seemed like a possibility.'

On his desk, Cole heard the ping of an incoming email, picked up his iPhone and saw there were images attached to the incoming message. *Barney, please circulate the attached images of Marta Ondřej to the whole team. Eve.*

Cole opened the first image and again muttered, 'Shit!'

Winters moved to Cole's side and looked over his shoulder at a close-up of Marta's head and face, her scalp littered with rough patches of stubble.

'Why would they do such a thing?' asked Winters.

Cole moved to the next image, a full shot of Marta, head to toe. In profile, Marta's face had an air of defeat that made Cole recall his own teenage sons, smiling past themselves because being alive was such a wonderful thing, and he hoped that they'd never have cause to look as forlorn as this girl.

Beneath the stubble on the back of her head, there were natural bumps and hollows that gave her skull the appearance of an alien planet created by a sick and twisted god.

Taking a deep breath, he sent the images to the whole team.

Cole felt the weight of Winters's hands as he patted him on either shoulder.

'Come on, mate,' said Winters. 'She's still alive, right?'

'Right,' said Cole, with as much positivity as he could muster. 'Where there's life there's hope and all that jazz, eh?'

Chapter 3

9.15 am

Clay looked up and down Picton Road, from the sealed-off end at the junction of Rathbone Road and Wellington Road to the Picton Clock Tower at the other. An airplane sobbed above her, and the noise drew her attention to the open window on the first floor of the Polish delicatessen. The deadness of the blackened glass made her shudder.

She scanned the shop fronts stretching away from the delicatessen and saw a single CCTV mounted above a mini-market, pointing directly at her.

Footsteps approached, and DS Karl Stone walked towards her.

'What's happening?' asked Clay.

'Mr Zięba, the deli owner, is at the crime tape by the clock tower. He confirmed to me that the flat above the deli is his property and that the people who live in it are his tenants. He understands that he can't cross the line but he's understandably rattled. I've got his full contact details.'

'Karl, tell him he'll be the first civilian to come back into Picton Road when we're done here and we're working hard to make that sooner rather than later. Go back and ask him about his tenants and see if you can get him to spill the beans on them, please.'

'Anything else?'

'There's one CCTV camera working in our favour.' She pointed. 'Track down the owner of the mini-market and pull all the footage from the last twenty-four hours. Send anything from it to Barney Cole and ask him to get Sergeant Carol White to drop what she's doing and focus on what that camera comes up with.'

As Clay walked to the back of the stationary fire appliance, a pair of firefighters stepped out of the narrow front doorway leading to the flat above the deli.

'Eve?'

She recognised the voice: Steve Doyle, a senior firefighter, who beckoned the two scouts towards him.

'Beat me to it, did you, Steve?'

Steve Doyle indicated the fire appliance. 'When it comes to clearing traffic...'

'Yours is bigger than mine. I know, you've told me many, many times.'

As the firefighters walked towards them, they lifted their visors and Clay was surprised at the contrast between the youth of the woman and the maturity of the man: two people at opposite ends of the career spectrum.

'Thank you,' said Doyle. 'Thank you for going in.'

Clay saw the distress on both their faces, the sweat in their hair and on their foreheads. She showed them her warrant card.

'Was the window open when you went into the building?' she asked.

'I opened it,' said the man. 'The fire's burned out. It's contained to one room, the room with the open window. It's a bedroom.

There are two bodies in there. There's also a kitchen, a bathroom and a box room. No other bodies in those rooms. There's some evidence of graffiti on the wall of the bedroom. It looks like whoever's killed these people has tried to burn out any evidence leading back to them.'

'What's your hunch on the fire accelerant?' asked Doyle.

'Petrol,' said the young female firefighter. 'But we won't know for sure until the fire investigator has a chance to look inside.'

'Are you sure it was murder?' asked Clay. 'Not a case of joint suicide or an accident?'

'Wait until you go inside,' said the woman. 'It's so strange. You'll see how the bodies have been arranged.'

Clay nodded and said, 'Thank you for that.' She focused on Doyle. 'How long before I can go in?'

He pointed at a firefighter setting up a large red fan in the main doorway to the flat and replied, 'Once there's a channel of air running through the building and I've filled in the incident hand-over form, you're in charge, Eve, but we need to make absolutely sure that it's safe for you to go in first.'

Clay looked around and noticed a tall, dark-haired woman standing on the pavement four doors down, staring into space.

'Is she our 999 caller?' asked Clay

'Yes,' said Doyle. 'Her name's Aneta Kaloza. She's Polish.'

Clay heard the chopping of the silver blades inside the red fan's cage.

'Does she speak English?'

'Fluent.'

As if alerted by some primal instinct that she was being discussed, Aneta drifted out of the daydream and looked across at them.

'She knows the blokes who lived in the flat above the deli,' said Doyle. 'They're her friends.'

'Aneta?' said Clay, keeping eye contact with the woman as she approached her. Attractive and in her early thirties, she carried a leather holdall; beneath her smart black coat, she was dressed casually in jeans and trainers. 'I've heard they were your friends?' Clay spoke softly, seeing the woman was trying hard not to crack.

'Are they dead?' There was hardly a trace of accent and her voice was strong, in spite of the massive pain that registered in her eyes.

'There are two bodies in the flat. It's been burned out. I'm sorry.'

Clay showed Aneta her warrant card and said, 'I'm DCI Eve Clay. I'll be leading the inquiry into what we're pretty certain is a double murder.'

Aneta looked away, as though searching for comfort from the ice and snow that lined the pavement. 'What makes you think it's murder?' she asked.

'A detail. I can't discuss it with you, Aneta. I'm sorry.'

Cold wind blew across Aneta's head and the ends of her neatly bobbed hair shook, releasing an aroma that Clay recognised as an expensive perfume.

'I'd like you to come to my car. So we can talk.'

Aneta looked directly at Clay. 'I want to talk to you, DCI Clay. They're my friends. I'll tell you everything I know. But I'll tell you right now, Karl and Václav Adamczak had no enemies. They were good men – the best.'

Chapter 4

9.20 am

Through the wall that separated the vestry from the church, Father Aaron heard the sound of an old lady walking down the aisle to a pew near the front, her heels clicking against the battered parquet flooring: footsteps that he recognised.

'That'll be Iris, always third to arrive every weekday morning...'

He looked at a statue of the Virgin Mary, dressed from head to foot in white, only her face and feet exposed to the cold air.

'My heart's heavy today, Mary.' He wished that the Virgin would speak to him but all he heard was the movement of his parishioners inside the church. 'I reckon that's three in so far for morning mass, five if you include you and me. Now, if you don't mind, Holy Mother, I need to get dressed for mass.'

In spite of the drab walls of the vestry and all the old brown wooden furniture, the room was brought alive with a row of vivid colours hanging from a tall aluminium clothes rail.

Father Aaron walked to the vestments and admired the colours of the chasubles: red, purple, black, violet and green, ritualistic robes that he had designed himself. He picked up the green chasuble and admired the grasshopper and the cricket, small creatures that were great symbols to him of God's creation. Putting it back, he took the violet chasuble and stole and began to robe himself in the vestments required for the time of year.

'That makes four, Mary, unless one of the three changed places to get out of the draft. No, they're always in the same places. Creatures of habit. Keepers of the faith.'

As Father Aaron dressed himself, he looked at Mary and smiled. Her face and feet were pink and radiant. He looked at her eyes and noted that time may have dimmed the blue light that had once radiated from them, but her gaze was still hypnotic and chaste.

He knelt down on the cushion on the floor at the Virgin Mary's feet. 'This morning, Mary, I bring before you Lucy who is close at hand, I bring before you Kelly-Ann who is so far away, I bring before you Iris and Kate, and Mr Rotherham and all my other parishioners. Be with all of them this day, but mostly Kelly-Ann.'

He stood up and walked around the room to shift the stiffness from his knees.

'Our Father who art in heaven, hallowed be thy name. Thy kingdom come, thy will be done on earth as it is in heaven... And I know what your will is, Holy Father, you made your will clear to the Israelites…' His mind was dancing. 'Just as you made your will clear to Mary and she obeyed you as must I… Make me obedient always to your will, speak your will in my heart and give me the strength to follow Abraham's example and be ever-obedient to you…'

He stopped and listened to the passage of time in the ticking of an old clock.

'Where was I? Give us this day our daily bread and forgive us our trespasses as we…' He looked to Mary for strength. 'As we forgive those who trespass against us. Lead us not into temptation… yes, but deliver us from evil…'

In the top right-hand corner of the mirror, Father Aaron caught sight of an ageing picture of a youthful Jesus, the Sacred Heart, his long flowing hair and neat beard almost blond, his eyes blue like Mary's and his skin pale with a rosy blush on either cheek.

In his head, he finished off the Lord's Prayer. Looking around the vestry, and noting that nothing seemed out of place, he offered up a silent Hail Mary in front of her statue.

'Bless me, Holy Mother.' He bowed and kissed her feet, looking into the eye of the parasitic serpent trapped beneath her toes, a beast destroyed by the power of God and the virtue of the Virgin.

He opened the door into the church, picked up the bell and rang it, a sound that deepened the solemnity in his heart. He heard the creak of pews and bones as his parishioners stood up to welcome him.

Father Aaron walked towards the altar with his hands joined and his heart sealed in sorrow. Standing behind the altar, he faced the congregation of three with a combined age of over two hundred and forty years: Iris at the end of the front pew, left-hand side; Mr Rotherham in the middle of the third pew, left-hand side; and Kate on the very last pew halfway in, right-hand side, close to the church door.

Father Aaron drew a deep breath and said, 'The grace of our

Lord Jesus Christ and the love of God and the fellowship of the Holy Spirit be with all of you.'

In one voice the three answered, 'And also with you.' But their voices were lost in the vastness of the dome above their heads.

Chapter 5

9.20 am

Jack Dare stepped out of the kitchen and into the small garden of the three-bedroomed terraced house he shared with his mother and younger half-brother Raymond, closing the door without making a sound. He stepped across the ice-bound lawn and headed for the domed barbecue on the patio in front of the ragged leylandii at the bottom of the garden.

He carried a black bin bag between the index finger and thumb of his right hand, holding the bag away from his body.

You stupid idiot, thought Jack, looking up at the window of Raymond's room where the blinds were still drawn. He estimated the teenage cretin was no doubt dreaming of the ever-shifting harem of sex slaves who would service his every need when he was running the country.

Jack wiped the snow from the dome of the barbecue and, lifting it, saw that it was dry inside, with a thick dusting of ash dotted with fragments of black coals – a leftover from a summer that felt like years ago. He looked at the tops of the leylandii that ran down the left- and right-hand side of the garden and at the back: a shield of dense green that meant the garden was not overlooked by any of the neighbours.

Not far in the distance, a bus ploughed through the sleet on Park Road and he wished that he was on board, travelling away from the Dingle in the direction of Liverpool John Lennon

Airport, but the reality was he was stuck in the house he'd been born into twenty-three years earlier.

He placed the bag on the icy patio and felt the first flake of a new snow shower landing on his nose. Digging his hands into the bag, Jack pulled out a white firelighter and charcoal briquettes that he'd found under the sink. As he put them inside the barbecue, the smell of smoke from Raymond's clothing drifted from his hands like an old curse.

Rooting through the bag, Jack did a mental inventory. Black North Face padded coat; red socks; blue jeans from George at ASDA; stained boxers; T-shirt decorated with a photo of a virtually naked woman, and a blue Le Coq Sportif tracksuit top.

Jack struck a match and touched the firelighter, then watched as thin ribbons of small blue flame raced down either side of the rectangle.

Too much to be burned in one session, thought Jack, eyes entranced by flame.

He dropped Raymond's socks and boxers onto the fire. A wave of disgust at the dry semen at the front and the skid mark on the back sent his eyes skywards, where the falling snowflakes danced to earth like malevolent shadows.

Jack looked at his younger brother's boxer shorts and was surprised to see a small twig and half a rotted leaf stuck to the elasticated waistband. 'Just *exactly* what did you do last night, Raymond?' he asked.

From his coat pocket, Jack took out a Stanley knife and slashed the stitching around the left armpit of the North Face coat, then set about cutting the garment down into manageable fire-friendly pieces. And his heart turned inside out at what lay ahead.

Jack felt the first stinging of cold in his ears and decided to bag up the partially dissected coat and stash the remaining clothes in the miniscule shed to his immediate left. As he did so, a memory assaulted him from nowhere, of the day he'd come home after being away in the Young Offenders Institution at Altcourse.

He remembered standing in the doorway of Raymond's bedroom for the first time since his arrival.

On the wall facing Raymond's bed was a hand-painted collage of thousands of people packed together in disciplined ranks with beams of white light pouring from the ground to the night sky.

'Did you paint this?' Jack had asked.

'Yeah,' Raymond had replied.

Jack looked closer at the wall, saw that each individual head was represented by a dot of paint, and that the dots around were all different shades of black and grey, to make each person in the crowd stand out. Looking deeper into the picture, Jack saw that to the right of each head there was an upturned diagonal line, a dash of paint.

'What's this, Raymond?' he'd asked, though he already knew the answer.

Silence.

'If you don't know what this is a picture of, why have you taken such time and trouble to paint it on your bedroom wall?'

'I've been doing the Second World War in school. I'm dead interested in it, all of it like. The Nazis. See the picture there, I did it from a photograph that was taken at a rally in Germany before the war, it was called the Nuremberg Rally.' Animation kicked into Raymond's monotonous nasal drone. 'Hitler made this speech, right, and everyone got carried away because it was so brilliant, he had the masses in his hands…'

As Raymond grew more excited, his words turned into a stream of meaningless babble.

It had been a hot day in June with no movement in the warm air. He'd walked to the window and looked out into the garden where his mother was pinning clothes to the washing line. She'd paused and looked up at the window. Jack raised his arm to acknowledge her, and wondered why she had allowed Raymond to put up Nazi imagery in his bedroom.

He turned back to his brother, who half-shrugged his shoulders and said, 'Well…'

'Well?' pressed Jack. 'The Nazis?'

'I'm interested in them.'

'What about your mates?'

'They're interested in them as well.'

Jack had walked to the bedroom door, stopped and pointed at the Nuremberg Rally. 'How long did it take you to paint that?'

'Three months,' replied Raymond, with barely concealed pride.

'You're not *interested* in the Nazis. You're obsessed!'

Jack tossed the bag of Raymond's clothes onto the pile of junk in the shed. As he walked away he saw his mother walking down the garden through the thickening smoke escaping from the burning barbecue.

'What're you doing, Jack?'

'It's Raymond. He's up to something. Again. I know he's heading for big trouble so I'm burning the clothes he wore last night.'

'Jack? You don't know that...'

'I do know that, Mum.' He looked at his mother closely. 'Trust me. You look really sad. What is it?'

'I got a call from the doctor at Broad Oak yesterday. Raymond stopped going to his therapy three months ago. They wanted to know how he was, if he was still alive even.'

Jack drank in the distress in his mother's eyes. 'I'll take him to the GP and get Doctor Salah to fix an appointment at Broad Oak. I'll frogmarch him there if necessary.'

'You're a good lad. We can't give up on him.'

Jack kissed his mother on the forehead. 'I can't give up on him, Mum, even though he drives me mad. When he got sick, I wondered if it was me going away that tipped him over the edge.'

'Jack, it wasn't your fault. It's nothing to do with you. Don't torment yourself with shadows.'

'Thanks, Mum. Leave him with me. Do we know if he's been taking his medication?'

They looked at each other in silence.

'I'll deal with that one before I go to work,' said Jack.

'How is Father Aaron?'

'He's good. He's got a few jobs for me to do, cash in hand.'

Jack saw his mother shivering in the cold air.

'Thank God that priest believes in you, Jack.'

'Yeah, he does. I just wish others were like him. Come on, Mum. Let's get indoors. It's freezing out here.'

Chapter 6

9.21 am

In the back of her car, Clay took out her iPhone and showed it to Aneta. 'I'm going to record our conversation, is that OK?'

Aneta nodded.

'How far did you get inside the building?'

Aneta looked out at the front door leading up to the flat.

'Take your time. How close did you get to the room where the fire was?'

'I opened the front door and there was thick smoke on the stairs. I climbed up until I could see the door leading into their flat and smoke was coming out from the gap at the bottom, like the fire was dying. I turned around, walked outside and dialled 999.'

'Why were you there, Aneta?'

Aneta looked at Clay. 'I've got a key to the flat. They pay me to clean twice a week. They're construction workers and they both get up and leave early for work – here, Manchester, St Helens, anywhere and everywhere.'

Aneta looked directly ahead, her brow creasing into a pained frown; Clay wondered if it was from the physical effort of forcing herself not to cry. She took in an Olympic-sized lungful of air and breathed out very slowly.

'Construction workers?' asked Clay.

'Both. Karl was a bricklayer. Václav a joiner.'

The thought chased round Clay's mind. Two physically fit construction workers murdered in the same narrow space? *This isn't the work of an individual*, she concluded.

'On the pavement, I looked up at Karl and Václav's bedroom window and it was jet black like something from a horror movie.' Aneta shook her head. 'But I realised that something was horribly wrong before I even arrived. I saw their van still parked in Wellington Road. It was just after eight o'clock. They're working in the Anfield district at the moment. They should have been long gone. They never miss a day's work, they never have. And they're never, ever late, not for anything, but especially work. When I arrived at the building, I opened the front door leading to the stairs and in the smoke there was another smell. Like cooked meat.'

'They must have trusted you to give you the key to their flat.' Clay offered a thread of comfort.

'We're all from Pruszków. It's not a big city. It's near Warsaw. I went to school with the Adamczak twins.'

'Is there a chance we could be looking at more than just Karl and Václav in the flat?'

As Aneta considered the question, Clay took her in. Although dressed for a cleaning job, her bag and coat and the attention she had put into getting her hair right spoke of a woman who took great pride in her appearance.

'The boys would never have anyone over their doorstep. Except me. Karl used to say, once the front door is closed, the world outside is closed. *To nasz dom.*'

'*To nasz dom?*' asked Clay.

'This is our home. I called 999. And then I called Karl Adamczak on his mobile phone, hoping against hope, but it was turned off. Karl never turns his phone off. He was the go-between for his brother in finding work because he had better English. Then I tried Václav's phone. Off.' Aneta took out her mobile phone, unlocked it and scrolled. 'I waited outside the building for the firefighters to arrive. And the police. And the ambulance, even though... I knew in my heart it was too late.'

She stopped interacting with her phone and asked, 'Would you like to see a picture of my friends?'

'Yes, please,' said Clay.

Aneta handed over her phone, then turned and faced out of the open window.

Clay looked at the picture: two men dressed up in smart jeans, designer shirts open a button too many, the same silver crucifixes nestling on the chests of identical twins out for a night in Liverpool city centre, standing in front of the Pumphouse near the Albert Dock. She saw a human chain made of two identical links: hands on each other's shoulders and bottles of beer in their free hands, smiling as the sun went down behind them on the River Mersey.

'You took this, Aneta?'

'Yes. It was my birthday in July. They take me out. They treat me as a queen.'

'Do you mind if I zoom in on the image?'

'Do whatever you have to do, Detective Clay.'

Clay focused on their faces and saw how handsome and just how identical they were.

She scrolled down the picture and zoomed in on their silver crucifixes – Jesus nailed to a cross. Panning out, their arms were knotted with muscle and they both had powerful V-shaped torsos. The shapes of their thighs were visible through their denim jeans, as if the muscles were straining to get out.

You must have met up, thought Clay, *with someone or some people with considerable power to have attacked you.*

'Aneta?'

The woman looked directly at Clay. Clay saw the onset of tears and the deepening of the knot in her brow.

'Did you see anyone around about here on your way to the flat?'

'Lots of people heading into town for work, and the other way. People waiting for buses, people getting off buses. Picton Road in the rush hour.'

'Can you send this picture and any other pictures you have of your friends to my iPhone?'

She nodded. 'There are many – over twenty, I think.'

'Send them all.'

Clay handed the mobile phone back to Aneta and reeled off eleven digits. 'All the pictures of your friends and pictures of anything in your gallery that relates to them, no matter how small it may seem. Everything you have on Karl, Václav or any of their associates.'

She looked out of the window; DS Bill Hendricks was approaching her car and another firefighter was emerging from the building.

Clay pointed at Hendricks. 'Aneta, he's going to come and sit with you, take your contact details, chat a little bit more.'

'I want to get away from here.'

'Soon enough.'

Clay stepped out onto the pavement and turned her back to the car.

'Bill, Aneta Kaloza. Talk to her. She's our 999 caller. I've got what's happened so far today. I want you to go back and get the wider picture. We need to know who their enemies were. She says they have none. But I'd put my house on it. This has been premeditated and well planned. I'll ask Barney Cole to contact the police in Pruszków to run a background check on them. They're identical twins and jobbing construction workers. Try to get a picture of where they've been working, and if they've had any static on the building sites they've been on.'

As Hendricks got into the car with Aneta, Clay looked up at the blackened window behind which two corpses awaited her, and in a niche in her head an image formed of a tiny silver Jesus on a small silver cross, a tear rolling down his face; and she filled in the silence around him with a blunt observation.

'Jesus wept!'

Chapter 7

10.05 am

At the end of mass, Kate Thorpe remained on her feet at the back pew and watched Father Aaron leave the altar, pausing at the door of the vestry to glance at the back of the church. When his eyes connected with hers, he gave her the smallest of smiles before disappearing inside.

'Morning, Kate,' said Mr Rotherham as he struggled up the left-hand aisle towards the front door of the church. She watched his lips move and raised a hand in acknowledgement, made her way to the altar and saw Iris sitting still in her place on the front pew.

As she came closer, Iris turned to her and said, 'There was one time in my life when I'd taken Holy Communion and I completely felt the presence of the Holy Spirit.'

Kate stopped and read her friend's lips.

'And the Spirit was so strong that my senses played tricks on me. I heard a choir of angels. When the Holy Spirit is in us, powerful and strong, It shows us things that aren't really there, to teach us that there is much more to this world than the things around us. I understand that now after all these years. Father Aaron helped me to understand. He came to my house and he spent two hours explaining everything away. Has he been to your house?'

Kate shook her head.

'I can talk to you about these things because I know you see visions of angels and saints. Oh? Yes, that's what he said, Father

Aaron. *Sometimes, the Devil places visions in our way to confuse us and take us away from Jesus.* But not you, Kate. God has blessed you. I can feel the Holy Spirit around you. Pray for me. Please pray for me.'

As Iris headed to the door, Kate made her way to the chapel of the Virgin Mary on the left of the altar. Passing the communion rail, she recalled receiving communion from Father Aaron ten minutes earlier, and it was this memory on which she intended to meditate.

She dropped a few coins into the slot and, taking a candle, lit it and placed it before the statue of the Virgin Mary. She knelt on the pad and held on to the small lectern, looking the Virgin directly in the eye, and praying silently for the strength and courage that had suddenly and recently deserted her.

Kate closed her eyes and bowed her head.

During communion, Father Aaron had paused in front of her at the rail, and said, *The Body of Christ.* She had mouthed the word, *Amen*, and held out her hands, right supporting the left. She had glanced along the communion rail but Mr Rotherham and Iris were already back in their pews.

Father Aaron had looked her in the eyes as he placed the communion wafer on the palm of her hand. She held his gaze as she took it and placed it on her tongue, *The Body of Christ is in you and so is the Holy Spirit, Kate. Long may it remain so.*

In the chapel, she opened her eyes and had the strangest sense that time had turned inside out and she wasn't sure whether she'd been praying and meditating for minutes or hours. Kate looked to the altar where Father Aaron was watching her, smiling.

'You're one of God's most beloved, Kate. When I gave you communion just now, I too could feel the power of the Holy Spirit around you that Iris constantly speaks of. But more than that, I can feel the grace of Our Lord Jesus Christ coming through you. That makes you a very special woman. Your obedience to the Lord and your unshakeable faith have been rewarded. It is this obedience and faith that has led you to having visions. When God in his infinite wisdom took language and hearing away from you, he replaced it with something much more profound. However, the world is an utterly cynical and mean-minded place. There are millions of people who would love nothing better than to laugh at you because of your gift. I can hear them now. The godless. *Dotty old woman!* The mockers. *Religious nutcase! Let's make a chat room on the Internet and mock her even more.* Kate, I don't ever want you to become a laughing stock. You must protect yourself from the world. Wait until the Lord has completed the cycle of your visions and then I can help you work out the best way to communicate safely about what you have seen.'

Kate got onto her feet and nodded.

'I'm sorry, Kate,' said Father Aaron as he walked beside her up the aisle. 'I know you'd love to stay and pray some more and I'd love for you to spend as much time as you like in this church but I have to lock the front door. There's very little here of material worth, but if I left the door open, someone would come in and steal what little we have.'

In the cold morning air, Kate walked slowly back to the quiet solitude of her home on Grant Avenue, with Father Aaron's words spinning around her brain, and her own words drowning them out.

I know what I saw. I saw what I saw. I saw what I saw and what has been seen cannot be unseen.

Chapter 8

10.06 am

The door of the incident room at Trinity Road Police Station opened and Sergeant Carol White asked, 'You wanted to see me, Barney?'

'Come in, Carol.' He rolled out a seat for her and she smiled as she sat down. 'What are you working on?'

'CCTV from the armed robbery on the jewellers in Liverpool One.'

'Eve wants you to drop that and base yourself up here with me. We're currently harvesting CCTV from the Picton Road scene.'

'The double murder?'

'Yes. This is the thing. I've had a call from the scene. There's one CCTV camera pointing at the entrance to the flat on a wall of a mini-market. It's relatively far away from the flat but if the perpetrators walked or ran away and towards the mini-market, there's a good chance we could get a decent image.'

'Do you want me to look through the footage with a view to seeing anyone entering the flat, Barney?'

Cole noticed the way Sergeant White held on to the base of her third finger, left hand, where there had once been a wedding ring.

'Eventually, yes please, Carol. I've thought this through. Start simple and work our way up and outwards. We'll start with late evening in to the early hours and hope for a hit. That's our best shot. I'm hoping there'll be other footage coming in.'

'I'll go and tell my colleagues on the ground floor.'

As Sergeant White headed out, Cole asked, 'How's your little lad?'

She turned at the door. 'Missing his dad. I'm not. The bastard.'

'I can't begin to imagine how hard things have been for you, Carol. I'm truly sorry.'

'Every time I wake up, it hits me hard like it's the first time over and over again. Still, I console myself with this. It can't be much fun being a disgraced copper on a segregated wing with the sex offenders in Strangeways. I'm sorry to sound so bitter, but I am. Be back soon. I won't mention him to you again.'

Nor will I, thought Cole, as the door closed after her.

Chapter 9

10.10 am

In Alder Hey in the Park Hospital, Detective Sergeant Gina Riley stood in the corner of the curtained-off space in which Marta Ondřej was being examined by an A & E consultant and a young paediatric nurse. The translator Kate Nowak stood at the side of the couch on which Marta lay, holding her hand and feeding her the comfort of her mother language. Each question the consultant asked of Marta was met with the same response. Silence. And what little light was in her eyes sank further and further away.

Suddenly, Marta sat bolt upright and snatched her hand away from Kate. She looked around as if she'd just been reminded of an abominable truth. Her eyes settled on the jug of water to her left.

Hands in the air, she lurched to her right and, picking up the jug, she slurped water from the rim, drinking with wide eyes and mouth and spilling the water down the loose blue NHS gown she had been changed into by the nurse.

When the water was gone, Marta looked inside the hollow vessel and dropped it onto the floor, then flopped back onto the couch.

The consultant turned to Riley and said, 'The initial examination's shown she has no visible signs of abuse. But she's clearly been left short of food and water and is dehydrated. No obvious broken bones, bruising or abrasions.'

Riley looked at the smudge of ink on the girl's left wrist. *It looks like the person who held you captive*, she thought, *drew on you with washable felt pen. Unless you did it to yourself.*

'Kate, could you please ask Marta again who drew on her arm and wrist and what it was?'

'I've asked her that question several times and in as many

different forms as I could think of. I'm sorry. It's like she's deaf.'

Riley turned to the consultant. 'Are you going to admit her?'

'She has a room of her own on the third floor. We need to do an MRI scan to see if there's any damage to her internal organs or her brain, and I've alerted the consultant psychiatrist. Is she capable of speech?'

'According to her mother, yes.'

'What about security arrangements for her?'

'I'm going to be with her permanently, and when I can't be here there'll be another plainclothes officer.'

'I'll send a nurse to take you to her room. I'll leave you to it, DS Riley.'

The consultant and the nurse stepped out through the curtains.

'I don't want to be the bearer of bad tidings...' said Kate.

'Go on?'

'Even if she can talk, I don't think she's going to for some time. I helped the police up in Bootle on a similar case and it took the boy three weeks to speak. In that case, the person who kept the boy captive told him that if he spoke, made any sound with his mouth or shouted for help, he'd track him down and cut his tongue out. It was only when I convinced him that his tormentor was banged up and out of reach that he started speaking.'

Riley looked at the bagged-up clothes Marta had been wearing – striped pyjama bottoms and a matching top. 'Marta?'

Slowly, Marta turned towards her, and Riley was filled with sadness and compassion. Head shaved and in a baggy, blue NHS gown, the girl looked at Riley and Kate in turn; silent tears rolled down her face.

'Kate, tell her that she's perfectly safe now. That she's going to be staying in a nice room in Alder Hey, a hospital especially for children. Tell her that there will always be a police officer guarding her room as long as she's in here.'

Kate spoke calmly and kindly to Marta but fear mounted in the girl's face, her eyes darting left and right as if looking for somewhere to run to. As she walked to the bottom of the bed, Riley hoped that the girl's mother would turn up soon and bring comfort to her daughter. Discreetly, she took a string of pictures. Slowly, the girl turned her head to look at her; seeing what she was doing, she frowned, held her arms out in Riley's direction and made a shield of her upturned hands. She lowered her face behind her hands and fell onto her back, her thin legs and bony knees making her appear even more vulnerable. She placed her hands over her face and started sobbing. As Riley moved the hem of the gown over the girl's knees, a heavy stream of urine flooded from her body, soaking the trolley and the gown she was wearing.

'Kate, can you do me a favour, please? Can you go and ask the nurse if we can have another gown? I'll stay here with Marta,' said Riley.

'Sure.'

As Kate left the cubicle, Riley stroked Marta's head. She patted the water from Marta's face and neck and, as she wrapped an arm around her shoulders, the girl rested her head against Riley's shoulder.

'You're safe now, Marta. You're all safe with Gina.'

Chapter 10

10.15 am

As she stepped onto the bottom stair leading to the flat above the deli, Clay felt the strong pulse of air from the fan at the front door and drank in the leftover cocktail of smoke and petrol. She focused on her breathing as she walked up the stairs, and told herself she was imagining the aroma of cooked human flesh that crept into her nostrils and the back of her throat.

Near the top of the stairs, her skin puckered into countless goosebumps and she imagined the pure despair that the victims must have felt when they were faced with death. And although she was very cold, Clay felt a bead of sweat roll down her forehead.

Reaching the top of the staircase, she stopped and looked at the open doorway to the flat in which two dead bodies lay waiting. Crossing the threshold, she saw two pairs of well-worn boots lined up neatly near the door. She looked down the dark, windowless corridor and flicked on her torch.

'Police!' she called, and wished in vain that a voice would come back to her, hoping that the firefighters had got it wrong and that one or both of the Adamczak brothers had somehow survived.

She glanced into the kitchen and saw a clean and tidy space with a poster on the wall of the Polish national football team; there were handwritten notices around it. She flicked her light onto the writing and saw the men's names: Karl. Václav. And underneath, days of the week, writing against each man's name. Rotas for cooking and washing dishes, guessed Clay.

Looking in the bathroom, she smelled the freshness of lavender in the space, saw that there were no splashes of urine around the toilet and that the seat was down. She came to a door with a key in the lock. She turned the key and saw an empty box room.

As Clay made her way to the bedroom, the air felt warm and gritty. She stood at the open doorway and threw a beam of light into the charred darkness of the men's shared bedroom.

She looked at the positioning of the two bodies in the centre of the room and the aroma of burned flesh was now undeniable.

The twin single beds were blackened pits and there was a charred line leading from the bed to the two interconnected and burned bodies.

She used her torch to explore the floor and walls and couldn't see a single drop of blood. Clay sent the beam onto the first fire-ravaged head and then the second skull.

They hit you with a blunt instrument, thought Clay. *Maybe.*

You didn't die where you've been positioned. Or you were strangled? Manual strangulation or ligature? In her mind she was now absolutely certain: this couldn't have been the work of one individual.

She saw an empty bottle of Jack Daniels and wondered if the brothers had been weakened by drink before they were attacked. She moved closer to the remains of the Adamczak twins. One of them was on his back on the floor and his brother lay face down across his centre: two bodies in the single shape of an X, the flesh of their separate cores melted into each other.

Together, thought Clay. *Together in the womb, together in death. You were dead when they set you on fire. Or did they leave you barely alive to watch you dying of smoke inhalation? Someone must have hated you. What did you do to deserve this?*

She lit up the charred head of the twin lying across his brother's centre and drew the torch light down his body. Just below his knees, she saw patches of pink flesh that the fire hadn't reached and she was filled with an almost unbearable sadness.

'Eve?' Detective Sergeant Karl Stone's voice drifted from the front door of the flat – a welcome sound. 'You OK?'

Clay called back, 'I'm fine!' through the poisoned air. A couple of seconds later, Stone appeared in the doorway. 'As soon as Terry Mason and Paul Price have gathered all the evidence, you can call the mortuary. We need Harper and another APT here as quickly as possible to remove the bodies and get them to Doctor Lamb.'

She looked at the fusion of two cremated human bodies and turned away. As the full horror of the twisted human sculpture hit her, her intestines tightened and her scalp crawled.

Something dark appeared at the edge of her vision and she moved to face it.

One wall was largely untouched by the fire; even though the striped wallpaper was darkened by several shades of smoke, she made out a distinct shape that made the pulse in her ears throb and the pace of her heart quicken.

She trained her light along the wallpaper and came to a piece of black graffiti: a dark, smoke-obscured circle with intricate geometric shapes inside. She stayed where she was, sensing in her bones that in finding one thing, she was overlooking something obvious.

'Karl, how did you get on with their landlord, Mr Zięba?' she asked, as she combed the walls from ceiling to skirting board with torchlight.

'They were model tenants, always paid their rent on time, took care of any repairs or decorating that needed doing. Respectful and hard-working men.'

'Did they have any enemies?'

'Not according to Mr Zięba. His words were, *How could such men have enemies? How could they meet such an end? Why? They bought from me to give to the food bank, not just a couple of cans but bagloads of provisions for the poor.*'

Slowly, Clay turned, training her torchlight on each and every square centimetre of the walls, ceiling to floor.

'Oh my, my, my!' she said, pausing her light just above the skirting board beneath the blackened window. *You really do mean business,* she said to herself.

'What's happening?' asked Stone.

'Step inside, Karl, see for yourself.'

On the space between the bottom of the window and the skirting board, she kept the light on six neatly painted words. With Stone at her shoulder she read them out: '*Killing Time Is Here Embrace It.*'

She caressed the dark language with light. 'This reads to me like a gun going off on the starting line.' Turning, Clay picked out the esoteric circle on the wall facing six spray-painted words. 'They've also left us something a little less obvious.'

They looked at the geometrical graffiti in silence.

'What's your hunch, Eve?'

'There's no sign of a forced break-in. The men who lived here trusted the perpetrators, let them into their personal space. Even though their friend Aneta said they didn't have people over, she wasn't with them all of the time. How could she *know*?'

Clay walked down the narrow hallway and noticed that the walls were interspersed with framed portraits of the Virgin and Child. Clay focused on the first image, a mosaic made of brightly coloured cubic blocks. The Virgin Mary wore a vivid red head dress and gown, and the infant Christ, in a pale blue tunic, looked up at his mother with great love, holding his little arms and hands out as if trying to climb his mother.

Clay counted six such images in the hall.

Familiar footsteps ascended the stairs and, before she could see him, Clay said, 'Terry, brace yourself.'

Scientific Support officer DS Terry Mason and his assistant Sergeant Paul Price appeared at the head of the stairs.

'What do you want us to focus on, Eve?' asked Mason.

'The bedroom to begin with, and the symbol on the wall facing the window. Clean the wall as best you can and reveal the graffiti that the perpetrators left behind. And check the writing on the opposite wall. *Killing Time Is Here Embrace It.*'

'How do we know it wasn't the victims who wrote on the wall?' asked Sergeant Price.

'Look around the flat, Paul, and you'll see that the people who lived and died here were neat, tidy, house-proud and well organ-ised. They weren't the type to write on the wall. These poor men were decent. It appears they were religious. Faith in action – they fed the hungry. Try and find evidence that will give us a picture of what was important in their lives. Find any contacts, address books, notes to self...'

As Mason and Price moved past her, Clay began descending the stairs and welcomed the draught of air from the powerful fan and the weak daylight at the open front door.

'What do you want me to do, Eve?' asked Stone.

'Stay here, and hot-line me any significant finds as and when they crop up. Find out if they have a priest, where they worship.'

As Clay left the flat, the words *Killing Time Is Here Embrace It* raced in a loop through her mind.

Who, Clay wondered, *have you enraged? And what have you done to provoke this barbarity?*

Chapter 11

10.28 am

As Jack Dare passed the closed living room door, he pictured his brother Raymond behind it, lapping up a single voice spouting from the television like toxic gas, and in his mind's eye, he could see the silent, hypnotised horde listening to that hate-fuelled noise.

The letterbox opened and a parcel landed face down at the bottom of the front door. When Jack picked it up, it felt thick and heavy; he turned it over and felt what appeared to be a book in an envelope addressed to Mr Raymond Dare. As he walked to the top of the stairs, from behind the living room door, Hitler finished speaking and, after a split-second silence, the masses found their collective voice.

'*Sieg Heil! Sieg Heil! Sieg Heil!*'

At his door, Jack unlocked the padlock and listened to his mother in her bedroom singing along to *Chain Reaction* on the radio, drowning out the mass hysteria playing out downstairs from another time and place.

He entered his bedroom and bolted the door, opening the parcel as he made his way to the gym bench in the tight central space.

Jack looked at the cover and title of the book: *White Supremacists* by an author called Dwayne Hare, sitting above a group of mugshots of sour-looking men whose eyes all had one thing in common. Something essential was clearly missing from inside each one.

Jack opened the book and saw from the contents page that each individual or organisation formed a separate case study.

In the first chapter, he looked into the face of a man not much older than himself, looking depressed as if the truth had finally ambushed him: life was over before it had had a chance to begin. Dressed in an orange jump suit, surrounded by prison guards and being led to a high-security van, his hands were cuffed and his feet chained. Beneath the picture was a bland-sounding name. Timothy McVeigh.

Jack skimmed the writing beneath the picture and picked out the words: *McVeigh said, 'I do believe in God, yes. But that's as far as I want to discuss it.* Beneath the writing was a colour picture of a modern building wrecked by a bomb blast.

Flicking past McVeigh, he looked at the pictures of Waco and saw what looked like a mild-mannered man in glasses with his name beneath the picture: David Koresh. Alongside this image was a picture of an American tank outside a burning compound.

He continued to flick through and saw the heading: 'The Woman Who Killed For God'. Sarah Sarah. There was a colour picture of her in court being led away to the cells in an orange jump suit, hands cuffed, feet chained.

Jack slipped the book back inside the envelope, took it to his small pine bookcase under the window and slotted it in a gap between two titles: *The Everlasting Man* and *The Lamb's Supper*.

He lay down on the bench and gripped the bar with a forty-kilo weight on either side, and wondered how much Raymond knew about those people. Jack lifted the bar from the stand and positioned it in the air above his chest. He lowered the bar to his chest, lifted it into the air and pulled off another fourteen repetitions. The words McVeigh, Koresh and Sarah chased after each other through his head like bluebottles on a hot, bone-dry day.

Replacing the bar on the stand, Jack sat up and felt the muscles in his arms pulsing with power, and a flash of inspiration that linked all the people in the book he'd just confiscated.

So, little brother, Jack concluded, *it looks like you're no longer just a run-of-the-mill Neo-Nazi. You're a wannabe white supremacist.*

Chapter 12

10.35 am

In the incident room at Trinity Road Police Station, Detective Constable Barney Cole listened to the computer-generated voicemail message on Lucy Bell's iPhone for the eleventh time in twenty-five minutes.

'The person you're calling isn't available to take your call right now. If you'd like to leave a message after the tone, please do so, or simply hang up after the beep.'

And after the tone, for the eleventh time, he said, 'My name's DC Barney Cole and I'm calling you because you contacted emergency services after you'd come across the missing child Marta Ondřej. Please contact me immediately on 0151 706 2341 and...'

The landline telephone on his desk rang out. He disconnected the mobile call and picked up the receiver.

Behind the caller's silence, Cole heard the competing voices of what sounded like a call centre. 'Detective Constable Barney Cole, Merseyside Constabulary.'

'I'm Alan Davies, returning your call, from O2.'

'What have you got for me, Alan?'

'Because of data protection...'

'No offence, Alan, but I'm going to stop you right there. We're investigating the abduction of a minor and your client is a key witness in that investigation. I need a name. I need a number. Pronto.'

'I'll put you on hold.'

Dance music invaded Cole's ear and he held the receiver away from himself, his frayed patience further unravelling as the seconds flew by. The music stopped and Alan came back on. 'Thanks for waiting.'

'What's the news, and make it *good* news?'

'Under the Data Protection Act of 1998, we can only release personal information about the account holder if the account holder has given his or her express permission. As you're a third party, you need proof of the account holder's permission before we can release data to you.'

'She's not picking up for me. I suggest you get your customer services to get in touch with her and see if she'll pick for them. Like in the next minute. Are you going to do that for me, Alan?'

'Yeah.'

'That wasn't a bit convincing,' said Cole, his grip on the receiver tightening.

'I'll put you through to customer services.'

He held the receiver away from his ear, heard the music stop and listened.

'Georgina Grey, customer services. Am I speaking to DC Cole?'

'Give me your email address please, Georgina. I'm going to email you a picture of my warrant card...'

'You're looking for a name and address of one of our customers, correct?'

'Correct. Please don't quote the Data Protection Act at me. I know her name's Lucy Bell but I need her home address or the address of her place of employment from you. If this is too big for you, put me onto a supervisor or someone who has the authority.'

'No need. I can help you with that. Email me your warrant card and I'll do what I can as quickly as I can. We'll get back to you the instant we have positive information.'

'Thank you.'

Georgina hung up and, as Cole replaced the receiver, a middle-aged constable who wasn't based at Trinity Road Police Station entered the incident room.

'Detective Constable Barney Cole?'

'Yes. You have something for me?'

The constable handed Cole a carrier bag. He looked inside and whistled at the collection of tagged pen drives.

'This is all the CCTV footage from Picton Road and the surrounding neighbourhood, from the Royal Liverpool Hospital to the Fiveways roundabout at Queens Drive.'

'Thank you,' replied Cole, the potential scale of the task kicking off a low-level headache. 'You've kept the one nearest the scene separate, the CCTV from the mini-market?'

From his pocket, the constable produced a pen drive in a small plastic bag. 'I've heard there may be more coming in,' he said.

'Thank you very much.' Cole picked up the landline and dialled Sergeant Carol White. As the call connected, he said, 'Carol, bring your eye drops with you. I've got the CCTV footage from Picton Road.'

Chapter 13

10.45 am

Detective Sergeant Karl Stone stood in the doorway of what used to be Karl and Václav Adamczaks' flat, and called their landlord on his iPhone. After three rings, Mr Zięba picked up.

'Who is this, please?'

'Hello, Mr Zięba. It's Detective Sergeant Karl Stone. We spoke earlier about Karl and Václav.'

'Yes. Are you telling me I can come back to my shop now?'

'Not yet, sorry, Mr Zięba. As soon as you can return, I'll let you know immediately. I was phoning with a couple of questions, if you don't mind.'

Stone looked right at the Wavertree Library in the distance and to the left where the Picton Clock Tower stood over the entrance to the main road, and saw it was a quarter to eleven.

'Fire away, Mr Stone.'

'When we went in to the flat above your deli, we found several images of the Virgin Mary with the infant Jesus. We assumed that these are Polish religious icons.'

'You assume correctly.'

'Did you put them there, or did the Adamczaks put them up?'

'The Adamczaks put them up. I'm not a religious man.'

'They were both religious?' asked Stone.

'To different degrees. Karl was a practising Catholic. So was Václav. Václav, though, he was a very, very religious man. I have a cross on the wall in my shop. This is to bring me good luck more than anything else, and to please the old ladies who come in for provisions. Václav thought I too was very religious and started talking to me about praying to the Virgin Mary to intercede to God, and how if everyone prayed to the Virgin, the world would heal itself. I'm summing up. It was a long, passionate speech. At the end I didn't have the heart to tell him I'm agnostic. Maybe I should have just been honest. Every time he came into the shop, it was God the Father this, the Holy Father that, the Virgin Mary the other—'

'Do you know which church they went to?'

'Different ones. The Metropolitan at the top of Brownlow Hill was a big favourite of Václav. They worked away some weekends so they had to go on Saturday evenings to whichever Catholic church was closest. They sometimes went to local churches. They were good men. They didn't deserve this. I am saddened beyond words. There was a priest who came into my shop sometimes. He knew Václav.'

'What was his name?'

'I don't know.'

Stone put himself in Mr Zięba's position, and wondered what he would be thinking and feeling if it had been his property where murder and arson had happened.

'You know your property...'

'Yes.'

'Above your deli, there is some damage. There was a fire but it was contained in one room. The rest of the flat is unharmed.'

'On a day of incredibly bad news, that is a crumb of comfort. Thank you for that.'

As Stone prepared to close the call down, Mr Zięba said, 'I will talk to people who knew the brothers and see if they have any idea about why this happened.'

'And I will call you the moment you are free to return to your shop.'

Chapter 14

11.06 am

On the third floor of Alder Hey, Marta Ondřej lay on top of her hospital bed with Detective Sergeant Gina Riley sitting door-side to the right of her and Kate Nowak by the window to the left.

'Marta,' said Riley. But the girl stared straight ahead and appeared not to hear.

'When's the shrink coming?' asked Kate.

There was a knock on the glass door and a nurse came into the room, carrying a tray of food covered with a metal dish.

'After the food,' smiled Riley.

'OK, Marta,' said the nurse. 'Seeing as you demolished the cooked breakfast, the chef thought, why wait until lunchtime for the next meal? As you wouldn't tell us what you wanted I made an educated guess based on what most of the other kids on this ward ask for...'

He waited for a reaction from Marta and, when he didn't get one, looked at Riley.

'She doesn't understand English.'

The nurse placed the tray down on the bedside cabinet in line with Marta's head. Lifting the metal dish, he said, 'Fish and chips. Enjoy!'

As the nurse left the room, Marta sniffed the air. She sat up suddenly and, looking at the food, plunged her hands into the plate. In one bite she took a third of the battered cod and stuffed a handful of chips into her mouth.

Riley checked her watch and timed her. It took Marta fifty-three seconds to demolish the food and start licking the grease from the plate. Then, slowly, she placed the plate on the bedside cabinet.

Riley moved her face close to Marta's and pointed at the toilet cubicle in the corner of the room. 'Come with me, Marta.'

She helped the girl to her feet and guided her to the toilet. For half a minute, Marta stood looking down at the toilet, as if it was an abstract sculpture. Riley walked into the space and turned Marta round by the shoulders. She gathered the hem of Marta's gown and placed it in the girl's hands. Gently, she placed her hands on Marta's shoulders and the girl offered no resistance as Riley sat her down on the toilet.

As water hit the pan, Riley turned her back on Marta and smiled at Kate.

'You're very good with children, Gina.'

'Thanks.'

When Marta had finished, Riley turned and lifted her from the seat. She took the girl's hands away from the hem of the gown and the garment fell, covering her legs to the knees.

Riley mimed washing hands by rubbing hers together, and turned on the tap. She placed Marta's right hand under the soap dispenser, filled her palm with foam and guided her hands to the stream of water.

Marta's hands were as still as stone. Water poured through her fingers and over the backs of her hands.

'I'll help you.'

Riley turned the girl's hands in the stream, rubbing soap into each hand and rinsing off the bubbles. She took Marta's hands to the air dispenser and watched her face as the warm breeze flooded her hands and a brief flash of pleasure crossed her features.

As Marta followed Riley out of the toilet, she paused in the doorway and her face filled with a look of pure uncertainty. She turned a quarter circle to face the toilet wall, and as Riley moved closer, she saw Marta looking at her own reflection in the mirror.

She appeared to be looking at someone she vaguely knew but didn't completely trust, and confusion swept over her face. As if her arms didn't quite belong to her body, she raised her hands to her head and patted the patches of stubble and baldness.

Marta fell still, staring hard into the mirror, and drew a deep breath through her nose.

Riley stood behind her, placed her hands on her shoulders, turned her round and wrapped her arms around her.

Marta let out a stuttering and laboured breath.

'Let it out, Marta, let it all out!'

The scream that she let out sounded too loud and intense to come from such a frail body. And it went on and on, dissolving into sobbing that subsided into a silence that was as deep as it was dark and filled with a horde of faceless demons.

Chapter 15

11.06 am

Raymond Dare sat between his friends CJ and Buster, staring in mutual silence at the plasma television mounted on the wall of his mother's living room. On-screen, behind a vicious barbed-wire fence, a camera panned across a line of emaciated and harrowed faces, eyes stamped with horror and lost in terror.

Raymond turned left and right, made eye contact with CJ and Buster.

'The fucking joke of it, Raymond,' said CJ, 'is that none of this Holocaust shit ever actually happened in the real world.'

'Yeah, I know that,' said Raymond, smiling as the footage unfolded and German civilians from a village near the death camp were forced to dig up the dead.

'All these films were propaganda, made by the fucking commie bastard Russians to make them look good and the Germans who were defending democracy look like shite!' Buster spoke with infectious confidence.

Raymond heard the creaking of a floorboard near the top of the stairs and recognised his older brother's footstep, a sound that split his brain in half.

'Right, get up, lads!' said Raymond, with mounting urgency.

CJ and Buster followed Raymond to the double-glazed door leading out into the garden.

'Fucking Jack,' said CJ, stepping out into the garden after Buster.

As Raymond slid the door open, he said, 'Get out through the back gate. I'll call you when he's not here!' He shivered in the cold air as he shut the door after his friends, softly as it connected with the plastic frame, so that no one could hear.

Jack's footsteps came down the stairs. Raymond hurried to the couch and changed to an MTV channel. Raymond muted the sound for a moment, listened to Jack taking a diversion into the kitchen and Jasmine barking with delight at the arrival of her master. He unmuted the sound and did his best to make a show of being engrossed in the music.

The sound of his brother's pure white pit bull terrier sparked a vision of her, bloodshot eyes staring at him, teeth bared and muscular legs ready to pounce. Fear invaded him, sickness followed as an ever-present rage simmered beneath his skin.

As the living room door opened and Jack stepped into the centre of the room, Raymond Dare looked up at his brother who took the remote from him and turned the television off.

From the other side of the door, his mother spoke as she walked from the stairs to the front door.

'Jack, remember what you said you'd do!'

'Don't worry, Mum,' replied Jack. 'It's just about to happen. I'll message you.' When the front door closed, he asked. 'What are you watching on TV, Raymond?'

'This music channel.'

'Right. When I was coming down the stairs I heard you moving around all of a sudden.' Raymond stared at his brother's feet. 'OK, no response, fine. So, what's this I hear about you dealing weed to ten- and eleven-year-olds on Otterspool Promenade?'

'Honest to God, Jack...'

'By the skateboard park, just inside Otterspool Park, to be precise.'

'How do you know?'

Jack shrugged. 'I just do. What's this, Raymond?' He shook the yellow and white box in his hand and the contents banged against cardboard, a small sound that erupted in Raymond's head like an explosion in a glassworks. Jack opened the box, took out four empty foil trays, and held the first one up in the air. 'Look at them, Raymond! Look at them!'

One by one, Jack showed the foils.

'All the Risperdal tablets have been popped from the foils, but you haven't been taking them, have you, Raymond?'

'I haven't. Somebody threw them away.'

Jack laughed bitterly. 'There are three of us in this house. You. Me. Mum.'

'It wasn't me threw them away.'

'So, are you telling me that Mum put them down the toilet? Are you telling me I put them down the toilet?'

'Maybe, yeah.'

'That's right, Raymond. I put them down the toilet because Mum told me to. Is that what you're going to say next? Me and Mum ganged up to withdraw your medication from you. You really are off your head! You put them down the toilet, didn't you? Didn't you?'

Raymond looked at him as if peering through a cloud, a look that told Jack he'd hit the bullseye.

'I don't... I don't remember doing it...'

'Why did you do it?' pressed Jack.

After a painful silence, Raymond said, 'I'm feeling really well.'

'You don't look well to me.' Jack looked at the box. 'Six milligrams, Raymond, that's a very heavy dose of anti-psychotic medication. The doctors started you off at a conservative one milligram, then two, three, four, five, six. Six did the trick. And you were feeling well because I was giving you the pills. Then your cognitive therapist at Broad Oak insisted you take responsibility for administering your own medication, and you stopped taking them. I've been watching you sliding down the slippery bank ever since.'

'All right, all right, I'll take my medication.'

'You can't today. You've flushed it all down the pan. And you stopped going to Broad Oak for your therapy. Don't lie. The medic spoke to Mum. Three months you've missed.'

Raymond opened his mouth to speak.

'No, shut your mouth and listen. You're going back in to therapy, and I'm going to take charge of your medication, and I don't care what your therapist says. Mental note to self. Bin off the therapist and insist on a new one. I've made an appointment for you with the GP, tomorrow at 4 pm, and I'm coming in with you, no argument. You'd better get that into your soul.'

'Who's the appointment with?'

'Doctor Salah,' replied Jack.

'That fucking bald Paki...'

'Cut that talk out right now. He's not from Pakistan, he's from Egypt, ignorant.' Jack put the foils back in the box and tossed it to Raymond. 'Read the information sheet inside. It might remind you how serious your condition is.'

Jack took a box of matches from his pocket.

'What are you doing?' asked Raymond.

'I'm going to check up on a job I'm doing in the back garden. I'll be back in a minute. There's something else we need to talk about.'

'What?'

'I want to know what you were doing last night, Raymond. And I want to know who you were doing it with. And you'd better not lie to me. Get that into your soul.'

Chapter 16

11.28 am

As Clay walked up the stairs of 682 Picton Road, she called, 'Terry, it's me!'

The skin on her arms puckered as the fan behind her poured cold air at her back, and she noticed how much the smell of smoke and cooked flesh had lessened.

'We're in here, with the bodies.'

Clay stepped into the bedroom and looked at the intriguing graffiti on the wall.

'It's looking a lot cleaner. Thank you both,' said Clay.

She scrutinised the graffiti, which was now blurred and distorted.

'Don't thank me,' said Mason. 'If you're looking for a very thorough cleaner, Pricey's your man. I went through the rest of the flat while he cleaned.'

'Anything?'

He handed her a black address book. Clay flicked through it, saw that most of the names and places in it were Polish.

She looked at the graffiti, a series of three concentric circles, black at the centre and another circle in the middle with a crowning circumference. Within the circles were dark, crooked symmetrical lines penning in chunks of empty space.

'I'm sorry for the distortion,' said Price. 'I used a Q-Tip to clean the wall around the graffiti but, even though I'm working with heavily diluted trisodium phosphate, the wallpaper's absorbent and it's sucked the cleaning fluid into the picture on the wall.'

Clay looked to the window and read the graffiti beneath it. *Killing Time Is Here Embrace It.* Any more messages like this, Terry?'

'None,' he replied, showing her the image on his iPhone of the black globe before and after cleaning.

'I'd like you to send these images to Riley, Stone, Hendricks and Cole, everyone directly involved. Ask if this symbol means anything to anyone. I'll ask Barney Cole to start digging into what it is and what it signifies. OK. Any thoughts?'

'Whoever's done this,' said Mason, 'must've been acting in a hurry. We've been speculating. We reckon they've used a card template with an ink roller and a pad, or maybe even a spray paint. If they'd painted it freehand, they'd still be here now.'

'Are you ready for the mortuary technicians to take the bodies?' asked Clay.

'I'd appreciate more time in this room and the others, Eve. Just to double-check everything, make sure we haven't missed anything.'

Mason pointed towards the criss-crossed and charred men, a ghoulish pair of Siamese Twins. 'How are they going to be parted?' he asked.

'I've no idea, Terry. I've never seen anything quite like this.'

As Clay scrutinised the central place where the bodies were joined, her iPhone rang out.

'Hi, Barney, what's happening back at the ranch?'

'You'd better get here as quickly as you can, Eve.' The excitement in Barney Cole's voice was infectious.

'What's happening, Barney?'

'Lucy Bell's shown up at reception.'

Clay shot towards the stairs. 'Where is she now?' She rushed down the stairs, passed the fan's turning blade and towards the muddy light of the world outside the house of death.

'Interview Suite 1.'

At the bottom of the stairs, Clay said, 'Call Bill Hendricks and ask him to sit with her until I get there. I'll be there in twenty minutes, sooner if I can. How's she presenting?'

'Half-detached, half-anxious, back and forth.'

Clay ran across the frozen pavement, directly into a fresh band of sharp, diagonal snow, thinking, *Lucy Bell, half-detached, half-anxious, back and forth like a human pendulum.*

Chapter 17

11.28 am

Riley could hear voices and footsteps coming towards Marta Ondřej's hospital room. Homing in on their voices, she identified one as Marta's mother, Verka. Two women came into sight through the glass wall of Marta's room – Verka and Sergeant Samantha Green from the family liaison team. Green placed her hand on Verka's arm to stop her in her tracks.

Verka had a handkerchief pressed to her face and her eyes were red from weeping.

'Hang on a second, Kate,' said Riley. 'I'll be back in a moment.'

Outside Marta's room, Riley introduced herself. 'My name's Detective Sergeant Gina Riley. I'm looking after Marta.'

'I want to see her now.' Streaks of mascara ran down Verka's cheeks and her eyes were raw.

'Soon, Verka. We need to know. What language does Marta speak?'

'Little bits of Czech. Little bits of Roma. A lot of words no one understands.'

That's why they let her go, thought Riley.

'OK, Verka. I've got something to tell you, something I want you to think about when you go to the toilet down there to wash your face. I don't want you going in there looking all cried out.'

'I understand. I'll clean myself up.'

'When she was in captivity, the person or people who held her captive cut her hair off.'

'Her hair? Much off?'

'Pretty much all of it. When you first go in there you mustn't react. You've got to keep your face straight. She saw herself in the mirror and she was hysterical.'

'I will try my best.'

'You're going to have to help us get through to her. She's proving hard to reach at the moment.'

'Marta is hard to reach, Detective Riley.'

Riley watched Verka follow the signs for the ladies' toilet.

'Her English is really good,' observed Riley.

'I said that to her in the car coming over,' agreed Green. 'She spent a couple of years in the south of England when she was growing up, and some time in Northern Ireland.'

Green moved to the glass wall and looked inside Marta's room. 'Jesus, what have they done to her head?'

'You might as well ask Jesus, because I certainly can't explain it away apart from the obvious – they've taken it as a trophy.'

'Is that the translator?'

'Yeah, and she's staying put even if Verka's got good English. I don't know Verka, so I can't trust her to tell me everything Marta says.'

Chapter 18

11.28 am

Raymond stood in the bay window of the front room, his heart falling as he heard the back door shut and Jasmine's paws scratching against the laminate flooring in the hall as she followed Jack to the living room. She sounded like ten mad dogs rolled into one and the noise her paws made ran through him, set his nerves jangling.

Why do you always keep me fucking waiting? Raymond thought to himself. *You fucking dickhead, Jack!*

Jack's voice entered the room before he did. 'Sit down, Raymond!'

Obediently, Raymond sat on the couch as Jack entered the room, dominating the space.

'What?' asked Raymond.

'What did you do last night?'

'Why?'

'It's a really simple question, Raymond.'

'Nothing. I didn't do nothing.'

'Why're you up so early after such a late night?'

'Just am.'

'You were buzzing past yourself last night when you came home and you're never up this early. I know you slept for a few hours because I looked in your room. Have you been doing speed?'

'Don't like speed, gives me a headache and makes me itch.'

Jasmine trotted to the double-glazed door leading out to the garden and barked aggressively.

'It's OK, Jasmine. Come on, back to me!'

Jasmine hurried to Jack's feet and sat facing Raymond, staring into his eyes with a look that pushed his heart and pulled his brain in the same instant. He looked at her face and then at

Jack's, back and forth, again and again, until their faces melted together, half Jack, half Jasmine, divided dead centre.

'It's only smoke, Jas... You've been lucky so far, really lucky, Raymond. Your mates. Remind me. What're they called?'

'CJ and Buster.'

'You've been pulled in by the cops a few times but they could never make anything stick on you. Right?'

'Right.'

'When it does stick and you get sent to a young offenders' institution, how do you think you'd get on?'

'Fucking well. I've won plenty of fights. I'm hard, me.'

'No, you're not hard, Raymond. You're vicious. There's a difference between hard and vicious. I'm very good at violence but I don't take any pleasure in it. You enjoy it – that's what makes you vicious and me hard. Stick to the question. What did you do last night?'

'Went to Sefton Park to smoke weed. Why? What's up, Jack?'

'I'll tell you what's up, Raymond. When you got home, early hours this morning, I went straight to the wash basket to see if I could work out from the state of your clothes what you'd been up to. Your clothes stank of smoke.'

'We robbed a car. From The Elms. We drove it for a couple of hours round Sefton Park. We siphoned off the petrol to torch the car and destroy the evidence. And that's why we haven't been caught, because we're fucking clever, cleverer than you think, Jack. It's not luck. It's being street smart.'

'Where'd you burn the car out?'

'Ullet Road.'

'More?'

'By the Gate House into Sefton Park, near Bellerive School.'

'I'll check it out. You had a bath since last night?'

'No. Haven't had time.'

'You need a bath. You smell of smoke on your skin.'

Raymond sniffed his hands. 'Can't smell nothing.' There was a bleak silence. 'Why are you looking at me like that?'

'The night before last, you came home spliffed off your head, ended up unconscious on your bed. You left your laptop on. I watched that film you downloaded, the one where the black woman gets violently raped by three white excuses for men. Recommended viewing for white supremacists.'

'That was Buster, I didn't—'

Jack held his hand out to slap Raymond's face, then held up a warning finger instead.

'Ow! What did you do that for?'

'I didn't touch you, Raymond.'

Raymond held his hand against his cheek, felt a burning sensation down to the muscle against his teeth.

'You end up inside, you'll be like the woman in that film. You'd better get that into your soul. You're lying to me, Raymond. That wasn't all you did last night. I watched you when you came home. You couldn't see me because I was in the shadows. You didn't go joy riding!'

Jack watched Raymond withering before his eyes. A look of sheer confusion crossed his features.

'What's happening with your art these days?'

'Can't be arsed!'

Jack picked up Jasmine, carried her to the kitchen and settled her in her basket. Raymond trailed after him.

'Can't be arsed... Can't be arsed,' Jack carried on. 'After I've fed Jasmine, I'm going to work. I'm running there via Ullet Road and the Gate House. If I don't see any sign of a burnt-out vehicle there, it'll tell me what I already know. You've been lying to me. Get that right into your soul.'

As Jack scooped Winalot into Jasmine's bowl, he said, 'There's something else I want to talk about.'

'What?' Raymond sounded completely defeated.

'The other night when you left your laptop open, your iPhone was next to it. You'd written down the four-digit pass code on a piece of paper. Why?'

'Because... the last time I changed the code to stop CJ from fucking with my phone, when I woke up in the morning, I couldn't remember the new code and I had to take it to a shop to get it unlocked…'

'Who is she, Raymond?'

'She? Who? Who do you mean?'

'You're a catch, aren't you?'

'I don't know what you're talking about, Jack.'

Jack shut the kitchen door in Raymond's face.

When Jack left the house, Raymond counted to one hundred in his head, then thought, *Fuck you, Jack. And fuck Risperdal…*

He took out his mobile phone and dialled.

'Buster, it's me. He's gone now, the bastard.'

Chapter 19

11.29 pm

As Marta Ondřej woke up, her mother Verka held onto her hand and gazed at her with a mixture of unconditional love and deep sorrow.

'Verka, remind Marta she's in hospital and that she's perfectly safe,' said Riley.

Verka spoke to Marta, but the girl didn't look at her or appear to be listening. Instead, she looked directly up at the ceiling, her free hand pressing against her head, as if she was trying to stop it falling from her neck.

'Verka, keep talking to her, please. Reassure her. Talk about happy times you've had as a family, good memories, birthdays, Christmases, anything,' insisted Riley.

Riley felt her iPhone vibrating in the inside pocket of her jacket. She moved away from the bed and on the display saw 'Eve'.

'How is she, Gina?'

'She's coming round. She's eaten, she's slept, she was shocked by her own reflection which shows self-awareness.'

'Is Verka still there?'

'She's not moving from her bedside.'

'Gina...' said Kate urgently.

'Excuse me, Eve. What is it, Kate?'

'Look!' She pointed at Marta, who was struggling to an upright position on the bed, her lips moving but no sound emerging from her mouth.

'It looks like she's starting to verbalise, Eve.'

'Film it for me, Gina, send it to my phone.'

Riley pressed record on her iPhone video and zoomed in on Marta's face. She watched the girl's lips moving, her mouth opening wider, bit by bit, as the volume of her speech rose. She looked at Kate, whose whole attention was focused on Marta, her brow lined, her eyes drinking in the shapes that her lips made and swallowing the sounds coming out of her mouth.

Unable to understand a single word the girl was saying, Riley focused on the emotion behind the language and guessed that Marta was in no-man's land.

Time passed as she carried on speaking, stopping only to draw breath.

Her eyes rolled as the volume rose and lowered, up and down, eyes and speech synchronizing, until her voice dipped and slowly sank back down into silence.

And in that silence, her arms and hands came to rest, crossing each other on her chest.

When Riley was confident that the girl wasn't about to break into speech again, she stopped recording and looked at Kate.

'Six minutes, thirty-one seconds.' She took out her notebook, clicking her pen into action, and read bewilderment on Verka's face.

'It's not good news, Gina,' said Kate. Riley waited. 'She was talking gibberish. It was like a crossover of Czech and some

Roma dialect from the region. You've got to understand, different Roma groups have different dialects. Roma Group A meets Roma Group B, there might be certain bits of language they have in common but it's possible that they just won't understand each other at all.'

'Maybe Verka can shine a little light on this,' said Riley, more in hope than reason. 'Verka, what did you make of all that?'

Verka looked at Riley. 'Upside-down talk. I didn't understand.'

Riley walked to Marta's bed and said, 'Marta?'

The girl opened her eyes and looked up at her. She held out a hand and grasped Riley's fingers with a sparrow-like grip. She opened her mouth but no sound came out.

Then, drilling her eyes into Riley, Marta whispered, '*Tma*.'

'*Tma*?' Riley echoed back the sound.

'*Tma*. That makes sense. It's Czech for darkness,' said Kate.

Marta let go of Riley's hand and shuffled down the bed, under the covers, hiding from sight.

Riley sent the film of Marta to Clay's iPhone and attached a message: *Eve, Marta has spoken but it all appears to be meaningless, except for one word. Darkness. The first drip before the tap flows? I hope so. Gina.*

She looked at Marta's shape, her entire body covered by bedclothes.

Darkness, speculated Riley. *Back to the sheltering darkness...*

Chapter 20

11.30 am

Father Aaron Bell lifted the tenth clear plastic lid from the Perspex cage on the plain oak table in front of him and dropped in the grass and leaves he had harvested from the garden.

He stooped and looked at his pets – five grasshoppers and five crickets that lived with him indoors, alongside the dozens who lived outside in the garden.

He sat at the table that had been in the kitchen of St Luke's Presbytery for over one hundred years and poured tea from a heavily chipped brown pot and milk from the bottle.

He unfolded the *Daily Telegraph* and, ignoring the economic gloom on the front page, scanned through the domestic news on the following pages until he reached 'The World In Brief'.

His eyes were immediately drawn to an image of a woman on the cusp of middle age, in an orange jump suit, handcuffed and foot-chained, being led into court by police officers. Her dark but greying hair was tied back, and no emotion showed on her narrow face.

Father Aaron drew in breath and prepared to read the paragraph.

> Kelly-Ann Carter, 58, has lodged a final appeal with the governor of the State of South Carolina to commute her death sentence into life imprisonment. Carter was convicted in 1990 of the triple murder of three teenagers from the same family. She has written at length about her remorse for her crimes and has spent the last thirty years alongside other women facing the death penalty on the Mountain View Unit in Huntsville. A demonstration outside the maximum security unit is set to go ahead if her plea for clemency is denied.

Closing the newspaper, Father Aaron placed it on the table and brought his hands together in prayer. 'Lord, please speak to the heart of the governor of South Carolina when deciding on Kelly-Ann's life. May he be obedient to your will. Please be with Kelly-Ann as she waits on death row. Amen.'

He looked at the image of Mary on the wall above his head.

'Mary, Mother of Jesus, mother to all of us who believe in you, intercede on my behalf with God. May his voice be powerful and clear in the governor's heart.'

In his mind, Father Aaron conjured the picture from the newspaper of Kelly-Ann Carter and words rolled around in his head like millstones: It's not going to be granted, it simply isn't going to go her way.

Chapter 21

11.35 am

'Lift the seat up if you're going for a piss, Buster!' On the upstairs landing of his house, Raymond looked through the open door of the bathroom at the end of the corridor, where his friend stood at the toilet with his jogging bottoms and boxers around his ankles. 'Last time you used the toilet, you managed to piss all over the floor and I got the blame.'

Buster flipped the seat up and a stream of bright yellow urine hit the water.

Just behind him, the sound of metal hitting wood drew Raymond's attention and he turned to see CJ flipping the padlock on Jack's door, up and down.

CJ nodded at the door and the secrets that lay behind it.

'Why's he need to padlock his door?' asked CJ.

Raymond looked over the banister into the hall below, convinced that Jack had somehow sneaked back into the house to try to catch him out. The unnerving sensation this possibility caused just under his scalp made him want to spark up a joint the size of a ruler.

'Because when he was in prison, he said there was no privacy. That's why he locks his door.'

'Have you seen that thing on the internet about Jack?' asked Buster.

'I have, yeah. Is it true, Raymond?' said CJ.

'Is what true?'

'That when he went to the nick, everyone was respectful to him because he battered three Pakis by himself, but he wasn't happy with just that. He wanted to be top dog, so he followed the hardest lad in the place into the showers, called him a cunt and a queer, then laid into him.'

'It's true,' said Raymond, with a glow of pride and an explosion of fear and envy. 'He told the lad that if he grassed to the screws that's exactly what he would be in everyone else's eyes. A fucking grass. He told the lad that if he did grass, he'd come after him again and that he'd *really* lay into him next time. The lad told the doctor he slipped and banged his face on the shower floor.'

'That part wasn't on the internet,' said Buster. 'Go on then, Raymond. What's in his room?'

'Weights. I can hear the clanging of the bar on his bench press.'

'How long's he work out for?'

'Hours and hours, every single day.'

'Yeah but that's not all he does in there, right?' asked Buster.

'There's this kind of smoky smell comes out from time to time.'

'Weed?'

'It's not weed. It doesn't smell like weed. He doesn't do weed. He doesn't do anything. I've never seen him shit-faced.'

'Boring fucker!' CJ laughed and Buster joined in as Raymond looked down into the hall once more, and tried to delve under their noise as deep as he could into the house. He had looked the feelings up on the internet. *This is pure fucking paranoia*, he told himself, but knowledge of what it was called didn't help.

CJ lifted the padlock and dropped it against the door to Jack's room. Over and over, metal banged against wood and Raymond's anxiety spiked with each unpleasant beat.

'Fucking stop doing that, CJ, you're getting on my nerves!'

Buster pulled up his jogging bottoms and boxers, turned and said, 'You know, I remember what Jack used to be like before he went away. He was as fucking sound as anyone could be. But then he goes away and comes back fucking changed into this twat who thinks he's like better than everyone else put together. He doesn't even sound like he used to.'

'I thought that, exactly,' said CJ. 'It's like he's been brainwashed, like... Did he get brainwashed?'

Buster and CJ were now shoulder to shoulder outside Jack's door, facing Raymond.

'Ask him yourselves!' said Raymond.

'Fuck off,' said CJ. 'I'd sooner eat shit than do that. He'd twat me round the block.'

Without moving his head, Raymond glanced down but he couldn't see anything; he just had the clearest sense that something was moving with slow stealth up the staircase.

'You know what I don't get about him,' said CJ. 'He's been offered really good money by every gangster in town to go and work for them, and he's turned them all down flat. He might be hard but he's a fucking dickhead.'

'What about the cage-fighting promoter he turned down?' asked Buster.

'And then he goes and gets a job as a gardener for some melt of a priest in Wavertree,' added CJ.

'Yeah,' replied Raymond, heavily, recalling how Jack had turned down this legal option to work as a professional cage fighter and how he'd hoped with all his heart that his brother would say *Yes* and end up battered and broken by someone harder and quicker than him. The stinging on his cheek intensified and the words *I didn't touch you* blossomed inside his brain. Raymond felt pulsing in his marrow; something was drawing nearer, but the dark music in his bones left him unable to move.

'Shall we talk about last night?' asked Raymond, eager to change the subject.

'No!' said CJ.

'No fucking way.'

'I mean as in like, where was we *all* last night?' asked Raymond.

'We were round at my Ma's,' said CJ. 'She let you both in. You both came up to my room and we stayed there all night playing on my X-Box and smoking weed.'

The sound of metal against wood made Raymond want to scream, but he caught himself on the inside, laughed and said, 'Is correct! Leave his fucking padlock alone.'

'OK.' CJ looked at the padlock as it remained against the wood and said, 'You know, I could get that open with a paperclip. Bet you any money I could do it in ten seconds flat, no shit.'

Raymond's eyes were drawn to the corner of the landing at the head of the stairs. He felt as if an invisible vice was turning on his skull as he peered into Jasmine's accusing eyes, Jack's white pit bull terrier, who stared back at him with contempt and accusation.

She remained perfectly still, but the growl in her throat hit the air like an ominous prophecy. CJ turned to the sound and said, 'I'm not standing round here like an arsehole chatting shit all day.'

No one moved.

Jasmine let out a single menacing bark, turned and bounded down the stairs.

Raymond's phone vibrated in his pocket and it felt as if it was pulsing poison into his marrow.

'Fucking hate that fucking dog,' said Buster.

Raymond took his phone out, saw that it was Jack and connected immediately.

'Are they there?' asked Jack.

'No, I'm alone.'

'I can smell them from here. Tell them to get out of the house right this minute.' Jack disconnected.

'I'd love to slit her throat.' CJ stared at the space where Jasmine had just been standing.

Be careful, thought Raymond, *she might hear you*. 'You've got to go, the two of you, right now,' he said, as the sonic poison travelled from his hip through his spine and into the plates of his skull.

As CJ and Buster walked downstairs, Jack's voice scratched the bone beneath his skull. *Better get it into your soul. Better get it into your soul. Better get it into your soul.*

Chapter 22

11.55 am

Jack Dare circled the area around the Gate House on the edge of Sefton Park and Ullet Road, looking for signs of scorched tarmac on the pavement. As he did so, he pictured his brother Raymond and the way he walked, shoulders rolling back and forth and legs moving as if his feet were on little springs.

'Liar!' he said, as a stream of traffic turned from Ullet Road onto the road that ran round the park.

A park ranger pulled up at the lights across the road and Jack caught his attention, flagging him down when the lights changed to green.

The ranger wound down the window and asked, 'Can I help you?'

'My car got robbed last night.'

'Sorry to hear that.'

'I know. I know. I was told that someone'd burned a car out right here, but there's no sign of a fire. I was wondering have there been any burned-out cars in Sefton Park, last night?'

'Absolutely not!' the ranger fired back immediately.

'Absolutely not?'

'No way. The police would've called me to attend. It's happened in the past but not last night.'

'Well, thanks for that, much appreciated.'

'You're welcome. I hope your car turns up.'

Jack watched the ranger drive away, filled with cold contempt for Raymond.

He took a series of cleansing breaths, boxed off the anger in his head and his heart and tried to think positively about the day that lay ahead. Turning his back on his brother's latest lie, he ran as quickly as he could in the direction of Wavertree.

Chapter 23

12.05 pm

At the door of Interview Suite 3, Clay took a few deep breaths to calm the antagonism she felt towards Lucy Bell. Walking inside, she weighed up the woman facing Detective Sergeant Bill Hendricks. Lucy didn't move at the sound of the door opening, or turn to look at Clay as she moved to sit down next to Hendricks.

Clay noted the curve of fat on Lucy's back beneath the rich purple fabric of her T-shirt, and the sleek, shiny quality of her jet-black hair, cut straight across the centre of her forehead and styled into a shoulder-length bob. Her face was round and there was a wedge of unshiftable fat under her chin.

As she sat next to Hendricks, Clay saw that Lucy looked puzzled and anxious. *Homely girl*, she thought. The negativity she had felt towards her since she had left Marta alone in the Wavertree Mystery was punctured by a note of compassion. She noticed her stubby, ring-free fingers and concluded, *Late twenties, early thirties and probably convinced she's on the shelf.*

'My name's DCI Eve Clay,' she said evenly, showing Lucy her warrant card.

Lucy glanced at the card and seemed to look through it.

'Thank you for finding Marta and calling 999. Lucy, I want you to sit back and focus. I'm getting the feeling that this event is leaving you a little stressed out.'

'I'm very stressed out,' said Lucy, blinking slowly, drawing Clay's attention to the precise but vivid black eye-liner around her deep brown eyes.

'This is Detective Sergeant Bill Hendricks,' said Clay.

'Yes, he told me his name while we were waiting for you.'

Clay glanced at the dominant image on the front of Lucy's T-shirt, the palm of Jesus's hand with the fingers and thumb stretched up. At the dead centre of the palm was a perfect hole forming an O; on either side of it were three other letters making the word 'LOVE' –Jesus's punctured hand post-crucifixion, and a message that could have been a personal cry for help.

Christian, thought Clay. 'Tell me what happened, Lucy? This morning?'

'Where's my dad?'

'Your dad?'

'When the woman from the O2 shop came to the uni to ask my permission to pass on my contact details to you, I said *Of course*, I understood that you'd probably want to speak with me in relation to the little girl I found in the Wavertree Mystery Park, so I said *Yes, give them my details by all means but in the meantime I'll go and see the police myself directly*, and I asked who is it exactly who is looking for me and where is that person based to which she told me...' She looked at Clay and said, 'Detective Constable Barney Cole at Trinity Road Police Station in Garston. I came immediately from Abercromby Square. And here I am. Where is Detective Constable Barney Cole?'

'He's busy.'

Lucy gripped the edge of the table with both hands and leaned forward as if she was about to stand up and leave the room, job done.

'Lucy, please,' said Clay. 'Relax. You're helping us with our enquiries and we appreciate that greatly.'

'Where's my dad?' She let go of the table and, as she folded her hands across her swollen middle, Clay thought, *Here is a young woman who carries chocolate bars in her pockets wherever she goes.*

'I don't know where your dad is, Lucy,' said Clay.

'He should be here. I phoned him and left a message on his answer machine saying where I was going and what I was doing. He should be here to support me.'

'Perhaps,' said Clay kindly, 'he's on his way. Tell me what happened this morning, Lucy.'

'I left the house.'

'Where's home?'

'The house next door to St Luke's Roman Catholic Church, the presbytery. Albert Edward Road.'

'The priest's house?' Clay double-checked, hearing a small noise in Hendricks's throat, a note of incredulity from a man whom it was almost impossible to surprise.

'My father's a Roman Catholic priest, Father Aaron Bell. I was in my early twenties when he was ordained,' said Lucy. 'Where was I? I walked across the Mystery as I do every day to get the bus into work...'

'One moment, please, Lucy.' Clay turned to Hendricks.

'Lucy told me she's a lecturer at the University of Liverpool, history department,' said Hendricks. 'I did check it out, Eve. She's also a PhD student. I asked a few other questions about you, Lucy, and your colleague speaks very highly of your teaching ability and your fairness in marking your students' assignments.'

Lucy blushed and looked visibly calmer. 'I do my best.'

'Go on, Lucy,' said Clay. 'Tell me about this morning?'

'It was misty. I saw the little girl standing stock still in the middle of the Mystery and, when I came closer, I recognised her face from the picture in the paper and on TV, though I noted with alarm that her head was shaven and she was very scared. I gave her the chocolate I was going to eat at morning break from my bag. I phoned 999 but then had to leave her because I was going to be late for the lecture I was due to deliver. I can't be late for anything.'

'Why can't you be late for anything, Lucy?'

'Because that's the way I am.' She folded her arms under her breasts, blocking out the message on her T-shirt. 'I was diagnosed as being on the autistic spectrum when I was nine years old. I have Asperger's syndrome.'

'Your condition, Lucy, affects your life on a daily basis?' asked Clay.

'That's right, DCI Clay. I have learned many hard lessons and have had much assistance to help me fit in, things that other people take for granted and learn easily.'

Clay noticed the dense meatiness of Lucy's arms and the smallness of her breasts. Body and brain, left hook followed by a right. 'Did Marta speak to you?'

'Not a word. Just gobbled down my chocolate. *Let the little children come to me, and do not hinder them, for the kingdom of heaven belongs to such as these.* That's all I know and that is all I believe. When I heard sirens coming towards the Mystery, I felt easier about walking away because I knew help was coming fast. The child was so still, I knew she wouldn't be walking or running away.' Lucy touched her head. 'I worked out it was safe for me to go and safe for her to be there. Outside of my work, teaching undergraduates, I am very shy, DCI Clay. I do not seek attention or thanks. My encounter with Marta lasted less than one minute.' Lucy sat back, as if exhausted by the effort of speaking.

'Did you see anybody else?'

'She was alone. If I had seen someone, say, the person who may have kidnapped her, I would have challenged them or taken a picture. But it was just me and Marta.'

Lucy looked into the space between Clay and Hendricks, and nodded as if listening to some invisible person whom only she could hear. Slowly, she stood up, pushing the chair away from her with the backs of her legs.

'We haven't finished yet, Lucy,' said Clay. 'Sit back down, please.'

Lucy sat down on the edge of the seat, her backbone like a weather vane.

'As I said earlier, you've been through a stressful experience,' Clay continued. 'Stress plays tricks on the mind. I'm handing you my card, my contact details. If you remember something you've failed to mention now, I want you to call me immediately.'

Lucy took the card without looking at it and slipped it into the pocket of her jeans. 'There is nothing. I wish I could help you more.'

'Did you not think that maybe being late was preferable to leaving a missing child on her own, even if only for a minute?'

'Of course I thought about it. But as I say, I was confident that she'd soon be in your care. Oh? Another thought I had about the child was that she had some sort of global delay. She had a look on her face that I've seen on many, many such children. She wasn't going anywhere. I didn't want to stay and answer questions there and then because, like I say, I had a lecture to deliver and you surely would have made me late.'

There was a sudden knock on the door.

'Come in,' said Clay.

Sergeant Harris stepped into the room.

'Hello, Sergeant Harris,' said Lucy.

'I have something else to ask you, Lucy,' said Clay. 'Why did you turn your phone off?'

'When I'm not making calls, I always do. I turn it on when I need to make a call. And when I do that, I return any calls I've missed, if any, and there aren't many. I have to have it that way. Has my dad arrived, Sergeant Harris?'

'Sorry, Lucy. No, he hasn't.'

She looked disappointed to the core, and the last hot ember of Clay's frustration towards her turned to ash.

'I've got to ask you, Lucy. How do you get on in a packed lecture theatre? It must be stressful.'

'Yes, but not like this. In front of a crowd, I talk history and when I talk history, I know what I'm talking about, be it to one person or two hundred. That makes me happy. This is the up-side to my condition. My confident streak comes out and God gives me any other strength I need.'

Clay held Lucy's gaze.

'DCI Clay,' said Sergeant Harris. 'I've had a call from DS Mason at the scene of...'

Clay walked into the corner of the interview suite, behind Lucy's back, and Sergeant Harris followed.

'What's happening?' asked Clay.

'Terry Mason's ready for you to OK the removal of the bodies by the APTs to the mortuary.'

'I want to be there when it happens.' She looked at Lucy's back. 'I'll suspend the interview.'

Returning to the table, Clay said, 'We're going to catch up with you at some point later, Lucy, but for now you're free to go. There are plenty more questions I want to ask you.'

'I understand.'

'Where and when's your next lecture?' asked Hendricks.

'This afternoon, 19 Abercromby Square, two o'clock. Why?'

'We just want to get an idea of your whereabouts,' said Clay. 'We're all done for now. I know you don't want to, but I need you to promise me you're going to keep your phone on.'

'I. I—'

'Lucy, we could have been really cross with you for walking away from Marta!'

'Then I promise I'll keep my phone on.'

'Come on, Lucy,' said Sergeant Harris. 'Just a few questions from me at the desk and then you can go.'

She stood and followed Harris to the door and without a backward glance, left the room.

As the door closed, Clay turned to Hendricks. 'We need to check what Lucy Bell's told us against what Marta comes up with. I want you to find out as much as you can about Lucy.

Go and catch her lecture this afternoon. I want to know how she holds up in front of a crowd. It could be crucial when all this winds up in court.'

Clay weighed up the interview as a whole and the work that lay ahead of her. 'I'm going to visit her father. Father Aaron Bell. Let's see what that throws up.'

Chapter 24

12.45 am

Alone in the house, Raymond Dare lay on his unmade bed and looked at the screen of his phone. As he pressed the green messages icon, he debated whether to delete the messages and pictures he had been sent. He felt his cheek sting and a surge of rage overwhelmed him. He put the phone down on the duvet and walked out of his room to Jack's bedroom door.

Looking over the banister, there was no sign of Jasmine.

'I've put your fucking mutt in the kitchen, you arsehole, so what are you going to do about that?' he seethed at the door, squeezing the padlock and wishing it was Jack's throat. 'You'd better get that into your fucking piece of shit soul, twat.'

He heard the roar of traffic on Park Road and entered a regular daydream about Jack.

Jack would be mown down by a bus, not killed because that would be too easy for the bastard. No, he would have to spend months in hospital, paralysed from the neck down being spoon-fed by pretty young nurses, one Asian, one African, who as soon as the feeding was over would hoist him to the bathroom to remove his shitted-up pad and smile at each other behind his back as they wiped his now sagging and bed-sore-covered arse.

In his mind, Raymond opened the door of Jack's room with

the invisible key he now had in his control. It was a plain white room, the way Raymond had designed it, and there was a narrow bed with railings up the side to stop Jack falling out onto the bulging bag of bright yellow piss at his side.

He entered the room and turned on the bare red light bulb, then walked over to his brother who lay motionless on his back, staring up at the ceiling. Raymond picked up the switch next to the catheter bag and elevated his brother so that he was at an angle that would allow him to see into the room.

'Hello, you crippled sack of shit. We've got visitors. Get in here now, bitches!'

The African nurse followed the Asian nurse into the room, and Jack made a noise that signified the onset of tears.

'Let me see,' said Raymond, eyeing the women up and tormenting Jack with a glance. He pointed at the African nurse. 'You wipe his arse!' He prodded the Asian nurse under the chin, forcing her to look directly at him. 'Bend over, look back up at me and smile as I fuck you up the arse!'

The sound of Jasmine growling up the stairs brought the vivid fantasy to a crashing end, and he bounded for his own bedroom door.

As her breathing came closer his heart pounded. From his doorway, he saw she was watching him with evil in her eyes. Raymond tried to stare her out, but she remained perfectly still, growling at him, glaring up at him, daring and goading with defiant dog eyes.

Raymond slammed the door and, sitting down on the edge of the bed, felt his palms turn clammy as he pressed CJ on speed dial. The phone rang out and CJ's answer service kicked in.

'It's CJ. Leave a message, like...'

Yeah, you dickhead, thought Raymond. *For the coppers to listen to. Oh, God, shit, shit, shit. My phone's been bugged by the police.*

He dialled Buster and after three rings, Buster connected with, 'Right, la!'

'Where are you?'

'At the lock-up.'

'Who you with?' Raymond found a roach on his cluttered bedside table and sparked it up with a disposable lighter.

'Who the fuck do you think I'm with?' asked Buster.

'CJ?' Raymond frowned, sucking on the roach 'Like, CJ and you went to the lock-up without me.'

'You said you didn't want to go. When you chucked us out from yours. We asked you to come with us.'

Raymond had no recall of the exchange. He held a ball of smoke deep in his lungs and wracked his memory.

'You said, *I'm knackered.* I said, *I don't want to be around your house if Jack shows up. Come to the lock-up with us, bag up some weed and make some money.* And you said, *I can't be arsed.* You don't remember us talking?'

'Yeah, yeah,' he lied.

'You don't sound right, lad. What's up?'

'Can you and CJ get back to ours as soon as you can?'

'So Jack can kick our arses? What's up with you, Raymond?'

'I'll tell you when I see you.'

Behind the door, Jasmine's growling grew louder and she started scratching on the wood. *If my phone's been bugged*, he concluded, *why not the rest of the house?* The red-raw thought made Raymond feel like his bones had turned to Vaseline.

'Fuck it, I'll meet you at the lock-up, Buster. Keep your mobile on, lad.'

Raymond saw snow falling past his bedroom window and it reminded him how cold a day it was. He went to the wash basket in the corner of his room for his black North Face coat, and felt an ever-deepening sickness when it wasn't there. He rummaged but none of his clothes were there.

Mum's washed them and put them away, he hoped. He opened his wardrobe and the sickening inside him mushroomed when his coat and clothes just weren't there.

Outside, Jasmine's growling developed into barking, and she

clawed and clawed and clawed at the door. He dropped the roach onto the laminate flooring and crushed it with the sole of his trainer.

Raymond walked to the door, placed his fingers round the handle, and summoning up all his strength, opened it wide quickly.

Silence.

He looked down.

Jasmine wasn't there.

He moved to the head of the stairs and looked down into the hall.

Jasmine was at the bottom of the stairs.

Better get it into your soul... The words drifted from the surface of the dog's skin as if Jack himself was standing there. Calmly, she turned away from Raymond and made her way back to the kitchen.

Something shifted on the surface of Raymond's brain and everything suddenly seemed massive, the stairs river-wide, the ceiling where the sky used to be. He hung on to the banister and, for a moment, felt like broken glass was flowing through his veins.

He struggled but had no memory at all of his conversation with Buster, absolutely no memory of choosing to stay in the house while they went to the lock-up.

Memory? Memory...

No memory.

Chapter 25

1.30 pm

Cole got up and stood behind Sergeant Carol White as she stared at her laptop. On her screen was a stretch of shops on Picton

Road, with the door to the Adamczaks' flat next to Mr Zięba's Polish delicatessen far from the eye of the camera.

'How's it going, Whitey?'

'Lots of people have walked past the door in both directions but no one's come out of the flat and no one's gone in. It's half-past one in the morning and the volume of people passing the door has thinned to a trickle.'

Cole's landline rang out. When he saw the +22 followed by seven digits on the display, he lined up his notepad and pen and picked up the receiver. 'Detective Constable Barney Cole, Merseyside Constabulary.'

'Hello, my name is Deputy Commissioner Aleksandar Kasprzak from the Pruszków police, Poland.'

'Thank you for returning my call so promptly, Deputy Commissioner.'

Eyes still on the screen, White gave Cole a double thumbs-up and said, 'That was a quick call back.'

Cole noted the man's voice. He spoke English confidently and with a minimal accent, and sounded like he was in his late forties or early fifties. 'Can I just confirm that you are in overall charge of the police station in Pruszków?'

'I am in charge.'

'And that you have a picture of my warrant card with you?'

'Yes, I am confident that you are who you say you are.'

'We're looking to run a background check on a pair of identical twins who are...' Cole chose his words with infinite caution '... in the UK for the purposes of work...'

'Karl and Václav Adamczak? The junior officer who took your call did pass on their names to me. Are they in trouble?'

'They're not in trouble.'

'So why're we having this conversation?'

'They've been murdered.'

In the briefest of silences, Cole heard fleeting voices in the background and, beyond that, the rumble of traffic.

'This is an investigation at the very earliest of stages, sir, and we're looking for any information that could help us build a picture of the victims.'

'Karl Adamczak has no connection with the police in Pruszków. His identical twin Václav is known to us but has no criminal record. When their names were passed to me, I instructed two of my officers to build a detailed picture of exactly how and why Václav Adamczak was on our radar before he left Poland to live and work in the United Kingdom. In the interests of clarity, I want to be as precise as I possibly can be with you.'

Cole heard a deep intake of breath and the fizz of a bottle of carbonated liquid being unscrewed.

'Could you give me an idea of why Václav Adamczak was known to you?'

'An *idea* is simply that. What you need is a fully factual record of what we *know*.'

Cole held the receiver away from his ear and bit down on the frustration he felt at Deputy Commissioner Aleksandar Kasprzak's teasing precision.

'Are you still there, Detective Sergeant Cole?' His voice leaked from the receiver like a prayer lost on the west wind.

'Yes, Deputy Commissioner Kasprzak. Could you give me a time scale on when you'll be able to supply me with a full and accurate account of why Václav Adamczak is known to you.'

'Hours. Today...'

'You couldn't give me a hint...'

'Do you know every issue that is brought to the attention of the police on Merseyside?'

'No.'

'If you were asked for information from the police in Pruszków, would you inform them with poorly-sourced intelligence?'

Cole imagined his emotions if he turned in to work at Trinity Road one morning and Deputy Commissioner Kasprzak had performed a three-hundred-and-sixty-degree life swap with Detective Chief Inspector Eve Clay.

'Do you want to know the circumstances in which Karl and Václav Adamczak died?'

'Death is death. Murder is murder. The end, don't you agree?'

'With the greatest respect, no, I don't agree. But I appreciate you returning my call and the professional rigour with which you are dealing with our request for information.'

'I'll phone you as soon as my officers have briefed me on what Václav Adamczak did to bring himself to our attention.'

'According to people who knew them, Karl and Václav were watertight close, Deputy Commissioner Kasprzak. Was Karl involved in Václav's activity?'

'Wait on my call.'

'When?'

'When I know what I'm talking about.'

The line died and, as he put the receiver down, Cole soothed his frustration by looking at the sharpened-up diagram of the blurred graffiti that he'd been working on.

He started at the centre with the solid black circle at the heart of the symbol, and worked his way out to the edge. A band of black surrounded the central circle and this was mirrored in the dark band at the circumference. Cole counted the twelve lines that linked the circumference to the centre; each line was made of three parts. A short vertical line turned at a right angle into a horizontal line and this gave way to another vertical line that formed a link to the centre.

All that was left for him to do was to shade in four of these lines that he had outlined with his fine black line pen and ruler and to complete the last part of the circular circumference.

Cole picked up his pen, turned on his desk light and wondered what Google Reverse Image would throw up of this thing that looked like a cartwheel with crooked spokes, but was surely so much more.

Chapter 26

1.45 pm

The fire was blazing nicely.

Jack looked around the frozen garden and wondered for the thousandth time if he would ever live in a house that had such a beautiful space at the back door. The trunks of the skeletal apple trees and two pear trees that lined the bottom of the garden against the tall sandstone wall were lined with drifts of snow, and something deep in the pit of his heart sank.

He warmed his hands on the fire and walked past the life-sized marble statue of the Virgin Mary standing next to a frozen fountain that he'd turned off because of the bitter cold. Jack listened to the music of the garden, the birds in the trees and Father Aaron's beloved crickets and grasshoppers in the vegetation.

As he walked to the shed he reminded himself of Father Aaron's instructions for the day: *If it can be burned, please burn it. If you think it's of value leave it in the shed and we'll have a table sale to raise money for the good women running Levene House* – the hostel in Garston for battered and vulnerable women and their children.

Jack picked up an armful of wood that was cracked and buckled. He walked towards the fire in the rusting brazier and watched the sparks rise from the belly of the blaze.

Back in the shed, he looked around. On top of a brown single wardrobe was a wicker chair, which looked like it would sell easily. He stretched up, but on dragging the chair down, immediately saw that the seat and backing canes were mostly broken.

'For the fire, then,' said Jack, walking the chair down the garden and snapping its arms and legs, folding it as small as he could in preparation for the flames. The fire roared and the flames danced as Jack fed it into the brazier.

He passed the Virgin Mary, her saintly face blank of the fine detail that paint could add to a statue; but he felt her eyes were following him, reproaching him for not offering a prayer up to her. He stopped, bowed his head and offered a silent Hail Mary.

Walking back to the shed, Jack looked at the tall rear elevation of the huge Victorian house, and saw Father Aaron standing at the kitchen window, at the sink with a cloud of steam rising from the hot tap, gazing into the garden with the look of complete sadness that filled his eyes when he thought no one was looking at him.

Behind a stack of rusting garden tools, Jack's eye was drawn to a two-shelf bookcase on which sat rows of well-preserved leather albums and scrapbooks. He picked up the first album. On the first page were old colour photographs of Father Aaron with a handful of other men outside a church beside a huge cross. It was a hot day and they all wore the same short-sleeved black shirts and trousers. Jack realised this was the first time he had seen his employer without a bushy grey-black beard.

He closed the album, putting it back where he found it; there were ten of them on the top shelf and eight on the one below it. He ran his fingertips over the spines on the top shelf and squatted to comb them with his eyes.

Jack stopped at the eighth spine, his attention focused on the neat black handwriting that was almost lost in the deep blue of the spine.

Kelly-Ann Carter.

He opened the book and saw a newspaper clipping with the headline: 'TRIPLE MURDER OF SIBLINGS'.

Flicking through, he saw the scrapbook was dedicated to an American serial killer living on death row.

Jack heard Father Aaron's footsteps coming towards the shed.

'How's it going?' asked Father Aaron.

'There are some books here. I haven't looked through them all. I think they're photograph albums and scrapbooks.'

He extended the scrapbook to Father Aaron, who turned the pages slowly.

'Kelly-Ann Carter?' asked Jack. 'Who is she?'

'I write to several men and women on death row. Kelly-Ann Carter's one of them. She's going to be executed by lethal injection in a matter of weeks.' Father Aaron clasped the scrapbook to him. 'I'll keep this one. Burn the rest, Jack.'

'But they're old photographs of you.'

'Remember that little chat we had a few days back? What did I say about the past? The past doesn't exist. Erase any trace of it and don't speak of it again. Listen, Jack. I'm taking this scrapbook back into the house for now. The reason I kept it out in the shed was Lucy. You know how sensitive she is. What's about to happen to Kelly-Ann would give her nightmares. Please don't mention her or this book to her.'

'I won't say a word. What do you want me to do with the garden tools? Keep them or burn them?'

'Burn them.' Father Aaron looked closely into the shed. 'I'll leave it up to you, Jack. Like I said, if you think we can raise some money with them, keep them. If you don't, burn them. You can do what you want with everything. Well, would you look at that, Jack.'

A cricket chirruped from inside the garage, sitting on the photograph albums and rubbing its back legs together. Father Aaron chirruped back, an uncannily good impersonation, and the cricket flew onto his outstretched finger, landing on it. He admired it and then blew on it, sending it on its way into the garden.

'Are you sure about the photograph albums, Father Aaron?'

'Absolutely. Let's have a fire that would put Old Nick to shame.'

Chapter 27

1.45 pm

Outside 682 Picton Road, Clay stopped between two black mortuary vans parked near the entrance of the building and saw a pair of ghost-like pictures of herself reflected in the sheen of their surfaces.

Looking away from the double mirage of herself and up at the blackened window, she heard voices drift from inside the murder scene.

'Who's inside now?' she asked the young constable running the log at the door.

He double-checked his log. 'DS Terry Mason and Sergeant Paul Price from Scientific Support. Harper and Kline, the APTs from the mortuary.'

The wind howled as she walked up the staircase. Over the force of the weather outside and the turning blades of the fan in the doorway, Clay heard the unzipping of a body bag.

'Terry?' she called.

'Eve,' replied Mason. 'Wait at the top of the stairs, please.'

She stopped on the top stair and looked down the length of the corridor, the gloom of the windowless space now dispersed by a powerful arc light at the far end that made the pictures of the Virgin Mary shine on the walls.

Clay walked to the door and made eye contact with Mason in a room where the living narrowly outnumbered the dead.

'We'll help you take the bodies away from each other, Harper.' For a micro-beat, Mason raised his eyes to the ceiling. 'But how are we going to do it?'

'Brute force,' replied Harper. 'There's no other way.'

He crouched down to get a closer look at where the bodies had melted into each other, and Clay joined him. Fire had turned their clothes to dust and the flesh around their abdomens and ribs had fused together.

'Think of it this way, Eve. If you cooked two sausages across each other in a very hot oven and doused them in fire accelerant, they'd cook into each other where their skins and the meat beneath were exposed. But what would happen to the space where they were unexposed – where the sausages, or bodies in this case, were connecting?'

Clay thought about it and replied, 'They'd remain raw on the inside.' She looked at the bodies and took a huge breath. 'Let's just get on with this. Tell me what to do.'

'Terry,' said Harper. 'Put your hands under the top of the upper cadaver's thighs. Eve, the same but the right arm, right up into the armpit, I'll do the same on the left-hand side.' He looked at his young assistant and said, 'Kline, take a step back and watch how this is done, in case you ever have to call the shots at a scene like this.'

As Clay felt the cooked meat of his armpit, she noticed how her other senses were suddenly sharpened. She smelled and tasted pork, and bit down her gagging reflex.

'Are we all in place? Are we all secure and ready to tear them apart?'

'Yes,' said Clay, looking at the graffiti on the wall, the blurred geometric globe, and thought about the language on the wall behind her. *Killing Time Is Here Embrace It.*

'On the count of three, then,' said Harper. 'Ready? One, two, three, lift.' At first the weight of the man on top of the human sculpture and the glue of two melted bodies caused a stubborn resistance.

'Brute force. Just keep lifting,' said Harper.

Out of the corner of her eye, Clay saw Mason lifting the thighs higher as the skin above the pubic bone ripped away from the body beneath it; it sounded like Velcro being torn apart. From the pubic bone to the base of the ribs, flesh tore away from flesh as they separated the two bodies.

'Get those thighs as high up as you can, Terry,' said Harper.

Beneath the latex that gloved her hands, Clay felt a dampness in the roots of his armpit that made her skin crawl. Mason's elbows jutted out and his shoulders rose as he raised the thighs. Clay summoned all her strength and the flesh in her hands rasped away from the flesh beneath it.

As they lifted the body clean away, it felt like a dead weight in Clay's hands, a single body that felt like ten.

'Lay him down,' said Harper. 'On his back.'

With her iPhone, Clay took pictures of both men. She selected the clearest pictures and sent them to Hendricks, Stone, Cole and Winters. She looked at the bodies in turn and back again, half-cooked and half-raw. She heard blood thumping in her head and, as the wind whipped the building outside, she imagined a stormy red sea lashing the darkened heavens.

What kind of savages are we dealing with here?

Chapter 28

3.20 pm

Detective Sergeant Bill Hendricks sat at the centre of a crowded lecture theatre in Abercromby Square, watching Lucy Bell give a lecture about Joseph Stalin's rise to power. He looked at the faces around him and it wasn't the fact that he was the oldest person in the room that caused him a momentary melancholy; it was that Lucy Bell's students were mostly young enough to be his children.

Lucy was perfectly still, her voice level and loud enough not to need a microphone. With her back straight, she looked around the room as if trying to make eye contact with as many students as she could.

He looked at the screen behind her head, split down the middle by two portraits of the same man. Joseph Stalin. The young man, thin-faced, wide-eyed and with a mop of black hair swept back into an unruly quiff. The older man, his face filled out, eyes narrowed by time and greying hair slicked back.

Checking his watch, Hendricks saw that the lecture was due to wind up soon. He turned on the video on his iPhone and zoomed in on Lucy Bell, filming her as she rounded up what had been an entertaining and informative lecture on the brutal rise of an absurd but ferocious monster.

'As historians you must never seek to avoid analysing the psychology of the leader. Stalin did what he did through choice, and his choices were beyond mitigation. Never allow yourselves to shift the blame to abstractions or make excuses based on faceless historical forces. Stare the evidence in the face and base your conclusions on facts, but never ever allow your subject off the hook. Essays in a week Monday, 10 am. No extensions. No excuses.'

Hendricks watched the students as they filed out in front of Lucy, but none of them stopped to engage directly with the young lecturer, to ask a question or seek clarification of some difficult point from the hour-and-a-half lesson.

Watching her through the eye of his iPhone's video, he recorded reversible change. Ninety minutes earlier, she had transformed just as quickly from a wallflower to a full-on and confident teacher; now she switched back to a woman who looked uneasy with who and what she was. Her head, which she'd held so high during the lecture, drooped as she focused on placing folders and books inside her brown leather satchel. The ramrod spine started to bend and her shoulders developed a stoop that reduced her in height.

'Excuse me? Can I get past please?' A timid female voice at Hendricks's side sent him straight to the inner pocket of his coat for his warrant card. Keeping the iPhone on Lucy, he glanced sideways at a tall wholesome-looking girl with pigtails, the nineteen-year-old manifestation of the fictional child Pippi Longstocking.

'Do me a favour,' said Hendricks. 'And please don't take this the wrong way.' He showed her his warrant card. 'This is nothing to worry about, but please sit down. I've got a few questions I'd like to ask you.'

He sensed a sudden infusion of low-level panic as the student sat next to him.

The flow of human traffic passing Lucy Bell thinned and, as she finished placing the last of her papers and books in her bag, Hendricks noticed she had fully completed the metamorphosis: the confident and assertive spirit fled her body and the soul of a diffident and doubt-ridden loner had resumed its tenancy.

She turned a chair round so that it faced sideways-on and sat down with her back to the door.

Hendricks kept filming as she placed the satchel on her knee and stared into space, her lips moving slightly as if she were talking to herself, praying to a God he guessed had allowed her to be that other person as she got on with her job. He pressed stop, feeling utterly sorry for her, understanding how her lack of confidence may have led her to walk away from Marta Ondřej.

Smiling, he turned to the young woman at his side and said, 'My name's Detective Sergeant Bill Hendricks. I'm with the Merseyside Constabulary. And you are...?'

'Jenny. Jennifer White. Jenny.'

'Thanks, Jenny.'

Lucy stood up and, with her back to Hendricks and Jenny, walked towards the door, her movements mechanical as she left the lecture theatre.

'I – I saw you filming Lucy with your phone,' said Jenny. 'She's not in trouble with you, is she?'

'No. We're at the very earliest stages of a complex investigation and I really can't divulge any information to you. But please don't worry about Lucy. Really. She's done us a favour this morning.'

Hendricks smiled and felt Jenny softening as she looked at him, weighing him up, reassured by the genuine kindness he felt towards a young woman with an openness that could make her a very useful witness.

'I need to know a little bit about Lucy,' said Hendricks.

'Such as?'

'Is she forgetful?'

'Forgetful? Why do you ask that?'

Hendricks indicated the space that Lucy had just vacated.

'She's left her satchel behind.' *Just like she left Marta Ondřej behind*, thought Hendricks. 'What's she like as a teacher?'

'She's a brilliant teacher but when she's not teaching she's massively shy. She's like…'

'I think you're going to say an actress, but didn't want to use that word because it sounds like she's some kind of fake.'

'That's exactly right,' she confirmed, with the air of a woman on the receiving end of a deep secret at a séance.

'I knew a girl when I was at uni in Cambridge,' said Hendricks. 'She was totally withdrawn, so much so she used to go to a counsellor. No one heard her speak for eighteen months. Then, on her counsellor's suggestion, she joined the Drama Society, and when the spotlight hit her on stage, she turned into this colossus of confidence. Three months after joining, she played the lead in John Webster's *The Duchess of Malfi*. Once the greasepaint was off, well, she wasn't as quiet as she had been, but she was still pretty much withdrawn. It's not unheard of.'

'I asked my academic tutor about her.' Jenny's voice dropped and her hand rose to her mouth, shielding her lips as she spoke. 'She's on the autistic spectrum. She has Asperger's syndrome. Which means she wants to belong but finds it very hard, unlike people who are plain autistic and usually don't care if they do or don't belong. My sister's got Asperger's, that's how I know about it.'

As Hendricks considered the information, he asked, 'She's outstanding in a large room full of students like this. How does she hold up in a small room for a symposium?'

'The same. Great. When she's talking history, she's fine. Ask her the time of day on the corridor and she'll run away like she's seen a vampire.'

'She's marked your work?'

'She's a fair marker. Diligent, conscientious. She gives lots of constructive criticism. I wish they were all like her.'

'Do you know anything about her life outside the University of Liverpool?'

'I've heard she's very religious and she lives at home with her father, but that's as much as I know. I really don't know anything else about her.'

'Thank you, Jenny,' said Hendricks, handing her his contact card. 'If you find anything out or anything seems... unusual, call me on my mobile number. I'll take her bag to her. Can you tell me where her office is?'

'On the third floor, next door.'

Hendricks turned to the voice in the doorway and saw Lucy Bell looking directly at him. There was something in her voice like she was breaking up inside.

'You came in here very quietly,' said Hendricks, standing and making his way to the aisle. *Like the creeping Jesus.*

Lucy moved to the spot where she had just been teaching, both hands on the handle of her satchel which she now held in front of her like a piece of armour.

'I'll go now...' Jenny hurried down the aisle to the door.

'I was very impressed, Lucy – you nailed so many good points about Stalin.'

Lucy nodded her head once, let out a soundless, 'Yes...' and started walking towards the door. 'He trained to be a priest but failed. So he turned to politics and did the same again. Only this time, the suffering he unleashed...'

As Hendricks made his way towards her, he smiled, but she took a backwards step as he came close.

'Why are you asking questions about me?'

'You're very important to us, Lucy, and we need to find out as much as we can about you so that we can get the best from you and support you to the best of our abilities.'

'I haven't done anything wrong.' She sounded like a small girl wrongly accused in the head teacher's office.

'No, Lucy, you've helped us.'

'Will you go and see my father?'

'One of us will.'

'He's cross with me. He said I should have stayed with her. How I wish I had now.'

'We'll call you, Lucy. Keep your phone on at all times, OK?'
'DCI Clay told me to do that and I promised...'
'Brilliant lecture, Lucy, I learned so much. Thank you.'

Chapter 29

4.15 pm

'I'm looking for Father Aaron Bell,' said DCI Eve Clay to the young man shovelling snow at the gate of St Luke's Roman Catholic Church.

He smiled as Clay showed her warrant card and said, 'Father Aaron? He's in the church.' He put down his spade. 'Let me help you.'

He skipped up the gritted steps towards the church's front door and took out a huge metal key.

'Are you Father Aaron's curate?'

He laughed and glanced over his shoulder at her. 'I wish. Nothing quite so grand. I do the garden and odd jobs.' He stuck the metal key into the large keyhole.

'What's your name?'

'Jack Dare.'

Jack opened the door and, as he stepped inside, classical music drifted from the altar. 'Father Aaron! Father Aaron!'

The music stopped.

'Father Aaron, you have a visitor. Nice to meet you, DCI Clay. I'll leave you with Father Aaron – it's back to the snow for me.'

As she entered the church, the smell of wax threw Clay back to her early childhood in St Clare's under the loving care of Sister Philomena. In her mind, she saw a picture of herself kneeling next to Philomena in the chapel at St Clare's, feeling the sister's protective arm settle round her shoulders as together they sounded the last amen: a woman and her surrogate child at one with each other.

The memory filled her with the urge to go home and be with her son Philip and her husband Thomas. She fought down the desire this stirred and told herself to get on with the job in hand.

In front of the altar, a tall man dressed head to toe in black and with a head of thick grey hair pushed a mop up and down the wooden floor. The words *poverty*, *chastity* and *obedience* crossed Clay's mind.

Leaving her open umbrella at the church door, she walked down the side aisle.

'Father Aaron Bell?'

The man stopped mopping, fell silent and looked at Clay as she advanced. He stuck the mop head back in the bucket and propped the handle against the front pew.

He nodded. 'I am.'

Clay showed her warrant card to the priest.

Father Aaron indicated the front pew, said, 'Let's have a seat.'

'Father Aaron, I can hear a hint of an accent there.'

'I thought it was altogether gone. I'm from Scotland originally. Edinburgh, to be precise.'

Around the intricate stained glass on the wall above the altar, swathes of green paint hung in curls away from the bare plaster beneath.

Father Aaron genuflected slowly and the effort showed in his face. He settled his large frame on the pew and Clay wondered if the wood was going to support the weight of a man who looked like he'd played a lot of rugby in his younger years. When he folded his hands together, the muscles in his forearms tightened; and as he looked up to the crucified Christ above the altar, Clay knew that the old man was offering up silent prayers.

Father Aaron turned and looked directly at Clay. She made out a bend in his nose that looked like an old break; either side of his misshapen nose, the man's eyes were deep brown and had an indelible smile stamped on them.

'You don't have anyone to help you with the cleaning?' asked Clay.

'There are some female parishioners who have volunteered to help clean the church and my house next door, but I don't believe it's right or decent to expect other people to perform menial tasks that I'm still capable of. I'm not a young man. There may be a time when I have to take up that offer, but at least I'll know that when I could do it, I did it myself. Jack helps me with the heavier chores.'

'The young man who showed me in here?'

'He's a good boy. But you've come to talk to me about Lucy, right?'

'Right.' Clay processed a thought. 'How about Lucy helping you out?'

Father Aaron laughed and gave the domed ceiling and the heavens beyond a brief but knowing glance.

'She's just not domesticated. Her head's full of books. She simply isn't practical. If I gave her a mop and bucket and asked her to clean the church, she'd end up flooding the building. I gave her a paintbrush and a pot of varnish once and more varnish ended up on her than on the garden fence.'

'Are you sure she didn't do that so that you wouldn't ask again?'

'Maybe.' He smiled and said, 'I guess you must think it rather odd a Catholic priest having a daughter.'

'I'm clued in. I know you didn't adopt her.'

'The church wouldn't have allowed that for many obvious, shameful and alarming reasons. I wasn't always a priest. I was a married man most of my adult life and Lucy was our only daughter. When Lucy's mother died, just before she started at Cambridge University, and I was left alone in a big old house in Cressington Park, I felt God calling me to the priesthood. So when she started her second year, I started my training at Ampleforth. They accepted me even though I was in my sixties. I was relatively fit and healthy and there's a great shortage of priests, so beggars can't be choosers.'

'What did you do before you were a priest, Father Aaron?'

'I was an entomologist. Insects were my general love, crickets and grasshoppers my greatest passion. As I'd retired and Lucy had left home, I ended up volunteering in the University of Liverpool Veterinary Laboratory Services, Parasitology and Entomology Department.' He pointed at his head and said, 'I'm still an entomologist, and always will be. The detail of God's creation never ceases to amaze me.'

'My son Philip, he's four. He's obsessed with insects. He'd love to meet someone who could answer his thousands of questions.'

'That can be arranged, DCI Clay.'

Father Aaron turned to face the altar again, his brown-eyed gaze filled with love. Clay marked him down as a man who took better care of his church than of his own personal appearance.

'At this moment in time, I'm not exactly happy with Lucy, Detective Clay. She told me what happened and how she'd walked away from the little one. I couldn't believe it. Lucy is on the autistic spectrum but that's no excuse. She was trained rigorously by her mother and I on what to do and what not to do in social situations, and she knows what she did was wrong. She didn't tell me about it until the situation was over and there was nothing I could do to help. She was already on her way to Trinity Road when I found out. How did she get on, DCI Clay?'

'She was very nervous. I interviewed her.'

'DCI Clay? *Eve* Clay?' It was as if the old priest had been struck by lightning in the deepest seat of his memory. 'My oh my... You're that Eve Clay, aren't you? It said in the paper, you're leading the investigation into Marta's disappearance?'

'I am.'

'We have a mutual friend. A nun called Sister Ruth.'

'Sister Ruth who spent two years in St Clare's when I was four or five?' Memory flooded Clay, filled her with a silence that made her reticent.

'Did she?' The priest smiled, and her reticence was overtaken by the need to know.

'Yes. We met again a few years later when she came to work at St Michael's, the children's home I moved into after...' Eve paused.

'Yes, DCI Clay?' prompted the priest gently.

'After Sister Philomena died and I was moved to my second childhood home. She came to St Michael's a couple of years after I arrived there and left a few years later. I wasn't allowed to keep in touch with her. Please, tell me more about Sister Ruth.'

'Her whole life was devoted to caring for orphaned and abandoned children. She was an unsung saint.'

Was? thought Clay. 'Is she still alive?'

'Yes.'

'And you're in touch with her?'

'She lives in Aigburth, in Bethlehem House off Dundonald Road.'

'Is she in good health? Mentally and physically?'

Father Aaron touched the side of his head. 'As bright as a newly minted penny.'

'Could you give me her contact details so I can offer to visit her?'

The smile on Father Aaron's face faded and he shook his head. 'Not right now, no. I'd have to speak to her first.'

'Of course.'

'And if Ruth wants you to contact her, I'd have to deliver the request directly. The human touch. I can get the ball rolling today.'

The door of the church creaked open and Clay listened to the uneven approaching footsteps heading towards the altar. For a moment, she wondered if the person was crippled.

Without turning his head, Father Aaron said, 'Hello, Lucy.'

'Hello, Dad.'

Father Aaron spoke softly. 'She's a slave to the rigid lines in her head. She has improved with age and she'll be full of remorse for what she did earlier, or rather didn't do. I hope that confirms the impression you have made so far of my Lucy.'

As she sat in the pew behind them, Clay turned to look at Lucy and saw her father's eyes in hers. Her jet-black hair glistened with melting snow and when she looked at Clay, her breath condensed on the air.

'Second time we've met today, Lucy.' She showed her warrant card, but Lucy didn't look at it – just straight through her, as if focusing on the space behind her head.

'DCI Clay, why are you here?'

'Lucy, it's DCI Clay's job to ask the questions...'

'I came here to speak to your father. To learn more about you. And to talk to you if at all possible.'

Clay looked down at the satchel on Lucy's lap, almost overflowing with books, and then up at the intensity on her face.

'We're going to be asking you in for another interview soon.'

'I've already told you everything I know. What on earth do you want to talk to me about?'

'Lucy! Enough.'

'Sorry. I'm sorry.'

'Thank you for your time, Father Aaron.' Clay stood up. 'We'll be in touch, Lucy. It's really nothing to worry about.'

As she walked to the front door of the church, she listened hard, but neither father nor daughter so much as whispered. Acting on instinct, Clay stepped into the shadows around the door, waiting to see what would happen. She opened the door and closed it with a thud.

Time passed and nothing was said until Lucy broke the silence. 'I'm sorry, Dad, for leaving that poor little girl on her own.'

'It was a foolish and unkind thing to do, Lucy. What question do I always ask you to ask yourself? Ask yourself the question now and tell me the answer.'

After a handful of heavy moments, Lucy said, 'Jesus would not have left that poor little girl's side for one second.'

'If you'd have acted like Jesus this morning and handed the child over to the authorities, you wouldn't have the police on your back now.'

Clay felt something in her heart bend when she heard Lucy sobbing. As the sobs echoed, she felt her shoulders sag with an invisible burden of sadness.

'Dad, I want you to take me for confession.'

'Now?'

'In the confessional box, not face to face.'

She listened as the priest and his daughter shuffled towards the box, and heard the front door of the church creak open. As he entered the building, Jack propped the snow shovel against the wall.

'DCI Clay, are you waiting for someone? Something?'

She picked up her umbrella and said, 'I almost forgot this on my way out.'

The young man smiled, and Clay noticed how the beads of melted snow on his eyelashes gave his eyes an angelic but distinctly sad cast.

What's your baggage, Jack? she wondered. *Why are you here in St Luke's with an elderly priest and his autistic daughter?*

'It's been nice to meet you, DCI Clay.'

'Likewise.'

'Father Aaron? He's not in trouble again, is he?' laughed Jack. 'Joking aside, no, not at all.'

Clay looked at her watch and said, 'I've got to go.'

She watched the young man walking towards the pews. He genuflected and took a place kneeling at the end of the last pew, falling into silent prayer with his head down on his folded hands.

She listened and heard a sound that felt completely out of place in a church. Somewhere, a grasshopper or a cricket was rubbing its back legs together and chirruping.

She opened and closed the main door with infinite care, then walked out into the slanting snow with her cheeks burning and a worm turning in the centre of her brain.

The unspoken question that Father Aaron had posed to his daughter worked deeper inside her head.

What would Jesus do?
And Lucy's answer echoed against the plates of Clay's skull.

Chapter 30

5.15 pm

On Facebook, Detective Constable Barney Cole found three matches for Lucy Bell in Liverpool: a twelve-year-old girl; a woman in her fifties and, bang in the middle of her namesakes, *the* Lucy Bell he was looking for.

He got onto her home page and saw that the profile picture was quite old – she looked ten years younger, thinner, and the camera had caught her in a good light. The common links between the profile picture and her current appearance were the jet-black hair and the vivid eye-liner.

Cole made notes in his spiral-bound pad. Lucy was a Eucharistic minister in the Roman Catholic Church and had studied history at King's College, Cambridge. Her hero was the historian Eric Hobsbawm. She volunteered at Levene House.

He looked at the door of the incident room as it opened.

'Hey, Barney...'

'Clive!' Cole raised a hand but kept his eyes on the screen as Winters walked towards him, passing behind Carol White as he did so.

'Hello, Carol. What are you doing here?' asked Winters.

'It's nice to see you too, Clive.' She tilted her head back and squinted at her laptop screen.

Winters looked at the paused image, and groaned. 'CCTV from the Picton Road scene. You have my sympathies, Carol.'

He pulled a chair up and sat next to Cole. 'You on Facebook in work time, *again*? What you looking at?'

'Lucy Bell. Eve wants background information before she pulls Lucy in again.'

Cole scrolled down the page and saw a handful of photos in the gallery. In the first picture she was around three years of age with a man in his late forties.

'I guess that's her father, the priest.'

'Sergeant Harris said she was asking for him like a little kid,' said Winters.

With Lucy aged five and in his arms, Aaron Bell had a short back and sides, jet-black hair and was clean shaven. As she progressed through single figures and into her teens, his hair turned white.

Cole focused on a picture of Lucy in her early teens, her father standing behind her next to a waterfall.

'Notice anything odd, Clive?'

'Two things. What do you see?'

'There isn't a single picture of either of them smiling,' replied Cole. 'What's the second thing?'

'There was a mother on the scene. She died when Lucy was eighteen or thereabouts. No sign of a mother in the pictures.'

Cole scrolled and saw an image of Lucy at the front of a small group of women arranged in layers on the stone steps of the Metropolitan Catholic Cathedral. At the base of the image was the subheading 'Easter 2012'.

Dressed in a black shirt, cardigan and dog collar, Lucy was the youngest in a group of odd-looking female misfits of all shapes and sizes. He noticed how, for the first time in the photographs she had posted on Facebook, she smiled like all her Christmases had come together in a series of faith-inspired moments, and his head connected with his heart.

'First picture without daddy,' observed Winters.

Cole moved onto the next image.

Lucy knelt at the altar rail in front of the same group of women, her eyes closed and head tilted down. In front of her a bishop wearing a gold mitre had his hands on either side of her head and face, fingers spread to reach as much surface area as possible, his mouth open speaking the words of ordination, drawing Lucy deeper into the circle of the church. And Cole noticed, in the group of priests to the side and back of the bishop, Father Aaron Bell watched his daughter with a look of grim determination.

He scanned the next set of pictures and noticed that she was either on her own or with people who were considerably older than her.

'Bingo,' said Winters. 'Ballroom dancing with another woman. Eating cream tea in the parochial club. Watching paint dry in the church hall. And there I was thinking ET was the only image system that could make me want to cry.'

There was a picture of Lucy with a group of women and children outside a tall building with a sign by the front door: Levene House.

'She volunteers there,' said Cole.

'I'm Googling it,' replied Winters, nimble thumbs on his iPhone. 'Got it. It's a refuge centre for women and children who've been on the receiving end of domestic abuse. They also take in women who are vulnerable because of homelessness and mental health issues.'

Cole moved to the right of the page to check out Lucy's fifteen friends. They were all young people, late teens to mid-twenties, posing into the camera, male and female giving their profile picture the best possible shot. He scrutinised each image for anything that jumped out. Smiling female, Mary O'Learey; pouting female, Jac Rivers; poker-faced male, Tom Head.

'These won't be real friends,' said Winters, as Cole scrolled through the faces. 'These'll be her students trying to blow smoke up the crack of the lonely woman marking their assignments.'

'I'll email it all to Eve, and copy everyone in on what we've seen,' said Cole.

'What do you make of Lucy Bell?' asked Winters.

Cole made a note on his spiral bound pad and read it out loud. 'Not a lot of joy in this lonely woman's life.'

Chapter 31

5.30 pm

In the viewing gallery of the mortuary at the back of the Royal Liverpool Hospital, Clay looked at the photos of the two dead Polish men she had just taken on her iPhone. Above the white sheets that covered both of them from the necks down were two charred faces, identical in death as they had been in life: the murdered twins, Karl and Václav Adamczak.

She heard footsteps approaching the viewing gallery and, recognising Aneta Kaloza's voice accompanying Detective Sergeant Bill Hendricks through the wall, felt a dead weight descend from the centre of her brain to the pit of her being.

As Clay looked through the glass at the bodies on the table, pictures from religious books from her childhood flooded her mind. Jesus wrapped in a shroud. Jesus laid to rest in a shroud in a cave, then the entrance being blocked with a huge stone; the stone rolled aside and Jesus gone, the white shroud discarded on the ground just inside the cave.

You see, Eve, not even death could defeat the redeemer.

Sister Philomena's voice was alive inside her, supporting her as she made a sudden and unwanted imaginative leap. She could not stop seeing the shape of her husband Thomas under the white sheet, his face burned out, bones and teeth exposed to the air; and then, rolling on fast-forward into the future, seeing her son Philip's grown-up form, horizontal and dead in the viewing room. As the painful pictures faded from her mind, she was grateful for the memory of her surrogate mother and knew that the thought of Philomena would help her face Aneta Kaloza in the next few moments.

As the voices came closer, Clay was glad that the mortuary manager Barbara Peters had taken charge of the viewing.

She spoke to Barbara on the other side of the glass. 'Turn off the light, please.' And the room in which the bodies lay was filled with deep darkness.

The door opened and Detective Sergeant Bill Hendricks said, 'Step this way, please, Aneta.'

Clay turned. Since she'd last seen Aneta outside the crime scene in Picton Road, it was like she had aged several years.

'Thank you for coming to identify the bodies, Aneta,' she said. 'I know they're your friends and I appreciate how difficult this must be for you.'

Aneta nodded. 'Where are they?'

'They're behind that glass partition,' said Clay. 'When you're ready to see them, Barbara will turn on the light.'

Without hesitation, Aneta said, 'I'm ready.'

As the light came on and the shapes of their bodies became clear beneath the sheets, Aneta appeared to be punched on the jaw by an invisible fist. Her head moved up and away as her eyes stared at the ceiling above her.

'Oh...'

Then she looked down and directly through the glass.

'I'm sorry, Aneta,' said Clay, placing her hand on the woman's arm. 'Barbara can fold down the sheets covering them to show you any distinct marks on their bodies,' said Clay. 'But I have to warn you, Aneta, just like their heads and faces, much of their bodies have been badly burned.'

Aneta wiped both eyes at once and took several breaths.

'Did they have any identifying marks on their bodies?' asked Clay.

'Karl has a tattoo of the white eagle from the Polish flag on his left upper arm. Because the tattoo ink is white and he is white, it makes it look like the tattoo is raised from the skin,' said Aneta.

Barbara positioned herself at the head of the table and, as she folded the sheet down to reveal each of the victims' upper torsos, Aneta fell forward onto the glass partition, stopping herself with her hands. Clay looked at Hendricks, who placed his hands on Aneta's shoulders, raising her from the glass and supporting her.

'It's either Karl or Václav Adamczak.'

'Aneta, if you can't make an identification, we can always check their dental records and do it that way.'

Aneta looked like she was desperate to say something, but that the words inside her head were moving at such speed that she couldn't pin them down into speech.

Clay caught Barbara's attention. 'Can you look very closely at both of their upper left arms, please?'

Taking a torch from the pocket of her blue tunic, Barbara shone the light on the upper left arm of the victim furthest from the glass. She repeated the search on the next victim and, looking at Clay, stepped forward to the glass.

'Both upper left arms are completely burned,' she said softly. 'The skin of their arms has melted into the flesh of their torsos.'

'Absolutely no sign of a white eagle?' Clay hoped out loud.

She shook her head. 'Sorry.'

'Aneta,' said Clay, 'can you think of any other distinguishing features? For either man?'

'Well...' Aneta looked at the bodies behind the glass. 'Karl.' She turned to Clay. 'Karl. His left ankle. Has this been burned to nothing?'

'From the knees down there was very little damage to either man,' replied Clay.

'Let me see his left ankle.'

Barbara moved to the other end of the table and, lifting the sheets back, revealed feet and ankles untouched by fire.

'Excuse me,' said Aneta. 'Can you see a tattoo of a spider on the inner ankle of either of my friends?'

Barbara turned the left foot of the body furthest from the glass and said, 'No.'

Then she turned the ankle of the next body.

'Yes...'

'Don't say what kind of spider it is!' Aneta turned to Clay and Hendricks. 'Can you see it from here?'

'No,' replied Clay.

'It's a tarantula,' said Aneta.

'Yes, it's a tarantula,' confirmed Barbara.

Aneta pointed at the body nearest the glass and said, 'This is Karl Adamczak. And the man lying next to him is almost certainly his twin brother Václav.'

'So, definitely Karl,' said Clay. '*Almost* certainly Václav? We'll assume it's Václav. But we'll have to check his dental records.'

'Karl got the tattoo on his eighteenth birthday against his mother's wishes. When she found out, Mrs Adamczak was furious and threw him out of the house. He stayed a while with my family. Václav begged his mother to forgive his twin and in the end she gave way and took him back home.'

'Was there any significance to the tattoo being a tarantula?' asked Clay.

'It was his nick-name in high school. Tarantula.' A fleeting smile pierced the depths of sadness in her eyes and then sank under the weight of her grief.

Barbara covered their ankles and feet and lay cloths over each of their charred faces.

'Why Tarantula?' Hendricks's voice was just above a whisper.

'Because he was hairy and scary to look at, but he was completely harmless. There was no…' Aneta paused, looking for the word, '… venom in him. He was a lovely boy. And as he grew older, he became an even lovelier man.'

In the silence that followed, Barbara looked at Clay and said, 'Can I take them to the autopsy suite now?'

As Hendricks led Aneta out of the viewing room, she broke down into hopeless sobbing. Alone, Clay looked into the empty space where Karl and Václav Adamczaks' bodies had been and felt a rush of bitter sadness.

They should have been working, joking with each other and drinking tea on the building site, sending money home to their mothers and families, planning on where and when to go for a few pints and to watch a football match at the pub.

Instead their lives had been stolen. *Killing Time Is Here*, thought Clay. *Embrace It*? She had no choice. She was certain other bodies would show up in an open season for slaughter.

Chapter 32

8.30 pm

Father Aaron Bell was woken from a disturbed slumber on the couch in his living room by the ringing of the phone on the table in front of him.

In the corner of the room, disjointed modern classical music drifted from Radio Three. Father Aaron reached out for the receiver and when he placed it to his ear, knew immediately that the call was from far away.

There was a pause and in that second, Father Aaron looked at the time on the small grandfather clock on the wall opposite him.

Eight-thirty UK time. He did the maths. Six hours ahead here. Two-thirty in the afternoon in South Carolina.

'Aaron Bell?'

He recognised the voice of Simon Wheatley, the Welsh human rights lawyer who had handled Kelly-Ann Carter's appeal for clemency for the last ten years.

'Simon, thank you for calling,' said Father Aaron, making it to an upright position. In the background, he heard voices chanting a slogan – a demonstration in progress.

'I'm sorry, Aaron. It's bad news. The worst. Kelly-Ann's appeal to the governor of South Carolina has failed. She's going to be executed by lethal injection in a little over three months' time.'

Father Aaron stood up and turned off the radio. 'How did she take the news, Simon?'

'As she always does. With dignity and self-respect. It was the last chance, and it's gone.'

'I suppose it's inevitable,' said Father Aaron. 'Unfortunately.'

'She still provokes a lot of anger here,' said Simon. 'She's a hate figure. The governor knows, everyone knows, that if he'd given her clemency there'd have been race riots on the streets. He did the thing the British government would have loved to have done to Ian Brady and Myra Hindley. But they didn't have the luxury of the death penalty.'

'So she's still hated that much?'

'More so with the passage of time. She's the bogey woman. People don't believe her remorse; they don't buy that she's changed.'

'What did she say?' asked Father Aaron.

'That she will welcome death as a bride meets her groom, and that she hopes the Lord will take mercy on her embattled soul. She will spend the next three months in constant prayer. She thanked me for trying to save her life. She asked me to pass on her remorseful apologies to the families of her victims. And she had a message for you, Aaron.'

'What was that message?'

'She says she's grateful to you for all the letters you wrote to her while she was on death row, that your words of comfort helped her get through some dark times. She's sorry that you never managed to visit her in person but she understands why you couldn't, and she wants you to forgive yourself for not making it over. She wants you to pray hard for her and she says that she'll pray for you until the last moment.' The line crackled. 'Will you make it over to visit her during the next three months?'

'I doubt it. Can you tell her that I am praying long and hard for her and that I will pray for her just as I have been doing for the last thirty years.'

Behind the silence between himself and the lawyer, the demonstrators were now singing, and Father Aaron could hear bitter tears being shed outside the jail.

'No more words for now then, Father Aaron,' said Simon Wheatley. 'I don't care what time it is. I'm going for a beer.'

Father Aaron heard him hang up and for many moments kept the phone pressed to his ear, listening.

The dead tone.

Chapter 33

8.30 pm

The only sound breaking the peace in Levene House was a baby crying in one of the upstairs bedrooms and, from the large living room at the front of the hostel, the television set, where the older children were enjoying cartoons.

After two hard hours of giving their mothers a break, bathing younger children and settling the little ones down for the night, Lucy Bell poured herself a cup of tea and helped herself to a chocolate digestive from the biscuit barrel. She dunked the biscuit into the hot tea and enjoyed the moistness of the base and the creamy, melted milk chocolate on her tongue.

'You did so well to give up chocolate, cakes and biscuits for Lent, Lucy.' Elsa Warwick, the hostel's duty manager, came into the kitchen and closed the door.

Lucy, who had fallen several times in the run-up to Easter, blushed a little. 'It's warm in here tonight, Elsa.'

Elsa sat across the wooden table. Lucy poured her a cup of tea, and eyed the biscuits in the barrel with anticipation and pleasure.

'I really appreciate you coming in at such short notice to help out,' said Elsa. 'We've had an outbreak of flu, and we're so short-staffed.'

'You can't expect mothers who've been beaten black and

blue within the past few days to take full responsibility for their children. They don't just need counselling, they need someone to give them a lift with their kids,' said Lucy, taking another chocolate digestive.

'I wish we had three Lucy Bells volunteering here. Life would be so straightforward.'

Lucy looked at the closed door, and then at Elsa. 'You don't normally close the kitchen door. Is something the matter?'

'She's gone missing again.'

'Who?'

'Dominika Zima. She slipped out last night without telling anyone. One of the other mothers saw her from her bedroom window, heading away from the house, across Garston recreation field. She said Dominika was dressed extremely provocatively.'

Lucy pictured Dominika's three-year-old son. 'Has Luka asked for his mother, or where she is?'

'Once or twice. He's grown up with her frequent absences.'

'She'll come back with her tail between her legs. She always shows up. At least she's consistent in that.'

'Yes, but there's a massive problem this time. I know the rule, you know the rule, and Dominika certainly knows the rule because I spelled it out in no uncertain terms the last time she flitted off for over twenty-four hours. Three strikes and you're out. This is her third disappearance.'

'You could choose to overlook it and say if this happens again, there just will not be another chance. I think that's what Jesus would do.'

'Jesus with all his godliness didn't have the problem of running a women and children's refuge where nobody misses anything. If I flouted the three strikes rule, every wayward woman in the house would start taking the mickey. I throw Dominika out, I throw Luka out with her. I couldn't sleep last night, worrying about her and worrying about what must happen when she turns up, God willing.'

The quiet in the kitchen was disturbed by the sound of

chirruping from the Welsh dresser along the back wall, and Lucy's attention was drawn to the large green cricket in a transparent plastic box.

'The children love Buddy,' said Elsa. 'I'm going to write to your father and thank him for his thoughtful gift.'

'He'd like that. Why did you call him Buddy?'

'Buddy Holly and the Crickets.'

Lucy frowned and looked questioningly at Elsa.

'They were a rock 'n' roll group in America in the 1950s. Buddy Holly was the leader of the Crickets.' There was a sharp spike in the laughter from the children in the front room. 'You've never heard of them?'

'No. Buddy Holly? Was he an Afro-American?'

'No, he was white but he played black venues at a time when it was utterly frowned on to do so.'

'How bizarre,' said Lucy. 'Is he still making music?'

'He died in a plane crash aged twenty-three or thereabouts.'

Lucy offered the biscuit barrel to Elsa, who shook her head. 'Now that you've explained it to me, I can see that you have no choice, Elsa.'

'Are you having another biscuit? You deserve it.'

'My appetite's suddenly vanished. For once in my life.'

'Dominika likes you, Lucy. She always takes you to one side to talk. Have you noticed anything strange? Has she said anything odd?'

The cricket rubbed his back legs together and the sound evoked the darkness of night and the loneliness of vast open spaces.

'Yes,' said Lucy. 'I did notice. She started wearing a lot more make-up. And. And carrying her mobile phone around with her all the time, in her hand, like she was waiting for someone to call her.' Lucy drew around the top circumference of the biscuit barrel with her right index finger. 'I should have told you, but I didn't want to cause trouble.'

'Told me what?'

'I was walking past her room a few days ago. I can't remember the day exactly. But she called me in, asked me if I wanted to see some new pictures of Luka on her phone. I was busy but I didn't want to be rude. She showed me the pictures of him and then a picture came up on the screen of Dominika. Naked. I was really concerned but she just smiled and showed me another sexually provocative picture of herself. I said, *Stop, Dominika. You must delete these pictures and stop taking any more.* She told me she had a new boyfriend, and that she liked sending them to him and that he liked receiving them.'

'She's not going to attract the right kind of man with these antics,' said Elsa.

'Word for word, that's exactly what I told her.' Lucy sipped her tea. 'Have the other mothers commented about her?'

'That's putting it mildly.'

'Then I believe you really have no choice, Elsa. Dominika simply has to go, or you'll quickly lose control of a difficult environment. Do you need me here tomorrow for bath and bedtime?'

The kitchen door opened slowly, with a long-time squeak. A little boy in Teenage Mutant Ninja Turtles pyjamas rubbed his eyes as he walked towards Lucy. She picked him up and, stroking his head, spoke with the kindness she thought Jesus would offer to a little boy who couldn't sleep.

'Come on Luka, I'll put you back in bed and stay with you until you fall asleep.'

Day Two

Friday, 2nd December 2020

Chapter 34

7.15 am

Eve Clay sat at the table in her morning room looking out at the ice-capped rose bushes, and the small lawn outside the window under the brick wall at the back of their garden, where the deep snow covered every single blade of grass.

'Oh, I forgot to tell you, Philip's teacher called me yesterday in the surgery,' said Thomas from the adjoining kitchen.

'Is everything all right?' Anxiety that she had learned to hide so well beyond her front door marbled her voice.

'No worries. They're rehearsing the nativity play pretty much all morning. They're going to make an exception for you in case you miss the full production next week. You can go along and watch the rehearsal. Will you be able to go?'

'I'll do everything I can. And unless another body shows up before twelve...'

Upstairs, the water pipes rattled as Philip turned on the tap to brush his teeth.

'So, Philip doesn't need waking up in the morning anymore?' Eve double-checked.

'He's become really independent in the past few days.' Thomas came into the room with two mugs of tea. 'He uses the toaster, butters his own toast, pours his own milk, goes upstairs, washes himself and gets dressed. He's got a self-reliant streak this wide.'

'He doesn't use the kettle, does he?'

'He wants to, but I've told him he needs to grow a few more inches.'

Eve opened her mouth to speak.

'Don't worry, Eve, when the time comes I will supervise him very closely.'

The rattling stopped and moments later, Eve heard Philip bounding down the stairs. She picked up his reading bag and looked inside.

'Oh my goodness,' she smiled, and felt a mixture of pride and dismay.

'Hi, Mum, you're still here?'

'Of course I'm still here. Are you using gel on your hair now, Philip?

'First time today. I've got to look smart for the rehearsal.'

'I'm sorry, I forgot to run it past you, Eve.'

'That's OK.'

Philip climbed up and sat on his mother's knee.

'The last time I heard you read, Philip, you were on reading book Pink Band Level 1. I see you're now on a Yellow Band Level 3. I missed out on a whole level, Red Level 2.'

'I like reading. I read every night. With Dad, twenty minutes. Every letter has a sound. Ah, eh, i, oo, uh. I know a lot of words.'

'Well, I'm very proud of you.' She spoke with pride. *And*, she thought with dismay, *I'm so sad I'm missing out on so much*. 'How about I take you to school today?'

'That'd be great, Mum.' He laughed.

'What's so funny?'

'Your face yesterday when we were on the yard and you got that phone call.' He pulled a deeply serious face, underpinned with the need to move swiftly, and in his features she saw her own.

'I see why your teacher's given you a lead role. Hey, how about we go and get the Christmas tree on my next day off? We can get a really big one from Woolton Village.'

'That's a good idea,' said Thomas.

'Have you written your letter to Father Christmas yet, Philip?' He wriggled a little on her knee.

'I will do. When the play's done.'

'What would you like?'

'Well, I know I can't have a dog because we're all out most days. How about... half-season ticket for Everton, money, books, and games for my X-Box?' Philip slid off his mother's knee and she looked at the sharp parting in his hair and the slick brush strokes as his hair moved from right to left.

'What do you want for Christmas, Mum? I know dad wants a half-season ticket for Everton...'

'I didn't say that.'

'No, but when I mentioned it to you, there was this look on your face, like, *That's a good idea, I wouldn't mind one of them myself.*'

Thomas looked at Eve and, behind Philip's back, she smiled and nodded, raised an approving thumb.

'I'll sort that out today, Eve.'

'What'll you sort out today, Dad?'

'Something your mother and I were talking about when you were getting dressed. Really boring grown-up stuff.'

'Mum, you haven't answered my question yet.'

'Oh, right, yes. What do I want for Christmas? Well, this is like Christmas to me right here and now, the three of us sitting together and catching up. So I guess I've already got it, I just don't get enough of it all the time.'

'Is there anything you'd like before then?'

'Yes, Philip. I'd like you to read to me and I'd like to fill in your reading diary. Is that OK?'

'Not a problem.' He reached inside his bag and took out the book and home reading diary and headed for the two-seater couch in the middle of the room.

Eve sat next to him and placed her arm around his shoulders.

'I'll begin at the beginning.'

'Always a good place to start.' In her heart, where the weight of the world constantly dragged her down deeper and deeper, there was complete love and a peace that part of her had almost forgotten.

'The title,' said Philip, looking at the cover. '*The Rainy Day.*' He turned to the opening page and read fluently.

'Keep going, Philip, that's great reading.'

She planted a kiss on his head, felt the gel against her lips and stored the moment in her heart against whatever the future was going to throw at her, or what horror was around the next crooked corner.

Chapter 35

10.15 am

As Clay walked towards the school hall of St Swithin's Infant School, she heard the opening notes of 'Little Donkey', her childhood favourite Christmas carol, drifting down the corridor from a slightly out-of-tune piano.

A memory flashed through her mind. She was three or four years old. Sister Teresa's back was hunched as she played the piano in St Claire's. She looked down at her own thin legs dangling from Sister Philomena's knee as her surrogate mother sang the song to her.

The collective sound of barely more than baby-like voices singing in harmony threw Clay back in general to the Christmases of her later childhood in St Michael's Catholic Care Home for Children and, in particular, to the one when she was ten years old and it was her turn to take on the role of Mary.

As she came closer to the school hall, she felt a smile break out on her face, just as it had all those years ago when she carried a Tiny Tears doll wrapped up in a sky-blue crocheted blanket, and remembered the clarity of her child-like thought.

I want to be a mother when I grow older.

Clay stopped at the glass door, saw the boys and girls massed at the back of the stage, singing their hearts out to the piano played by a young teacher she didn't recognise. In front of the infant choir were two children, one dressed as a donkey, the other as a cow. Between the donkey and the cow, a small blonde girl dressed as an angel with a tinsel halo stood on a podium and picked her nose.

Clay's focus drifted to the right of the stage, and her heart turned to ether.

Philip, dressed in a Joseph costume, helped a classmate called Sarah towards the steps at the side of the stage. She was dressed from the head down in a lovingly made blue and white Mary costume, and was carrying a doll wrapped up in a lilac blanket.

The choir and pianist stopped as Philip and Sarah reached the steps.

Clay opened the door wide enough to hear the line Philip had practised hundreds of times at home.

'This is the stable, Mary, where we will stay tonight and welcome our baby Jesus into the world!'

Philip's voice was loud and slow, each word audible and clear. As pride flooded Clay, she looked at the large empty space that would one afternoon be filled with adults come to watch the nativity play, and pride gave way to fear.

What if, she thought, he is overwhelmed with nerves and forgets his line? What if he falls over and people laugh? What if the enormity of the occasion gets to him and he runs off in tears and gets teased forever about it?

She blinked and in the micro-beat of darkness her mind was filled with the distorted and smoke-darkened geometric globe painted on the wall in Picton Road.

The piano music started again and the children's choir

supplied the story as Philip led Sarah and her doll to the centre of the stage.

'Ring out those bells tonight, Bethlehem, Bethlehem...'

Philip helped Sarah to sit beneath the angel whose arms were now stretched up and out in the direction of heaven. As he settled next to Sarah on the stage, and the music and singing carried on, Clay realised that she had taken several steps inside the hall.

Philip stared lovingly at the bundle in Sarah's arms and Clay felt a tide of tears rising as the music and singing came to a close. She fought down the emotion, keenly aware that the last thing Philip needed was a weeping mother letting him down in front of his classmates.

Silence, a room full of children and complete peace and quiet.

Without warning, the bell rang for playtime, and beneath the sudden shrill din, Clay heard, 'Mum?'

Philip was on his feet. He jumped down from the stage and sprinted across the space towards her. Children's voices built as the teacher called, 'The sooner we quieten down, the sooner we can have our milk! The sooner we have our milk, the sooner we can get back to our nativity play.'

The noise of the children's voices softened as Philip reached her. She crouched down to his height and he threw his arms around her neck and planted a kiss on her cheek. As she held him, she imagined that she could feel his heart beating inside his body and into hers.

'Mum, will you be coming with Dad to watch the nativity play?'

'When is it happening?'

'Not this week – next week, on Friday in the afternoon.'

'I'll do everything I can to be here, Philip. You do know if I don't make it...'

'It's because something very important cropped up.'

She felt a knife straight beneath the place where her ribs met.

'Mum, you're giving me the sad eyes.'

'The sad eyes?'

'Yes, the sad eyes.'

'I didn't know I had sad eyes.'

'When you can't do something for me because of work. It's OK. Don't have sad eyes. I understand. Dad's job as a GP doctor gives him...' He searched for the right word.

'Flexibility?' suggested Eve.

'Flexibility. Catching bad men and women doesn't give you that *flexibility*. I like those eyes better. Happy eyes.'

'Philip!' The teacher's voice rose above the noise of the children's and she waved a carton of milk above her head.

'Thank you, Miss Carter! Who are you trying to catch today?'

'I'll tell you when you pass your driving test.'

'That's ages away, mum.'

She felt the ping of an incoming message on her iPhone.

'I've got to go, Mum, and get my milk. Miss Carter's mad keen to get started on the rehearsal.'

She gave him a hug, drew him as closely to her as she could and smelled the freshness of his skin.

'Mum, other kids are watching.'

Clay let go of him and, watching him walk away, knew there would come a day when she would wake up and mourn all the moments of his life that she had missed because of the demands of her job.

Philip looked over his shoulder and his parting smile made the back of her eyes prickle.

She took out her iPhone and saw the message was from Mason: *Eve – Please come back to Picton Road immediately.*

As she walked out of the hall, she called him. 'Terry, what is it?'

'I want you to see it.'

'One to ten, how big is it?' asked Clay.

'Twenty-five.'

'I'll be there as soon as possible!'

Chapter 36

10.15 am

Sergeant Carol White drained the last mouthful of coffee from the fifth mug she had consumed in as many hours and, adjusting her glasses on her nose, returned to the CCTV footage from Picton Road. With the exception of a dog and a man on a bicycle, the stretch of road she was watching had been like a ghost town.

She pressed play and watched, resisting the temptation to check her phone for messages, reminding herself that this task was infinitely easier than the two years she had spent watching child pornography.

A car approached from the junction of the Picton Clock Tower and took a right turn into Frederick Grove. As she tracked the vehicle's progress and disappearance, in the bottom right-hand corner of the screen a door opened next door to Mr Zięba's Polish deli, and a snowflake landed on the CCTV camera lens.

She banged pause and looked across at Barney Cole. He was watching twilight footage from 6.30 pm, looking for someone or some people entering the Adamczaks' front door, just as she was looking for those same people leaving. White rewound the footage and focused on the door.

A black figure emerged, looking like a moving matchstick man on the pavement. It was impossible to tell if it was a man or woman.

She focused on the doorway and thought she could make out two more figures, but the snow was falling faster and she couldn't say for sure there were three. She rewound and paused just where the figure emerged from the doorway, fixed on the best shot and noted the time on the screen in the lower left-hand corner: 3:02:13 am.

She imagined the scene that the figure had left behind, and

knew that as this sequence was being recorded, in a room above and to the right of the front door, a fire was raging and two men were being partially cremated.

The definitive figure had one of two ways to go: into what was probably the CCTV oblivion of residential Grove Street, or towards the general direction of the city centre and the eye of the CCTV camera above the mini-market.

'Thank you, God...' she said, as she watched the figure start its journey.

'Why are you getting your rosary beads out, Whitey?'

'Give me a minute, Barney.' She could hear in her own voice a smile breaking out.

The figure walked in the direction of the CCTV camera. She paused and rewound to the beginning of the passage.

'It could have been three coming out of the flat. But there was clearly one person who walked away from it.'

Barney stood up and walked over.

'Look at this, please,' said White. 'I'll narrate it for you. Ready?'

'Shoot.'

'Keep your eye on the door, bottom right-hand corner. Ignore the car coming towards the camera. One figure emerges, then maybe two more. Snow on the lens. What shit timing was that? Then the one perpetrator we're sure of comes out and walks in the direction of the nearest CCTV camera. He's dressed head to foot in black with a black hood up. He's carrying a black bag. The snow on the lens melted and, as the suspect comes closer, his form becomes clearer.'

'I agree with everything,' said Cole. 'Look at the way he's walking. Women don't walk like that. It's a male. He's walking like he's got something hard and metallic stuck up his arse. Closer and closer he swaggers towards the camera and he looks up, directly into the lens, but he's wearing a balaclava with holes cut out for his eyes. And then he's gone. Play it back for me again, please, Whitey.'

They watched together in silence and, when the sequence

finished, Cole said, 'That's a gangsta stroll. Yo! Look ata me, I looka like I need seriuz spinal surgery, bruv...'

'Yeah,' White agreed. She wound the footage back and froze on the clearest image of the coat he was wearing. There was a white logo on the left of it, but it was blurred. 'The clothes as well. I couldn't make out a logo on the coat but I'll bet you twenty quid that coat's a North Face or some such brand that the kids hoover up.'

'Show me the sequence again.' Cole watched as the figure marched casually towards the camera, wondering if he was well aware of the CCTV and was showing off. 'Age-wise, I'm putting him at anywhere between fifteen and twenty-five, maybe up to thirty. Show me him swaggering again.'

He watched the killer walk towards the camera. 'He's buzzing. Look how he's walking. He thinks he's in an East Coast gangsta movie. Great work, Whitey, and this is where the good news piles up. We've got footage from Wellington Road if he took a left at the next junction. If he took a right at Rathbone Road, we haven't got anything until Long Lane. But we've got a time window now, so no more hours of watching endless nothing.'

Cole and White went back to his desk and looked at the tagged and labelled pen drives laid out in neat lines. He picked up two and, handing them to her, said, 'Wellington Road and Rathbone Road at the junction with Long Lane.'

'He could have carried on straight down Wavertree Road and into the city centre.'

Cole considered the idea and the geography of the neighbourhood he'd grown up in. 'He'd had his moment of theatre in front of the CCTV on Picton Road.' He picked up the receiver of his landline phone and dialled. 'If it was me, I'd turn into Rathbone Road and take a left down North Drive. That would give him multiple getaway options.'

'Let's go with those scenarios first.'

He called Clay. 'Eve, it's Barney. Whitey's come up trumps on the CCTV from Picton Road.'

Chapter 37

12.03 pm

In Autopsy Suite 1 of the Royal Liverpool Hospital mortuary, Detective Sergeant Bill Hendricks stood on one side of the board facing the pathologist Doctor Mary Lamb and her APT Harper.

Harper nodded and looked down at the body of Karl Adamczak.

'Why are his arms bent at the elbow and his hands bunched into fists, Doctor Lamb?' asked Hendricks.

'You may well have also noticed a less defined bend at his knees.'

Hendricks looked at the knees and thought that they looked like they were about to attempt a fuller bend, to kneel and pray perhaps.

'It's a pugilistic attitude. It happens to the human body when it's exposed to extreme heat. After Mr Adamczak died, the muscles in his body contracted because of their exposure to fire.'

Hendricks looked Karl Adamczak's body up and down.

'We performed an autopsy on his twin Václav yesterday. It took eight hours from start to finish. He was exactly the same.' Doctor Lamb indicated Karl Adamczak's throat. 'Put a light there, please, Harper.' She pointed at a brown discolouration, where the scorch marks on his neck ended and there was a small patch of unburned flesh.

As Harper illuminated it with his torch, Hendricks examined the curve of the shape.

'I think that's a thumbprint,' said Doctor Lamb. 'If yesterday was anything to go by, I think the cause of death is going to be strangulation.'

Hendricks looked at her and tried to conceal the horror and utter sorrow he felt for Karl Adamczak and his twin brother.

Her elderly face was solemn but in her blue eyes, there was a permanently imprinted smile, and he knew that she could see through his bravado.

'Doctor Lamb,' said Hendricks. 'Are you certain that the Adamczak brothers didn't die in the fire?'

'Oh, absolutely sure. Yesterday, when I opened Václav Adamczak's throat, I was looking for two things. There was no soot in his windpipe so he can't have breathed in smoke. Therefore he died before the fire was started.'

Briefly, Hendricks worked out the logic of the scene from the killers' point of view. In setting fire to a living human being, they were risking getting burned themselves. Setting fire to them after death gave them time to stage the bodies and get out fast before they placed themselves in danger of smoke inhalation.

'I was then looking for evidence of strangulation, so I took out his larynx and hyoid bone with his tongue attached. I found deep tissue contusion and fracturing to his laryngeal bone.'

Hendricks's phone rang out. Seeing Clay on the display, he made his way to the viewing gallery overlooking the autopsy suite; as he connected, he looked at the specimen jars on the wall of the autopsy suite.

'Where are you driving to, Eve?'

'Picton Road.'

As he looked at the body parts across the room, the visual effect of twisted spines, skulls marked with the black brand of syphilis and a human heart suspended in formaldehyde made the idea in his brain solidify.

'As soon as you're able to, leave the autopsy and join me at the murder scene. Anything, Bill?'

'Václav Adamczak was strangled and set alight after death. It looks like it's going to be the same story for Karl. I can come and join you right now, Eve. What's happening in Picton Road?'

'Terry Mason and Paul Price have found something. Terry was cagey about it. Sounds like matters have just got a whole lot worse. Meet me there.'

Chapter 38

12.30 pm

As Clay climbed the stairs to the flat above the Polish delicatessen, the brutality of the premeditated violence that had occurred there hit her hard. She felt like she was reliving her first encounter with the conjoined bodies of the Adamczak brothers.

Walking into the flat, she tried to imagine what the men had been doing twenty-four hours earlier and wondered if they had thought about death as they went about their daily work.

The speculation triggered a childhood memory.

Aged five, she had stood at the partially open bedroom door of an elderly and dying nun called Sister Agnes as Sister Philomena prayed and read from the New Testament at the old lady's death bed.

'Now, brothers, about times and dates we do not need to write to you for you know very well that the day of the Lord will come like a thief in the night.' Then Sister Philomena had stopped reading and, with her back turned to Eve, had spoken softly and kindly. 'This is no place for you, Evette Clay. Go to your room, please, pray for Sister Agnes, and do your best to go to sleep.'

It was as if Sister Philomena had an additional sense that told her exactly where Eve was at all times. Clay smiled at the memory, but her smile dissolved as the words *like a thief in the night* invaded her head. She recalled the graffiti in the room where the Adamczak brothers had died: *Killing Time Is Here Embrace It.*

She heard Mason and Price's muffled voices inside the flat and, from the bottom of the stairs, Hendricks.

'Are you all right, Eve?'

'I'm... fine.'

Hendricks hurried up the stairs behind her. 'I've just had a call from Doctor Lamb.'

'What's happening in the mortuary?'

'She's removed Karl Adamczak's larynx. She's looking for deep tissue contusion to see if the cause of death was strangulation. She's found just that. Identical twins, identical causes of death and post-mortem abuse. How's Barney doing with his search for the source of the graffiti?'

'Google Reverse search isn't playing ball.'

'We're in here, Eve!' Mason's voice came from the box room down the corridor.

Clay and Hendricks arrived in the doorway of a space that was almost completely filled by DS Terry Mason and Sergeant Paul Price. The floorboards were all up and stacked neatly against the wall. Mason and Price knelt on the rafters, exploring the space between them with a torch.

'I think this room is probably where they kept her,' said Mason.

'Who?' asked Clay.

'Definitely nothing else here, Paul?'

'Definitely nothing else.'

Mason rose to his feet and tiptoed along the rafter to the door. 'The evidence we found is in the kitchen, Eve. I want you to see it with your own eyes before I say anything. I don't know whether you're going to love or hate us.'

On the table in the neat and tidy kitchen were a ketchup bottle, a teapot, two mugs and two evidence bags. Clay pointed at them.

'We couldn't unlock the phone,' said Price, sliding an evidence bag towards Clay.

'Poppy Waters will have it open in the blink of an eye,' she replied. She picked up the brown evidence bag and saw a dirty and much-handled iPhone through the central transparent strip. 'Bill, can you please take this to Trinity Road and give it to Poppy?' She was filled with foreboding, her senses charged up. 'As soon as she's cracked it she's to send all relevant images, films or evidence directly to me.'

As Hendricks took the evidence bag, Clay asked Mason, 'Where did you find it?'

'Under the boards in the box room.'

She picked up the next, face-down evidence bag and turned it over, the pulse rising in her ears.

Hendricks said, 'How about that?'

She placed her right index finger on the transparent strip and felt the material within: the silky texture of human hair. She moved her finger along the length of it, felt the width of a thick clump of hair.

'Bill, we need to take Aneta Koloza to Trinity Road for questioning. Can you organise that now? I want you to stay there for the interview. Call Karl Stone and ask him to pick her up. I'll be there as soon as I can. And can you ask Clive Winters to pull in Lucy Bell? We need her to account fully for her movements over the past eight days.'

Clay lowered her nose to the open evidence bag and drank in an oily aroma of what appeared to be half-a-head of hair. She turned to DS Terry Mason, listened to Hendricks following Price out of the house, and said, 'This is Marta Ondřej's hair. Tell me why you lifted the boards in the box room, Terry.'

'Top of the door, left-hand corner, I saw a few long black hairs stuck to the woodwork and trapped there by a crack in the surface of the paint. I'd have missed it if I hadn't seen that,' said Mason.

Clay walked back to the box room, looked at the space and pictured herself locked inside it for eight days and nights. She felt the scale of the trauma that Marta had been through. *They'd have done it to Philip if it suited their ends*, she told herself, feeling her skin turn hot and cold, over and over, and a ball of black anger expanding at her core. 'Great work, Terry, thank you. Get the rest of the boards up, please – the whole flat.'

'No problem. Where are you going, Eve?'

'Trinity Road. I'm going to talk to Aneta Kaloza!'

Chapter 39

12.30 pm

For the second time, Detective Constable Barney Cole uploaded a picture of the blurred and smoke-damaged graffiti from the Picton Road murder scene onto Google Reverse Search, and for the second time drew a blank.

The incident room was empty and had been for hours, which was the way he liked it when he was hunting down information for Eve Clay. He went through the process again and, finding no match, felt his breath escaping from his lips like steam from a fractured pipe. He wondered if the image was nonsense, the invention of the killer to send those in pursuit down a dead end.

Cole drifted towards the large plate-glass window and, looking long and hard at the image in the light of day, tried to visualise it without the smoke damage and with its lines crystal clear.

'Barney!' Behind him, Poppy Waters's voice was calm and quiet. 'I'm sorry, I've alarmed you.'

'No worries.' He turned. 'I thought I was on my own. I didn't hear you come in.'

'You've been standing at the window for more than half a minute – the time I've been here.'

'I was lost in an idea.'

A cool breeze from the air conditioning system pulsed through the warm room; as he indicated for Poppy to sit at his desk, Cole unknotted his tie and opened the top button of his shirt.

'So, Poppy,' he smiled. 'What's happening?'

'I've been told to wait here for Bill Hendricks. There's a phone from the Picton Road scene needs opening. You?'

'Having a bad time with the distorted graffiti from Picton Road and Google reverse image search,' said Cole. 'It's like putting a buckled coin in a slot machine.'

'Call in a civilian artist...'

'I thought about that one, Poppy. But I can sort out the image myself.'

'You're good at art?'

'Don't sound so surprised. I've got an A-level in it.'

'Me, too. You still painting, drawing?'

'The job, the family… time's not on my side. I'll get back to it one day. Probably pick it up again when my eyesight's so bad I'd flag down an ambulance thinking it was a bus.'

He leaned over her and produced a compass and pencil from his desk drawer.

'You keep a compass in your drawer?'

'If I use something during the course of an investigation, Poppy, I keep it, and if I can't keep it in my drawer because it's too big, I keep it in my locker.'

She stood up and moved out of his personal space. 'So if I need a magnifying glass…'

Cole produced a magnifying glass from his drawer, and she laughed in her mellow, almost child-like way. 'That's amazing.'

He laughed with her and looked at her for a moment too long as she backed away from the desk. It occurred to him to ask her if she wanted a coffee, but the urgent need to get a handle on the graffiti kept him silent.

Cole tightened a pencil into the compass, took a piece of A4 paper from his rack and proceeded to draw the outer circle of the graffiti.

'Let me see the image, Barney.'

Cole showed her the image of the blurred graffiti he had printed off from the wall in the flat on Picton Road. 'Any ideas?'

'It looks sinister to me, but apart from that no, sorry. You?'

'I can see a solid circle at the centre, a concentric circle within the shape and the outer wheel. I can estimate the nature of the recurring geometric shapes within the wheels. It might take a few reconstructions or more.'

The door of the incident room opened quickly and Hendricks walked directly to Poppy. 'This is the phone, Poppy.'

There was a rustle as an evidence bag was passed from hand to hand.

'My God,' she said. 'It's filthy. It looks like it's been on a building site.'

'It probably has been on a building site.'

Cole looked at Hendricks as Poppy headed for the door.

'It almost certainly belongs to either Karl or Václav Adamczak,' said Hendricks. 'It looks like our murder victims are responsible for the abduction and kidnapping of Marta Ondřej.'

Chapter 40

1.01 pm

Kate appeared in the doorway. 'I'm going to the shop on the ground floor. Do you want anything, Gina?'

'I'm on a diet.' Riley stroked Marta's face, looked at the patches of stubble on her head. 'I'll have a Mars Bar, a big bag of Revels and a two-litre Diet Coke. To share with others, of course.'

A man appeared at the glass wall of Marta's room. Behind the turned-up lapels of his heavy black overcoat, Riley caught sight of a band of white at his throat. She walked out to the corridor and he held out his hand and smiled.

'I've got a present for Marta,' said the priest. Riley's hand felt swamped in the largeness of his, but she also felt relieved from the difficulties of the day by the kindness he radiated and the compassion stamped in his eyes. 'It's all over the hospital chaplaincy about the little girl staying in for tests. Not exactly the ideal start to a new life in a new country.' The priest released Riley's hand. 'How is Marta?'

'She's on the mend, I think. I hope.'

'I don't wish to intrude and cannot stay, but I have something for her. I'd be grateful if you could pass it on.'

'Sure.'

The priest looked into the room. His face creased with sadness, he folded his hands together and closed his eyes. His lips moved; when they stopped, he made the sign of the cross. 'This is a very blessed hospital. The best medical care to cater to the children's physical needs and the best chaplaincy for the spiritual needs of the children and their families.'

As Marta turned her eyes towards the priest, he waved his right hand, head high, with the steady rhythm of a windscreen wiper. Then he turned to Riley and, reaching into his pocket, handed her a small silver box with a blue image of the Virgin Mary on the lid.

'Rosary beads, for little Marta. Maybe you could give them to her. It might help.' The priest smiled. 'Has she spoken?'

'She has difficulties in communicating.'

'God bless her.'

He turned and, as he walked away, Riley looked inside the box at the tangle of rosary beads. By the time she'd replaced the lid, the priest was gone and Riley, who still felt the warmth of his hand in hers, was left with the distinct impression that even though she had touched his hand, she had just had an encounter with a ghost.

Her iPhone pinged with an incoming message and then rang out with an incoming call. On the display: 'Eve Clay'.

'Eve, anything?'

'I've sent you a photo of Karl and Václav Adamczak. They've just become red-hot prime suspects in the abduction and kidnapping of Marta Ondřej. Can you show the picture to Verka and ask her if she knows them? Don't tell her why.'

'I'll call you straight back.'

'I'll keep my line clear,' said Clay.

As Riley returned to Marta's side, Kate Nowak appeared in the doorway with a carrier bag half-full of sweets, crisps and sugary drinks.

'Come in, Kate. There's something I have to ask Verka.'

The translator stepped inside and closed the door.

'Verka,' said Riley. 'I have a picture to show you. Would you take a look?' She held out her iPhone.

Verka's brow creased into a frown. 'I know these faces,' she said. 'I saw them. The first week I was here, living on Smithdown Lane. They were working three doors down – and then they did some repairs in our house. The same landlord, you see. At first...' Verka smiled a little. 'I thought it was just one person. This man, he was amazing. He could appear in two different places at once – he'd be up the stairs one minute and ten seconds later coming in through the back door of the kitchen. Then one day, I saw them together, and it made sense.'

'Do you know their names?'

Verka shook her head. 'No. And I couldn't tell them apart at all. One of them was a bit distant but one of them was lovely to Marta. On the day they finished working, the nice one gave Marta sweets. And a £10 note.'

'Thank you, Verka. That's all.'

Riley went back out into the corridor and called Clay.

'What have you got, Gina?'

'The Adamczak brothers knew where Marta lived, had direct contact with her. Listen to this.'

Chapter 41

2.15 pm

From the door of the lock-up he shared with CJ and Buster, Raymond looked out across the River Mersey and pictured Jack hanging on to the flashing buoy in the middle of the water, his wet fingers losing their grip as the water chopped around his head and swamped his face. He swallowed a mouthful of water and in the fierce attack of coughing that followed, his fingers slipped from the wet surface of the buoy.

To his right, Jasmine cried and whimpered as her head dipped under the rough surface of the river, and when she was thrown up into the air by the power of the water, her face turned into Jack's and his face turned into the bitch's.

Raymond laughed his loudest as their faces switched back, each to his and her own.

'*Raymond, I'm begging you, save me, save me, Raymond!*'

Jack's fingers and hands came away from the buoy and he thrashed in the water, desperately trying to hold on and screaming at the top of his voice.

Raymond opened the door of the lock-up and, turning on the light, looked back at the water.

Something white and mobile moved through the dark water towards Jack. The white thing swelled up like a living balloon and then shrank back into a cylinder.

Raymond closed the door, walked to the punch-bag in the corner of the lock-up and drank in the aroma of sweat and damp that always clung to the wooden walls.

He closed his eyes and the jellyfish came closer to Jack. Swelling itself up to its largest proportions, it pulled its hood down over Jack's face and head, making him look subhuman and distorted, and then like a freak with a cowl where his face should have been. Jack grabbed the jellyfish by the arms that dangled from its body and in trying to pull it from his head, pulled himself and the creature under the water.

He looked around the lock-up at the plasma screen televisions, laptops, iPhones and Wii consoles. In a series of jewellery boxes items were separated out: rings, chains, bracelets and watches, other people's shit from other people's houses.

Raymond punched the bag with his right fist and then his left, right, left, right, left, Jack, right to Jack's head, right to his fucking smug face, left to his windpipe.

There was a noise outside. Raymond stopped and recognised CJ and Busters' voices.

'Is that you, Raymond?' asked CJ.

Knuckles stinging and grazed, Raymond opened the door and let his friends in. CJ walked to the corner and picked up a cardboard box that Raymond hadn't seen before. He placed it on the work surface and took out a litre bottle of clear fluid with no label.

'What's that?' asked Raymond.

'Vodka,' said Buster.

'But we don't drink vodka,' said Raymond.

'Maybe we should start, broaden our tastes,' said CJ, unscrewing the cap.

'Where's it from?' asked Raymond.

'Dreyfuss, the gimp who lives in that flat in Princes Road. He makes it himself and sells it to winos for jack shit money but gets to shag their women. He's got a fucking brewery in his kitchen. I threatened to blow him up to the cops if he didn't give me a batch. And that's the way it's going to be from now on. We're expanding our business, Raymond.'

'What's the plan?'

'The plan is,' said Buster, 'we're not selling this shit to winos. We're going to stick Smirnoff labels on the bottles and go round the pubs on Park Road near closing time when they're all bladdered, and sell them fake vodka. A tenner a litre. Here's to our new business venture.'

CJ took a swig from the bottle and, passing it to Buster, said, 'Not half bad at all.'

Buster drank from the bottle, three hard glugs, then let out a satisfied, 'Aaaahhh!!' He handed it to Raymond.

'Come on, Raymond,' said CJ. 'Down the fucking hatch, old bean.'

Raymond swallowed a mouthful of tasteless vodka and as it went down, his throat burned, but something deep inside him made him take a second and then a third hit.

'We can't sell weed on the prom anymore,' said Raymond. They both looked at him, silent and incredulous. 'Jack's on to it. He didn't say as much but he kind of...' He searched hard for the right word. 'Implied he'd kick our fucking heads in if we dealt it to junior school kids.'

'Fucking St Jack come to save the planet single-handed,' laughed CJ.

The alcohol kicked in to Raymond's veins and he felt a glow at his centre that caused him to laugh along with his friends, and take another hit before passing the bottle to Buster.

'How many cases a week is he giving us?' asked Raymond.

'Two cases of twelve which works out at £240 a week, nearly a grand a month. We can buy a lot of weed, coke, ecstasy, smack with that money. We could make a fucking fortune. We haven't got enough cash flow to make a big success of our dealing,' said CJ, taking the bottle from Buster.

'It's too hit and miss at the moment,' said Buster. 'We're smoking more than we sell.'

'You two sound like you've been binge-watching University Challenge,' laughed Raymond.

'We need a plan,' replied CJ.

'I'm fucking tired of being skint.'

'I can get with that,' said Raymond. 'Shall we all take one bottle home with us, so we can have some when we're round at each other's houses?'

'Sure.'

'How come I wasn't there when you went round to Dreyfuss's flat?' asked Raymond.

They looked at him and then at each other.

'You *were* there!' said Buster.

'I'm shitting you!' It came flooding back to Raymond. 'I kicked Dreyfuss in his bad leg when he objected to giving us the booze. It was all my idea, right?'

'You're the ideas man, Raymond,' said CJ, lighting up a joint and handing it to him. 'Your idea to break into this empty lock-up. Your idea to change the lock and make it our own private business premises.'

The glow inside Raymond was growing. He took a hit and passed it on to Buster and, although he didn't say anything, and never would, he was glad that they were his friends and counted himself lucky that he was not alone. There was a bond between the three of them and love was not a word to be thrown around lightly, but every time he was with CJ and Buster, that feeling grew stronger.

Chapter 42

2.15 pm

On the ground floor of the Novotel Hotel overlooking Liverpool One, Detective Sergeant Karl Stone followed Neville Pearson, the duty manager, into the lift. As the doors closed, Pearson pressed seven and the lift started its smooth ascent.

'How long has Aneta Kaloza worked here?' asked Stone.

'Two years.'

'What's she like?'

'Pretty strange to begin with, cultural differences I guess. But as time's moved on she's become a model employee. I wish they were all like Aneta. She hasn't had a day off sick. I mean, she's in today, for God's sake, after what happened. Awful.'

Stone noticed the way Pearson seemed to drift into himself as he imagined the scene.

'Neville!' said Stone, with a hint of steel. 'Tell me about Aneta, please.'

'She always works hard and is extremely good at what she does. She's polite to the guests and she's respectful to her colleagues. She's worked her way up. She supervises the domestic staff but she's not afraid to roll up her sleeves when we're short-staffed.'

Stone looked above the door, saw they were at the fourth floor. 'So, you're saying she's a saint?'

He heard a catch of laughter in the duty manager's throat.

'Dish the dirt, Neville!' said Stone, seeing the fifth floor fly by. 'We're going to be seeing her soon. What made you laugh when I said *saint*?'

'My dad was a copper and he drilled it into me: if the police come asking you questions, tell it as it is. They'll find out in the end anyway. First couple of months she was here, she liked to spread her favours with the men and women she worked with. She was promiscuous.'

Stranger in a strange land, thought Stone, feeling nothing but compassion for Aneta. Throwing sex at people as a means of finding friendship or even love.

'Was? You know what, Neville I heard a silent *and* in that statement.'

The lift doors opened with the merest sigh. Stone stepped out, looked up and down the corridor and saw a domestic loading bed linen onto a large metal trolley, well out of hearing range.

'OK.' Neville dropped his voice into confidential mode. 'It wasn't just the sleeping around that made her stand out in her early days here. Some of the political and racial views she expressed were really out there.'

'As in?'

'She was a little to the right of Mussolini. When she first came to work here, days after she'd stepped off the plane from Poland, when she obviously didn't understand what was and wasn't acceptable here, she made some massively racist remarks to another domestic.'

'Did she racially abuse her colleague?'

'Her colleague was white and from Liverpool. She was on about people from the Czech Republic and Slovakia being lazy good-for-nothing scumbags. She had a particular downer on the Czech Roma population. Thieves, liars, murderers and rapists down to the last man and woman. The children were no better.

Hitler had it right in taking gypsies to the death camps. Blah, blah, blah!'

'What happened?'

'Her colleague reported her. She was hauled into the general manager's office. I was there in the room as a trainee manager, I hadn't been here long myself. He confronted her, read back every word that had been reported by the other domestic. She stood there with this look on her face. I read what was going on in her head and it was, like, *Why are you bothering me with this?* The general manager...'

'What's his name?'

'He's not here anymore. He said *What have you got to say for yourself, Aneta?* She said, *Well, it's the truth. Don't you agree with me?* He told her that such talk was unacceptable in England and that if it happened again, she was facing the sack on the spot. She looked at me and then at the general manager and said to him, *Can I speak to you in private, please?* He asked me to leave. I stood outside the office and a minute later, the general manager sticks his head round the door and says, *Stay there. If you want a career in hotel management, you stay right there – you're not to let anyone knock on my door under any circumstances. I don't care if World War Three breaks out. Stay there!* Five minutes later, the door unlocked and she came out with this triumphant look on her face. *I've been informed*, she said, *I understand how things work in England.* He told me to come in and close the door. He was a big bloke and his face was bright red. *I've dealt with it*, he said. *Neither of us saw or heard a thing. It's her word against her colleague. And I believe her. Who do you believe, Neville?*'

'So what happened to the racism and over-friendly behaviour?' asked Stone.

'She canned the racist, right-wing talk as soon as she'd had that meeting with the boss. She was still sleeping around for two or three months after that. She went off on leave one Thursday with long peroxide-blonde hair and came back on the Saturday with jet-black hair in a shoulder-length bob. All the sexual shenanigans stopped and she started projecting this aloof and ladylike version of Aneta the Artiste, formerly known as the Novotel Bike.'

In a fragment of a moment, Stone weighed up each and every word that Neville had said and asked, 'What did you say when the general manager asked you who you believed over the racist shite?'

Neville's shoulders sank slowly as he said, 'Aneta.'

As soon as Pearson said her name, the padded quiet of the corridor was disturbed by the creaking wheel of an approaching trolley, and a female voice. Stone turned and saw two women approaching: a domestic pushing a trolley and another woman in a smart uniform walking slightly behind her.

'When you've finished helping Carys on the seventh floor, I need you to go to the eighth to help Julie, please. Alexa has called in sick.'

The woman in the uniform spoke precisely and with a small hint of a foreign accent, but with the air of a woman who took *No* for an answer like a personal insult.

The domestic's face was stony, but her voice was light when she responded, 'Yeah, sure, Aneta...'

Stone made eye contact with Aneta. She eyed him up and down in a glance, and said, 'You're from the police, right?' She didn't blink or break eye contact with him and he thought, *Born with a face to play poker.* 'Have you caught the people who murdered my friends?'

Stone showed her his warrant card. 'No, not yet. I've come to collect you for questioning at Trinity Road Police Station.'

'But I told your colleague, DCI Clay, everything I know.'

Silence fell on the corridor, but Aneta defied Stone with eyes that swam with confidence and anger.

'I see,' said Aneta, folding her arms across her middle. 'You think I'm somehow responsible, don't you?'

'Change into your day clothes, Aneta,' said Neville Pearson. 'You're not walking in to Trinity Road police station wearing a Novotel uniform.'

Chapter 43

2.35 pm

After uploading the reconstructed image from the Adamczak murder scene onto his YouTube account, Detective Constable Barney Cole took a moment to look at it. With its central black circle and concentric circumference, the circular line close to the centre gave the overall image a sense of order that was in direct opposition to the twelve crooked blocks of black that linked the circumference through the smaller dark spoke to the centre.

The broken spokes caused the blocks of white between their crooked neighbours to form a recurring image. The twelve white blocks looked like an abstract representation of a dozen people kneeling to be beheaded.

With his picture on-screen, Cole went on to Google Chrome and clicked Search by image. He right-clicked, and clicked Search Google with this image.

In under one second, Cole had a direct match.

Black Sun.

Cole pulled up a range of pictures that made his spine tingle. He patted himself on the shoulder when he saw that he had matched the other esoteric wheels on the internet. There were some in black and white like his, and others with the sun blazing, fires shooting up from the wheel imprinted on its surface.

He scrolled down and saw an increasingly bizarre range of images. A stag with its skeleton exposed inside its body. Subhuman warriors from the world of fantasy. Superhuman men with bodies carved out of muscle.

And then a familiar face from the dregs of twentieth-century history. An insipid-looking man, balding, middle aged, rimless glasses, weak chin, arms folded across his chest.

He dialled Clay and, as she connected, he heard that she was driving at great speed.

'What's happening, Barney?'

'I've got a match for the symbol at the Picton Road murder scene. It's called Black Sun. It looks like an occult symbol, and I think it's going to prove beyond anything that the murder of the Adamczak twins was racially motivated.'

'How so?'

'I need to research it, Eve. I've only just this second cracked it.'

'Great work, Barney. I'm on my way in. Where are we up to with Aneta Kaloza?'

'Last thing I heard, Eve, she's sitting in reception with Karl Stone, waiting for you like a good girl.'

'That's good, because she's going to be booked in, swabbed and fingerprinted within the hour. She's a suspect in the abduction and kidnapping of Marta Ondřej.'

As soon as Cole placed the receiver down, his desk phone rang out.

'Detective Constable Barney Cole speaking.'

'Hello, Detective Sergeant Cole.'

'Deputy Commissioner Aleksander Kasprzak, you have some information for me about the Adamczak brothers?'

'Yes, indeed I do. Are you listening, Detective Sergeant Cole?'

'I'm listening...'

Chapter 44

2.45 pm

In Interview Suite 1, Aneta Kaloza and her solicitor sat across the table from DCI Clay and DS Hendricks. Clay looked at the solicitor's visitor badge and said, 'Welcome to Trinity Road Police Station, Ms Jennings.'

Ms Jennings looked up from her spiral-bound pad and said,

'My client has lost her two best friends in what is most likely a racially motivated double murder. I'll be listening very closely to your questioning, Ms Clay. It's common knowledge that the Merseyside Constabulary is an organisation plagued by institutional racism.'

'Listen for as long and as hard as you like, Ms Jennings. You won't hear a racist word from me or my colleague, Detective Sergeant William Hendricks.'

Clay formally opened the interview, looked directly at Aneta and counted to ten in silence.

'Why have you brought me here, taken me away from my work?' asked Aneta.

Clay glanced at the evidence bag face down on the table and asked, 'On a scale of one to ten, Aneta, one being minimal and ten being completely intimate, how close were you to the Adamczak twins, Karl and Václav?'

Aneta looked at the evidence bag, glanced at Ms Jennings and said, 'Eight, I'd say.'

'Your relationship with the brothers was platonic?'

'Yes. There was never any question of a romantic or sexual relationship. They were like brothers to me. Had there been a sexual relationship between me and, say, Karl, I'd have answered ten for Karl and eight for Václav. In reality, it was eight for both.'

'Aneta,' said Ms Jennings. 'Just answer the questions flatly. One word would have been sufficient to respond to that question. Eight.'

'Aneta?' Clay drew her in with her name and when she had full eye contact, she said, 'Aneta, it's clear to me that you are eager to cooperate. Your solicitor's here to intervene in case we step over the edge of what's right and professional. You're an intelligent woman. Use your own judgement to answer our questions in as much detail as you think appropriate. If you want to, give us a *no comment* interview. Your call.'

Clay looked at Ms Jennings, then carried on. 'Context

is everything,' she said, sliding the evidence bag in front of Hendricks. Aneta's eyes tracked the movement of the brown paper bag.

In the inside pocket of her jacket, Clay felt her iPhone buzzing, and the still silence in between the blasts of vibration felt deep and dark.

'You were close to both the brothers?'

The silence deepened and the tremor grew stronger through her clothes, against her skin and into her blood.

'Yes, I was.'

'So you'd notice if anything unusual was going on, Aneta?'

'Yes, of course.'

'Did you notice anything unusual going on, say in the last eight days?'

'No, everything was normal. I'd arrive at their place, let myself in because they'd long gone to work. I'd clean the flat. I'd pick up my money at the end of the week. And I'd speak to them on the phone every other evening or so.'

'Did they appear agitated?'

'No.'

'Did they follow their usual routine?'

'As far as I know, yes. I wasn't with them twenty-four/seven.'

'How thoroughly did you clean their flat?' Silence against her skin; the phone stopped vibrating.

'Thoroughly. Each room from top to bottom.'

'And there was no one else in the flat with you?'

'Excuse me,' said Ms Jennings. She turned to Aneta. 'If DCI Clay or her colleague DS Hendricks refuses to name the linked child abduction case to the murder of the brothers, I'm instructing you to put in a *no comment* interview.' She looked directly at the camera up in the left-hand corner of the room. 'Did you get that? I instructed her to go *no comment*. *No comment* does not equate to guilty. This is not a fair interview.'

There was a sharp and rapid succession of knocks on the door and, before Clay could respond, the door opened. Sergeant

Harris stood in the doorway, and the look on his face told Clay it was serious.

'Eve? A moment please.'

Clay stood and said, 'DS Hendricks, show Aneta and her solicitor the evidence.' She heard the bag rustle as Hendricks turned it over.

'What's this?' asked Aneta.

'What does it look like?' replied Hendricks.

Aneta looked inside the evidence bag and said, 'Human hair.'

'We're sure it belongs to Marta Ondřej,' said Hendricks. 'Do you know where it was found?'

Sergeant Harris drew Clay out of the interview suite and spoke quietly. 'Eve, there's been a body found near the railway bridge in Otterspool Park. Female. In her thirties or thereabouts. She's been set on fire.'

'Phone whoever's at the scene and tell them I'll be there in ten minutes. Wait a moment, please.'

Clay returned to the room, her head rammed with the figure *twenty-four hours*, the need to buy time and a growing number of spinning plates.

'Aneta?' said Clay.

'Yes?'

'I have to go now.'

'You do?'

'Something very serious has happened. I need to talk to you as soon as possible. But for now, you're free to go.'

Clay looked at Aneta's solicitor and addressed her directly. 'We have evidence in the bag in front of you. Karl and Václav Adamczak are directly linked to the abduction and kidnap of Marta Ondřej. Your client had the key to their flat. Do you want to advise your client or do you want me to do so? We're not keeping her in custody for now.'

'Make yourself fully available for questioning, Aneta. Go to your workplace or stay at home, nowhere else. Keep your phone on at all times. Do not attempt to travel.'

'Good advice, Ms Jennings. Because, Aneta, in the last days of their lives, it looks like your friends abducted Marta and kept her prisoner in their flat.'

'They… they wouldn't do such a thing. Never,' said Aneta.

'Really?' asked Clay. She looked at her watch, felt her pulse quickening and blood pounding in her head as she moved closer to Aneta.

'What do you *need* to do, Aneta?' pressed Clay.

'I'll do exactly as Ms Jennings has said.'

'Good. I'm circulating your picture to all ports and airports.' Clay stood across the table, leaned closer into Aneta's face.

'Running away's an admission of guilt. Run away if you want to, but we will catch you.'

Chapter 45

2.45 pm

Poppy Waters stood at the window of her office and looked at the iPhone found under the boards at Picton Road. On the surface of the cement-flecked and soiled device, she saw remnants of white fingerprint dust and sections that had been covered in sellotape to lift the prints at the scene.

There was a knock at the door. Instinctively covering the phone with her other hand, she said, 'Come in!'

The door opened and a tall man with jet-black hair and sky-blue eyes stepped into the room.

'Poppy?' His voice was gentle, and accented. He walked towards her, smiled and held out his hand, a visitor badge hanging from his neck. 'I'm Robert Baliński.'

'Much as I'd like to shake hands with you,' said Poppy, 'I'm in the middle of something.'

He looked at her hands in latex gloves. 'I understand.'

'You're my Polish translator?' she asked.

'I am.'

'Can you do me a favour, Robert? Could you go to the canteen and have a coffee? I need to look at something before you help me with the emails and other documents that are in Polish. Twenty minutes, say?'

'I'll be back then.'

As she watched him leave, she thought, *Handsome and nice manners with it.*

She used her right index finger to unlock the iPhone. At first, she typed in her own password; it was declined.

'Here we go then,' she said, pressing Emergency and 9111. She pressed the green call button several times and each time she did so, the red close call sign came on-screen. *911#. 108. As soon as her call to 108 connected she declined the call and waited, counting to five in her head, and watching a band of snow advance inland from the Mersey estuary.

She smiled as the screen saver came up along with a set of icons. She remembered the instruction Eve Clay had emailed to her as she waited for the iPhone to come in: look at the photographs and videos first.

She looked at the screen saver behind the icons: two identical men on either side of a woman. Poppy guessed they were the victims and the woman who had called 999.

She pressed photos and a camera roll with sixty-five pictures and My Photo Stream with eighty-two items appeared. *Not prolific photographers*, she thought, hoping as she brought the camera roll on-screen that she wasn't about to see something that would come between her and her sleep.

Slowly, she scrolled through the images and quickly saw a pattern of five. She went back to the bottom and saw that the first set of five was a single building in various stages of construction, from the flattened ground to the finished item, with the rising exterior and the roof either side of the midway stage.

The next set of five followed the same pattern; scrolling through the camera roll, she did the maths. The dead men had worked on thirteen building sites.

She pressed Albums and then My Photo Stream.

Pictures of the two men with the same woman at different places around Liverpool. The three at the Albert Dock, outside both cathedrals, in the Echo Arena at a concert – three nice-looking hard-working people having fun.

Poppy pressed the videos icon and saw eight jet-black boxes in two rows with various timings in white in their lower left-hand corners.

She pressed the box on the top row, left-hand corner, marked 4.32.

She counted five seconds and the on-screen blackness gave way to an image of a bare light bulb hanging from a white ceiling, crackling as it came to life. There was a noise like choking as the camera panned down the wall and around the bare walls of a room not much bigger than a cupboard with a door.

The camera panned down and Poppy said, 'Oh no! No! No! No!'

She paused the image and, taking out her mobile, called Eve Clay. Her phone rang out and, after several rings, went to the answer service.

'Eve, it's me, Poppy Waters. I've opened the phone from the crime scene. I'm going to send you footage I've found on the phone. It's Marta, Marta Ondřej.'

Chapter 46

2.48 pm

'Thank you for attending, Lucy.'

In Interview Suite 3, Detective Constable Clive Winters sat

across the table from Lucy Bell and smiled at her as she sat down.

'This isn't the same room that DCI Clay interviewed me in.'

'We have more than one interview suite because there are times when more than one interview is taking place. But it has exactly the same features.' He pointed at the video camera in the left-hand upper corner and the audio recorder on the table.

'I've formally opened the interview, Lucy, but I'll ask you again. Would you like legal representation?'

'I've done nothing wrong.'

'I know all about the events around your discovery of Marta Ondřej, but what I need to find out is what you were doing during the eight days leading up to your 999 call.'

'Where's DCI Clay?'

'She got called away to another matter, so I'm sitting in for her.'

'It's just that she said *she* would speak to *me* next time.'

Winters kept the words *You can't take everything literally* inside his head and said, 'If she'd been available, she would have spoken to you personally because you are an important witness. However, she can't.'

'The last eight days leading up to my 999 call? Yes, I can tell you absolutely everything, more or less.'

'Go on, Lucy.'

She bent down and placed her bulging leather satchel on the table.

'Marta went missing on Monday, 24th November 2020. On Monday, I was teaching all morning from 9 am until 12.30 pm with a break at 10.30 until 11 when I drank a cup of tea and gave an academic surgery for...' She took an A4 blue hardback notebook from the satchel and flicked through the dog-eared pages. 'A good diary is like a much-loved Bible, a little the worse for wear around the edges. Here it is. 10.30 until 11, I spoke to James Wade, Eileen Penn and Rupert Ross, all first-year undergraduates.'

She placed the satchel back on the floor and pushed her diary towards Winters. He scanned the first page marked Monday,

24th November and took in all the details, that she got out of bed at 6.30 am, prayed in her bedroom until 7 am; from 7 am until 7.30 am, she showered and dressed; 7.30 am until 8 am, she made tea and toast for her father's breakfast and a single serving of cornflakes with 220ml of milk for herself, and home by 6.13 pm as she did each and every night.

'That's not much of a breakfast, Lucy.'

'I cannot cook. I am not domesticated.'

'Tell me what happened after 12.30 pm.'

'I went to the sweetshop in Mountford Hall, the student union building across the road from the Tate Building near the top of Brownlow Hill, and purchased four bars of chocolate for my lunch. I do this every weekday. The lady who served me, Madge, doesn't even have to ask me what chocolate I eat, and she says she can set her clock by me. I got there on Monday at 12.41 pm – it's a three-minute walk from where I was teaching.'

'Thank you for that, Lucy. Would you mind if we photocopy pages from your diary?'

'Of course not. But you'll only need to copy the pages that cover those eight days.'

Winters took out his phone, and got through to Sergeant Harris. 'Could you come to three, please, Sarge. I need a favour.'

'I ate the chocolate bars going back to Abercromby Square where I had a meeting at 1 pm until 3 pm with my academic supervisor, Dr Ben Reid.'

He glanced down at Lucy's perfectly formed handwriting, skimmed 1 pm and scanned Dr Reid's name and room number – 103.

'We discussed my ongoing PhD thesis, with which he was pleased.'

'What's your subject, Lucy?'

'How twentieth-century political ideas and doctrines were influenced by classical and ancient theories. I still haven't formulated a well-balanced conclusion but that will come with time.'

'I'd like to come back to that later, if you don't mind. It sounds fascinating.'

There was a knock on the door and Sergeant Harris stood in the doorway.

'Excuse me for a few seconds, Lucy.'

Winters took Lucy's diary out of the interview suite and, closing the door, handed it over.

'This is her diary,' he told Harris. 'As a priority, I need you to arrange a photocopy of Monday 24th November until Monday 1st December. But I'd like the whole thing copied. I'll keep her talking. Thank you.'

He returned to the suite and sat across from Lucy again. 'Thanks for that, Lucy.'

'As I understand it, Detective Constable Winters, from what I've heard through the media, Marta went missing at around 2 pm from the Smithdown Lane area of Edge Hill.'

'Yes'

'I was with Doctor Reid at that time, in room 103 in Abercromby Square,' said Lucy, sitting up a little. 'I have a solid alibi from an utterly reputable witness.' She spoke with mounting confidence. 'I had nothing to do with the disappearance and kidnap of Marta Ondřej. I just happened to chance upon her and alert you to my discovery. If I'd have harmed the child in any way, would I have phoned 999? I don't think so, Detective Constable Winters.' She looked at him without blinking and said, 'May I ask you a question?'

'Go on?'

'Isn't it rather difficult at times for you in the police?'

'How do you mean?'

'Being a black man in an institutionally racist organisation like the Merseyside Constabulary.'

'Things are not as bad as they once were, Lucy.'

'I wrote an article for *History Today* about the policing of the Toxteth Riots in 1981, and how the police used the sus laws to police the black community. It was policed on a colonial model. I'm still shocked at what I discovered.'

'Lucy, the Toxteth Riots happened nearly forty years ago.'

Lucy was quiet for a few moments but maintained eye contact with Winters. 'The chief constable at the time said the black population of Liverpool was a result of sexual encounters between black seamen and white prostitutes. Which was not true and was not nice.'

'If any chief constable said such a thing now, they'd be out of the door before they drew their next breath.'

She nodded. 'I guess so. But...'

'But?'

'Do you know how many people were employed by Merseyside Police in 2017? Over seven thousand, including police officers and people in a wide range of roles. In 2017, there were twenty black police officers in Merseyside Constabulary.'

'It's not a good statistic. I was one of the twenty. What can I say? I've got two or three more questions to ask *you*, Lucy.' In his mind he saw pages from her diary mounting up in the photocopier tray. 'So, I had a brief look at your diary, at the entry for Monday, 24th November, and it seems clear you have an alibi. But what happened on the following days, leading up to Monday, 1st December? Would you like to give me a little précis while Sergeant Harris copies the pages for those days?'

'Yes. But can I ask you a question first, Detective Constable Winters?'

'Yes.'

'If I had anything to hide, would I have handed over my personal diary?'

'No.'

'My life consists of two parts. Domestic and university. Domestic. I can tell you, I am either at home with my father or in church or performing duties related to my work as a Eucharistic minister or helping out in a women's refuge. University. I am either teaching or with Doctor Reid or studying in the Sydney Jones library. In between domestic and university I am on public transport, invariably the 86 bus or the 86A.'

'You didn't learn to drive?'

'No. I had one lesson. I couldn't stand it one little bit.'

'OK, Lucy. I see. Now, DCI Clay asked me to ask you about Jack Dare. How do you know him?'

'He works for my father, performing heavy chores around the house and in the garden. My father is getting very old.'

'Is he your friend?'

'No. I like him. He is a good worker. He is polite.'

'Thank you. Well, that's it. But we ask you to make yourself available for interview, if—'

'I know. I've already promised DCI Clay I'd keep my phone on at all times and that is a promise I will keep, in spite of my own personal wishes on the matter.'

Winters sat back in his chair and formally closed the interview. As he turned off the audio recording, Lucy asked, 'Am I free to go now?'

'Yes, by all means. However, I'm intrigued by several details in your diary – one detail in particular. 6.13 pm. You always arrive home at the presbytery at 6.13 pm, come hell or high water. Why?'

'6.13 pm was the time I was born many years ago. To arrive home any earlier or any later strikes me as too early or too late.'

'I see what you mean. One other thing. Twentieth-century political doctrines. How were they influenced by ancient and classical ideas? It sounds fascinating.'

She smiled and lit up like the seafront at Blackpool in early autumn. 'Where, oh, where do I begin?'

Chapter 47

3.15 pm

The violent snowstorm that had hit Garston in the previous hour, had not yet arrived in Aigburth Vale. Needle-like arrows of sleet fell slowly and in random diagonal lines, tossed by the wind that whipped from the River Mersey.

As Detective Chief Inspector Eve Clay parked her car at the top of Jericho Lane, she noticed tyre-width indentations in the snow, and guessed that whoever had parked there had performed a three-point turn to get away from the place. She looked at the broad marks and was sorry that a coating of fresh snow from the on-off showers had covered the tread of the tyres.

Dipping under the crime scene tape at the Aigburth Vale entrance to Otterspool Park, Clay looked at the email, and eight attached videos Poppy Waters had sent to her iPhone as she travelled from Trinity Road to the scene at Aigburth Vale.

Grim news, Eve. The words in Poppy's email ran around her head as she hurried deeper into a park that was part woodland. *But great news for the inquiry. Eight pieces of film of Marta in captivity.*

She felt like a malicious hand had fallen from the sky, splitting her through the centre of her being.

It'll have to wait, thought Clay, frustration rising, prioritising the new murder scene over the films.

Up ahead on the snow-locked path, Clay saw something small that drew her full attention. It was a robin, the natural blush of redness on its breast in life made vivid in death. The wound was deep and, as Clay passed, she observed that it had been made by another, larger bird.

Clay headed towards the gathering of officers at the bottom of the bank near the railway bridge. On the bank, there was a white tent in which a dead and burnt body lay. In the group, she picked out Detective Sergeant Karl Stone talking to a paramedic at the back of an ambulance.

The paramedic walked away from Stone and into the back of the ambulance.

Above the group, she saw the top of the bridge and thought for a moment she was seeing things. Lined up along the straight line of the bridge's top were several crows, a macabre audience standing in the balcony, watching a real-life tragedy unfolding as they perched on the wild ivy that hung down in ragged clumps.

'Karl?' she called, slowing to a vigorous walk as he walked towards her, away from the small crowd. He turned and, as their eyes connected, the small light of hope that someone somewhere down the line had made an error was snuffed out.

'Walk with me, Karl.'

'Sorry, Eve,' said Stone. 'It's a female, thirties, forty maybe, naked and face down on the embankment close to the railway bridge. She's been set alight. There's a distinct smell of petrol in the air.'

'Same as our Picton Road scene then? Only one body less and a different gender. Where's the woman who found her?'

He nodded in the direction of the ambulance. 'I've called Doctor Lamb. She's already sent the APTs down here.'

'Where are they up to with the Adamczak brothers?'

'She's done enough work in both autopsies to leave it for a colleague to dot the is and cross the ts. She's ready to work on our Otterspool Park victim as soon as she arrives at the mortuary.'

'Any obvious racial indicators with the victim?'

'Her skin, the skin that hasn't been burned, is dark olive. She's not white.'

Clay observed the rear of the ambulance, the doors closed against the fierce cold and said, 'OK, Karl, we'll leave it at that for now.'

She knocked on the ambulance door and said, 'DCI Eve Clay...'

The door was opened by a female paramedic and, as Clay showed her warrant card, she looked past her at the woman sitting on the bed wrapped in a blue blanket, shivering and face beaded in moisture.

'Kerrie,' said the female paramedic. 'This is DCI Eve Clay.'

The woman didn't speak or look up from the space she was staring into.

'Hello, Kerrie,' said Clay. 'Thank you for alerting us to your discovery.'

Slowly, Kerrie turned to Clay and looked through her as she struggled to find words.

'I need to have a quick word with you, Kerrie. Did you see anybody else around in the park?'

'No. I saw the odd dog walker on the prom but I didn't see anybody at all in Otterspool Park. It was desolate. It was just me. And her.'

'What drew your attention to her body?'

'It was pretty well-hidden, high in the bank between the trees... It was the crows eating her, their hunger, their noise...'

Clay turned to the paramedic, spoke softly with compassion borne from the depths of unbridled hope. 'Has she said anything to you? Anything?'

'Nothing.'

'If she does say anything, try to record it on your iPhone or write it down, please. Kerrie, just one thing before I leave you. This is your regular running route?'

'Yes.'

'Was anything out of place? Did you notice if anything was not right or different?'

'The... writing... on the wall, on the inside arch of the railway bridge. I missed yesterday. *Killing Time Is Here Embrace It.* It's very recent.' She sounded like a spirit trapped in a bottle. 'And that strange looking circle, that's brand new.'

Kerrie closed her eyes and her chin dropped to her collarbone.

'I'm sorry you had to see this. But thank you for alerting us to it.'

Walking towards the bridge, Clay said to Stone, 'I want you to call Barney Cole and get him to pull any CCTV from Otterspool Promenade and Aigburth Vale. Whoever's done this had two ways in. Top end of Jericho Lane facing the shops in the Vale. And from the prom.'

Clay walked under the arch of the bridge and saw the words *Killing Time Is Here Embrace It* spray-painted just above the tarmac on the lower right hand wall. The writing was identical to the graffiti she had seen at the Picton Road murder scene. Above the writing on the wall was the geometrical Black Sun logo.

As Clay walked away from the bridge and up the bank towards the tent, the victim's body was partially concealed by Detective Sergeant Terry Mason crouched on his haunches and taking close-up photographs of the murdered woman.

'Terry?'

He looked over his shoulder and, as he stood up, he nodded to Clay as she saw the extent of the fire damage to the woman's body.

All of her hair had been burned away and her scalp was blackened. Clay looked above her neck, and knew that her head and face had been doused in petrol, that this was where the fire had started. She looked down the length of her back and saw a huge burn-mark down her spine, stretching out to either side of her ribs, a wound that exposed her bones to the cold air. Where her flesh had melted, it gave her the appearance of a small fire pit in the earth.

Clay looked around up and down the woman's body and saw blood on the ground between her upper thighs. As she crouched to get a closer look at the woman's charred face Clay worked out the grim maths that, in a direct line, her home in Mersey Road was around eight hundred metres from the murder scene.

Clay scrutinised her scorched profile, lifted her head gently to get a view of her whole face and said, 'Karl? Come and look at this.'

Stone crouched beside Clay and looked at the victim's upturned face. He groaned as Clay lowered the woman's face to the frozen earth.

'What do you think, Eve?'

'I think they've targeted her face with petrol to disguise her identity and make life tougher for us.'

Stone turned and looked at Clay.

'Karl, give Scientific Support the heads up. I strongly suspect our victim has been subjected to a sexual assault.'

She pointed at the bush and the ground near it.

'Please stay here with Scientific Support and organise a finger-tip search of the embankment, both sides. There are tyre imprints as you come out of the park. Get them sectioned off, please.'

'Where are you going?' asked Stone.

'Poppy sent me some footage from the phone Terry found in the Adamczak brothers' box room. I'm going to look at it in my car.'

Clay walked carefully in a diagonal line down the frozen embankment and away from the bridge, watching her feet and hoping that she wouldn't tumble in front of the growing body of police officers.

As Clay walked along the path leading out of Otterspool Park, Poppy's words, *Grim news, Eve. But great news for the inquiry*, rolled around the inside of her head like a blessing housing a curse. Reaching the door of her car, she felt the temperature drop suddenly and with the savage touch of the west wind, the snow storm arrived, and the wind that came with it knew no mercy.

Chapter 48

3.18 pm

Walking away from Trinity Road Police Station, Lucy Bell was aware of the return of an old fear she thought she had long conquered: the irrational fear that she was being watched or followed.

She glanced over her shoulder and saw that there was no one behind her, only a CCTV camera mounted above the front door of the police station, pointed at her back. Looking ahead, she saw a wing mirror on the passenger side of a black car that she recognised immediately as her father's ancient Ford Orion. Reaching the door, she opened it and said, 'Dad, thanks for...'

'Sorry, it's not your Dad, it's me,' said Jack, smiling. 'Your father asked me to pick you up – gave me the keys.'

He turned on the engine to try to generate a little warmth in the cold car. She sat next to him, closed the door and said, 'Oh, no, I'm... I'm very happy to see you, Jack. I always am, you know that.'

'Likewise, Lucy.'

A painful silence fell between them and Jack read the depth of Lucy's neediness in her eyes.

'You're like a sister to me,' he said. 'Remember that conversation we had.'

'It's platonic,' she said. 'Our relationship.'

She felt a blush rising and knew that within seconds her face would be crimson.

'Tell me what happened in the police station?'

'I'm frightened I'm making a fool of myself. You're a very handsome young man and there are other women out there who'd agree with me...'

'There are loads of women out there but, my mother excepted, you're the only one who stood by me in my darkest days.' He changed the subject. 'Want me to drive you back to the uni?'

'Yes, please, Jack.'

'You seem very tense. Relax, Lucy.'

She looked in the wing mirror. 'I keep thinking we're being watched.'

'By?'

'I don't know. My father. The police.'

'That's not the case, Lucy. Trust me.'

'Please drive away, Jack.'

He pulled away from the pavement and felt the momentary touch of Lucy's fingers on the back of his hand as he shifted into second gear and turned the corner.

They travelled in silence for a few blocks and Jack recognised a catch in Lucy's breathing, the fighting down of tears.

'Do you remember when we first met, Lucy? When I was in

the Young Offenders Institute at Altcar and you used to come and visit me, even though I was a complete stranger to you? You used to write to me, telling me never to give up hope, and that the time might drag but one day I'd be free. It wasn't any of those women *out there* who kept me sane when I was locked away. You were one of the few people in this world who believed my side of the story, and you told me over and over that one day I'd be vindicated. You showed me by the things you did and said that there is a God of love, and that God loved me.'

Jack kept his fingers on the gearstick, but he could still feel the weight of Lucy's hand on the back of his hand.

'I'd love you to be my boyfriend but I understand. The love you have for me is the love of a brother for a sister. Do you think that might change one day?'

Jack pulled up at a red light outside St Austin's Church, and smiled at her. 'How can I ever be your boyfriend? I'll never have a full-time job. I've got no prospects. I can't afford to take you out. Things are the way they are...' Jack pulled away as the lights turned green. 'Did Clay interview you?'

'No, it was a man. He was polite, well spoken, and took a keen interest in history. He asked me questions about my thesis. He was exceptional for another reason. He was a black officer.'

'A police constable?'

'No, a detective constable.'

In silence, Jack pulled up at a red light at the junction of Aigburth Road and Jericho Lane. Lucy looked straight ahead at the two police officers in high visibility jackets pointing a speedometer and a camera at the traffic coming towards them.

'Are you all right, Lucy? You look a bit anxious?'

'Why are they taking pictures? They don't normally do that at speed traps.'

'Look!' Jack pointed at three officers dressed in white protective suits emerging from Otterspool Park. 'It's a crime scene.'

Lucy glanced up at the red light.

'I'm going to be late for work.'

'Lights are changing already. There, green, go...'

'It's just...'

'Just what, Lucy?'

'I'm sick to death of seeing police officers.'

'Everything will go back to normal, really soon. Trust me.'

Chapter 49

3.38 pm

With the engine running and her windscreen wipers working at top speed, Clay prepared to look at the footage from the Adamczak brothers' phone.

As she pressed play, a black mortuary van pulled up at the scene-of-crime tape. Clay drew the passenger window down and called to Harper at the wheel of the van, 'You'll have to wait there until Scientific Support give you the all-clear. You'll probably have to carry the body from the railway bridge to where you're now parked. You know the drill.'

Looking back at her phone, the camera panned down, past a bare light bulb and a blank wall and straight into the face of Marta Ondřej, her mouth covered and silenced with a black gag. Marta blinked hard, the bright light hurting her eyes after the complete darkness she had endured. The end.

She pressed play on the second film and saw a direct close-up of Marta's face and head, this time without a gag. Marta opened her mouth to speak and an androgynous voice shushed her harshly, waving the black gag before her eyes. Marta closed her mouth, and her eyes filled with tears as the film ended abruptly.

Ragged snowflakes danced in the wind above the empty passenger seat and Clay shivered as she wound the window up.

As she pressed play on the third film, Clay guessed correctly that it would be another close-up of Marta's face. This time a black-gloved hand appeared on the right of Marta's hair, slapping and prodding her cheeks viciously. The girl sat in silence, blinking when the fingers came near her eyes. Although she appeared unafraid, Clay could see she was numb with terror. There was a final freeze frame on Marta's face as the hand vanished off-camera.

Eight days missing, thought Clay, *and eight pieces of film. A video diary of oppression.*

The fourth day's footage was a close-up of Marta's face with the gloved hand snipping and cutting her hair, the black gag on her mouth forcing her to scream in her throat as her eyes bulged with terror.

She was now halfway through and Clay feared the worst was still to come.

In the fifth sequence, in the close-up of her face, her head was shaven save for the patches of stubble that Clay had first noticed in the Wavertree Mystery. She paused the film, looked closely at Marta's face. Her cheekbones were now sticking out and dark circles were forming around her eyes. After three seconds, the film ended.

They didn't feed you. Clay couldn't help but imagine Philip in Marta's place. Bleak anger rose up inside her. 'Who would do this to a child?'

'Why did you do it to her?' Clay could hear outrage in each rising word.

On the sixth day, Clay noticed that Marta's face was now in the early stages of emaciation, and her lips were dry and cracked. The black-gloved hand came from the left this time with an uncapped bottle of water. Marta raised her hand to take the bottle but it was snatched away. Then it reappeared, *Come and get me!*

Clay wound her own window down, this time to allow the cold air and snow into the car, to cool the prickly heat in her face.

She called Hendricks on her iPhone. 'Bill, it's me.'

'What's wrong, Eve?'

'I've got the footage of Marta Ondřej from Václav Adamczak's phone. There are eight pieces. I've just finished the sixth.'

'Bad?'

'Bad, and getting worse by the day. I'll send it to your phone. I need to get back to Trinity Road and sweat down Aneta Kaloza. Has she said anything since I left?'

'No. Sorry, Eve. She's refused to leave the station. She's sitting in reception, telling everyone she's going to clear her friends' names.'

'She's not going to do it. You'll see why when I forward these films to you. But for now, their contents stay between you and me.'

'OK, understood.'

She sighed as she prepared to play the seventh piece of film, terrified to see what pain and suffering awaited her.

Chapter 50

6.00 pm

When Jack opened the front door of his mother's house the smell from upstairs was so bad that he thought Raymond had died and was decomposing in a room full of electric fires, but he quickly dismissed this as wishful thinking, and smiled when he heard Jasmine barking for his attention. He opened the kitchen door and she trapped her face between his ankles, licking his feet.

'Come on, Jas.' She followed him as he took the stairs two at a time. 'Raymond, hey, answer me!'

Reaching Raymond's bedroom door, Jack looked in and saw his brother fully clothed and curled up in a foetal ball. He looked around the squalor of his brother's room, the clothes strewn across the floor, the tangle of sheets stale with bodily fluids beneath his unwashed frame, the brimming ashtray, matches and Rizla papers at the side of his bed.

His eyes settled on a forgotten box in an ignored corner of the room. In an unloved and chaotic space, it was the only window onto anything good. Jack walked over to it and lifted the lid.

The plastic bottles of poster paints and tubes of oil paints sat next to pots of immaculately clean brushes, set out in order of size. There was a range of palettes for mixing colours, empty jars for watercolours and a thick roll of quality art paper. Thick coloured card poked out from a blue plastic wallet at the back of the box, next to spray paints and cardboard templates. Jack reached down the side of the wardrobe and pulled out a wooden easel and placed it back.

Then he went to the bathroom and turned on the hot tap.

In Raymond's room, he pulled back the curtains and opened the window as wide as it would go. He sat on the end of Jack's bed and Jasmine climbed up onto his knee.

'Wake up, Raymond!'

But his brother didn't flicker until Jasmine barked three times at top note. Raymond lifted his head and looked at Jasmine and Jack as if there was a dense fog in the room.

'What's that noise?'

'It's the bath running. You stink, Raymond.'

'I'm not well.'

'Tell me about it.'

Jack saw Raymond's phone on the mattress, close to where it had fallen from his limp hand as he'd fallen asleep.

Raymond squinted and rubbed his eyes. 'What do you want, Ja-Ja-Ja...'

'Here it comes. The return of the childhood stammer, as in don't bother asking me anything because you'll have to wait till Christmas for an answer.' Jack picked up Raymond's phone. 'Who is she?'

'You... ask me th-that... be-be-before?'

'Yeah.'

'Who do you mean?'

Jack started unlocking Raymond's phone.

'Give it back to me.'

'If you leave your number lying around, what can you expect? She says her name's Dominika,' said Jack.

'Give it to me.'

Jack showed Raymond Dominika's Facebook profile picture. 'Who is she?'

Raymond looked around, covered his face with his hands and talked to the ceiling. 'She sent me a friend request on F-Facebook last Wednesday. I didn't know who she was but her profile picture was nice, she was fit. I accepted. She sent me a message, asked me where I lived. She told me she lived in Garston and that maybe we should meet up. I said, *Yeah*. Then she didn't get back in touch for a couple of days and I thought, *Well fuck that then*. Then on Saturday night, she asked me if I wanted to see a picture of her? *Yeah*.'

'You didn't think it was odd?' Jack turned Raymond's phone towards him, showed him the image of Dominika with her back to the camera, bending forwards and looking through her parted legs at the viewer. 'She looks nothing like Dominika in the profile picture you were sent. She's a good fifteen years older, Raymond, and judging by the look of her she's from one of the Eastern block...'

'It's my business.'

'You to her: *Send me a film of yourself*... Her to you: *Shall we meet first?* You to her: *Yeah, when?*'

'Stop it, Jack.'

'She told you she's from the Czech Republic. I don't get it, Raymond. I thought you hated all immigrants?'

Raymond turned onto his side and buried his face in the pillow. A stream of language flooded from his mouth and was lost in the pillow slip.

'Look at me, Raymond!' Jack grabbed him by the shoulders

and hauled him up into a sitting position. 'Didn't you think it was just a little bit strange this woman who you've never met is sending you pornographic images of herself?'

Raymond placed his hands over his eyes and dragged his fingers down his face.

'You came in here the night before last, early hours, full of yourself.'

'But you didn't see me.'

'I did see you. I watched you come in like you were the king, and I thought, *What's he been up to?* You won't tell me what you did which is unusual because you can't hold your own water when you've pulled some stunt, so I can only conclude you've done something really heavy duty. Are you going to tell me what?'

'I told you, we robbed a car and torched it.'

'I don't believe you. You hardly slept, you woke up and were still full of yourself. But look at you now. You're an open book, Raymond. You're traumatised.' Jack tapped Raymond's forehead with his index finger. 'It's hit home. You and your goons have punched above your weight this time. Haven't you?'

'It's freezing, Jack.'

'Put your clothes in the basket and get in the bath.'

'We robbed a car, that's all.'

'Raymond, I've had this conversation with you for Mum's sake. Why don't you stop your stupidity for her sake?'

Raymond sat up on the bed and kicked off his trainers.

'I'm going to open a few windows downstairs to let the stench out. One thing. Have you met up with Dominika yet?'

As Jack walked out of the room, Raymond spoke.

'What was that, Raymond?'

'I said, no I haven't.'

Raymond listened to Jack going downstairs. When he was safely out of earshot, he spoke softly to himself. 'Yes I fucking did meet up with her. When was the last time you got laid, dickhead?'

Chapter 51

6.03 pm

At the desk he'd requested for its closeness to the incident room's kitchen, DC Clive Winters turned over the last photocopied page of Lucy Bell's handwritten diary and said, 'You poor cow.'

'Lucy Bell's *Groundhog Day*?' asked Cole.

'It makes her Facebook page look like a wild night in Las Vegas. Jesus, the attention to detail's just mind-bending. Every day is the same. Every time is rigid. Wake up. Get up. Pray. Wash. Eat. Uni. Home. 6.13 pm each and every night. Eat. Then she's either marking essays by her students, working on her thesis, or skivvying at Levene House. Then it's go to bed. Pray. Sleep. Wake up, repeat...'

'Does she do anecdotes?' asked Cole. 'What are the weekends like?'

'Pretty much the same. Every other Saturday, she travels to HM Prison Liverpool where she visits prisoners who have no one else coming to see them.'

'One prisoner in particular?'

'No. I reckon after the first visit, the prisoners tell the screws not to let her anywhere near them. She must know they don't want to see her and yet she persists in going. I'll be honest with you, Barney. I'm sorry for her. She means well. But the road to hell and all that.'

'Did she write an account of finding Marta Ondřej?'

'Oh, yeah!' Winters consulted his notebook and read out loud, 'I found Marta Ondřej in the Wavertree Mystery and called the police. When I heard sirens approaching, I left her and went to catch the bus into uni.'

'Can I have a look?'

'Sure.' Winters stood and scooped up the photocopied pages. 'You think I've been bored into missing something?'

'No, it's just a second pair of eyes.'

Winters placed the photocopied diary down on Cole's desk.

'I feel like a massive shot of Jack Daniels,' said Winters.

'As soon as this is sorted out I'll join you, and it's on me.'

Chapter 52

6.15 pm

Detective Constable Eve Clay made her way from the car park of Trinity Road Police Station to the main building, shivering as she pressed her iPhone to her ear.

'Eve,' said DC Barney Cole, 'I've got two things for you. The graffiti from the Adamczak murder scene, first. Where are you?'

'Heading in to the funny farm. What's with the graffiti?'

'Well, you know I told you it represents Black Sun... I've found out more about it now. It's an esoteric symbol to do with old magic. It was seized on by the Nazis, Heinrich Himmler and the SS in particular. They were based in Wewelsburg Castle where they had a green sun wheel laid in the marble on the first floor of the north tower, which was the centre of the world according to Himmler. These lot were into weird mystical mind-fuckery. They'd plan archaeological expeditions to go and find stuff like the Spear of Destiny.'

'Good work, Barney. The only graffiti they could have left that was more screamingly Nazi was a swastika. Where are you now?'

'Heading down to reception to meet you. I've heard back from the Polish police about the Adamczak twins.'

'Eve,' said Sergeant Harris as Clay entered the building. 'You're popular today. You have a visitor.' He pointed at a row of blue seats attached to the wall with bolts. An elderly and burly man in a black coat, holding a grey trilby hat, stood up with a large Home Bargains bag in his right hand.

'Father Aaron, can I help you?'

'I've come to talk to you about Sister Ruth.'

'Shall we go somewhere quiet to talk?'

'One and Two are free,' said Sergeant Harris.

'Follow me, Father Aaron.'

Just then, Cole hurried into reception through the swing doors.

'Eve...'

'Barney, I...'

'I'll be very brief, I promise,' said Father Aaron Bell.

Cole raised a thumb.

'Step this way please, Father Aaron.'

As Clay took two chairs away from the table in Interview Suite 2, Father Aaron Bell said, 'I've never been in a police interview suite before. As a matter of fact, I've never been in a police station before.'

Clay set the chair down for the priest and sat directly in front of him.

'You have some news for me, Father Aaron?'

'Yes, I thought it best to let you know personally. Sister Ruth isn't in good physical health but her mind's lucid and she's as eloquent as ever. I went to see her after you visited me.' He looked at his watch. 'Your colleague requires your attention. So. Sister Ruth remembers you when you were a child in St Claire's and St Michael's perfectly. And she is more than happy to communicate with you. She has asked me, though, to act as intermediary for the time being while she gathers her thoughts, and so she can pray for a meaningful and rewarding journey into the past for you.'

He extended the Home Bargains bag and said, 'This is a small present for your little boy. The book's for when he's older.'

Clay looked inside the bag and saw the spine of an academic text book. *Entomology: Structures and Habitats. Aaron Bell.* Next to the book was a clear Perspex box with a cricket inside it.

'Philip will be thrilled with this. This is your book, right?' she checked.

He smiled.

'What a kind thought. Thank you, Father Aaron.'

Father Aaron Bell took a folded, snow-dampened piece of paper from his pocket and handed it to Clay.

'I'm sorry, I can't afford a business card. You can call me any-time except nine till half nine Monday to Friday, or twelve to twelve-thirty, when I say mass in my church or at Bishop Eton. Oh, and I take confession on Wednesday from two to four in the afternoon at the Metropolitan Cathedral, not that I get many people, but I make myself available just in case.'

He stood up and the melted snow on his coat glittered like distant stars.

'Thank you for your time, Father Aaron.'

Clay held open the door for him.

'Do you mind me asking you, Eve – do you still keep and prac-tise the faith?'

The temptation to lie was strong, but she was aware that bring-ing untruths in to the picture could harm the dynamic. 'I was six when I lost Sister Philomena, Father Aaron.'

He looked at her and radiated kindness.

'When she died, I lost my whole world and when my whole world was gone, my faith gradually went with it.'

He nodded. 'I understand completely. I do. Would you mind if I started praying for you?'

'That would be very kind of you. Thank you. I appreciate that.'

He looked at Clay and said, 'I can see myself out. You look like you could do with a few quiet moments. God bless and keep you, Eve, and all those you hold dear. Philomena would have...' He paused.

'Go on, Father Aaron.'

'She would have wanted you to have the comfort and support that faith gives to those who share it. I too would like it for you. I didn't meet Sister Philomena personally but I've met a lot of people who did know her, and I've learned much about who she was. We should make time to discuss those impressions.'

'That would be wonderful, Father Aaron. Thank you.'

As he shut the door, Clay sat on the chair and listened to the sound of her own breathing. Opening the paper he had given her, she read to herself, 'Father Aaron Bell 0151 496 0113.' She committed the phone number to memory, and felt the giddiness that always accompanied hope when it visited her heart.

Chapter 53

6.32 pm

Clay found Cole in the corridor outside Interview Suite 1.

'What have the Polish police dished on the Adamczak twins, Barney?'

She looked over his shoulder at Aneta Kaloza as Sergeant Harris accompanied her down the corridor.

'To all intents and purposes, Karl's as clean as the driven. Václav not so.'

'Really?'

Clay indicated Aneta coming towards them.

'I stayed here of my own will,' said Aneta, as Sergeant Harris opened the door and shepherded her into the interview suite.

'I'll be with you in a minute.'

As the door to Interview Suite 1 closed, Clay said, 'Go on, Barney?'

'Just over two years ago, a teenage girl went missing three streets away from where the Adamczak brothers lived with their mother and sisters. When she turned up four days after going missing, she pointed the finger at Václav – said he'd lured her into a lock-up garage and held her prisoner there against her will.'

'What happened during that time?' asked Clay, coldness spreading to her fingers and toes.

'Nothing was proved forensically, but she alleged he systematically sexually assaulted her. The police did issue formal warnings to Václav: keep away from teenage girls. There were a few reports to the police. One girl said he followed her home. Another that he was hanging around near the playground she and her mates went to. That he was watching them. Václav said, he walked the girl home for her safety. There'd been a fight on the playground the week before the girl reported Václav hassling her and her friends. Václav said he was protecting the girls from the violent youths who'd turned the playground into a blood bath.'

'Overprotective or downright naive? Where was Karl when all this was going on?' asked Clay.

'He was out of town, working in Krakow, waiting for his brother to get better and join him on the building site. Václav was on his own in his mother's house getting over a bout of flu. His mother and sisters couldn't corroborate his side of any of the stories and allegations against him because they were in Warsaw, setting up a flat for the twins. The Scientific Support team combed the lock-up she claimed to have been imprisoned in. There was no forensic evidence linking Václav to the garage, or any traces of his DNA. But they did find forensic evidence linking the girl to the place.'

'Did the lock-up belong to Václav?'

'No, to his friend George, a local hustler who used it to store fake designer brands sourced from China and what have you. The girl claimed she didn't know the hustler from Adam, but it was clear Václav had links to him. He had the key to the lock-up and was looking after it while George was on a buying trip abroad. When she was examined by the doctors there was no physical evidence of the assaults she alleged Václav committed, but she reported it two weeks after the so-called events.'

'What was the upshot?'

'The Polish prosecution services recommended that the police didn't have a case that would stand up in a court of law. Some other teenage girls stepped forward once the kidnap allegation hit social media. Václav had been seen around town with another girl, buying her ice-cream, cuddly toys, perfume and clothes. Maybe he was a victim of the 'no smoke without fire' argument. He had a seedy reputation and that reputation turned pure bad.'

'Anything else?'

'Ten days after the police investigation into Václav collapsed, the same girl was back in the central police station in Pruszków, making allegations against another man.' Cole shrugged. 'Anyway, it seems the final allegation and subsequent inquiry was instrumental in the brothers upping sticks from Poland and trying a fresh start in Liverpool.'

Clay pointed at the door, and Aneta behind it.

'She'll know all about this. Let's ask Aneta Kaloza about Václav's taste in young girls.'

Chapter 54

6.40 pm

Clay and Hendricks sat across from Aneta Kaloza, whose eyes were like windscreen wipers moving back and forth between them.

'I've done the formalities,' said Hendricks. 'Miss Kaloza has declined legal representation.'

'Aneta,' said Clay. 'I seriously advise you to have a solicitor—'

'No. This is madness. I've done nothing wrong.'

Clay turned her iPhone round on the table and showed Aneta the photograph of Marta that had been circulated after her disappearance.

'You know who this is, Aneta?'

Aneta looked at the image for a few moments and said nothing, but nodded.

'She's turned up.'

Clay watched Aneta but didn't detect any increase in the anxiety and confusion that were already in her face.

'Is she all right?'

'I don't know yet,' replied Clay, picking out on her iPhone the image she had taken of Marta in the Wavertree Mystery. She showed it to Aneta.

'What's happened to her hair?'

'The person or persons who held her prisoner cut off her hair and kept it as a trophy.'

Clay showed her another image on her phone. 'Do you recognise this phone?'

'It's Václav's.'

'Our IT expert unlocked it and found some very damning footage.'

'Ms Kaloza,' said Hendricks. 'We're going to show you a sequence of still images which we'd like you to narrate. But before we do so, we need to know about the dates and times you visited the Adamczak brothers' flat on Picton Road between Monday, 24th November this year to Monday, 1st December.'

'I clean for the brothers on Mondays and Fridays – Monday to make things spick and span, Friday to sort out any mess from their working week. So, Monday 24th November you say. Yes, eight in the morning until nine-thirty. Friday 28th November, same time slot. I turn up on Monday 1st December and they're both dead.'

'Tell me about last Friday,' said Clay.

'Friday. I cleaned their flat. Eight until nine-thirty.'

'Did you go into every room?'

'Of course.'

'Were you on your own, Aneta?' asked Clay.

'Yes, the boys were at work in Anfield.'

'Which company?'

'CJ Construction. On Friday, they were on a site near the football ground...'

'DS Hendricks, could you check that out, please.'

Within seconds, Clay and Aneta were alone in the room.

'I'm going to show you that sequence of images, Aneta. Tell me what you see.'

'I see the narrow hall of Karl and Václav's flat in Picton Road. Now, I see the door to the empty box room on the left of their hall. This is the inside of the box room.' There was a long silence. 'This must be the space under the floorboards in the box room, because they've been taken up...'

'Did you go into the box room on Friday?'

'Yes. I opened the door to air the room. That side of the flat gets damp.'

'And what was in there?'

'Nothing.'

'When our Scientific Support officer went in there, he saw something that made him lift the boards. When he lifted them, tell me what he found.'

'I can see a length of darkness and Václav's mobile phone. It's a length of...'

Clay opened the evidence bag and showed the contents to Aneta.

'It's almost certainly Marta Ondřej's hair,' Clay told her. 'It was found under the boards in the box room of your friends' flat.'

Something shimmered in Aneta's eyes and, for a moment, Clay thought she was going to faint.

'Marta Ondřej is small and frail for her age...' Clay carried on.

'What are you saying?'

'Based on video clips I've seen of Marta in captivity, the space in which she was imprisoned looks exactly like the box room in your friends' flat, where her hair was discovered along with Václav's phone. It's a compelling triangle. Box room... shaven hair... video evidence on Václav's phone.'

'I swear to God, I know nothing about this.'

'Box room, Marta… Shaven hair, Marta… video evidence on Václav's phone, Marta. Marta who'd fit into a box room that can be locked from the outside for a little over a week. She's got learning difficulties, she's like a lamb.'

'DCI Clay, she was not in that box room on Friday.'

'Did you see Karl or Václav Adamczak between Monday 24th November and Monday 1st December? Don't sit there in silence, Aneta.'

'No! No, I did not see them from that Monday to the next.'

'Did you communicate with them during that window of time?'

'Yes, I spoke with Karl on the phone, after they had finished work one night.'

'Did he sound odd, disorientated?'

'No, Karl was perfectly normal, as always – calm, polite, friendly.'

'Did he have a sexual preference for young girls?'

'No!'

'What about Václav?'

'You can say what you like about the dead because they have no voices to defend themselves. No, Václav did not have a preference for young girls.'

'Aneta, I'm working towards nailing down the truth here about an abduction in which your friends are heavily implicated. I'm also looking for a motive. Why would someone kill your friends? Help me out here. Tell me the truth.'

'I'm telling you the truth.'

'We've been in touch with the police in Pruszków.' Clay watched the colour rise from Aneta's throat and into her cheeks. 'There were several complaints about Václav. Bothering young girls.'

'None of which were prosecuted. Václav was over-friendly and under-intelligent, the opposite of Karl in spite of them being identical twins. These lying little sluts were trying to exhort money from him.'

'Do you drive a car, Aneta?'

'Yes.'

'Did you drive Marta Ondřej to Wavertree Mystery Park?'
Aneta spoke with quiet unbottled anger.

'Would you repeat that, Aneta, for the audio recording.'
Aneta sat back and folded her arms.

'Aneta, I heard you. If the machine didn't pick you up, we can enhance the sound quality. You just said, *fucking Roma.*'

'Yes, fucking Roma, wherever Roma goes trouble follows.'

'She's a fourteen-year-old girl...'

'Are you sure she's fourteen, these people aren't good with numbers, and they're even worse in telling the truth. Where was her birth registered? Get a DNA sample. She's probably in her twenties, but her mother's claiming child allowance. Do you know people all over Europe laugh at your country and the benefits it pays out. Stupid England. English dickheads, to use one of your words.'

In the silence that followed, Clay watched Aneta freefall from the heights of her rage.

'I-I-I didn't mean that. It was an outrageous thing to say about Roma. I am stressed. My friends are murdered. My friends stand accused. I am in a police station answering painful questions. I apologise. I am not a racist. I apologise for my outburst and retract what I have said in anger and through distress.'

'I understand, Aneta... I'm keeping you in custody for twenty-four hours.'

'Enough now. I want legal representation.'

'We can sort that out while you're in the cells.'

There was a sharp knock on the door and, as DS Hendricks entered, Clay dialled the desk for Sergeant Harris.

Hendricks faced Aneta. 'CJ Construction deny all knowledge of Karl and Václav Adamczak. As for the site manager in Anfield, not only have they never worked there, he's never even heard the names Karl and Václav Adamczak.'

Aneta looked like the marrow was setting fast in her legs.

'Did they work the weekend or did they have Saturday and Sunday off?' asked Hendricks.

'No, I didn't see them, but Karl told me they were taking the time off on Saturday and Sunday.'

'According to the site manager, no one had the option of taking the weekend off. The job's fallen behind and CJ Construction face a massive fine if they don't deliver on time. All hands on deck at the weekend.'

'This isn't happening.'

'The site manager's going to contact his CJ Construction colleagues across the northwest to check that the Adamczak brothers weren't on some other site.'

There was a knock on the door and Sergeant Harris entered.

'It is happening, Aneta,' said Clay. 'Choose a solicitor and have a good think when Sergeant Harris has taken you to the cells. Maybe your friends lied to you about where they were working because they were too busy – because they had company.'

When the door closed, Clay said, 'She had a racist outburst against Roma people.'

'I read up about this when Marta went missing. The Roma people are widely despised in Poland and other countries in central Europe. Just as the travellers are here. We've got the Racial and Religious Hatred Act 2006. Voice your racist views and it's up to two years in prison. The 2006 Act stopped millions of people from using the words nigger, gypo and ghost, but it couldn't do anything to stop people thinking those words or from having racist views.'

Clay's iPhone rang out; she saw it was an incoming call from Stone.

'What's happening, Karl?'

'Can you get to Otterspool Park, Eve?' He sounded excited, and the bitter cold put a tremble in his voice.

'What's been found?'

'Three items of the victim's clothing.'

'I'll be there as soon as I can, Karl.' Clay turned to Hendricks.

'I'll be back for Aneta as soon as she's had a chat with her solicitor.'

'What do you want me to do?'

'I'd be grateful if you'd stay here, Bill, in case she cracks.'

Chapter 55

6.45 pm

Father Aaron Bell placed the small colour photograph of Kelly-Ann Carter, clipped from the *Daily Telegraph*, on the table in the Chapel to the Virgin Mary and made the sign of the cross as he knelt before the statue. He picked the picture up and propped it against Mary's stone feet, obscuring the head of Satan in the form of a serpent writhing under her feet, allowing him to see Kelly-Ann handcuffed and in her orange prison uniform.

He looked at the image in the candlelight and then at Mary's beatific face, and the words of prayer that flowed from his heart and soul stuck inside him.

'I... I?' He stared into Mary's eyes for inspiration, but none was forthcoming. 'I will stay here until the words come out of me. In the meantime, Mary, I will pray with the words of prayers that I know until I find words of my own.'

The wind leaked in through a crack in a stained-glass window depicting Mary's ascension into heaven, and the candles flickered at his side.

'Hail, Mary, full of grace. Our Lord is with you. Blessed are you among women...' He stopped, listened hard, wondered if a mostly sleepless night and stress were ganging up to play tricks on his senses.

The sound came again, clearer this time, and louder. Someone was banging on the church door. Father Aaron got to his feet.

As he went to answer, the words of the Hail Mary flooded through his mind.

Bang! Bang! Bang! The person on the church steps tried to turn the circular handle.

'Who is it?' asked Father Aaron. Outside, the wind moaned around the sandstone walls but all else was silent. 'Who is it? If you don't tell me who you are, how can I possibly open the door to you? Tell me who you are and I will open the door if I know you.'

Bang! Bang! Bang!

'I'm going away now. I can't open the door to...' Silence. 'Is that you, Kate?'

Bang!

He slipped the large black key into the lock and turned it. As he opened the door, the words *Dear Lord, please make it Kate!* danced in his heart. Looking through the narrow crack, he saw that it was her.

'Come inside out of the cold, Kate! Come in! Come in!'

He closed the door after her and turned on the light around the font, casting them from darkness into half-shadow.

'I've been to your house a few times over the past couple of days.' He looked at her eyes, fixed on his lips. 'Yes, a few times. The light bell you have to alert you when there's someone at the door – is it working? I would check if I were you. I'm pretty sure you were in when I came to see you, but you didn't come to answer. That's never happened before, Kate. We've always been good friends, from my first day in the parish. You've been a good and faithful parishioner for years...'

She placed the index finger of her right hand to her lips and made deeper furrows in the wrinkles on her brow. *Silence, please!*

'What is it, Kate?'

Kate walked in front of Father Aaron, made a gesture with her hand. *Follow me!*

When she got to the very back pew, right-hand side, she stopped. She pointed to the place on the end of the pew where she always sat – seven days a week, twice on Sundays – and then at Father Aaron.

'Let me get this straight. You want me to sit in your place?'

She nodded and, as he sat down, Kate walked down the aisle in the direction of the altar. She walked past the altar rail towards the vestry and opened the door. In the doorway, she turned and looked directly at Father Aaron. He held her gaze and felt the rock at his core turning into quicksand.

Father Aaron stood up and moved as quickly as he could to the third pew on the left-hand side, Mr Rotherham's regular place. He turned his eyes to the vestry but could only see as far as the end of the altar rail. He moved to the front pew, to Iris's place in the congregation, and couldn't see the vestry door or Kate. Standing up, he hurried past the altar. When he came to the vestry door, Kate was gone. The door at the back of the church was closed and, when he looked for the key in the lock, it was gone.

Father Aaron turned the handle but the back door was locked from the outside. He listened and heard her feet shuffling through the cold gravel at the side of the church.

'No! No! No!' he called to himself as he rushed out of the vestry and up the aisle towards the front door of the church, blood pounding and his breath coming in sharp spasms.

He threw open the church door and looked both ways. Kate's shuffling was coming from the side of the building, and Father Aaron swallowed his mounting outrage.

As Kate reached the corner she stopped, staying out of sight.

'I can hear you, Kate. What's going on?'

He walked down the steps, hanging onto the rusted metal rail, and watching his feet against the frozen grit.

'You can hide there, but I'm coming now, so you won't hide forever. And I know you can't hear me, you deaf old bitch. I've humoured you for too long, you and your attention-seeking visions, and this is the way you repay me with this... this... god-damned nonsense.'

He reached the corner and, turning around it at speed, found Kate flanked by Mr Rotherham and Iris.

'How dare you speak to an old lady like that,' said Mr Rotherham, his voice filled with shock and anger. 'How dare you abuse her because of her disabilities?'

'Father Aaron, I am shocked that these words have come from the mouth of a priest.' Iris shook her head, tears in her eyes.

Kate handed the back door key to Father Aaron.

'This is all a big misunderstanding. I-I've been under enormous stress...'

Kate linked her hands into Mr Rotherham's and Iris's elbows.

'I've only just found out that a dear friend of mine has got weeks to live.'

'Iris, Kate, are you ready to leave?'

They walked towards the open gate.

'Give me a chance, let me explain. Come back, I can explain everything...'

They stepped onto the pavement and didn't look back.

Chapter 56

7.02 pm

From the viewing room of Autopsy Suite 1 in the Royal Liverpool Hospital, Detective Constable Clive Winters looked in dismay at what was left of the naked female on the aluminium table.

'I suspect we have the same mode of killing in this case and, almost certainly, the same perpetrators,' said Doctor Lamb, flashing a beam of torchlight onto the dead woman's throat.

Winters sighed bitterly as he looked at the woman's charred, unrecognisable features, and knew that getting an identification on her was going to be a major problem. Her face reminded him of a documentary he had seen about a man frozen in ice for over three thousand years, and it hit him hard that she had probably been alive and well only forty-eight hours earlier.

Doctor Lamb touched a section of unburned skin on the base of her throat at the windpipe and counted, 'One, two, two, one… She's been strangled by someone behind her. Two thumbprints on her windpipe, and I'm estimating four fingerprints either side of her neck, but three of those have been burned.'

Winters called Clay, who was evidently in reception at Trinity Road Police Station; he could hear Sergeant Harris's raised but calm voice trying to settle down a difficult customer.

'What's happening, Clive?' asked Clay.

'I'm with Doctor Lamb. She started an external inspection of the Otterspool Park victim, and it's looking like the same perpetrators as Picton Road. Manual strangulation and post-mortem burning. The fire damage is to her head, face, neck, back and both hands.'

'Has she said anything about the sexual assault?'

'She picked up on that straight away. It's either rape or incredibly rough sex. There are lacerations to her vagina. She's been penetrated in two orifices, her vagina and anus. How's the search going in Otterspool Park?'

'It's ongoing. Some personal effects that may well have belonged to the victim have turned up. I'm going to Otterspool Park now.'

'Has the CCTV footage from Aigburth Vale come in yet?'

'Yes. Carol White's on the job and Poppy Waters has stepped forward to help while the translator goes through all the documents on Václav Adamczak's phone.'

'Clive!' called Doctor Lamb, interrupting. 'Her hands have been burned. They're both clamped together into tight fists.' She turned to her APT. 'Harper, can you open the right-hand first using a scalpel?'

'Eve, there's an APT filming the autopsy,' said Winters. 'And Harper's about to prise open her fist.'

'Ask Doctor Lamb to—'

'As soon as it's over, Eve, I'll send it to you,' called Doctor Lamb.

'Clive, ask her to tell Harper to wait for a moment. I'd like to come into the suite and get some stills of the victim's body.'

'I can do that.'

'OK, thanks, Clive. Keep me posted.'

Winters headed back immediately to the foot of the aluminium table. He took pictures of the overall view of the victim's body, lingering on the purple thumb and fingerprints around her throat and neck. From the charred scalp to her bruised and dirty feet, he focused on her blackened and blistered right and left fists.

'Thank you, Doctor Lamb,' said Winters, considering the dark tone of her unburned skin; he was reminded of a mass-produced painting from his childhood of a young Spanish woman, which took pride of place in his grandmother's sitting room.

You have the same skin tone as Catalonian Maiden, thought Winters, *but you've got a few more years on her, for sure. Mid-thirties, more or less.*

Harper poked the tip of the scalpel into the knot of the victim's fist, where the stump of her little finger clung on to the outer edge of her charred palm. 'They've melted together, it's like it's become a single piece of the body, not fingers, thumb and palm.' Harper looked at Doctor Lamb questioningly.

'Well, we're not going to separate what's left of her fingers and thumb from her palm, so if I were you, Harper, I'd be as firm but gentle as possible. Left hand first, right hand second.'

As Harper pushed the scalpel into the victim's left fist, Winters heard the ripping of flesh; as her fingers moved away from her palm, it gave the eerie effect of the dead woman coming to life and moving what was left of her digits of her own accord.

The piece of her palm that her fingers and thumb had protected was bleached out and the lines like brown rivers. Winters looked at her palm closely and was disappointed that it was empty.

'Do you want me to straighten her fingers out further, Doctor Lamb?'

'No need, thank you, Harper.'

Harper walked around the aluminium table to attend to the victim's right fist. He stuck the scalpel between the little finger and palm and slid the blade into the melted fingers. He used a little force to prise flesh from flesh, and there appeared to be little difference between the open left and right palms.

He stepped back.

'Doctor Lamb,' said Winters. 'May I borrow your torch, please?'

She handed him the light. Winters ran it across the right palm, looked at the complex web of fine lines that ran into the deeper lines on the surface of her inner hand.

Doctor Lamb joined him to peer closely. 'Harper, there's a magnifying glass on the bottom shelf of the trolley. Could you bring it and hand it to Clive, please?'

Out of the corner of his eye, Winters noticed that the woman's inner thighs and pelvis were darker than the rest of her torso. He highlighted it with his torch and asked, 'What's this discolouration, Doctor Lamb?'

'She could only bruise while she was alive. It's livor mortis as opposed to straight bruising. I suspect there is bruising here, but after death blood accumulates beneath the skin because the heart can no longer circulate it. It'll help me to determine the time of death.'

Harper handed the magnifying glass to Winters, who shone the light on the woman's right palm.

And there, lying on the dry bed of her life line, was a single hair.

'Harper, can you get a series of still pictures of this palm and close-ups of the hair on the life line.'

Winters stepped back and listened to the clicking of Harper's camera.

'Is that enough?' asked Harper.

Winters checked the set of good-quality images of the woman's right palm. 'Thank you. Hold the light for me, please.' Winters swapped the torch for the tweezers and brought the silver tips to the centre of the woman's life line. He felt the pressure of contact and slowly lifted the hair and held it into the light.

'Pictures, please, Harper,' said Winters.

The ends of the hair were shrivelled by fire, but the body of it was thick and grey or fair, and appeared to be human.

'Bring an evidence bag, please, Harper.'

Harper held the small bag open and slowly Winters placed the top third of the tweezers inside the inner space. He opened them, lifted them to the top of the bag, and saw that the hair was no longer between their tips.

He turned the bag's transparent strip to the autopsy suite's fluorescent light and breathed a sigh of relief when he saw that the hair was safely inside.

'I'm going to call Eve,' said Winters. 'Thank you, Doctor Lamb. Can you please send your still pictures and videos to my phone and DCI Clay's.'

Doctor Lamb's voice followed Winters as he headed for the changing room.

'Strike while the iron's hot, Harper.'

Chapter 57

7.25 pm

Walking down the path leading from Jericho Lane to the railway bridge in Otterspool Park, Clay felt like she had never experienced such darkness. The branches of the trees above reached towards each other, creating a continuous canopy.

As she headed for the arc light near the railway bridge, she flashed her torch on the steep banks of earth to either side of the path. Then, under the light, she picked out Detective Sergeant Karl Stone. In each hand, he was holding a large evidence bag.

'Karl!' she called, as she walked towards the arch of the bridge. It was filled with a bizarre clash of light and shadows, like a scene from a living nightmare.

Clay looked at the bank where the victim's burned body had been discovered and the white tent that was now empty but still there. She recalled the fire damage to the woman's face, the way she had bled from her vagina and anus, and felt a combination of sorrow and horror that made the writing on the wall even more sinister.

Killing Time Is Here Embrace It.

Stone met her on the path under the bridge.

'What have you got, Karl?' Clay's voice echoed.

'Good news and bad news. When are the two ever apart?'

He handed over an evidence bag. As she looked inside, he said, 'It's a black corduroy jacket, not really suitable for this kind of weather. In the bag I'm holding there's a grey T-shirt with a lighter splash of colour and the word 'love' on that splash.'

'Who were they manufactured by?' asked Clay.

'The corduroy jacket is mass-produced – Primark. The T-shirt is by Mokles. It's a firm in the Czech Republic.'

'Show me, please.'

Stone opened the evidence bag and turned up the manufacturer's label on the neckline.

'Czech. Same nationality as Marta and her mother Verka,' observed Clay.

'What's the likelihood that Verka knew the victim?'

'Ex-pat Czech women in the same city in England. Verka's got to be our first port of call.' Clay turned a slow circle and weighed everything up.

'Tyre indentations just outside the gateway on Jericho Lane,' said Stone. 'The victim was brought here in a car to this secluded spot on a foul winter's night. Five metres from the bridge.' He pointed to the tent. 'The sexual attack and murder took place there. They left their written and symbolic graffiti and set her corpse on fire.'

'Where were the clothes discovered?'

'Left-hand embankment near the gateway, near where the car

was parked. They made an effort to cover them with a layer of dead leaves.'

Clay worked out the logic of the piece. 'So they took clothing away from the scene as trophies and when they got closer to the car, they either got cold feet or saw something that made them think, *This is a shit idea. This could implicate us.* You said there were three items of clothing, Karl.'

'The third one's being hotfooted down to the lab. It was a white denim mini-skirt. I've saved the best for last. There was semen on it. Not a trace – a substantial amount.'

'The poor woman,' said Clay. 'The stupid, evil bastards.'

She looked up at the ivy hanging from the top of the bridge and watched how at the top it stayed still, while the trailing ends rustled and shifted in the mean wind. In the arc light, it looked alive with an alien and malevolent intelligence.

'Thank everyone for me, Karl. Please call Carol White and Poppy Waters and send them images of the skirt, coat and T-shirt, so that they can look out for them on the CCTV from Aigburth Road.'

'Sure. Anything else?'

'Yes.' Clay felt swamped by darkness. 'Send the pictures of the clothes through to Gina Riley at Alder Hey right now. Verka's with her there. See if she can identify them as belonging to any-one she knows. If she can do so, we'll have to arrange for her to look at the victim's body in the mortuary.'

Chapter 58

7.53 pm

'Aneta, there are two photographs in front of you. One is of what is almost certainly Marta Ondřej's hair...'

'Where's the hair now?' asked Aneta.

'It's been sent away for DNA analysis,' said Hendricks. 'Please listen to DCI Clay and please don't interrupt.'

'The second photograph is of Václav Adamczak's phone. We've transferred the videos that we found on it onto this laptop.'

On the table between them in Interview Suite 1, Clay lined up one of two films on her laptop.

Hendricks made eye contact with Ms Jennings, Aneta's solicitor and said, 'We're going to show your client two films that were made of Marta when she was in captivity. They were on Václav's phone.'

'For the sake of the audio recording, Aneta, I'm going to tell you what's happening as you see it. These are the seventh and eighth videos in the sequence. Are you ready to watch?' asked Clay.

'Yes.'

Clay pressed play.

'Darkness,' she said. 'A light bulb crackles on suddenly and we see Marta's face, blinking hard against the harshness of the light. Her hair is shaven and she looks hungry. The camera pulls back from her face to get a full shot of her, head to toe. She is wearing striped pyjamas. The light goes out. In the darkness, she makes a noise. Listen.'

The sound of crying drifted from the laptop and stopped with the end of the film.

'Did you recognise the room, Aneta?'

'No comment.'

'Could it be the box room in Karl and Václav Adamczaks' flat on Picton Road?'

'No comment.'

'Why has her hair been shaven off?'

'I don't—'

'Excuse me, Aneta,' said Ms Jennings. 'What was my advice to you?'

'No comment.'

'Why has she been deprived of food and water?'

'No comment.'

'Why has she been kept prisoner?'

'No comment.'

Clay looked at Hendricks.

'Aneta,' said Hendricks. 'Did Karl or Václav Adamczak have strong right-wing views?'

'No comment.'

'Did either of them ever express racist views to you?'

'No comment.'

'Did either of them ever express specific racist views against Roma?'

'No comment.'

'Did either of them have views that were pro-Nazi?'

'No comment.'

Clay caught Ms Jennings's attention.

'Yes?' asked the solicitor.

'I think you've advised your client badly.' Clay looked directly at Aneta and waited until their eyes were locked. 'I've sat through all kinds of *no comment* interviews over the years, from the heights of hard-faced contempt to the depths of ineptitude, but yours is by far and away the most uncomfortable performance I've ever seen. I'm going to give you a minute to decide who you're going to listen to. Your solicitor, or yourself. Time starts now.'

Clay turned the laptop back to herself and lined up the next piece of film.

'I think,' said Clay. 'No, I believe you want to answer these questions, so I'm going to cut to the chase before I show you the next piece of film. Karl and Václav shaved her head, starved her, deprived her of water and dressed her in striped pyjamas because they were recreating a microcosm of the Nazi concentration-camp system. What do you think?'

'They would never do such a hideous thing,' said Aneta.

'The strange thing is, Aneta, Scientific Support turned their flat upside down and they couldn't find any sign of anything to do with the Nazis, apart from this.' Clay showed Aneta a photograph of the Black Sun graffiti. 'It's an occult symbol, seized on by the Nazis. Did Karl or Václav paint this on their bedroom wall?'

'It wasn't on the wall when I was last in their flat on Friday. Do you know how people in Poland feel towards the Nazis? There are still people alive who lived through the occupation – Karl and Václavs' grandmother being one of them. They hated the Nazis.'

'True. But a lot of Polish people collaborated with the Nazis during the occupation,' said Hendricks.

'You're not listening to me.'

'No, Aneta, we are listening to you. It's easy for anyone who lived through the occupation of Poland to say that they hate the Nazis. And that's especially true and convenient for people who collaborated with them. We want to hear what you have to say,' insisted Clay. 'While we're being as open-minded as we can, in the light of some pretty damning and compelling evidence, we've also got witness reports of you approving enthusiastically of the Nazis sending Roma to their concentration camps.'

'Where from?'

'Your place of work. And we know how and why you got away with it with the hotel's manager.'

Aneta's face turned light scarlet.

'And we know where to find the domestic who you told that Hitler was right to put Roma people in death camps.'

A look of complete sickness settled on Aneta's face.

'You are at liberty to deny you said such things, Ms Kaloza,' said her solicitor.

There was a deep and ugly silence.

'I cannot deny it.'

Ms Jennings said, 'All right, let's just move on, shall we?'

'Watch the next film, Aneta.' Clay pressed play, turned the laptop towards Aneta, stood up and walked behind her.

The darkness on-screen lingered for moments, and then the light came on.

'She's getting wise to it now. She's keeping her eyes tightly shut so that the light doesn't hurt them. We can see her face and head and the top half of her body. She is still wearing a concentration-camp uniform. A hand in a black leather glove comes into view and rolls up the right sleeve of the top Marta has been forced to wear. This reveals her right arm halfway up to the elbow.'

Clay leaned over and pressed pause on the image of Marta's arm.

'What's been written on Marta's forearm, Aneta?' asked Hendricks.

'A six-digit number.'

'What does that bring to mind?'

Aneta looked set to collapse. She put her elbow on the table and leaned her head on her hand. She closed her eyes. 'I don't know anything about what happened to this little girl. It's nothing to do with me, and I'm almost certain it had nothing to do with Karl and Václav.'

'You're *almost* certain? You were certain of their innocence in your last interview,' observed Clay, returning to sit across from Aneta again and drawing the laptop closer to herself.

Aneta sat back, her head flopping down, eyes on the floor. 'I didn't think they lied to me about anything. But it looks like I've found out that they did. They lied to me about working in the Anfield district for CJ Construction. They weren't there at all. Why? Why did they lie?'

She lowered her head as if it was a ton weight, looked at Clay and answered her own question. 'Because they were doing something else, maybe. Something they wanted to keep secret. Something shameful, I don't know. I've known them all my life and thought I knew them as well as I know myself, but they lied to me. And if they lied about one thing, why not about other things? Or anything? Why not about everything?'

Clay indicated the screen of the laptop, pointed at Marta's wrist. 'This is a six-digit concentration camp-style tattoo.'

'It's nothing to do with me. Maybe they were madmen, monsters hiding behind friendly masks. Monsters pretending to be decent hard-working men.'

'I'll be blunt with you, Aneta,' said Clay. 'Your problem is this. On Friday, 28th November, you were in the Picton Road flat. Marta was missing on that day. She was kept prisoner in the box room, a room you say you looked into, but you claim there was no sign of her. Do you want to reconsider your position on that one?'

'There's nothing to reconsider. I was there. She wasn't. If she had been I'd have taken her to the nearest police station and reported Karl and Václav. They have a white van. Maybe they moved the child when it was time for me to clean their flat.'

'But that would have involved them getting Marta in and out of the van on Picton Road, a major arterial road leading in and out of the city centre, a road crawling with pedestrians,' replied Clay.

'DCI Clay,' said Ms Jennings. 'Are you linking the murder of Karl and Václav Adamczak to their alleged abduction of Marta Ondřej?'

'It's early days yet, but we think whoever killed Karl and Václav did so because of Marta,' said Hendricks. 'That's one possibility. More will no doubt arise as we gather further evidence.' Clay turned to Aneta. 'Aneta, I'm going to close the interview now. When Sergeant Harris takes you to the cell, I'm going to ask him to give you pen and paper and I want you to write down the names of any of Karl or Václavs' friends, colleagues or associates. Put an asterisk next to the name of any individuals you know who were hostile to them.'

'Why?' asked Aneta.

Because whoever killed the brothers knew them, thought Clay. 'We want to talk to them. Have a think about what you've seen on the laptop, Aneta. You really don't want to be implicated in any of this, do you?'

Chapter 59

8.01 pm

Carol White placed a mug of coffee next to Poppy Waters and said, 'It's really decent of you to come and help me with the Aigburth Vale CCTV trawl.'

'Thanks for the coffee. Time goes quicker when you're busy.'

White sat across the table from Poppy, each at their own laptop.

'We've got three lots of footage,' said White. 'One's from the CCTV at the bus terminus near the subway under Aigburth Road. One's from the launderette on the way out of the Vale and leading onto the residential section. And one's bang in the middle, outside Gino's Bar.' She paused. 'Have you seen the Otterspool Park victim's clothes?'

'The pictures were sent to my phone,' replied Poppy.

'I printed them off. It gives you a better impression.' White handed Poppy three colour images. 'Her skirt's at the lab along with her T-shirt and jacket.'

Poppy looked at the top picture of the grey T-shirt and winced at the irony of the word 'LOVE' on the lighter part of it. She turned to the next picture, of the flimsy black jacket, and said, 'It was a cold night. What was she thinking of?' She held up the third image, of the white denim mini-skirt.

'I think she was thinking *Come and get it*,' said White. 'The poor woman. She got a lot more than she bargained for.'

'Any pictures of the victim?' asked Poppy.

'Brace yourself.' White pulled up an image of the woman's head and face, taken on the embankment near the railway bridge in Otterspool Park. Poppy said nothing as White moved on to a picture of her legs. 'On CCTV, we're looking for a woman with a dark complexion wearing a white denim mini-skirt, a grey T-shirt and a black jacket. Where do you suggest we look first?'

'The footage from Gino's Bar.' replied Poppy.

'It doesn't open until five, so I suggest we do this. You look from five to eight o'clock. I look from eight until eleven. Then we watch in half-hour blocks until Gino's closes at midnight and beyond as the customers drift back home. Good with that?'

'Good. She's going to be easily identifiable. I mean, other people who got caught on CCTV will be dressed for winter, not a walk on the beach.'

'You'd be surprised how many men and women under-dress when they're out on the lash. Whatever the weather. We're looking out for her entering the bar with or without company and, most significantly, when she leaves and who she leaves with. Ready to go?'

'Sure.'

'Happy hunting.'

Chapter 60

8.08 pm

In the reception area of Trinity Road Police Station, Sergeant Harris sipped tea and watched Aneta Kaloza in cell five on the monitor. She took the blanket from the bed, folded it and placed it on the floor.

The main door opened and Sergeant Harris looked across at an old woman standing in the entrance.

On the monitor, Aneta knelt down on the folded blanket and made the sign of the cross. She folded her hands and lowered her head in prayer.

Harris looked again at the old woman, dressed in a thick woollen coat, with trousers and shoes that looked more suited to a man. Her head was wrapped in a black scarf against the foul weather. He smiled at her, taking in her look of anxiety.

Aneta's back was turned to the CCTV camera on the wall across from her bed, but she appeared to be deep in prayer.

You haven't started that list for Eve Clay yet, thought Harris. *You'd be better off doing that to get yourself off the hook than praying for a miracle.*

He looked to the old woman and asked, 'How can I help you?'

She didn't move or speak, but looked at Harris as though weighing him up.

Harris eyed the paper and pen he had given Aneta and saw she had left them near the top of the bed. *When I get cover at the desk*, he thought, *I'll come and remind you to get on with it.*

He returned his attention to the old woman and, as he spoke, saw she was focusing on his lips. 'Would you like to step closer to the desk, please, Madam? I don't bite.'

As she came closer, he smelled the wetness of wool from her coat and a distinct note of lavender. She tried to smile and he caught a glimpse of her white dentures.

'My name is Sergeant Harris. Who do I have the pleasure of meeting this foul, foul night?'

She took a handwritten card from her pocket and placed it on the desk in front of him. *My name is Miss Kate Thorpe and I am a deaf-mute.*

Harris pulled a notebook and pen from under the desk and gave it to Miss Thorpe. He mimed writing and pointed at the empty pad.

She picked up the pen and frowned, looked at the blank page and then at Harris. Putting the pen down, she looked at the main exit.

'Miss Thorpe, you can lip read, right?'

She nodded.

'With respect, can you read and write?'

Annoyance flashed in her eyes and she set about writing. A few moments later, she showed her words to Harris.

I was at the top of my class at the Glasgow School of Art before you were born.

The writing was spidery but the message was clear.

'I apologise, Miss Thorpe. I had to ask because I want to help you. Write down why you've come in to Trinity Road Police Station.'

She picked up the pad and sat down across the space in front of the desk. With the pad on her knee, she looked into space and Harris was aware that his presence was making her self-conscious. He half-turned his back and returned his attention to Aneta Kaloza, who was still on her knees in prayer.

Out of the corner of his eye, he saw Miss Thorpe writing as DCI Eve Clay entered reception from the main body of the station.

Harris pointed at the image of Aneta on her knees.

'No list of names yet?' she asked. He shook his head. 'Can you go and have a word, please? I'll cover you here.'

As Harris went out of reception, Clay looked at the old lady and said, 'Good evening, Madam.'

She didn't respond, but a few moments later, she looked up and frowned on seeing that Harris was no longer there. Clay glanced down and saw the handwritten card on the desk.

'He's been called away,' explained Clay, as the woman made her way over, placing the pad down. She smiled at the old lady and read her words back to her.

'*I can't think why I came here. I simply can't remember.*' Clay looked into the sky blue of the old lady's eyes and saw a woman with huge depths. 'Well,' she continued. 'If you do remember, come straight back. Though it's not a very nice night.' Clay showed her warrant card. 'Would you like me to organise a lift home for you?'

Kate shook her head and, as she scrutinised the warrant card, a look of recognition filled her face. She hunched over the pad and wrote, then handed her words to Clay.

Clay read back, '*If I remember what I came here for, I will come back immediately.*'

The old lady nodded.

Clay pushed the pad and pen towards the old lady and said,

'Could you write down your home address for me please, Miss Thorpe. Maybe I could come by and jog your memory over a cup of tea.'

The woman took the pen and wrote: *131 Grant Avenue, Liverpool 15.*

'Your house overlooks the Wavertree Mystery Park?'

Miss Thorpe nodded.

'Did you see something in the Mystery? The front windows of your house must have a wonderful view of the park.'

Miss Thorpe's head stayed still, but she raised a hand. *Farewell.*

Clay watched her as she left Trinity Road. Looking down at her spidery writing, she was completely intrigued, and had the clearest sense that some light was about to appear in the dense bank of dark clouds that mounted up in front of her.

Chapter 61

8.45 pm

'You certainly had it nailed about the dress code, or lack of it,' said Poppy Waters from the screen of her laptop. 'I've just seen a woman go into Gino's looking like she's going for an audition in a lap-dancing club.'

'The men are as bad,' replied White.

'Short-sleeved shirts when there's a weather system sitting on us from Scandinavia. No sign of White Denim Woman yet?'

'No, plenty of short skirts but not our target.' White rubbed her eyes and hoped that they weren't chasing shadows.

They returned to their screens.

'Bastard,' said White.

Poppy looked across the incident room. 'Someone on-screen?'

'No, just thinking of my soon-to-be-ex-husband and that bitch

Alice who pretended to be my friend when we were assigned to trawl through child pornography together.'

'That must have been awful for you.'

'Still is. Worse for them though. He's going down for perverting the course of justice and she's been drummed out of the force. I still wake up in the middle of the night, thinking, did they really try to frame me? And the answer's always unfortunately, *Yes they did, and how.*'

Poppy poured the water and milk into the cups, not knowing what to say, but wishing she had words that could help a helpless situation. She put the drink down next to Carol.

'You've got a beautiful little boy, Carol.'

'One significantly great thing from a shite marriage that was built on a load of lies.'

'Everyone says how dignified and brave you've been.'

'Thanks.'

'Do you want to give your eyes a rest for two minutes?'

'I wouldn't mind a trip to the bathroom. Keep an eye on it for me, Poppy.' Poppy paused her screen.

White stood up and Poppy sat in her place, watching the footage from Aigburth Road outside Gino's Bar, and was impressed with the quality of the CCTV material.

A man and a woman came out of the bar and lit up cigarettes as a group of women entered. Poppy paused the tape and checked out the three women, but there was no sign of White Denim Woman. A man walked out on his own, worse for wear. To Poppy's eyes, the footage Carol was looking at mirrored what had been going on earlier in the evening. People walked into the bar. People walked out of the bar, some tipsy, some well-cut. People smoked outside and went back in. Then there were acres of nothing.

The door of the incident room opened and White asked, 'Anything?'

'No.'

Poppy stood up to allow White into her seat, but kept watching the screen.

'Wait, yes,' said Poppy, pausing the film.

As White sat down, Poppy touched the screen on the right-hand side.

'It looks like her, doesn't it?' said White, unpausing until White Denim Woman was clearly in the middle of the screen, heading for Gino's Bar.

'White denim skirt,' said White. 'Tick. Black jacket. Tick. Grey T-shirt. Tick.'

Her hair was thick, long and black, and as she came close to the CCTV camera, she looked up and blew the camera a kiss.

'She's not hammered,' observed Poppy. 'But she certainly looks like she's had a couple of scoops already.'

White paused the film and rewound it to the point where the woman's face was clear to see. 'That's what she looked like before they set her on fire,' she said. 'We'll print this off and circulate it.'

She unpaused the film and they watched the woman enter Gino's Bar.

'She's wearing a pair of black flats,' observed Poppy, recalling that no shoes had so far been recovered from the scene.

White took out her mobile and dialled Eve Clay, turning on the speakerphone.

'Hi Carol, any news?'

'We've got our Otterspool Park victim on CCTV. Identical clothing. And we've even got a shot of her face. She went into the bar at 8.44 pm; she's in there now on CCTV.'

'Was she alone?' asked Clay.

'Yes.'

'Send the image of her face to my phone, please. Very well done to both of you.'

'If it wasn't for Poppy, it'd have taken me a lot longer to find it.'

'I owe you one, Poppy,' said Clay. 'Is Barney around?'

'He's in the canteen. He should be back soon.'

'Are you going to be in the incident room for the foreseeable, Carol?'

'Yes.'

'Barney could do with some fresh air. I'll call him. I want him to go to Gino's Bar and find out what happened beyond the range of the Aigburth Road CCTV. I'm grateful to both of you for this. I'll call him now.'

Carol looked at the image of nothing much happening outside Gino's on a very cold night, and her own troubles fell into a form of perspective.

She pictured the woman blowing a kiss to the CCTV camera, an unwitting kiss of death.

Chapter 62

8.55 pm

When Riley's iPhone pinged with an incoming message, the sudden but slight noise drew Marta's attention away from the space into which she was staring. Her eyes connected with Riley standing at the glass partition.

Riley glanced up from her iPhone and smiled at Marta.

'Kate, can you tell Marta we'll have another go at trying to remember what happened while she was away.'

As Kate spoke to Marta and Riley checked the images on her phone sent by DS Karl Stone from the Otterspool Park murder scene, Verka spoke over the translator.

'DS Riley, my daughter, her mind is full of holes. She understands little and remembers less.'

'I understand that, Verka, but we've got to keep pushing on the door...'

'Pushing on what door?' Verka sounded perplexed.

'What I mean is, we have to keep trying to get her to remember, to speak. She was a victim but she is also the key witness to her own abduction, which is linked with some other serious crimes.

Kate will start things off after I've shown you these pictures. Could you come over here, please?'

Riley lined up the image of the black corduroy jacket and turned the iPhone screen to Verka, who looked intently at the Primark garment.

'Do you know anyone who wears a black jacket such as this?'

'No.'

Riley brought up the grey T-shirt with the forlorn message 'LOVE' on its lighter middle section. 'I'm asking you because it was manufactured in the Czech Republic. It belongs to the victim of a serious violent crime. And we think the victim may well come from the Czech Republic.'

'Is she alive?'

'Sadly, no, she's not alive.'

'How did she die?' asked Verka.

'I can't discuss the detail with you. I'm sorry.'

'Poor woman. Show me the next item of clothing, please.'

Riley showed her the image of the white denim mini-skirt.

'She went out in that, in this weather?'

'Yes. Recognise it?'

Verka shook her head. 'No, I don't recognise it. I own nothing like these clothes. Especially this short white skirt. None of the women I know own clothes like this. I am sorry for her that she was no doubt murdered. But she dressed herself like a prostitute. Was she a prostitute?'

'We don't know yet whether she was or she wasn't. Is it relevant, Verka?'

'I'm saying nothing. I was here as a child years ago. But I've only been in this country for three weeks. How do I know what your values are? Mine may be different. I don't want to argue with you. You are helping my daughter. That is all that matters to me. Thank you for that.'

'Thank you for looking at these pictures…'

'Mama!'

Verka hurried towards Marta's bed. The girl held her arms

out, as if a light had switched on inside her head and she now suddenly understood that the woman in front of her was her mother. Verka embraced her, sobbing and holding her tightly.

Marta pressed her lips against Verka's right ear and spoke a few words quietly.

'What did she say, Kate?' asked Riley.

'She said, ask the man to give back my hair.'

'Verka!' said Riley. 'Ask her who the man was! What did he look like?'

Verka spoke, and, as Marta looked over her mother's shoulder, she looked directly at Riley. The sudden light in her eyes faded as quickly as it had turned on, her mouth moving.

'*Tma, tma, tma...*'

Riley wished she could take hold of silence and shake it into sound. *Tma? Tma? Tma?* The words sank deep under Riley's skin. *Darkness? Darkness. Darkness...*

Chapter 63

9.05 pm

'Thanks for seeing me at such short notice, Gino. It's a really serious matter we're dealing with here,' said Detective Constable Barney Cole, shaking hands with the owner in the office above the bar.

'You're more than welcome, Mr Cole,' said Gino, in a broad Scouse accent. He sparked a cigarette. 'Do you want a drink, or something to eat?'

'No, but thank you for offering. I take it you're not actually from Italy?'

'My great-grandfather came here after the end of World War Two. I've tried to bring a little piece of Mediterranean sunshine to wintry Aigburth Road. How can I help?'

'Last night,' said Cole, showing him the picture of the Otterspool Park victim blowing a kiss to Gino's CCTV, 'this woman
entered your bar.'

'Entered? She more or less came in here like a lamb and transformed into a lioness. Oh!' Cole watched the silver dollar drop
in Gino's head as his eyes filled up with darkness. 'Otterspool
Park, right?'

'Right,' confirmed Cole. 'Was she a regular?'

'The one and only time she came in here was last night. I barred
her before I threw her out.'

'What happened?'

'You've got to understand, Mr Cole, my bar has a certain
sophistication. We don't have loud music that punters have to
shout over – we have the likes of Sinatra, Dean Martin and Nat
King Cole playing softly in the background. Couples come here
to talk, friends to meet. Zero tolerance for bad behaviour. There's
a notice above the bar: *Be Nice Or Leave*. So, when this woman
came in, I clocked her mini-skirt and T-Shirt that was way too
tight, you see what I'm saying?'

'She was showing off the goods.'

'Exactly. I mean, she was reasonably good-looking, thirty-
fiveish. I'll be honest, my very first impression was this: I'd give
her one. The trouble started when the men's heads started turning. You could see the women they were with getting really pissed
off by the silent attention she was drawing. There were a lot of
PMT and armed-with-a-machete faces. She went up to the bar…'

'You didn't get a name?'

'I'm sorry, no. She went up to the bar and ordered a glass of
Chianti which she paid for with a handful of ten- and twenty-
pence pieces. Tom, my head barman, caught my eye when she
was busy sorting out the money and mouthed, *She's already had
a few*. She wasn't pissed but she wasn't sober. *OK, lady*, said
Tom. *One drink and then that's it, off you go*. Tom reckons she
understood exactly what she'd been told, but started acting like
she'd just got off the boat.

'So, she sits at the bar on this swivel chair, kind of half-turning it and eyeing up the territory, picking out which bloke or blokes looked likely. But that was the joke of it. Every man in there last night was with his wife or girlfriend, and there were no pairs or groups of lads in the place.

'Terry Jackson, one of our regulars, a real gent, goes to the bar and she says, *Excuse me. Your aftershave. I like it a lot.* He thanked her for the compliment and she looked over her shoulder at Terry's missus, smirking at her, *Like I can have him off you in a flash.* She started rattling the bottom of her glass against the bar and Terry, being the gent he is, bought her a drink. She stands up and kisses Terry on the cheek. Tension was sparking off from table to table by this point.'

'Let me get this straight, Gino. She didn't ask Terry to buy her a drink? He offered?'

'Yeah, he offered, but she drew attention to herself.'

'So, it'd be wrong to state that she deliberately hit on a married man?'

'I wouldn't go that far but, you know, it was all in the eyes. Another couple are sitting there minding their own business and the lady gets up and goes to the toilet. Her bloke gets up and goes to the bar. He starts talking to her while Tom's pouring their drinks and they get laughing together and he offered to buy her a drink and she accepted but Tom said, *No, I said one drink, you've had two, you're taking the piss, love.* The bloke's girlfriend comes out of the toilet, sees her man rubbing shoulders with this woman and arguing the toss with Tom, so she walks straight out. He runs out of the bar after her. I said to Tom, *Ten more minutes with this bitch here and we might as well close up for the night.*

'I confronted her. *Get out! Don't come back! You're barred for life!* At this point, she suddenly loses her ability to understand or speak the English language which she'd just used so well. So I pointed at the door. I looked around. All the women looked a lot happier. And she says to me, *One phone call, then I go.*

'I walked to the door to let her out. She makes this really short call...'

'To?'

'Someone called Jay or Ray. According to Tom who listened in, she was pissed off with him because he was supposed to have met up with her in my bar. She asked him to pick her up and give her a ride home. When she closed the call down, I opened the door and she marched straight out. When I closed it after her, it was like the whole bar gave this massive sigh of relief.' Gino fell silent and then muttered, 'Otterspool Park? The poor cow.'

'Did you see the car that she was picked up in?' asked Cole.

'No.'

'Any internal CCTV?'

'I don't need it. This is a classy bar. We don't get trouble – well, hardly ever.'

'Is Tom around?'

'No, it's his day off.'

'Do me a favour, Gino. Call him up and pass him on to me.'

'Happy to help,' said Gino, dialling Tom's number on the land-line phone on his desk. 'Tom, sorry to bother you, mate. I've got a copper called DC Cole with me in the office. He wants to talk to you about that floozie who rocked up last night.'

Gino handed the phone to Cole.

'Hi, Tom, thanks for your time,' said Cole. 'The woman in the white mini-skirt.'

'Cougar, bit of a hottie.'

'Did you catch her name?'

'No.'

'What about when she spoke with the two men at the bar?'

'It was all very flirty. I'd say they were coming on to her rather than the other way round. A lot of the regulars come into the bar with their wives and girlfriends playing the happily-ever-afters card. They like Gino's because it's local, convenient and you don't get any out-and-out scallies. But I've seen the same men in city centre bars with other women.'

'She definitely didn't give anything away about who she was and where she lives or where she was from?'

'Nothing.'

'What about the phone call she made before Gino showed her the door?'

'I can remember it word for word because it was so short. *I'll be outside Gino's on Aigburth Road. Come and pick me up, Ray. You were supposed to meet me there. What do you mean, you forgot?*'

'Ray?'

'Yeah, yeah, definitely Ray. What's up?'

'She was murdered approximately three hundred metres away from Gino's Bar after she left. Absolutely and utterly beyond doubt, she said Ray?'

'On my daughter's life. Ray, it was *Ray* she asked to pick her up.'

Chapter 64

9.25 pm

'Take me for a walk. Take me for a walk.'

Jasmine's voice entered Raymond's brain through the bone-dead centre of his forehead.

'I can hear you loud and clear,' said Raymond, finding it hard to walk down the stairs, with one hand on the rail and the other clutching the almost-empty bottle of vodka.

'Take me for a walk. Take *me* for a walk *now*.'

'I'll take you for a walk now, just shut up, you've been nagging me for an hour.'

'What was it like last night? Did you feel like a really big man? Did you laugh? Did she cry? Did you feel pumped up after shagging that foreign slag?'

Raymond sat on the bottom stair and swigged back the last of the vodka.

A purple light flashed to the left of his vision and when he turned his head to look at it, it turned red and was dripping from thin air onto the laminate flooring, a crimson pool growing wider and wider as each drop fell onto the wood with a drip, drip, drip, drip that he believed would never end.

He stuck the index finger of his right hand into the pool and sticking it into his mouth tasted sweet, sticky blood that quelled the sourness of the vodka.

'Stop sitting on your arse on the bottom of the stairs like a fucking loser and take me for a walk now.'

He pictured Jasmine standing at the closed kitchen door, sharp teeth bared with two ropes of saliva hanging from each corner of her mouth, and the image sparked a wave of revulsion and terror, on a par with the grim emotions Jack provoked in him.

In pure and utter dizziness, Raymond fell forwards onto his hands and knees and, turning to the widening pool, lapped the blood to give him the strength he needed to face Jasmine.

'I am white, pure white,' said Jasmine. 'And my whiteness is supreme. How is your whiteness, Raymond?'

'My whiteness is supreme also,' said Raymond, through lips coated with dark red blood.

'I am as white as the white cliffs of Dover. We cannot have any more of these foreign scumbags coming here and taking over our white and pleasant land, even if we do want to shag them.'

He could feel the vibrations from the constant growl in Jasmine's throat in his spine.

'Take me for a walk. Not now. I am hungry. Feed me. Nothing from a can. Fresh meat. Carmel, I want to eat Carmel, the one who smells of cooking fat and sings like an alley cat. The one who claims to worry about you but she is just like Jack. She doesn't care. For you. Raymond. Raymond. Raymond, stop acting like a beast of the field and stand up like a white man on two legs, back straight, salute the sky, *Sieg Heil! Sieg Heil! Sieg Heil!*'

Raymond hung onto the wall as he made it to his feet and, once upright, felt a bolt of steel piercing the length of his spine and Jasmine's voice being drowned in a rising sea of human voices.

'*Sieg Heil! Sieg Heil! Sieg Heil!*' The music of Nuremberg cascaded over him and for a moment, he was shoulder to shoulder with the massed ranks of Nazis and the Führer himself was within touching distance, making eye contact with Raymond, who filled up with emotion, with love, with a certainty that everything he had done, everything he was doing, and everything he would do was completely righteous.

The sound of the crowd faded into a background hum as Hitler pointed at Raymond and Raymond said, 'Me?'

'Yes, you. They must be punished next and you must punish them. The Russians lied about the Holocaust. It was nothing to do with me,' said Hitler. 'They lied and made propaganda films about the treatment and murder of the Jews to make me look bad and themselves look good. Your next target is a Russian, the more the merrier.'

Hitler exploded into a million points of blinding light and as his vision cleared, Raymond saw everything in the hall as if a film of grit had been peeled from his eyes and the whole world was available to him in the brightest detail.

'Feed me! Feed me now!'

Jasmine's voice poured through the kitchen door, but it wasn't Jasmine's voice anymore, it was Jack's.

'Feed me! What about your art? Feed me now!'

And Raymond was astonished that the sound of Jack's voice did not deliver the usual sharp blow to his core, and the fear that filled his whole being like toxic water did not happen.

'Can't be arsed?' It was the voice of the weak and paralysed Jack filtering through the head, heart and mouth of a dog.

'You heard me.'

Raymond's feet tingled and the tingling rose up through his

legs and into his hips and balls, tingling power into his gut and his heart through his windpipe and into his brain.

'Feed me your art now, dot dash dot dash art, and take me for a walk.'

'You can't go for a walk, dickhead, because, because, don't you remember when the bus mowed you down, because you're a fucking cripple, big brother.'

'It's not Jack,' said Jasmine. 'It's me, me, me, me, me taking the piss out of the fucker.'

He felt his heart beating with immense power, the muscle squeezing between his ribs as each beat picked up strength. As he walked towards it, the kitchen door took on the surface of a coffin lid, something Raymond had never noticed before.

Upstairs, metal hit metal over and over in Jack's room as he pumped iron, grunted and raised the impossibly heavy bar up and down above his chest.

Raymond opened the kitchen coffin door and ignored the ringing phone in the pocket of his jeans.

'Leave a message and I'll get back to you.'

Beep. Silence.

'Feed me,' said Jasmine. 'I'm hungry. Feed me now.'

Raymond pushed the coffin lid with the bottom of his empty vodka bottle and looked into the corner of the cemetery where Jasmine lay sleeping in her basket in the reeds where baby Moses of the Holy Land had once been hidden from the fu-fu-fucking ph-ph-pharaoh...

Eyes shut and still as a corpse, Jasmine's voice poured from the hard muscles of her back, flanks and limbs.

'Go to the fridge, feed me now, go to the fridge, feed me now, *Sieg Heil*, feed me art...'

Raymond walked past the sleeping dog and to the white marble door of the fridge, to the plinth on which a sculpture of a white avenging angel stood looking down with a bow and poised to send an arrow of desire into his beating breast.

'Raymond,' said the angel. 'Tell them, tell them all, fuck off back to where you came from, all the foreign fuckers and the niggers as well, and do it now or else there'll be more blood, much more blood!'

The marble door opened to his touch.

'Feed me art now.'

At the front of the top shelf of the fridge was a brown paper bag and red fluid had leaked into the fabric of the paper. With both hands, Raymond lifted it from the fridge and felt the minced muscle within it. He squeezed the bag gently and felt a shimmer of blood on his fingers and palms.

As he relaxed his grip, the cold lifeless matter in the bag seemed to move in his clutch and sent waves of energy into his hands and veins, locking into the beating of his heart.

'Feed me, feed me now, feed me meat now.'

He looked down on Jasmine, asleep and at peace in spite of the voice that drifted through her flesh from her dreaming brain and, prodding her with his toe, watched the bitch stir from slumber.

Raymond crouched and dropped raw mince into her empty bowl.

He took an ecstasy tablet from his pocket and made a hole in the mince, concealed the tablet in the hole and covered it up with raw meat.

He placed the bowl near her nose and watched as Jasmine's senses came to life.

'Wakey-wakey, Jasmine...'

She blinked and, as she got to her feet, sniffed the mincemeat in her bowl. She looked up at Raymond, silent now, stripped of the voice and words that she had poured into his head.

Jasmine licked the meat and set about eating it in hungry gulps. Raymond walked towards the sink, to the drawer where sirens sang to him, ethereal music to come down to from the biggest high.

He looked back and saw Jasmine eating raw, fatty mince, turned to the drawer and opened it.

His eyes moved like table tennis balls. Jasmine. The open drawer. Jasmine. Jasmine. The things in the drawer. Jasmine. His hand. Jasmine. The carving knife in his hand. Jasmine.

Jasmine.

He stepped towards her.

Jasmine...

He looked at the whiteness of her neck and throat, and the redness of her eyes.

Jasmine.

He drew a line with his eyes as she wolfed down the last morsels of raw mincemeat, listened to her smacking her lips with satisfaction.

Jasmine...

She looked up at him and, for less than one second, she penetrated his head with one word made of three sounds, a blunt accusation.

'Time for your walk now, Jasmine. Come for a walk in Sefton Park with the murderer.'

Chapter 65

9.25 pm

'This is the picture we'll circulate for an identification on the Otterspool Park victim,' said Clay, showing a printed-off image of the woman in a white denim mini-skirt blowing a kiss to Gino's CCTV camera. 'OK, are we ready to roll with the pick-up?'

Clay stood next to Poppy Waters looking over Sergeant Carol White's shoulders at the screen of her laptop.

The door of Gino's Bar opened and a few moments later the Otterspool Park victim emerged into the cold night. The door was closed from inside and the woman stepped away from it.

Cars streamed past, and then a red Renault Mégane slowed down and stopped in front of her. She walked to the open window and had a brief exchange with the driver.

'We need the license plate on the Mégane,' said Clay.

'We've already got it,' said Poppy.

The woman stepped back from the car and threw her right-hand middle finger up and shouted at the driver as the car sped away.

The driver tried to pay you for sex, thought Clay, *the cheeky bastard. However, she concluded with mounting bitterness, if you had taken him upon his offer...*

The woman wrapped her arms around herself against the cold and didn't turn or react when the door of Gino's Bar opened and a couple emerged, then walked away in the direction of Aigburth Vale.

'It's coming up now, Eve. After this bus,' said Poppy.

Clay's iPhone vibrated in her hand with an incoming call from Cole.

'Can you pause this for me, Carol.' She put the phone to her ear. 'Hello, Barney. Anything from Gino's?'

'I haven't got a name for *her* but I do have a *name*. She turned up on her own and wasn't in the bar for long. Caused a bit of consternation with women and their partners, which wasn't really her fault or intention in my view. She left after a couple of drinks at Gino's insistence and called up a Ray or Raymond for a lift.'

'That's all we have?'

'She made a phone call and she was gone pretty soon after she hit Aigburth Road. No CCTV from indoors.'

'Thanks for that, Barney. We've got the external CCTV footage. I believe I'm about to see Raymond for the first time.' *But it won't be his last*, she told herself as she disconnected the call. 'Let's roll with it.'

A red minibus passed the woman and then she waved at a car that wasn't in shot, a car that slowed down and came to a halt.

'Licence plate?' asked Clay.

'We've circulated it already and we've had some information back fast. It's listed as stolen,' said Poppy.

On-screen, the woman got into the passenger seat and pulled the door shut.

'It's a ten-year-old white Fiat Uno and the owner's Milly Graves, 48 years old and living in the Holy Land off Park Road in Moses Street.'

Clay watched the stationary car and wondered what it was that the woman and the driver Raymond were talking about. She looked hard at the screen, could make out the woman in the passenger seat but not the man at the wheel. The back window was dark. 'There could be two more people in the car – back seat, driver's side and middle.'

'The Holy Land?' asked White.

'There's a cluster of streets running parallel to each other off Park Road. They're all named after Biblical figures,' explained Clay.

'Her car went missing from outside her front door,' Poppy concluded.

The car drove off in the direction of Cressington Park and Garston. Clay looked at the scope of the CCTV camera and was disappointed to see that it went as far the central island that separated the lines of traffic travelling to either Garston or the edge of the Dingle and Toxteth. 'Rerun it for me, please, Carol, from the point where the white Fiat Uno comes into shot.'

As she watched the footage for a second time, Clay worked out the options in terms of time and directions to Gino's Bar.

'So this Raymond travels to pick up the woman from either Aigburth Road heading to Liverpool 8, from Jericho Lane turning right onto the dual carriageway or Ashfield Road turning left. The other option's Sefton Park, running onto the dual carriageway from the slip road to the left of the subway. She made the call just before she was thrown out of the bar and she didn't have to wait too long for him to pick her up. Can we get a precise timing on how long she waited from the door of the bar to the door of the stolen Fiat Uno? Add on half a minute for the call to Raymond. He doesn't live that far away from Gino's Bar and the crime scene over the road in Otterspool Park.'

How long did you live after stepping into that car? Clay wondered.

'Carol, can we look at the next two minutes after the white Uno went off screen.'

As Clay watched, she counted in her head, made a mental journey to the junction near St Anne's Church and pictured coming back the other way along Aigburth Road towards the top of Jericho Lane and Otterspool Park.

'Stop there, please. He performed an illegal U-turn by the church.'

On-screen there was no traffic passing Gino's Bar or pedestrians on the icy pavement.

'What are we looking at, Eve?' asked White.

'We're looking at the moment, or as close as can be to it, when the Fiat Uno was taking the woman back down Aigburth Road and to her death in the park. We can't see it for sure but we can be pretty certain that just out of the CCTV's range there's our quarry.'

'What do you want us to do, Eve?' asked Poppy.

'Poppy, once Barney gets back, ask him to track the white Uno on the automatic number plate recognition cameras going back along Aigburth Road to the Dingle and Toxteth. Carol, can you circulate the picture of the woman from Gino's Bar's CCTV. We're going to give this poor woman a name, and have this Raymond character in Interview Suite 1 within the next few hours.'

Chapter 66

10.15 pm

In her room in Alder Hey, Marta Ondřej was asleep and having bad dreams.

Riley watched her mother Verka stroking her head and making comforting noises that did nothing to quell the torment that Marta was going through. As the rising sounds from Marta reached screaming point, she stopped suddenly and opened her eyes wide, like she'd hauled herself out of the void and had landed on the other side, where the light was brightest.

'*Matka…*'

'She's just acknowledged her mother,' Kate whispered to Riley. '*Matka*. Mother.'

Marta looked away from her mother and around the room. When her eyes settled on Riley, she said, '*Policistka.*'

'Yes, Marta, that's right,' replied Riley. 'I'm a policewoman.'

Marta's eyes filled with light as she pulled down the bedding and swung her legs out. As her feet touched the floor, she supported her weight by holding onto the mattress.

'This is what she is like,' said Verka. 'She is often scared and she understands little.'

'Maybe she understands more than we think – she just can't put it into words that well,' said Riley.

Marta knelt down and looked under the bed for several moments. As she rose to her full height, she said, '*Nic tam není.*'

'She said *There's nothing there,*' said Kate.

Marta walked towards the toilet, opened the door and had a good hard look at the space around the sink. She stood and faced the mirror. Riley took a deep breath, expecting her to start a prolonged bout of screaming, but instead she remained calm and silent.

She looked at Riley and made a motion with her hands for her to come and join her. '*Policistka!*' She waved her hand rapidly and, as Riley did as she asked, noticed that her mother was coming, too.

She held up a hand in a stopping gesture. '*Ne!*'

'Sit back down please, Verka,' said Riley.

At the mirror, Riley stood behind Marta who continued staring calmly at the mirror. In the reflection, her eyes sought out Riley.

'*Nic tam není,*' said Marta, her voice measured but loaded with sadness.

'It will grow back,' replied Riley, moving her fingers from her scalp down to her collarbone. Marta copied the mime and Riley turned her round, placed her arms around her and felt the child's hands copying her and patting her back as if she were a baby.

'Gina Riley,' said Marta. She pulled away from Riley's arms and looked at the translator sitting by the door. 'Kate?'

'*Ano.* Kate.'

'Kate, *je policistka?*'

'*Ne.*'

She looked at her mother and said, '*Matka.*'

Verka smiled and pointed at herself. '*Ano, Matka.*'

Marta hobbled back to her bed and looked around the bedside table. She picked up the small silver and blue tin of rosary beads that the priest had left for her and, holding it to her left ear, shook the box, making the beads rattle.

As she walked to the glass partition, Marta opened the tin with her thumb and dropped the lid to the floor. She stood at the glass looking at the corridor outside. A look of immeasurable sadness crossed her features and it struck Riley that the girl had run out of tears. The lost and haunted look in her eyes made her appear a lot older than fourteen.

Marta sighed, and the whole weight of her recent memory was registered in the sinking of her shoulders. She looked into the corridor at the same spot with growing intensity, as if she could see someone who was invisible to everyone else's eyes.

Verka stood up.

Instinct told Riley to hold up her hand and say, 'Please Verka, no!'

As Marta stared out, she removed the rosary beads from the tin and allowed the base of the tin to join the lid on the floor.

She twisted the rosary beads around her fingers, rubbed and pulled them.

Her breathing grew louder and quicker as the seconds ticked by.

She pulled with growing force and one of the small metal clasps that linked the beads snapped. Marta whipped the broken rosary to the floor and her breathing grew quieter and slower as she stared out into the corridor.

'Gina Riley,' said Marta. '*Chyťte toho ďábla. Chci svoje vlasy.*'

Riley looked at Kate.

'She said, *Catch the Devil. I want my hair.*'

Marta looked away from the corridor and at Riley.

'*Toho ďábla. Muže.*'

'The Devil is a man?' asked Riley.

'*The Devil. Man,*' said Kate.

Chapter 67

11.59 pm

Detective Sergeant Karl Stone placed the third sugar in his mug of coffee, stirred it and congratulated himself on cutting down from four spikes in his ten-a-day caffeine regime.

He looked at the document he had printed off from the internet and settled back to double-check the information he had discovered about Black Sun before firing off his round-robin on the fascist organisation to the team.

Stone confirmed the origin of the far-right sect, the way it spread across the globe after the fall of the Nazi regime, its criminal activities, its secrecy, the racist and anti-left engine that drove it and its ultimate demise as a force of any reckoning.

He heard a thin whistle five desks away and saw a broad smile lighting up Barney Cole's face.

'Good news, Barney?'

Cole dialled Clay's number on his desk phone. 'The very best, Karl...' He hit speakerphone. 'Hello, Eve.'

'What have you got for me?'

'Really great news. Data from the automatic number plate recognition cameras track the Fiat Uno. Going backwards from Aigburth Vale, I get a hit on Aigburth Road by the TA Barracks. I get a hit by the library. Is he coming in from Lark Lane and hence from Sefton Park? No. Is he driving at over forty and getting clocked by the speed cameras? Yes. I get a hit from the camera at the top of Aigburth Road at the junction. Is he coming from the Dingle or Toxteth? The Dingle. I get a hit on Park Road by Tesco. And then he hits a speed camera as he turns out of Dell Street. We're looking for a man called Raymond who probably lives or is staying in or around Dell Street. He stole the Fiat Uno from Moses Street which is a two-minute walk from Dell Street. My next trick's to narrow down the Raymonds in the neighbourhood, starting with those who live on Dell Street. I'll try peopletracer. co.uk and dive into the electoral register. It'll be quick, Eve.'

'I'll wait for your call and then go pay a visit to the Dingle. Who's with you?'

'Karl Stone.'

'Ask him to wait for my call. I need him to come to the Dingle with me.'

'I caught that, Eve,' called Stone.

Cole placed the receiver back.

'How about you, Karl?'

'I've been looking up Black Sun, seeing if I can shed a bit of light on the graffiti at both murder scenes.'

'What have you got so far?'

'Black Sun grew out of a far-right group called New Order back in 1973. It had lots of cells all across Italy, but they wanted to expand. By the late 1970s they had spread across Europe and into the USA, Japan, Brazil and Nigeria. They bombed public places, robbed banks and hijacked airplanes. They didn't care who they killed but, here's the irony, they had a strong Christian identity. Killing was acceptable because they were at war with governments who were agents of Satan. They did exceptionally well in the USA, sucking in all the anti-government, anti-gay, racist, gun-lobbying religious zealot meatheads.'

'Any names jump out at you, Karl?'

'Not yet. I'll send you my email with a bit more detailed information.'

He looked at the email on his laptop screen and pressed send.

He stood up and put on his coat from the back of the chair.

'Where are you off to?'

'Park Road. To put myself in position for Eve when she calls. You?'

'I'm tracking down our Ray or Raymond. I'll be in touch.'

Chapter 68

11.59 pm

Carmel Dare held on to her son Jack's arm as he walked with her round the corner towards their home.

'How's Raymond been?' she asked.

'Doctor Salah told him off. I've taken his prescription to the chemist's. Doctor Salah's referring him back to Broad Oak, and wants to see him on a weekly basis.'

'Thank you so much, Jack. You're so good to me and your brother.'

He drank in the relief in his mother's face as they arrived at the gate.

'How's he been this evening?'

'Asleep as far as I know. Last time I saw him he was spread out over his bed. I think he'd been drinking vodka or white rum by the kip of his breath. I was working out in my room.'

Jack turned the key in the front door lock and felt his heart freefall as he put on the hall light. Something was wrong. The house was unnaturally still.

'Wait here, Mum.' He looked at the kitchen door, where Jasmine would normally be scratching the paintwork to attract his attention as soon he stepped over the threshold.

'Jasmine?'

Silence and no barking.

'Jasmine?'

He opened the kitchen door and scanned the room but there was no sign of her.

'Raymond?'

Jack ran up the stairs two at a time.

Raymond was not in his room.

He rattled the lock on his bedroom door, and the room was secure.

Carmel was at the bottom of the stairs. 'There's no one downstairs, Jack.'

He checked the bathroom and his mother's room and there was nothing and no one there.

'If anything's happened to my dog, if he's harmed her in any way, I swear to God, I'm going to kill him. Wait a minute. Wait a minute.'

Jack hurried down the stairs, to the kitchen and the door leading into the back garden. He looked at the hook on the back door and felt a surge of anger and a physical pain in his core like a smack from a baseball bat.

Jasmine's lead wasn't there.

'What's he thinking of?'

He opened the back door and tripped the security light.

'He's left the back door unlocked,' said Jack, walking across the grass to the bottom of the garden in seconds.

He tried the shed door and found it locked. Taking his keys from his jacket pocket, he found the shed key and unlocked the door.

He looked at the floor-to-ceiling junk, but there was no sign of Jasmine.

'He's taken her out, the idiot,' said Jack, marching back to the house.

'Try not to be too angry with him, Jack.' Carmel blocked the back door. 'Tell me you won't be too angry with him!'

'Mum, please get out of the way. I need to go out and look for her.'

Carmel moved to one side and said, 'I'll come with you.'

'No, you stay here in case he shows up with Jasmine. If he does, call me straight away.'

As he ran down the street, he looked in one direction and thought of Sefton Park. Then he looked the other way at Otterspool Promenade.

He headed for the vastness of Otterspool Promenade, seven kilometres long and half a kilometre wide.

Day Three
Wednesday, 3rd December

Chapter 69

00.25 am

At twenty-five minutes past midnight, Clay received a call from DC Barney Cole. Someone called Raymond who wasn't on the electoral register had shown up on People Tracker.

She drove down Park Road followed by Detective Sergeant Karl Stone in his car, and a pair of constables in a third vehicle as back-up. She turned left into Wellington Road and picking up the even side slowed down, looking for the door to 102.

'108, 106,' she said to herself. '104.' She parked her car to block the vehicles in and around 102 Wellington Road, and felt adrenaline pump through her body as she approached the frosted PVC front door.

Ringing the bell, she heard Stone getting out of his vehicle, and the constables splitting up to block the alleyway behind the houses at the top and bottom ends. In houses on either side of 102 Wellington Road, lights went out as the neighbours prepared for a better view.

Clay kept her finger on the bell and banged hard on the door. A light came on in the bedroom above her and a woman's voice filtered into the night.

'All right, all right, for fuck's sake, I'm coming!'

The downstairs hall light came on and feet hurried down the stairs. The woman opened the door but kept the chain on, poked her pudgy face into the gap.

Clay showed the woman her warrant card and said, 'Detective Chief Inspector Eve Clay.'

'Oh, he's done something really serious this time, for the likes of you to be coming to the door at this hour.'

'Your neighbours are watching, Terri.'

'Nosey bastards,' she observed, unchaining the door. 'How do you know my name?'

'Electoral register.'

'What the fuck's he done now?' asked Terri, moving aside to allow Clay and Stone over the doorstep.

'Who?' asked Clay.

'Benji.'

'We're not here about him. We're here about Raymond.'

Terri leaned her bulk against the banister rail, folded her arms and looked utterly confused. 'Raymond?'

'Is he here?'

'Of course he's here. Come on, I'll show you.'

Clay followed Terri up the stairs as Stone stayed put at the bottom to catch any runners.

'Raymond's in there,' she said, pointing at a closed door across the narrow corridor from a bathroom. 'Benji's in the box room, next to mine.'

Clay looked into Terri's bedroom and was shocked at the depth and variety of pinks in the space.

'Benji's asleep in there. He's out for the count. Shouldn't tell you this but... weed.'

'Can you wake Raymond for me, Terri?'

She opened his door and the first thing Clay noticed was the ventilating machine to which the old man was attached.

'Dad was a heavy smoker for years.'

Clay nodded, felt claws of disappointment running down her back.

'Show me Benjamin.'

As the door opened, Clay noticed that the bedside lamp was still on, picking out a skinny boy of about twelve years of age.

'He's scared of the dark, but he thinks he's a big man now that he's started smoking weed. What can I do? I can't keep him locked up in the house twenty-four/seven.'

Clay looked around the room, saw the walls were covered with pictures of skaters and snowboarders.

'Could you come and have a word with him when he's a full shilling in the morning? Put the living shits up him!'

'I'll send a community officer round.' Clay stifled the urge to scream with frustration, and headed back down the stairs. 'We're looking for someone called Ray or Raymond who lives locally. Ring any bells?'

'Oh, yeah. Don't I fucking just know for a fact he was the cunt who broke into my house when I was on holiday. Same cunt who gave Benji free weed for a couple of weeks and then started charging him down at the skateboard park in Otterspool.'

Clay sensed that Terri was on the verge of a long and passionate rant, so she intervened. 'We're in a hurry. Name and address?'

'His name's Raymond Dare and he lives in the Holy Land, at 62 Jeremiah Street next to Moses Street.'

Chapter 70

00.45 am

After running for fifteen minutes along the concrete promenade, Jack Dare had not made out a single human form on the path that followed the winding River Mersey. Dark water lapped at the concrete beneath his feet, a melancholic sound that spiked his desperation and mounting anxiety.

He stopped when his phone rang out. 'Mum, what's happening?'

'You sound out of breath, Jack.'

'I've been running.' He looked up at the globe of the overhead street light and wished that Jasmine would come trotting down the grassy slope to him.

'Raymond's showed up at home.'

'With Jasmine?'

'No. He says he took her to Sefton Park and she ran away.'

'I'll meet you there, Sefton Park. Bring soft lad with you.'

'He's rambling.'

'Just do it, will you!'

'Jack, no, I'm sorry. He's not well.'

Disappointment stabbed his heart and split it into two cold halves. 'Did he say where he lost her?'

'He said something about the lake near Aigburth Vale.'

Silence.

'Are you there, Jack?'

'Stick with him then. I hope you'll both be very happy.'

He closed the call down and sprinted up the path towards Sefton Park.

Chapter 71

00.50 am

Carmel stood over Raymond as he rinsed his hands under the hot tap in the kitchen.

'Why have you got blood on your hands, Raymond?'

'When Jasmine... when I dropped the lead... and... she ran away, I ran... after her, fell over like, cut my hands on the gravel...'

Carmel squeezed washing-up liquid over the backs of his hands and said, 'Rub them together, do the backs of your hands and in between your fingers.'

'He's going to fucking kill me!' said Raymond. As the last

sound left his lips, a stream of green vomit left his mouth and covered the bottom of the sink.

'Jesus, that stinks. What have you been drinking?'

'He's going... to kill me!'

'Yes, if anything's happened to Jasmine, he'll kill you. Why did you take her out in the first place, you bloody idiot?'

'She was being nasty to me, Mum.'

'Pardon?'

'Really nasty. Looking at me like she was going to attack me. I thought, if I feed her and take her for a walk she might get more friendly towards me.'

Carmel shook her head and thought out loud. 'Yes, but where can I hide you? Who'll have you? You've alienated everyone I know.'

She paced up and down the small kitchen, imagining the front door opening and Jack coming into the kitchen. She turned off the tap and, inspecting the palms of Raymond's hands, saw no grazing or cuts. She moved the tap left, right and back again to rinse the fetid vomit down the plughole.

Raymond sat on the floor with his head in his hands.

'Tell me the truth, Raymond. What did you do to Jasmine?'

'I took her to Sefton Park and she ran away.'

Carmel slapped him hard on the top of his head.

'What was that for?'

'For not taking your medication and stopping going to therapy. For buying and selling drugs and taking drugs and thieving from people and for all kinds of other reasons...'

The doorbell rang and Raymond scrambled to his feet.

'I'm dead, I'm dead, I'm fucking dead!'

'That won't be him. He's looking for Jasmine in Sefton Park, and... he's got a key.'

'Don't answer it, Mum. Please.'

The doorbell sounded again and this time the caller kept their finger on the bell. Raymond looked in the direction of the sound and started crying.

'My head's going to explode! Stop ringing the bell!' Raymond held onto the sides of his skull, digging into the skin and bone with the tips of his tensed fingers and bitten nails.

'I need to see who it is!' said Carmel, walking to the kitchen door.

'No!'

'Shut up!'

As he watched his mother leave the kitchen, Raymond felt a weight pressing down on his head, a weight that sapped him of any strength and pushed him down onto the ground. Instead of the tiles of the kitchen floor, he felt a softness and a warmth beneath his bottom, as he heard his mother open the front door.

The ringing of the doorbell stopped. He heard voices, his mother and another woman, and he felt colossal relief. A man's voice filtered to the kitchen, and it spiked his nerves for a moment, but it wasn't Jack.

As the front door closed and the voices came closer, Raymond wished with all his might that he was invisible and as light as helium so that he could float up to the ceiling and be unseen by whoever was in the house.

His mother came into the kitchen first, and then a smart-looking woman with a man.

'It's the police, Raymond.'

'Raymond Dare?' said the woman walking towards him, holding out a warrant card. 'My name is Detective Chief Inspector Eve Clay, and I'm going to take you in to Trinity Road Police Station in relation to a serious criminal offence.'

The man came to Raymond and gave him a colour picture, blurred shapes that swam before his eyes. He put the picture on his lap and wiped his eyes, blinking to try to get a little focus. Looking at the image closely, he wondered if he were dreaming.

'Do you know her, Raymond?' asked DCI Clay.

It was a CCTV picture of Dominika blowing a kiss to the camera.

'Her name's Dominika Zima,' said Clay. 'You appear to be in a relationship with her.'

'What?' said Carmel, astonished.

'Who is she to you, Raymond?' asked Clay.

'She… kind of… well, no, she, she's my girlfriend. I guess.'

The man took the picture away and showed Raymond a second picture of Dominika getting into a white Fiat Uno outside Gino's Bar. He blinked into focus.

'Who's the driver, Raymond? Who's picking her up?'

He looked at his mother, who raised her hands in mystified horror at the CCTV image that Stone showed her.

'She's old enough to be your bloody mother. What the bloody hell's going on here, lad?'

'Come on, Raymond,' said Clay. 'Who's the driver?'

'No, I'm not answering any more questions. Are you arresting me? I want a solicitor.'

'We can sort that out for you when we get you down to Trinity Road Police Station,' said Clay. She looked down at Raymond, cowering in a dog's basket.

'I know my rights,' said Raymond, feeling a dark heat in his bowels.

As Raymond got to his feet, he looked at his mother and she said, 'You've just got lucky.' He looked at her as if she was insane. 'You're much better off in police custody than you are here.'

'Carmel, we've just applied to the duty magistrate for a warrant to search your house. That search will begin shortly. Your son is still a minor…'

'I've got another son. He needs me.'

'You look distraught, Carmel, torn in two,' said Clay with sympathy from one mother to another.

'Jesus, what a horrible night,' said Carmel, her eyes filling with bitter tears. 'I'll accompany Raymond to the police station. What's he done now?'

★

Raymond and his mother sat in silence in the back of Clay's car. As she fired up the ignition, Clay said, 'It's impossible to unlock from the inside. So if we pull up at any red lights, don't even think about doing anything stupid.'

'He won't,' said Carmel.

Raymond looked out of the window and appeared, to Clay's eyes, as she watched him through the rear-view mirror, to be sinking into a world of his own.

As she turned right onto Park Road, he muttered, 'OK... OK...'

A group of young men walked the pavement, hoods up and hands buried against the cold, trailed by two stragglers at the back.

'OK. OK, what?' asked Carmel.

'Just thinking... out loud...'

'Save all your thinking out loud for when we get to Trinity Road, Raymond.'

He breathed on the window and drew three circles in the mist. Carmel leaned over him and, as she wiped the window clean, said, 'Have some respect for DCI Clay and her property.'

'I will, I will, trust me, I will...' said Raymond, staring out at Park Road as the lads on the street sank into the ever-deepening past. And he slumped back on the seat like a man who had just run a marathon.

Chapter 72

00.50 am

As he followed the curves of the lake, Jack Dare got further away from the streetlights at the entrance to Sefton Park. To his left the park was dense with trees and deep shadows that blocked out all illumination.

'Jasmine! Jasmine! Jasmine!' He had long lost count of the number of times he had called her name, but there was no response.

Jack felt sick and tearful in huge and equal measure.

'Carmel! Where are you, Carmel?' He looked at his iPhone. 'You can't be bothered to ring me but you're probably giving tea and sympathy to that other son of yours.' In anger, he switched it off and put it in his pocket.

The wind picked up and he tried to make out a dog barking somewhere in the woods, but all he heard was the thin misery of the wind dipping and raking the long grass.

He felt a surge of rage towards Raymond as he called, 'Jasmine!' He punched the palm of his left hand with his bunched right fist and he pictured Raymond picking his broken teeth from the tarmac.

Behind him, the wind carried the sound of a dog barking. His heart rose and fell back down because it wasn't Jasmine, and he had the sense that tonight God was mocking him, laughing in his face.

He thought about the story of Job, the one he'd read in the Bible Lucy had given him when he was in jail and wondered if God and Satan were having another wager at *my* expense this time? *God, I am not going to curse you, but please, please, please let me find Jasmine, safe and well.*

His capacity to pray fully spent and the cold eating his bones, he picked up his pace into a trot, calling her name, over and over, wondering if he'd ever see her again and thinking that if she was walking the streets or wandering in the dark in the huge park, someone would find her, an expensive pedigree dog, and take her back to their house and keep her.

'You absolute idiot!' he said to himself. 'You should have got her tagged!' And his self-reproach was followed by the bite of bitter reality. He simply couldn't afford it.

He was silenced by something small and fast flying towards him, its wing brushing his scalp and sending a shiver through him.

Another bat came, and another, squeaking as they swept over his head.

Jack made out a natural cave fifty metres away on his side of the lake.

He slowed down, the ground on this side of the lake icier than the wooded side, snow and ice crunching beneath his trainers, the whiteness of the ground picked out by the streetlights from Sefton Park Drive.

'Jasmine?' he called. 'Jasmine! Jasmine...'

It looked like a cherry, the dot of red on the ice in front of him, then a bowl of cherries. He bent forward and put his index finger in the redness, explored his fingertip in the second-hand streetlights. He rubbed his thumb on his index finger and the colour came off on his thumb.

Jack smelled his finger and thumb and he knew it was blood.

His pulse raced as he saw a trail of darkness in the snow and ice along the curving path, and felt like the breath had been sucked out of his body. His scalp came alive, as if one of the bats had settled on his hair and was rubbing its claws against his head.

The trail of blood grew wider as he came closer to the cave's entrance.

'Oh no? No, no, no...'

The blood stopped on the path as the trail disappeared into the darkness of the cave. He looked into the entrance and saw a void that could never be filled, the void that was growing inside him across his whole being, a Jack Dare-shaped void that was masked by his skin, hair and nails.

He got down on his knees and crawled into the darkness, his hands following the sticky wet surface of the cave's floor.

When he touched something solid, he stopped, no longer touching the wetness of blood; his fingers now were on a soft, smooth surface.

'Jasmine,' he whispered, stroking her flank in the darkness. His fingers rose towards her collarbone and he felt tears falling on the back of his hands. 'Oh, Jasmine?'

He reached her throat and stopped when he touched a gaping wound that separated fur and the muscle beneath. He ran his fingers along the wound and knew that she had been cut from ear to ear.

Tenderly, Jack placed his hands under Jasmine's body and lifted her from the blighted ground and said, 'OK, OK, OK,' because the silence around him was dismal.

He shuffled backwards on his knees holding Jasmine close to his body and weeping as he emerged from the cave. Closing his eyes, unable to look, he got to his feet, with the last of Jasmine's warmth fading off into nothing.

'I've got to look at you, Jasmine. It's the least I can do. I'm so, so sorry.'

He opened his eyes and her face was the one he saw when she was sleeping, but beneath her ears there was a wide wound, and her body was limp and without life.

Jack Dare held Jasmine tightly in his arms, looked up to the sky and howled at God in his heaven and cursed Lucy Bell for fooling him into believing that God was a God of love.

Chapter 73

1.01 am

DCI Eve Clay and DS Karl Stone watched Raymond and his mother at the desk with Sergeant Harris.

'Have you been drinking or taking drugs, Raymond?' asked Sergeant Harris.

'Yeah, I have, yeah. Weed, vodka...'

'Have you got mental health issues?'

'No, I'm cool—'

'No, you're not cool, Raymond,' said Carmel Dare. 'He hasn't been taking his medication. He's got a psychotic condition that makes him delusional. And he'll take any drug he can lay his hands on. Ecstasy. Speed—'

'Are you trying to get me sent away forever? I want a lawyer.'

'How are we going to do this?' asked Stone.

'I've called the duty medic in to look him over. I hope we can talk to him first thing in the morning, let him sleep it off. He was mostly lucid in the car on the way here.'

'Where's your coat?' asked Carmel.

'I lost it when I was running after Jasmine in the dark, in Sefton Park.'

'I did say *mostly* lucid,' muttered Clay.

The front door opened and Dr Baker the duty medic entered, looking around and catching Clay's eye. She pointed at Raymond as he came over.

'What's the problem and when do you want me to examine him?'

'Weed, booze and not taking his anti-psychotic medication,' said Clay.

'How badly and how soon do you need him?'

'He's up for murder, one count for sure, probably three.'

'I can prescribe anti-psychotic drugs right now but it takes time for them to build up in the body and take effect.'

'Empty your pockets, Raymond,' said Sergeant Harris. He dug his fingers into the pockets of his jeans and put a mobile phone, a disposable lighter and a handful of change on the desk.

'Sergeant Harris,' said Clay.

Raymond turned to look at her.

'Can you pass his phone on to our ICT expert Poppy Waters.'

An expression of deep unease crossed Raymond's face.

'We've got access to anything that's on your phone, Raymond,' said Clay.

He turned and looked at Sergeant Harris, who tapped the desk. 'And the rest.'

Raymond produced two joints.

'Strange as it may seem, Mr Dare, we aren't too keen on our clients possessing drugs in the cell. As the custody sergeant responsible for your wellbeing while you're my guest, I'd be very remiss in my duties if I didn't say either hand it all over or we'll strip-search you.'

Confused, Raymond looked at his mother.

'Give it all to Sergeant Harris or he'll have to look up your crack!'

He dipped in and produced a small plastic bag containing several white pills.

'It's ecstasy. I don't do it, I just…'

'As in you don't do it, you just sell it?' asked Sergeant Harris.

'I don't do it, like regularly, I just take it… every so often.'

'That was some mental about-turn,' said Dr Baker. 'He's lucid enough. I think he's all yours first thing in the morning, Eve.'

'I'll book the interview suite for eight am,' said Clay.

Raymond looked at her with an expression that was filled with both mental darkness and light, like there was an automatic switch going on and off repeatedly in his skull.

'Any jewellery?' asked Harris.

'Nah!'

'Nah? What's that chain around your neck?'

Raymond looked blank as he touched the back of his neck and said, 'Oh, yeah!' He unclasped the chain and handed over a silver crucifix.

'Sergeant Harris, can I have a look at Raymond in the medical room?' asked Dr Baker.

'Don't be putting me on any medication or shit,' said Raymond.

'Eight am. Interview suite 1. And hope for the best,' said Clay, as Sergeant Harris escorted Raymond and his mother away from the desk, following Dr Baker.

Chapter 74

1.34 am

As he turned into Jeremiah Street, Jack Dare wondered if the sheer weight of his sorrow had somehow affected his senses and tipped him over into the first stages of lunacy.

At the end of the street, there were marked police cars and a white Scientific Support vehicle. Officers in white protective suits came in and out, and across the street neighbours had assembled to watch.

As he came closer, a non-uniformed officer stopped him and said, 'Can you not see the Do Not Cross tape?'

Jack looked and saw that the tape started where his house ended and the neighbours' house began. The officer showed Jack his warrant card.

'Yeah, I see it now, DS Hendricks.'

'My God, what's happened here?' Hendricks nodded at Jasmine in Jack's arms.

'I live there, Mr Hendricks. What's happening?'

'What's your name, lad?'

'Jack Dare.' He held on a little more tightly to Jasmine.

'Have you got a brother?'

'Yes. Raymond. I need to take my dog inside to wash her in the bath.'

'I'm sorry, you can't go in. Your whole house is being searched. Your brother Raymond and your mother are at Trinity Road. He's in big trouble.'

'He killed my dog, my Jasmine.'

'He did?'

'He slashed her throat and hid the body in Sefton Park.'

'He's going to be questioned about the murder of a human being, maybe more than one. You don't look surprised, Jack.'

Jack looked down at Jasmine and then at Hendricks, tears streaming down his face.

'OK, Jack, I'm sorry, truly I am. How about this for a plan? I've got a really nice travel rug in my car.' He pointed across the street at a red Audi. 'How about we go to my car, and you wrap Jasmine up in the rug. We'll lay her on the back seat. I'll ask one of the neighbours to make you a hot drink. We go to my car, we sit up front and have a conversation.'

'Mrs Miller at 42 is a good neighbour. She'll make coffee. You look cold, Mr Hendricks. You could do with a hot drink. I'm happy to talk to you. I'll tell you everything I know.'

Chapter 75

1.36 am

Sergeant Paul Price stood in the middle of Raymond Dare's bedroom, taking pictures of the walls, and listening to his boss Detective Sergeant Terry Mason opening the padlocked bedroom next to it.

'Right, Paul. So we've got mum's room, Raymond's Nazi shrine, and the older lad's room with a padlock on it. Fancy a small wager. What are we going to find behind this door?'

'Porn or drugs?' said Price. 'My ten quid says one of them.'

'Firearms or cross-dressing,' Mason speculated. 'Can you smell the incense?'

'Yes, fragrant. Come on, Terry, put me out of my misery.'

Mason opened the door and, stepping inside, said, 'We both keep our money.'

'Jeez,' said Price, following Mason into the unlocked bedroom.

On the wall facing the door was a collage that went from ceiling to floor, leaving no gaps at all.

'I feel like I should get down on my knees and start praying, Paul.'

'Now that is a labour of love.'

Price took a panoramic picture of the hundreds of images of the Virgin Mary and said, 'How about we do the bet on how many Virgin Marys are on this wall – the one who estimates closest gets a tenner from the other?'

'You're on. You first.'

'Two hundred and eighty-nine,' said Price.

'Three hundred and eleven,' countered Mason, turning to look at the opposite wall. 'Same again on this side, only this time it's Jesus. Where is he now?'

'He rocked up here after his mother and brother left with Eve,' said Price. 'Bill Hendricks is about to have a word with him.'

Mason took out his iPhone and took three rapid shots of the Virgin Mary collage. As Mason hurried down the stairs, Price heard him say, 'Bill, it's Terry. Are you with Jack Dare? Good. You've got to see this before you speak to him.'

Price looked around the room at the thin mattress, pillow and sleeping bag on the bare floorboards and near them, in stark contrast, a bench press, dumb bells, a chrome bar and circular weights of ascending size stacked up neatly under the bench.

Picking up a well-worn Bible from the pillow, Price flicked it open and saw copious lovingly hand-written notes in the margins.

He made a mental note of the garments on the clothes rail. Four shirts, three jumpers, one jacket, two pairs of battered trainers on the rack at the base of the rail next to a small collection of neatly folded underpants and paired socks.

On the small bookcase was a collection of religious titles. *City of God* and *Confessions* by St Augustine; *Introductory Guide to Reading the Summa Theologica of Thomas Aquinas*; *Theology and Sanity* by Frank Sheed.

On top of the bookcase was a wooden crucifix with a metal Jesus, an old statue of Mary that had been lovingly repainted, an incense holder and incense sticks and a cheap disposable lighter.

As Price turned away from the bookcase, something in the row of spines stood out and caught his eye. He saw a book in a brown envelope. He slid it out and saw the cover: *White Supremacists* by Dwayne Hare. From the front of the envelope, Mason learned that the book had been sent to Raymond Dare, the juvenile in custody at Trinity Road.

Price took a picture of the cover and, checking the row of theological titles, took a picture of their spines.

He composed a brief message: *From Raymond Dare's brother's bedroom. Holy books galore with one exception.* White Supremacists *which I believe is Raymond's property.* He sent it to Clay with images of the contrasting reading matter.

Turning slowly to look at the wall facing the bookcase, Price heard Mason coming back up the stairs at speed.

The wall was divided into two exact halves. On the left-hand side were floor-to-ceiling images of heaven: angels playing trumpets to Jesus sitting on a throne on a cloud, being serenaded by a heavenly choir, his apostles kneeling at his feet, their hands joined in prayers of supplication. On either side of Jesus Christ were images of the Virgin Mary and God the Father, while the Holy Spirit hovered about his head in the form of a white dove.

On the right-hand side of the wall were images of hell. Against a background of fire and darkness, devils in many guises tortured the damned with fire, hot brands, spears, knives and swords. Some of the damned were eternally drowned by laughing monsters, while others were nailed to a turning wheel and subject to the lash as a black-faced Satan sat above the scene, watching with the impartial desperation of one who'd seen it all before but would see it all again and again until the end of time.

At the foot of the imagery of heaven, by the skirting board, was a well-worn dog's basket.

'I feel sorry for the mother,' said Mason. 'A Neo-Nazi for one son, and a religious nut-case for the other.'

'It must be a barrel of laughs,' grinned Parker, imagining the tension between the two brothers. 'You're in a lifeboat with one place available. Both brothers are drowning. It's your call. Who gets saved? Which one?'

'Can I toss a coin?' asked Mason. Price shook his head and Mason thought about it. 'I'd take the Neo-Nazi.'

'Why?'

'Because he's probably got a better understanding of his motivations. I don't know where religious maniacs are coming from. In my view, nor do they, in the main. You?' asked Mason.

'The religious maniac. I reckon he'd provide endless hours of entertainment with the contradictions and wacky claptrap.' He looked at *White Supremacists* and the envelope bearing Raymond Dare's name and address. 'It looks like the Jesus Freak intercepts the Hitler Ghoul's mail.'

Chapter 76

1.38 am

Alone in the incident room, Clay looked at the clock as she listened to Sergeant Harris, and decided that she would go home for a few hours' sleep and see her husband and son.

'I want to interview Raymond Dare at eight. Can you get him up at seven, and make sure he's wide awake, fed and watered.'

'I'll put him in the yard outside after he's had his food,' said Sergeant Harris. 'It's going to be even colder later on than it was yesterday. I'll contact his solicitor. Tell him or her to get here way before eight, so the interview can start at eight sharp.'

'Anything to report on him?'

'He had his medical and fell asleep in the cell. I'm looking at him now on the monitor. He's sleeping like a corpse.'

'Thanks, Sarge. I'll see you in the morning.'

As soon as Clay put the landline receiver down, she noticed

that there was a message on her answer machine. She pressed play and listened to silence and then the slightly perplexed tone of an older person unused to the technology he was negotiating.

'Hello?'

More silence followed and then she heard the rustling of paper. Whoever was calling was going to read from an on-sheet script.

'DCI Eve Clay. My name is Mr Rotherham and I am phoning on behalf of a friend of mine, Kate, who is in the same congregation as me at St Luke's Roman Catholic Church.' Silence and the rustling of paper. Clay pictured the old lady in Trinity Road's reception. 'Kate does not have the power of speech or hearing but she would like you to come to her house. If you call me back, we can arrange a time and place to meet. My number is 0151 496 0260. Thank you.'

As Clay put her coat on she heard the sound of an incoming message on her iPhone. She resisted the huge temptation to ignore it, and looked to see it was a series of photographs from Sergeant Paul Parker from Raymond Dare's house in Jeremiah Street.

She read the message about Jack Dare's combination of theological titles and Raymond's copy of *White Supremacists* and looked at the images of the books.

She replied: *Paul and Terry, I'm coming to 62 Jeremiah Street. Eve.*

Walking to the door, she knew she wouldn't be going home or sleeping for the foreseeable future.

Chapter 77

1.43 am

Jack Dare sat in the passenger seat of Detective Sergeant Bill Hendricks's Citroën, holding a cup of tea between his hands and glancing back and forth between Jasmine, wrapped up in a travel rug, and the open door of his house with all the lights on and a constable at the door.

'That man you were talking to just now, the one in the white protective suit?'

Hendricks turned the light on above their heads.

'I'm going to record our conversation on my phone, Jack.'

'That's absolutely fine by me.'

'That was DS Terry Mason.'

'He won't be able to get into my bedroom. I've got a padlock on the door.'

'He already has been into your room. He says you're very religious.'

'I am very religious. I'm a devout Roman Catholic. My room is where I go to read, pray, meditate and work out. A sound mind and inquisitive soul belongs in a healthy body. It's my private place. But...' Jack looked back again at Jasmine.

'But?'

'How can God have allowed my brother to do such a thing?'

'As it hits me, God's not a puppet-master. People do bad things because they want to or they feel they have to. Don't join in!'

'What do you mean, Mr Hendricks?'

'You won't do anything silly to your brother if he's released from our custody.'

'*Vengeance is mine, says the Lord,*' replied Jack.

'Wise old sayings stay in our collective mind because they have depth and truth. Here's another one for you. *While seeking revenge, dig two graves – one for yourself.*'

Jack drank tea and Hendricks watched him slowly coming round to the realisation that he was being closely watched. Jack turned and looked directly at Hendricks.

'Tell me about Raymond.'

'He's mentally ill. He smokes too much weed and takes other illegal substances. And it looks like he's started hitting the booze with his mates.'

'Who are his mates?'

'CJ and Buster. I'm not even sure if they're their real names. If they're anything like Raymond, they'll think they're East Coast gangsta badasses. They're not. They're a gang of silly little boys who deserve to have their backsides kicked.'

'Where do they live, Jack?'

'Either with their mothers or in some sort of squat down by the River Mersey. That's all Raymond's told me, Mr Hendricks.'

'OK, Jack. We've got people on the ground with eyes and ears on what's happening on the street. CJ and Buster. They're pretty unusual street names. You've met them?'

'First time Raymond came home stoned on skunk, I asked him who he'd been with. He told me CJ and Buster. I told him if he ever brought them into our house, I would be forced to go to the police and turn the three of them in after I'd given them the kicking of a lifetime. It was a hollow threat.'

'If push came to shove, would you have done that?'

'No. Violence is against the principles of my faith. I thought the threat would be enough.'

'How's Raymond been the past few days?'

'He stopped taking his medication a while ago. His anxiety levels have been through the roof. I think he's been up to no good with CJ and Buster. Something heavy duty.'

'Go on?'

'They've been screwing people's houses. They're dealing drugs now.'

Hendricks sensed a tension in Jack – that he was struggling between holding back and telling the ugly truth.

'I'll be honest with you, Jack. I am interested if they're screwing people's houses, selling drugs and making misery money, but I've got to prioritise. We're looking at your brother being involved in murder. I'm going to show you a picture.'

Hendricks took out the printed-off image of the Otterspool Park victim blowing a kiss to the CCTV camera.

'Do you know this woman, Jack?'

'Yes. I've never met her, but I've seen more of her than I really ever want to.'

'Is this a riddle?'

'No. She friended Raymond on Facebook and started sending him pornographic images of herself. There was a bit of toing and froing between the two of them and talk of meeting up. I'm pretty sure he's still got the pictures on his phone. You have his phone?'

'We will have.'

'She's supposed to be called Dominika. Has she been murdered?'

'In Otterspool Park. Where was your brother on Monday night, Jack?'

'He went out at six o'clock-ish and didn't get home until four in the morning, maybe a bit later. I stayed up for him because Mum was exhausted. It's not just the hours she works, it's the mental stress Raymond puts her under.'

'Did you speak to him when he arrived home?'

'There was no point. He was high as the clouds and really excited and agitated. I observed him but he didn't see me. I spoke to him the next day, and he came up with a story about robbing a car and setting it on fire. That's his definition of being forensically aware.'

Jack looked back at Jasmine and Hendricks saw him go into the first stages of freefall.

'Jack, come on, finish your tea and talk to me. Please.'

Jack dragged his eyes away from his slaughtered pet and turned to Hendricks. 'He took all the wrong drugs and none of the right ones. Raymond wouldn't kill a human being. But he's not in his right mind. I don't know.'

'Did you ever think he'd kill Jasmine?' asked Hendricks.

There was a painful quiet in the car.

'No, I didn't.'

Hendricks watched Clay arrive, park over the road and get out of her car.

'Who's that?'

'DCI Eve Clay. She's the senior investigating officer in this murder inquiry.' Hendricks handed his card to Jack. 'This is how you get in touch with me. Give me your mobile and I'll store it in my phone.' Jack rattled off eleven numbers. 'We're going to need to talk to you again, Jack, in a more formal setting...'

'I understand that, Mr Hendricks.'

'You won't be able to sleep in your own house for the foreseeable future. Stick around, stay local and be ready to make yourself available at all times.'

'I want to cooperate. How did the woman...?'

'Let's leave it there, Jack. You've had enough upset for one night.'

'Can I take Jasmine from the back of your car, please, Mr Hendricks. Mrs Miller's said she'll take her in. She really is a Good Samaritan.'

Hendricks watched Jack carrying Jasmine's body to the doorstep of 42 Jeremiah Street, and listened.

'Jack, of course you can stay here, love.'

He carried Jasmine across the threshold and, as the front door closed, Hendricks's iPhone rang out. 'Hello, Eve. I'm over the road.'

'You've got to get over here now. We're home and dry with Raymond Dare.'

Chapter 78

5.59 am

The opening of the door into the incident room caused Clay to sit up sharply from the sleep she had fallen into over her desk.

'Sorry,' said Poppy Waters. 'Sorry for waking you.'

'It's me who should be apologising to you, Poppy,' said Clay. 'Bringing you in hours earlier than you should be. I called you because I had to, and I will find a way to make it up to you.'

'Coffee, Eve?'

'Please. Stick a couple of sugars in it, I need the energy.'

In the kitchen area in the corner of the incident room, Poppy flicked the kettle on, lined up a pair of mugs and asked, 'What's this phone you want me to unlock?'

'We're interviewing a prime suspect in the Otterspool Park murder at eight o'clock. He's a seventeen-year-old drug user with a history of severe mental health issues. If you can get anything from the phone that links him to the victim, you will be at the top of my Christmas card list. If you also find anything to relate him to the Picton Road victims, I will personally write to Buckingham Palace requesting you receive an OBE at the very least.'

'I'll crack it and I'll do my best to find what you need.'

On the desk in front of Clay were two sets of photographs. One set consisted of all the pictures of Karl and Václav Adamczak sent to her by Aneta Kaloza just under forty-eight hours earlier. The second set was of pictures of the Otterspool Park victim, taken from both the murder scene and the subsequent autopsy.

She started again with the pictures of the Otterspool Park victim and divided the set into two, the murder scene and the autopsy. Of the two sets, the autopsy photographs whispered a little more loudly to her than the Otterspool Park images.

Clay looked at the global images of the woman's body, charred head and face, and bunched fists. *Your hands,* thought Clay, *your poor, poor hands touched the killer, up close and personal.* She found the image of the victim's opened-up palm with a strand of hair on it, and set it in front of herself.

She put the pictures of the victim to one side and focused on the images of the Adamczak twins. Clay divided them into two sets, those from the Picton Road murder scene and the twenty-eight images of Karl and Václav Adamczak socialising.

Setting them out on her desk in seven rows of four, Clay asked herself, *Which ones stick in your mind? Which ones sing while others mutter?*

'There you go,' said Poppy, placing down a steaming mug of coffee near the edge of Clay's desk.

'Cheers, Poppy.'

Clay handed her Raymond Dare's mobile phone and Poppy lifted it to her nose. 'You could get high just holding this. It absolutely stinks of weed. See you later, Eve.'

'Poppy, do you mind working here instead of in your office? If anything comes from the phone, I need to hear it from the horse's mouth as and when it occurs. I need as much time as possible to compute information before the eight o'clock kick-off.'

Clay returned her attention to the photographs and considered the way the twins had been physically linked in death, into a human X. She turned over the fifteen images in which Karl and Václav were not physically touching each other and looked, one by one, at the images in which they were shoulder to shoulder, had their hands on each other or had linked arms.

She looked at the clock, saw it was seven minutes past six and heard the murmur of Poppy's voice as she talked to herself, unlocking the phone on the other side of the incident room. Her instinct told her she was missing something small but obvious. Clay turned over all the images in which the Adamczak twins were indoors.

Seven images that, after more than ten minutes, came down to three.

Karl and Václav Adamczak outside Goodison Park holding up an old-fashioned blue and white Everton scarf.

Karl and Václav Adamczak on the steps of the Metropolitan Cathedral with a small group of people around them and others coming and going, up and down the steep stone steps.

Karl and Václav Adamczak outside the Pumphouse at the Albert Dock, arms around each other, drinks in hand, smiling in the sunshine at Aneta as she photographed them.

One, two, three, four; one, two, three, four; one, two, three. She stopped.

Slowly, she drew the image of the identical twins outside the Pumphouse closer to herself, and smiled at the very first image she had seen of Karl and Václav Adamczak. Her mind skipped back to Raymond Dare being booked in by Sergeant Harris.

Oh, Raymond, she thought, *you are in so much deep, deep trouble.*

Chapter 79

8.00 am

Carmel Dare sat to Raymond's left and to his right sat Mr Robson, the duty solicitor. As DCI Clay formally opened the interview, Raymond looked down at three evidence bags on the table in front of him, Clay's laptop and his mobile phone.

'Mr Robson,' said Hendricks. 'Before DCI Clay starts the interview with your client, is there anything you'd like to lodge with us based on your discussion with the duty medic?'

'My client has major mental health issues and has electively not been taking medication to control the symptoms. There are also serious issues relating to substance abuse. I don't agree with the doctor. I don't believe he is fit to be interviewed. I'd like a second opinion from a doctor not employed by the Merseyside Constabulary.'

'Raymond,' said Hendricks. 'What's your date of birth?'
'October first, 2003.'
'Tell me something about the schools you attended.'
'Matthew Arnold when I was a little kid, then I moved on to Shorefields for secondary and, after they kicked me out...'
'Why did you get kicked out?' asked Clay.

'Arson. But it wasn't me. The police couldn't prove it was me.'

'So there must have been other issues?'

'Yeah, I nutted this teacher, Miss Nglove.'

'Why did you head-butt her?'

'Because she was a cheeky black bitch.' He examined the memory in a moment of silence. 'That's right. Then I went to a special school for bad boys.'

'How are you feeling?'

'All right.'

'He's on good form,' said Carmel. She leaned forward and addressed Mr Robson. 'He needs to get on with this. You don't need a second medical opinion. Ask me, I'm his mother, he can do this just fine.'

'When did you steal the white Fiat Uno from Moses Street, a few streets down from where you live?' asked Clay.

'No comment.'

Hendricks picked up Raymond's mobile phone and pulled up the gallery.

'Our IT expert came in at six o'clock this morning to open your phone,' said Clay. Raymond's mouth formed a little knot and his brow creased. 'How do you know a woman called Dominika Zima?'

'No comment.'

Hendricks turned the screen of Raymond's phone towards him. 'Is this the Dominika who sent you these self-portraits?'

'Oh my God,' said Carmel. 'The dirty old cow.'

'No comment.'

'We've got an incoming call on your phone at 8.30 pm on Monday, 1st December, two nights ago, from a phone registered to a Dominika Zima. Our IT expert traced it back to her.'

Hendricks showed Raymond a printed-off image of Dominika blowing a kiss to the CCTV camera outside Gino's Bar, as Clay pulled up the footage of her waiting outside on Aigburth Road on the laptop.

'Is this Dominika Zima?' asked Hendricks.

'No comment.'

'Same woman on your phone as the woman on the CCTV? Do you agree?'

'No comment.'

Clay turned the laptop around and pressed play. 'She's waiting for a lift here. You haven't arrived yet, but when she called you up from Gino's, the barman heard her address you as Ray, and ask you for a lift. She was annoyed with you.'

She stood up and walked behind Raymond. 'There you are. You've pulled up, and there she is, getting into the car.'

'How do you know that's me? You can't even see the driver.'

Clay paused the footage at the point where Dominika was sitting in the passenger seat with the doors closed.

'We know it's you, Raymond, because we found the car keys.' Hendricks picked up an evidence bag and poured the car keys onto the table. 'In your bedroom.'

'No comment.'

'We checked. There was a burglary at 101 Moses Street on Friday, 28th November. The car keys for the Fiat Uno were taken. Did you commit that burglary, Raymond?'

'No comment.'

'According to the barman, she was annoyed with you because you'd arranged to meet her in Gino's Bar but you didn't show up. But then you did turn up rather quickly to pick her up. We got you on every Automatic Number Plate Reader travelling from the street behind Tesco's on Park Road, where you left the Fiat Uno after you'd stolen it, to Aigburth Road, where you picked up Dominika.'

'No comment.'

'Has she been in touch with you in the last forty-eight hours?'

'No.'

'Do you know why that is?'

'No comment.'

Clay turned the laptop around, came out of videos and into the photo gallery.

'She hasn't been in touch with you because…' She turned the laptop back around, and showed an image of Dominika inside the tent in Otterspool Park. Raymond turned his face away and muttered, 'Shit!'

'Raymond,' said his mother, her face frozen, her words rising from her core. 'Stop messing around with *no comment* responses and start talking the truth. Was it the voices again? The voices in your head?'

'I'm going to draw a line under everything that's passed so far this morning,' said Clay, as Raymond looked anxiously at the other evidence bags on the table. 'Are you wondering what's in them? We'll come to that in time, but I will tell you that we found the contents of each bag in your bedroom.'

'What? What is it?'

'We ask the questions, Raymond,' said Hendricks. 'You answer them. This is your big chance. Talk to us before we charge you with the murder of Dominika Zima. Convince us that you didn't murder her, having raped her first.'

'I robbed a car from round ours and I gave Dominika a lift but that was all I did. I didn't kill no one. I'm not that violent. I wouldn't even hit a fucking woman, let alone… I'm a peaceful lad.'

'I don't think your brother would agree with you,' said Hendricks.

'What's Jack got to do with this?'

'You don't remember what you did to his dog last night?' asked Clay.

'I-I remember.'

'You took his dog to Sefton Park, slashed her throat and dumped her in a cave, lakeside.'

'Tell us about Monday night. Tell me about Dominika.'

Raymond looked at his mother. 'You'd better leave the room.'

Carmel looked at Clay who stood up and said, 'Come with me, Carmel.'

As Carmel followed Clay to the door, she looked back at Raymond and said, 'My God, you didn't, did you?'

Outside the interview suite, Clay said, 'There's a viewing room next door. Did you see the reflective glass on the back wall?' Carmel nodded, strangling the tears that stormed inside her. 'You'll be able to see and hear him. He won't know you're there. Ask Sergeant Harris to take you in.'

'Murder? My son?'

'I'm sorry, Carmel. I think you must prepare for the worst.'

Clay returned to the interview suite and sat opposite Raymond in silence, giving Sergeant Harris time to bring Carmel Dare into the viewing room.

'What's with the silence, all of a sudden?'

'I'm giving you time to process the information we have about your involvement in the murder of Dominika Zima. In thirty seconds I'm going to start asking you questions. The truth is your only option.'

Clay looked at Raymond's unfocused eyes, saw something behind them like a faulty fluorescent light.

'Ready to talk, Raymond?'

'Has she gone?' he asked. Clay nodded. 'I didn't ask Dominika out on a date. I'd just swapped phone numbers with her, and when she called me from Gino's Bar, it was, like, totally out of the blue. Yes, she was pissed off with me because she said we'd arranged to meet in Gino's and I didn't turn up.'

'Are you sure about that?' asked Clay. 'You sounded uncertain when you said *We'd arranged to meet in Gino's*.'

'I can be forgetful sometimes.'

Clay said nothing and stared him down hard.

'After she sent me the pictures of herself, we swapped phone numbers. We had a conversation on Sunday night, the first time I spoke to her on the phone. I smoked a lot of weed on Sunday, and I was half asleep when she called.' He blinked like talking was a huge physical effort. 'We might have arranged to meet, and I would have picked Gino's because they serve underage drinkers and don't ask for ID. It's kind of dark and quiet, lots of little corners...'

'So you've been before.'

'Yeah, not on a date.'

'Who do you go with?'

Clay looked in his eyes, saw him stifle the truth. 'I understand,' she said. 'You don't want to give away your friends' names.'

'DCI Clay,' said Hendricks. 'Their street names are CJ and Buster. Pretty distinctive. It won't take us long to track them down. You hearing me, Raymond?'

Raymond flashed a look at Hendricks, as if the man directly across the table from him had successfully read his mind. Hendricks smiled back at him.

'What are their real names, Raymond?' asked Clay.

He half-shrugged and muttered, 'Just Buster and CJ.'

'Were they with you on Monday night?'

'No, I was alone.'

'Why *did* you pick Gino's Bar, Raymond?' asked Clay.

He shook his head and swerved away from making eye contact.

'You must have known from the photographs that she was a considerable amount older than you. And like you said, it's dark and quiet, lots of little corners where you could hide with your cougar date. You were embarrassed about the age gap, weren't you?'

'I suppose.'

'OK, she phones you up, asks for a ride home. Take it from there, Raymond.' Clay sat back and kept her entire focus on Raymond as he shifted on his seat and drilled his eyes onto the floor. 'Raymond, you're about to be charged with murder. Now is not the time to clam up.'

'I-I robbed the car from Moses Street on Friday.' Raymond fell silent, looked up at the ceiling, head tilted back.

'I'm going to help you out, Raymond. You stole the car on Friday. Normally, you would have driven it round with your mates until the tank was empty and then abandoned it. But this time you parked it out of the way because you knew you were meeting up with Dominika and you wanted to impress her with your motor. *Look at me, Dominika. I'm a successful man of the world.* But you stood her up on Monday evening because you'd either genuinely forgotten the date due to the amount of weed you'd been smoking, or you plain bottled it.'

'I didn't bottle it.' He looked at Clay and said, 'I fucking forgot. I remember now. I did arrange to meet her in Gino's but then I forgot all about it.'

'Keep going, Raymond.'

'She called me, pissed off, and asked for a lift. I went to the car park behind Tesco's on Park Road where I'd left the car. I picked her up on Aigburth Road. She was a bit drunk. I was driving towards Garston when she put her hand between my legs and started talking really dirty, saying what she wanted me to do to her.'

'After you'd stood her up? She must have been a deeply forgiving woman.'

'I'd apologised and I told her she looked lovely. I said, *Let's turn around and go to Otterspool Park.* I was really pumped up at this point. She was kissing my neck and started telling me what she was going to do to me. I parked the car outside the entrance to the park, you know that bit that's just off the top of Jericho Lane. It was dark. We got onto the back seat and she said, *No, no, no, this isn't comfortable. Take me to the Travelodge.*' I told her I only had a tenner and I said, *Let's get out of the car and go into the park.*'

'And she agreed to that?' asked Clay.

'Yeah, she was well up for that.'

'On a night when the temperature was hovering over zero and you'd stood her up and you'd refused to pay for a room? Carry on, Raymond.'

'We walked towards the railway bridge, and went into the woods, where the sloping bit is. The embankment. We were there for, I'd say, the best part of an hour.'

'And what did you do during that hour?' asked Hendricks.

'I had sex with her three times.'

'In an hour.'

'I took a load of poppers with me. She took it up the arse and a couple of times up the minge.'

'Just for the sake of clarity, when you say *minge*, Raymond, are you referring to Dominika's vagina?' asked Hendricks.

'Her twat, yeah, whatever...'

'Was it your idea to perform anal sex?' asked Clay.

'It was her idea to do it up the arse. The poppers made it happen. After the third time, I'd pretty much run out of gas, so I said, *Thanks, I'm going now*. She started asking me for money, really aggressively, *Give me money or fucking else. Or else what?* I said. *Or else I'll tell the police you forced me.*'

'I gave her the tenner and started to walk off. She shouted, *Aren't you going to give me a lift home?* I said, *Where's home?* She said, *Garston*. I said, *No, where are you from in your country?* She was like *Zlin in the Czech Republic, why?* And I was like laughing and went, *You'd better get back there!* She started going crazy, running after me and calling me all the cunts under the sun. So I picked up a big branch and went, *Do you want some of this, slag?* She soon backed off. And that was the last I saw of her.'

Clay looked at the two face-down photographs in front of her. Hendricks pointed at an evidence bag and asked, 'Shall I?'

'Yes, please, Detective Sergeant Hendricks.'

'What else did you get up to on Monday night? After you'd walked away from Dominika?'

'I drove off and burned the car out. Then I went home and got stoned. And that's the truth.'

Clay pushed the face-down pictures towards Raymond.

'What's all this?' asked Raymond.

Clay turned over a photograph of Karl and Václav Adamczak; Hendricks emptied a small evidence bag, and the silver crucifix that Raymond Dare had handed over to Sergeant Harris tumbled onto the desk.

'Do you know these men?'

'No, I don't.'

'They're on a night out.'

'Looks like...'

'They're outside the Pumphouse by the Albert Dock. Arms around each other's shoulders, smiling, beers in hand. You don't know them?'

'No.' Flat and certain, Raymond looked at the picture and back at Clay. 'Don't know them from Jack Shit.'

'Have a closer look, Raymond. Look at the small detail.'

'What's your other picture of?'

Hendricks turned over the next picture and explained, 'This is a close-up of the crucifixes they were wearing.'

'Loads of people wear crucifixes. So what?'

'On the night that Dominika Zima was murdered and set alight, these men were murdered and set alight. When we pulled apart their flat on Picton Road, where their bodies were, the crucifixes in their photograph weren't there.'

Clay turned over the third and fourth photographs.

'This graffiti was found on the wall in the bedroom where the men died and were burned, post mortem. And this graffiti was found on the railway bridge in Otterspool Park where Dominika Zima was murdered and set alight earlier that evening.'

Hendricks picked up an evidence bag and asked, 'Do you recognise the graffiti, Raymond?'

'Yeah, it's Black Sun. Anyone who knows anything about the Nazis knows that. But what the fuck's that got to do with me?'

'I've seen a picture of the mural of the Nuremberg Rally that you painted on your bedroom wall. Detective Sergeant Mason sent the image to my phone. You're a talented artist,' said Clay.

'Thanks,' replied Raymond.

Hendricks took out a lovingly cut-out stencil stained with black spray paint.

'This was found in your bedroom, with your other art materials, including a black spray can.'

'That's *not* mine.' Raymond looked at his solicitor, his eyes filled with pleading and confusion.

'All right, Mr Dare,' said his solicitor. He turned to Clay and asked, 'Can I request a break from this interview, so I can speak in more detail with my client?'

'By all means,' said Clay.

'Are you trying to say I murdered three people?'

'Yes, that's right, Raymond,' replied Clay. 'But you didn't do it alone. You had two accomplices. After you've spoken with Mr Robson, and while you're waiting in your cell for this interview to recommence, I suggest you think about everything you've seen and heard so far, and think about telling us more about your friends.'

'Why would I murder a woman and two men?'

'Why would you stop taking anti-psychotic medication?' replied Clay. 'Why would you replace it with a cocktail of drugs? Why would you listen to the voices in your head? Why would you slit a dog's throat? Why would you do any of these things? You tell me, Raymond,' said Clay. 'You tell me.'

As Sergeant Harris arrived to escort Raymond back to his cell, Clay stepped to one side.

'You want to meet me and Raymond outside his cell, Sergeant Harris?' asked Hendricks. 'Come on, Raymond, walk with me...'

'Is his mother still in the viewing room?'

'No,' replied Harris. 'She turned crimson and started crying when he described his sexual encounter with Dominika Zima. She was mortified. It was awful.'

'I need to speak to her about Raymond.'

'What's your take on this?' asked Harris.

'He picked her up with two of his friends, so-called CJ and Buster. They took her into the park, raped her and murdered her. Then they moved on to Picton Road and carried on the blood-fest in the Adamczak brothers' flat. As soon as we pull in his friends, they'll rat out on each other and we'll know exactly what happened.' Clay indicated the viewing room. 'Did she say anything to you in there?'

'I asked her for the real names of CJ and Buster. She's never met them because the older son, Jack has barred them from the family home. And on the odd occasion when he refers to them, it's always CJ and Buster.'

Chapter 80

8.50 am

Detective Sergeant Karl Stone banged on the door of 103 Breck Road, headquarters of the Merseyside Anti-Fascist Coalition, and listened to the sound of approaching footsteps inside the building. Looking through the bay window he saw a huge picture dominating the wall of the front room.

It was a massive black and white image of the twentieth-century American folk singer Woody Guthrie singing at full pelt, the guitar in his hands bearing the slogan, *This Machine Kills Fascists*. The room was part-living room, part-office, with three very old filing cabinets lined up against a wall crying out to be decorated, and a photocopier from another era.

The front door opened and a hugely tall man in his seventies peered at Stone with a lifelong suspicion of everything in his eyes. With his beaked nose and aggressive stare, he looked like a hungry eagle.

'Karl Stone,' he introduced himself.

'Black Sun, Karl Stone?' Malcolm Charles responded with an ingrained public school twang in his voice.

Stone showed his warrant card. 'I need your help, Mr Charles.

You're an expert on fascist individuals and organisations. I'm a leading detective in a murder investigation and I'm trying to protect racial minorities.'

Malcolm Charles's eyes tick-tocked as he weighed the matter up and asked, 'If this is about the racist fucking fascists who killed the Polish building workers in Picton Road, you'd better come in...'

Stone followed him to a kitchen table littered with leaflets and card-covered files.

'Are you wired for sound, Detective Sergeant Stone?' asked Malcolm Charles.

Stone placed his iPhone in the middle of the table and said, 'Yes, Mr Charles, and this is it, but it's not turned on to record and nor will it be, because I haven't come here to interview you or in any way harass you. I've come cap in hand asking for your help. Black Sun?'

Something bright danced in the man's eyes, and he spoke after a significant pause. 'What links Black Sun to the political abomination on Picton Road?'

'At this point in time, Mr Charles, I can't directly reveal what links this murder has to the far-right organisation...'

Malcolm Charles held up a hand and pulled out a file from the chaos before him. 'It was like a virus,' he said. 'A far-right political version of McDonald's. They franchised their brand of hate across the globe. Everything that wasn't Eurocentric and white was simply wrong. But it translated into many markets. The Japanese Black Sun were anti-Chinese and Korean. Etcetera, etcetera. In Africa, it ran along tribal lines. Are you with me still, Detective Sergeant Stone?'

'One hundred per cent, Mr Charles,' replied Stone, focusing on the imperative to learn about communal madness. 'Everything has a purpose, right? What was Black Sun's objective?'

'It was simple: to stir up racial war and save the eventual fascist state the job of destroying the parasites within. Why kill the blacks, Jews, communists, gypsies, etcetera when you can create the conditions in which those savage minorities will wage a civil war of attrition and wipe each other out?'

Malcolm Charles stood up, marched to the sink and picked up five card files from the drainer. 'After you called me, I pulled together everything I've got on Black Sun. Why didn't you tell me you were an agent of the state?'

'Because I need your help and didn't want to alienate you. You're clearly the out-and-out expert in your field. Where else could I turn?'

'Black Sun was at its worst in four territories; Italy where it started, Nigeria, Georgia, and the USA, and at its most laughably incompetent in one: Japan. I've thrown that one in to show you how bloody stupid the whole thing truly was.' He walked across the small space, the five files in hand, and handed them to Stone.

'This is everything I've got on all five organisations. I was up until the early hours photocopying them. It was an expensive and time-consuming business, I can tell you that for nothing.'

'I can't thank you enough,' said Stone. 'You've kept your originals, right?'

'Of course. What are you doing?'

'The files you've kindly copied for me are evidence. I'm putting the evidence you've supplied against Black Sun into an evidence bag.'

'I suppose I should offer you a drink. Tea? Coffee?'

'I'm fine, thank you anyway. In your view, which was the worst of the five organisations?'

'They were all as bad as each other. But the American Black Sun came out on top in terms of the body count. The killings went well into double figures, and that was all the lying American media propaganda machine admitted to. I'm relying on you not informing anyone I've assisted you in this investigation. I did so not knowing that you worked for the state.'

'I'm assuming you're going to tell your comrades in the Anti-Fascist Coalition, just as I'm going to tell my colleagues in the murder investigation, and that's as far as it goes on both sides.'

'I used to have comrades in the Coalition. They've either died or moved on to politically less constructive things.'

Stone stood up, held out his hand and received no reciprocation.

'Don't pretend to be my friend. Just ask yourself the question. Why would a moribund fascist organisation suddenly reawaken now?'

'What's your view on it, Mr Charles?'

'By the pricking of my thumbs,' said Malcolm Charles. 'Something wicked this way comes.'

'It's already arrived, and's alive and kicking right here and now,' replied DS Karl Stone, heading to the front of the house, desperate to look inside the files in his hands.

Chapter 81

9.03 am

In front of a row of yellow-brick terraced housing, in the shadow of Liverpool Football Club's Anfield Stadium, sat a white Portakabin. Detective Constable Clive Winters looked out of its window at a hoarding proclaiming: *CJ Construction Respectful Development In The Community*.

A bulky young man with ginger hair stopped in front of the window, pointed at Winters and then back at himself. With the fingers of his right hand, he made a talking mouth and then walked away.

'So, what's it going to be when it's finished?' asked Winters.

The site manager, Damien Wright, scrolled through the laptop on his desk.

'A massive bed-and-breakfast facility for football fans from all over the UK and Europe.' He paused and pointed at his screen.

Winters looked over the site manager's shoulder.

'This is a list of everyone who was working on-site here in the week commencing Monday 24th November, and the weekend of Saturday and Sunday 29th and 30th November.'

Winters looked through the list and double-checked: there was no sign of the names Karl Adamczak or Václav Adamczak.

'I've asked around,' said the site manager. 'We've got work going on in Kirkby, Maghull, Widnes and Huyton at the moment. I can show you on the computer, the Adamczak brothers have never worked for CJ Construction. I can show you the rotas going back to late August when this project started if you want. But the men you've asked about simply didn't work here.'

'Thank you for your time,' said Winters.

'No problem.'

Winters smiled. 'I'm a big fan of the beautiful game,' he lied. 'Mind if I have a quick nosey at the hotel-in-progress?'

'You're all togged up so that's not a problem,' said Mr Wright, sliding a document towards him. 'Have a brochure. Pass on the good news.'

Winters closed the Portakabin door and saw the ginger-haired construction worker waiting inside the open doorway of the site.

'What's your name?' asked Winters.

'Mike Carlyle.'

He turned and walked deeper into the building, against a soundscape of electronic saws and heavy, repetitive banging. Winters followed him into the half-formed shell of an open-plan building, the former adjoining walls of the terraced housing supported by metal girders.

As he crossed the wooden boards, Winters checked his hard hat and followed Mike Carlyle into what looked like a future kitchen.

Winters showed his warrant card and said, 'You've got something to tell me.'

'I listened in when you were in Wright's office.'

Winters used silence against the background din.

'You're looking up Karl and Václav's recent history on the site?'

'Yes, did you know them?'

'They worked here. Wright's a fucking liar.'

'Tell me about them.'

'They were sound, both of them. They'd help anyone out, anyone who was struggling or needed a lift. When you heard they were on site with you, it was a morale booster. They were really hard workers and top notch at what they did. There are some slimy bastards out there.' A note of emotion crept into Mike Carlyle's voice.

'Is there something you want to tell me?'

'Remind me. What did Wright tell you about Karl and Václav's work on this site?'

'He didn't tell me anything. He showed me a list of all the people employed on this project. He showed me employee lists from other CJ Construction projects around Merseyside. Karl and Václav Adamczaks' names simply didn't show up on any of them.'

Mike Carlyle smiled bitterly. 'Can you cover my back?'

'If you've got information that will help this investigation, yes.'

Three construction workers walked into the space, and the oldest of the three asked, 'You're a copper, right?'

Winters showed his warrant card. 'Detective Constable Clive Winters.'

'Mike called us and said you'd shown up asking questions about Karl and Vác.'

'Karl and Vác who?' said Mike, his voice laced with irony. His colleagues laughed.

'Your site manager's adamant. They've never worked here.'

'He's been lying to you,' said Mike. 'CJ Construction's lying to you.' His voice dropped down further. 'You want to know the truth?'

'Yes, I do.'

'We haven't been paid for three weeks. Imaginary bonuses for patience and loyalty that never happen and when that scam runs out they start playing Russian roulette with us, making fucking heavy-duty noises about tax evasion, losing our houses and jail time.'

Winters drank in the sourness and anger bonding the men.

'They did work here, and they were good mates of ours.'

Chapter 82

9.15 am

'We didn't get any direct CCTV footage of you from the Otterspool Park murder scene, but we did find you on CCTV that directly links you to the double murder of Karl and Václav Adamczak in their flat above the Polish delicatessen,' said Clay, as Hendricks lined up the footage on his laptop. 'Raymond, are you listening to me or just staring into space?'

Mr Robson tapped Raymond's arm and he looked across the table at Clay as if she'd just descended from a passing cloud.

'Picton Road? I haven't been on Picton Road for years.'

'When was the last time you were there, Raymond?' asked Hendricks.

'When I was eleven. The school used to take us swimming in Picton Baths.'

'Are you sure about that?' asked Clay. 'You've already confessed to a leaky memory.'

'I'm sure about that though.'

'Well, we're not so sure what you're saying is true,' said Clay. 'DS Hendricks is going to show some footage of you walking away from the murder scene on Picton Road. We've already sent the footage to be cleaned up. While you're watching yourself, think of this. When our Scientific Support colleagues took your house apart, they found the partially burned remains of the clothes you were wearing in this footage in a barbecue at the back of your house. The coat you wore was a black North Face coat. The white logo didn't get burned. When we've cleaned up the footage we'll be able to highlight the North Face logo on the jacket you're wearing. Are you ready? Then we'll begin.'

Hendricks turned the laptop sideways. 'Can you see it?'

Raymond nodded, and Hendricks pressed play.

'There you are. We think you had two accomplices, but snow covered the lens of the CCTV camera. I suggest they went one way and you the other, right towards the camera above the mini-market on Picton Road.'

'Yeah, well, that's where you're wrong, because that's not me.'

Hendricks paused the film at the optimum shot of the figure walking towards the camera.

'Good idea to wear a balaclava, not a good idea to walk directly towards the nearest camera.' Clay leaned forwards. 'You must have been as high on blood as it's possible to be, you and your friends. CJ? Buster? Who are they and where do they live?'

'We were all at CJ's playing on the game station and smoking weed. His ma was in all night. She'll tell you.'

'Give us her name and address and we'll see if she can confirm your alibi.'

Raymond stared at the laptop screen and appeared to be fading away.

'Raymond, I'm waiting. A name and address. CJ's mother. If this is all a big mistake, she could be the woman who'll kick-start you on the road back to freedom. Who is she? Where can I find her?'

'No comment.'

'You murdered Dominika Zima in Otterspool Park and went directly to Picton Road to kill the Adamczak brothers.'

'No comment.'

'Three foreign nationals in one night.'

'No comment.' Raymond turned to Mr Robson and whispered behind his hand.

'I'm sorry, DCI Clay, but my client is refusing to answer any more questions.'

'Look at me, Raymond,' insisted Clay. When she had as much of his attention as she could, she said, 'I could charge you with murder right now, but I have time on my side, so I'm not going to. I'm going to give you the chance to confess. That way the judge will look slightly more favourably than if you carry on playing games with me and DS Hendricks. I'm cutting you some slack here, Raymond.'

Raymond turned to Mr Robson in silence.

'In protecting others, you're only harming yourself,' said Mr Robson. 'If I were you, I'd think carefully about what DCI Clay has said to you, and be proactive in protecting your own best interests. We'll talk some more before your next interview...'

'One last thing, Raymond. We know how you're connected to Dominika Zima. How do you know Karl and Václav Adamczak?'

'Who?'

'The brothers you and your friends murdered.'

Raymond raised his right-hand index finger to his temple and appeared to be tuning in to something inside his head.

'One voice is saying, *I can't remember*. One voice is saying... *No comment.*'

'I'm not buying this voices in the head theatre,' said Clay.

'*Repeat the question*, says a third I've not heard before. *Repeat the question.*'

'How do you know Karl and Václav Adamczak?' asked Clay.

Raymond nodded, spoke to himself, 'All right.' He looked at Clay and said, 'I'm listening. No comment.'

Chapter 83

9.25 am

Detective Sergeant Gina Riley hurried towards the main door of the chaplaincy at Alder Hey. A dark possibility had assaulted her minutes earlier and, in her head, its echo was loud and shrill. Who was the priest who left rosary beads for Marta?

She heard movement behind the chaplaincy door as she knocked loudly. It opened and an elderly nun smiled at her.

'How can I help you?' she asked.

Riley showed her warrant card and the smile on the nun's face turned into a frown.

She checked the NHS ID badge hanging from the nun's neck: Sister Agnes.

'Who are the Roman Catholic priests working in the chaplaincy in Alder Hey, Sister Agnes? I need to speak to them, to *see* them as much as speak to them.'

'Father James is in the chapel at the moment. He's the most senior priest. And then there's Father Mike and Father Timothy.'

Riley turned and saw Father James through the glass panels of the chapel, on his knees and apparently deep in prayer. From the back, he looked nothing like the priest who had visited Marta Ondřej.

'Detective Sergeant Riley,' said the nun. 'I'd respectfully request you don't disturb Father James at the moment. He's just come out of a seventy-two-hour vigil with a dying baby and her parents. The baby passed just over half an hour ago. He's praying for the baby and her parents as we speak. He is... emotional, to say the least.'

'I understand.' *I can almost certainly rule him out*, thought Riley, glancing back through the glass into the chapel. 'I don't think I need to see Father James.'

'Thank you for your understanding.' The nun's brow creased, as an idea formed in her head. 'Do you want to see pictures of Father Mike and Father Timothy?'

'Yes, I do.'

'Please step inside the chaplaincy. There are photos on the staff notice board.'

Riley followed Sister Agnes inside. Close to the door was a large board full of smiling faces arranged in panels according to faith, with the individuals' names printed underneath the portraits.

Riley skimmed and scanned the Muslims, the Sikhs, the Hindus, until she came to the Christian churches, and slowed down when she came to the three smiling portraits of Roman Catholic priests.

She looked at Father Mike Bolan, clean-shaven and half the age of Marta Ondřej's visitor. She double-checked Father James Dwyer; he was in the same age range as the priest bearing rosary beads, but he was bald and facially entirely unlike him. Under a picture of a smiling Sister Agnes, Father Timothy Jones had acne and looked like he was only weeks out of the seminary. There was no one remotely like the visitor to Marta's room.

Riley took out her iPhone and within three rings, DCI Eve Clay connected her call.

'Eve, I'm pulling CCTV from the third floor of Alder Hey on Tuesday, 2nd December, 12 noon until 2 pm. Marta's had a suspicious visitor. A priest, or a man dressed as a priest, brought her a gift of rosary beads. As more of her lights are turning on, the fleeting vision she had of the visitor has rattled her. She totalled the rosary beads. My alarm bells are ringing.'

'Mine are ringing just as loud. Did you get a name from him?'

'No.' Riley felt sick to her core. 'No, he was here and gone in under half a minute.'

'How much sleep have you had in the past seventy hours?'

'Not much.'

'Pull the CCTV as you've already suggested, and we'll see what we can nail down. Do you want me to put family liaison in for a few hours?'

'No, Eve. I'm bonding with this kid and... Like I said, she's coming out of her shell. I believe she's going to crack open on the fuckers who've taken her and I think I can help her to do just that. It's up to you. I think I'm of more use here than anywhere else. Your call? No right or wrong answer.'

'Stay put for now. Get the CCTV footage and email me everything.'

Chapter 84

9.45 am

En route to Kate Thorpe's house, Clay drove past St Luke's Roman Catholic Church on Albert Edward Road and looked at the dozens of terraced houses in Grant Avenue that had an uncluttered view of the Wavertree Mystery.

At the junction of Edward Albert Road and Grant Avenue, Clay stopped to let a car past. Looking at the presbytery, she decided she would rerun the interview with Lucy Bell and use the lecturer in a reconstruction of events on the morning Marta was discovered.

Clay turned onto Grant Avenue. Looking for Kate's house she was surprised to see the old lady standing on the step, her front door open. Clay pulled up and, turning off her engine, saw an elderly man shuffling along the ice towards her.

Kate looked at the man and then turned to Clay as she got out of the car, raising a hand in greeting.

'You wanted to see me,' said Clay.

Kate nodded.

'I'm Mr Rotherham,' said the old man. 'Are you DCI Eve Clay?'

She showed her warrant card and said, 'Thank you for your call on behalf of Miss Thorpe.'

'Thank you for calling me back and arranging this meeting,' said Mr Rotherham, following Clay inside Kate Thorpe's house. 'I know a lot of what Kate wants to talk about. She has written much of it down for me. She was not always deaf and she's good at lip reading.'

Kate Thorpe walked towards the kitchen at the back of the house.

'She's going to make us tea. She wants us to sit in the parlour.'

As she entered the room at the front of the house, Clay had the sense that she was walking into a religious art gallery. The three walls were lined with dozens of skilfully executed paintings of the Virgin Mary and the Sacred Heart of Jesus. In some pictures Mary and Jesus were on their own and in a few they were together.

Making her way to the bay window, Clay lifted the net curtain back and saw Lucy Bell coming out of the vestry next door to St Luke's Roman Catholic Church.

Mr Rotherham stood at her side. 'She's the daughter of our parish priest.'

'I've met both of them. Is Father Aaron a good priest?'

'Like all of us, DCI Clay, sometimes he is good and sometimes he is not. He has a flaw in his character, as we all do.'

'What is that flaw, Mr Rotherham?'

'It would be wrong of me to discuss it with you because Father Aaron is not here to defend himself. But he has disappointed us greatly of late.'

'I see.'

Clay watched Lucy Bell as she entered the Wavertree Mystery and saw her look back at Kate Thorpe's house as she pulled the gate after herself. She made direct eye contact with Lucy, tried to explore her features from over the road, and saw that she was emotional. The sorrow in her face stiffened into confusion when she connected that it was Clay in her neighbour's house.

Clay took out her iPhone, dialled Lucy's mobile, and watched her fumble through her coat pockets for her phone. She answered it with her eyes fixed on Clay.

'Hello, Lucy. I can see you.'

'I can see you, DCI Clay. What are you doing in Miss Thorpe's front room?'

'She invited me to come and see her.'

'About what?'

'I'm not sure yet.'

'She has no language and is deaf. Do you want me to come and help? I've known her for a long time and understand much about her.'

'Aren't you on your way to uni?'

'It's Saturday today. I'm going to the Sydney Jones Library to work on my thesis.'

'That's good,' said Clay. 'You won't be busy later on, will you?'

'I have things to do.'

'I'm organising a reconstruction of how you found Marta Ondřej. It's going to be staged soon. We need you to take part. Please make sure you're available and keep your phone on at all times. Goodbye, Lucy.'

She hung up but Lucy stayed where she was, looking back across the road. At the sound of teacups and saucers rattling on a wheeled trolley, Clay dropped the lace curtain but could still see Lucy as she walked into the park, moving at speed towards the spot where Marta was found.

Clay smiled as she turned. Miss Thorpe nodded towards an armchair, so Clay sat down as invited and looked around the walls at the framed religious paintings, noticing that they were all watercolours.

Miss Thorpe poured tea from a china pot and gave Clay a cup on a saucer.

'Thank you. Did you paint these pictures, Miss Thorpe?'

She nodded, with a small proud smile, and sat on the end of a sofa close to Clay, with Mr Rotherham in the other armchair. Miss Thorpe caught his eye and pointed at Clay.

'Miss Thorpe says she saw something on Thursday morning around the time the child was discovered by Lucy Bell.'

'What did you see, Miss Thorpe?'

She shook her head, half-raised her hands and stared at Mr Rotherham's mouth as he set to speak.

'It's too complicated for words,' said Mr Rotherham. 'She can't put it into words or signs but she can make a picture for you. She is making that picture today, and she needs to get it right. She saw something crucial.'

Miss Thorpe nodded and mouthed *Thank you* to her friend.

'Do you want me to tell her about the pictures on the wall?'

He looked at Clay. 'Go and have a close look at the picture above the fireplace, please.'

The heat from the real coal fire was welcome as the flames and smoke licked up the chimney.

Clay stood and moved to the painting. It was of the Virgin Mary, standing apart from people heading in both directions behind her. Dressed traditionally in blue and white with a veil around her hair, the thing that struck Clay was the Virgin's face. It wasn't the traditional beatific, unlined representation. She looked like many young mothers of small children, a little worn out and with the cares of the world upon her. Behind the figures was a stretch of water with the sun setting over the scene.

Clay turned and applauded Miss Thorpe, and enjoyed the smile on her face. 'Miss Thorpe, can you do me a favour? Can you get a pen and a piece of paper and write down a few words about what you saw on Thursday morning?'

She shook her head.

'I'm investigating a very, very serious crime and I haven't got time on my side.'

Clay waited, but the old lady didn't respond.

'When will the picture of what you saw be ready, Miss Thorpe?'

'She may be able to give it to you tomorrow,' said Mr Rotherham. 'She wants to know what you notice about the picture you've just been looking at?'

'I notice it is made with skill, love, care and originality,' replied Clay. 'What about the water and the sunset? Again, beautifully executed in its detail.'

'Sit down, please, DCI Clay,' said Mr Rotherham. 'I have something remarkable to tell you about Miss Thorpe.'

Clay took her seat near the old woman and smiled at her.

'Miss Thorpe saw the Virgin Mary at sunset by the River Mersey. What you can see on that wall was what Miss Thorpe saw with her own eyes two months ago near the Albert Dock. All of these paintings are representations of what Miss Thorpe actually saw.' He pointed at individual paintings as he spoke.

'The Virgin Mary walking the infant Jesus over the road at the lights by Penny Lane. The Sacred Heart of Jesus floating above the lake in Sefton Park on a hot summer's day. Look at the people lakeside. They're all looking at the lake but they cannot see like Miss Thorpe.'

'You've actually seen all this, Miss Thorpe?'

An enigmatic expression formed in her eyes and Clay picked out a picture on the wall behind her.

'You've seen the Virgin Mary standing on the top of the Radio City Tower? In the flesh?'

Miss Thorpe nodded and the hope that Clay had briefly entertained crashed. 'That's amazing, Miss Thorpe, simply amazing.' Clay drank two mouthfuls of tea and stood up. 'I'll leave you to it, and thank you for your hospitality. Let me know when you've finished your picture and we'll arrange to view it. No, no, Mr Rotherham. Stay as you are. I'll see myself out.'

On Grant Avenue, Clay looked at her watch and felt like some powerful energy at work in the universe was laughing hysterically at her expense.

Chapter 85

10.15 am

In the incident room at Trinity Road Police Station, Detective Sergeant Karl Stone and Detective Constable Barney Cole sat in front of five sets of documents on the global fascist movement known as Black Sun.

Stone looked up at Eve Clay as she approached.

'I got your call on my way over here, Karl. You told me you were ready to spill the gravy on Black Sun. I want to know what Barney's artistic skills have led you to track down. Well done, both of you.'

'The only cell that's of any interest, as I see it at the moment, is the American one. The four non-English speaking ones, including the original Italian group, were more like gangs than organisations. You'd be hard pressed to describe the Japanese version of Black Sun as a gang. It was a husband and wife who were so inept that the man they tried to kidnap ended up handing them over to the police within half an hour of the bungled snatch.'

Stone pushed four of the files away and pointed at the one marked 'USA'. 'This is a bit more interesting.' He opened it. 'Have a look at that.'

Clay picked up a black and white photocopy of a picture of four men and three women dressed in the same uniform, standing under a white flag bearing the Black Sun logo. They all wore black trousers, baggy at the hips and tucked in tightly at the knee into black boots, with black shirts and ties. Each of them had a handgun tucked into a shoulder holster. None of them was smiling.

She looked closely at their solemn faces and felt a sensation in her brain, like a light that wouldn't quite go on.

'I want to take this away with me,' she said. Folding the photocopy and placing it in her coat pocket, she made a mental snapshot of the picture.

Stone turned the page and showed Clay pictures of a couple of young black people in their front room, gunshot wounds in their backs, their heads incinerated. In another picture a man was being led away – handcuffed, foot-chained and in a baggy orange jump suit – by prison guards.

Cole read out the caption, '*Death sentence for Emanuel Emanuel*. Strange name, even for a fascist psycho.'

'The Black Sun movement grew out of a Christian fundamentalist group called The Covenant, the Sword and the Arm of the Lord, which was formed in Arkansas back in 1978 by a fundamentalist preacher called James Ellison. The CSA were heavy-duty right-wing religious militants. They used to steal...'

'Christian fundamentalists?' asked Clay.

'Stealing was perfectly justifiable. After David slew Goliath, the Israelites went and plundered the Philistine camp.'

'Thou shalt not steal?' said Cole.

'Don't be pedantic, Barney. Stealing was the bottom rung. They manufactured firearms and had a roaring trade going with all the other right-wing fascist militias and Christian fundamentalists. They burned down a church because it supported gay rights. They assassinated Louis Bryant, a black state trooper. At this point Governor Bill Clinton, as he was at the time, got onto their backs. Seven of the CSA faithful decided the organisation wasn't going far enough, so they left and formed Black Sun.'

'The seven smiley-faced ones beneath the Black Sun flag. They abandoned the names given to them by their parents and assumed Biblical ones. Emanuel Emanuel. Elijah Elijah. Ruth Ruth. Naomi Naomi. David David. Sarah Sarah. Abraham Abraham. At their peak they were thirty-five strong, and that's when things started going wrong. Two of their converts, Isaac Isaac and Micah Micah were FBI agents. Of the thirty-three kosher Black Sun members, twenty-eight are in jail to this day, either on life sentences or on death row. Four are dead and one remains unaccounted for.'

'So what was Black Sun's big plan?' asked Clay.

Stone handed Clay a picture of two people dressed entirely in black, their faces covered by balaclavas. Armed with high-calibre automatic rifles, they saluted with a fist held out sideways, the same fist on the flag above their heads.

'They created a fake black militia called the Black Hand of Justice, whose aim was to exact revenge on white bourgeois scum. Under this umbrella, they went into seven houses and killed seven white families over a two-week period. Thirty-two dead.'

'What were the undercover agents doing?' asked Clay.

'The whole BHJ thing was a secret to everyone in the group except the original seven members. The FBI were the latest recruits and therefore the most mistrusted. The leader of Black Sun, Christopher Darwin, AKA Abraham Abraham, ordered a stop to the killings while the two new recruits were tested out. To describe

Black Sun as utterly paranoid is a massive understatement. The original seven members had the plan and used the other members to do their dirty work. They wanted to spark a racial civil war. They wanted utter carnage.'

Clay worked to make connections with Raymond Dare. 'It's all bad *Boy's Own* stuff. I can easily see how a mentally ill pot-head like Raymond Dare could read up on all this and find it glamorous. All that death and glory nonsense, secrets within secrets, blood and honour, putting the world to rights with a powerful gun. I want to talk to him now.'

The mobile phone on Cole's desk rang out and he jumped to answer it. 'DS Barney Cole speaking. How can I help you?'

As he listened, Cole shifted his gaze from the mid-distance to Clay. 'Thank you, whereabouts did you say?' He smiled at Clay and Stone and held up a thumb. 'That's great, Constable Wilson. Stay with it, please, until we get there with the removal lorry. In the meantime, send me some images of the vehicle.' Cole put the receiver down. 'Burnt-out white Fiat Uno discovered at the site of the Festival Gardens, down by the river. It matches the plates for the one stolen from Moses Street, the one that Raymond Dare used to pick up Dominika Zima.'

'Let me take all the Black Sun files, please.' Clay picked them up. 'Great work, Karl. Could you get yourself over to the Festival Gardens? And Barney, copy me in on any images that come through.'

Chapter 86

10.18 am

'Now that Marta's talking, I believe it's safe to show her the photograph.'

Mr Edison, a tall, gaunt middle-aged man in a sharp black

suit, watched Marta sitting up in bed and colouring in a page on a pad of simple patterns.

Riley looked at the psychiatrist, and then at the random mess the child was making with the felt-tipped pens she had bought for her from Alder Hey's shop.

'Can you stay here, Mr Edison, while I do just that?'

From her bag, Riley took out the printed-off image of the Adamczak brothers, smiling in the evening sunshine at the Albert Dock, and looked at them with trepidation. She recalled Marta's hysterics when she had seen her own reflection in the mirror and dreaded a similar scene now.

She called Clay on her iPhone and was through in two rings. 'Eve, the consultant psychiatrist's said it's OK to show Marta the picture of the Adamczak brothers.'

'I'll stay on the line. How is she?'

'A lot better.' Riley looked at Marta and hoped that a vile memory was transforming with time into a bad and fading nightmare. 'I'll put you on speakerphone.'

'Thank you, Gina.'

Marta looked up at the new, disembodied voice in the room and then back down at her colouring book. She placed the green felt-tipped pen down, picked up a red and went over what she had already coloured and the lines she was supposed to be staying within.

'Kate?' Riley could feel the pulse inside her ears. 'Tell Marta to stop colouring and hold out both her hands.'

With the picture away from Marta's eyes, Riley sat on the edge of the bed and smiled as Kate spoke to the child and took the colouring book and packet of pens away from her. Then the translator pulled down the first of the blinds over the glass partition between Marta's room and the corridor.

'Tell Marta I'm going to show her a photograph of two men.'

The room darkened a little as a bank of cloud passed over the weak winter sun.

'Kate, ask her to tell you if she recognises the men.'

Riley placed her iPhone on the duvet and smiled at Marta as Kate spoke to her.

'Ask her if she understands,' said Riley.

Kate spoke and, after a moment, Marta nodded and almost smiled.

Riley placed the photograph face down on the bed and took in a huge breath. She picked it up by the top left- and right-hand corners and slowly revealed it to Marta.

For a few seconds, Marta's face was blank as her eyes drilled in to the picture of the Adamczak brothers. She looked at Riley and then back at the picture.

She reached out her right hand and touched the picture. Her head bobbed forward and her mouth opened into a crooked smile. She nodded and looked at Riley, who summoned up her willpower to ask, 'Are these the men who took you away?'

Kate translated.

The smile on Marta's face sank as quickly as it had formed, and she dragged her finger across the surface of the photographic paper.

Marta spoke quietly, in hesitant and pause-studded language.

'What did you say, Marta?' asked Riley.

'Two men... the same... the same... place. How can two men who are the same be in the same place?' said Kate.

Riley saw that there was no terror in Marta's eyes but, instead, a light built up.

'Ask her again, Kate. Did these men take you away?'

Marta took the edges of the paper and gently pulled it away from Riley. She shook her head and smiled.

Marta pulled the picture closer, so the tip of her nose was against the surface of the page. She kissed the picture twice and, Riley estimated, it was a kiss to both of their faces.

She sank back onto the bed, pressed the picture onto her chest and folded her arms over it.

Marta looked at Riley and spoke slowly and deliberately, three times.

'What did she say, Kate?'

'He's a nice man this two man one. He kind to me. I'm tired and want to go to sleep now.'

Chapter 87

10.18 am

As she rushed down the corridor towards Interview Suite 1, Clay came face to face with Raymond Dare, escorted by Sergeant Harris and his solicitor.

'No comment,' whispered Raymond, looking directly at Clay as Harris opened the door.

'You haven't listened to a word I've said, have you?' Mr Robson looked on the verge of losing his temper.

Sergeant Harris closed the door of Interview Suite 1.

Clay's iPhone vibrated in her jacket pocket, and she remained on the corridor as she connected to Winters.

'Clive, what have you got?'

'I went to Anfield to the CJ Construction redevelopment project and spoke to the site manager, Damien Wright. He showed me the rotas for the dates that Aneta Kaloza gave us, and there was no sign of the Adamczaks at all. So, it *looks* like they were lying to her.'

'*Looks* like they were lying?' asked Clay.

'After I was done in the site manager's office, I spoke to co-workers there. They told me quite the opposite. The Adamczak brothers were on site during the dates in question. They'd been on site going back weeks. CJ Construction is in a lot of financial trouble at the moment. The company's living hand to mouth. They're paying a whole raft of people cash in hand to cut financial corners, and two of them were Karl and Václav Adamczak. Three other workers confirmed that this was true. The Adamczak brothers even worked Saturday and Sunday the weekend before they died.'

'What kind of hours were they working?'

'Six in the morning until eight or nine at night.'

Coldness swept over Clay. She worked it out. Including travel, the Adamczak brothers were away from their flat for fourteen hours a day.

'Are you still there, Eve?'

'Hold the line for me, please.' A terrible possibility crossed her mind, and the answer lay behind the door of Interview Suite 1. 'The men you talked to – did any of them confirm if the Adamczak brothers had been on site on Monday, 24th November?'

'They hadn't had a day off in weeks.'

'You got names and numbers of these witnesses?'

'Yes, I've got the names and contact details of four people who've got a lot to lose with the Inland Revenue but who are completely at the end of their tether and grieving with it. They were with the Adamczak brothers on the afternoon Marta Ondřej was abducted.'

'Thank you, Clive.'

'You sound pissed off, Eve.'

'I am. The sewer rat in Interview Suite 1 who snatched Marta and killed the Adamczak brothers has been taking the piss out of us.'

As Clay hung up, she made her way towards the front reception desk. 'Sergeant Harris, please tell Aneta Kaloza to make herself available and stay within touch. But for now, she's free to go.'

Then, leaving the Black Sun files with Sergeant Harris, she marched back to Interview Suite 1.

Remaining on her feet, Clay leaned down over Raymond and said, 'I was going to ask you about Black Sun, but I've just learned something that not only says a lot about you, but it also makes it clear that you are sinking deeper and deeper down by the hour. I'm going to collect some evidence you need to look at. I'll be back shortly. While I'm away, I'd like you to think about why you kidnapped Marta Ondřej.'

'No comment. What are you on about?'

'You don't like foreigners, and you don't care how old they are.'

'No comment.'

'That wasn't a question, Raymond. It was a statement. A statement of plain and simple fact.'

Chapter 88

10.30 am

At Liverpool Festival Gardens, hungry seagulls drifting from the River Mersey outnumbered the humans by ten to one, their cawing and screaming loud and hysterical.

DS Karl Stone made his way from his car to the tape around a burned-out Fiat Uno. The two constables watching over the car were shivering, rubbing their hands together against the bitterly cold wind whipping over the water.

Stone snapped on a pair of latex gloves. 'Well done finding the car. What made you drive onto the site?'

'There was a burglary on Moel Famau Close. They took the car keys and the car from outside the house. It was probably kids because they drove the car they'd robbed five minutes earlier into a streetlight and must've escaped on foot. We've been looking for them on Riverside Drive and then we thought, see if they escaped through the Festival Gardens. That's when we came across this.'

'Well, if it's any consolation, you're involved in frying a much bigger fish with this find.'

Stone looked over the Fiat Uno on both sides, then at the front and boot at the rear.

The front end was badly damaged by fire; it looked like the majority of the petrol had been poured over the driver and passenger seats. Scorch marks tapered up the sides of the car but petered out in the metal of the back doors. The boot was relatively unscathed by fire, but had buckled near the lock in a collision of some sort.

Stone turned as a vehicle pulled up near him: DS Terry Mason's Scientific Support van. He continued filming inside the front, through the wound-down window, where oxygen had made its contribution to the blaze. The driver's and passenger's seats were like a hearth that hadn't been cleaned for a long while. The seats in the back were burned, but still kept some semblance of their shape.

He looked at the front of the Fiat Uno where the engine and electrics had been burned out, and listened to the rattle of what sounded like a vehicle carrier making its way deeper into the Festival Gardens.

'Karl?'

'Hi, Terry. You were quick.' Stone led Mason to the boot of the car.

'You were quicker.'

'Can you open the boot for me, please?' asked Stone.

'Paul!' Mason called to Price who was at the back of the Scientific Support vehicle, organising the necessary tools. 'Can you bring me black fingerprint dust and a crow bar. We'll open up the boot and after we've done that, we'll dust the lid for prints.'

A brown and off-white seagull landed three metres away and made a sound like a human being going out of their mind and laughing in the process.

Sergeant Price stuck the lip of the crow bar under the lock and gave it a heavy tug. Metal creaked but nothing shifted. He rubbed his hands and tried again, harder this time.

The boot of the Fiat Uno creaked open and the three men looked inside.

'Oh, well, would you look at that?' said Stone, smiling at the contents of the boot. He pressed record on his iPhone's video camera and thought, *Eve Clay, you're going to love this.*

Chapter 89

10.45 am

As Police Constables Andrew Jones and Sarah O'Neil came to the end of Jacob Street, she commented, 'We've asked forty-eight people so far and everyone hates Raymond Dare. That's quite an achievement. How many doors didn't open?'

Jones checked his notebook. 'On Jacob Street and Isaac Street, sixteen. We'll go back and knock them off when we've tackled David Street. Odds or evens?'

'Odds,' replied O'Neil.

They each went to one side of the road, and O'Neil knocked on 111 David Street. The door opened immediately, and a black teenage boy towered over her.

'I know why you're here. Social media's flying off its tits.' He looked excited and happy. 'How can I help you?'

'We have a Raymond Dare in custody at the moment.'

Two pairs of footsteps hurried down the stairs.

'Get in there!' said an advancing voice, as the other voice laughed.

Two boys and a girl, sixteen to nineteen, filled the doorway.

'Raymond Dare, the fucking fascist bastard,' said the girl. 'What's he done now?'

'I'm here to ask you questions, and I'm not at liberty to divulge information.'

'Facebook says he's been arrested for murder.'

'Do you want him nailed?' asked O'Neil.

'Sure as fuck we do,' replied the girl.

'We're looking for two people. We don't know their real names.

We do know their handles. CJ and Buster. Do you know anyone who goes by those names?'

They all looked blank.

'Do you know what,' said the boy who opened the door. 'I don't hate him just because he called me a fucking nigger every day when we were in the same form group in the same school, until he got sent off to that school for dickheads...'

'You didn't have to put up with that racial abuse from him.'

'Are you suggesting I should have grassed? I'm not a grass.'

'Is there any point in me talking to you?'

'Grassing doesn't apply to murder, especially when it's innocent people who've been killed by some Nazi psycho head-fuck.'

'Why do you really hate him?'

'He tried to make out that his brother was a political prisoner. He wasn't any such thing. He got sent away because he battered three Asian lads after he'd racially abused them. Not according to dickhead Raymond. The Asians started it, Jack finished it.'

As soon as they shut the door, thought O'Neil, *call DC Cole to tell DCI Clay.*

'What do you want to know?' asked the girl.

'Yours is the third street we've tried. No one knows them from their street names. You haven't answered my question. CJ and Buster. Do you know them?'

'No.' Each of them sounded solid, looked O'Neil in the eye as they replied.

'Everyone hates him round here,' said the girl. 'He robs from his neighbours, he sells weed to junior school kids and he's a Nazi. There's nothing at all to like about him. He has no friends round here. I reckon you're looking in the wrong place for these two mates of his. I know nearly everyone round here and there's no CJ or Buster. They probably live in some other part of the city.'

O'Neil knew the girl was talking sense.

'Thanks for your help. One thing. If anyone racially abuses you, tell us straight away. It's not grassing. How can we stop this if people don't report it?'

'You can't stop it. No one can. Ever.'

As soon as the door closed, she got out her mobile phone and called the incident room at Trinity Road Police Station.

PC Jones crossed the road. 'Have you got something?'

'DC Barney Cole speaking.'

'DC Cole, it's PC Sarah O'Neil. I think we need to run a background check on Raymond Dare's brother, Jack. And his mother, too.'

Chapter 90

11.03 am

Clay looked across the desk at Raymond Dare and said, 'Raymond, I want you to know that as you're sitting here with me, and as we speak, I've got a large contingent of police officers knocking door to door, starting on your street, and knocking on all the doors over your neighbourhood, looking for CJ and Buster. They will be found.'

'No comment.' He looked away.

'Look at the things on the table!'

On the table, next to the Black Sun files, were two small evidence bags, Raymond's iPhone, Václav Adamczak's iPhone and two photographs placed face down.

'You and Václav Adamczak have identical models of the same Samsung iPhone. Coincidence? Maybe?'

'No comment.'

'Maybe not?'

'No comment.'

'Do you remember what you were doing on the afternoon of Monday, 24th November?'

'No comment.'

'Let me prompt you, Raymond. You were in the Smithdown Lane area of Toxteth, quite close to the police station. It was day one of your Black Sun project to stir up racial violence...'

'No comment.'

'Black Sun.' Clay tapped the files in front of her.

He looked as if he'd been stung by a bee as he muttered back, 'No comment.'

'Let me tell you what I think's been going on. You abducted a Roma child from the street she lives on. You kept her locked up in a broom cupboard or a lock-up of some kind for eight days, during which time you tortured her and cut off all her hair.'

'No! No comment.'

'Where did you keep her?'

'No comment.'

'We've got footage of you abusing her.'

'No comment.'

'You then did several stupid things in a very short space of time, Raymond. You released Marta. You raped and strangled Dominika Zima, and then burned her. Then you went to Picton Road and killed Karl and Václav Adamczak. Well?'

'No comment.'

'You sent the footage of Marta Ondřej from your phone to Václav Adamczak's phone and planted it under the floorboard along with Marta's hair. You wanted to stir up racial hatred – Czech Roma killing Polish people, then the Polish would retaliate. You knew there was a raw nerve there, you're not as stupid as you're making out. Who were you going to go for next?'

'No comment.'

'But you also wanted to lead us astray. So you stole the following items from these men.'

As she turned over the photographs of Karl and Václav Adamczak, Hendricks poured out two silver crucifixes from the evidence bags onto the table.

'I've never met these fuckers in my life. No comment...'

She pointed to the blown-up photograph of the crucifixes on the Adamczak brothers' chests and pointed at the crucifix Raymond had handed over to Sergeant Harris at the desk.

'No comment.'

'Look at the silver hallmark on the backs of these crosses.'

He closed his eyes and placed his fingers in his ears. 'All the voices say, *Tell the bitch opposite you to fuck off and die.* Fuck off and die, bitch!'

'I'd like to take a pause in this interview,' said Mr Robson.

'I'm happy with that,' replied Clay. 'But first, Mr Robson, please look at the silver hallmark.'

He looked closely at the back of the crucifixes. 'I can see the letters K, W, the numbers 875 and a Romanesque head in profile.' Mr Robson looked back up at Clay, bewildered.

'It's a uniquely Polish silver hallmark,' said Clay. 'It enables us to trace the necklace to Warsaw, where the crucifix was made and hall marked. Karl and Václav Adamczak lived in Pruszków, a small city close to Warsaw.'

Clay and Hendricks sat in silence, creating a man-made void into which Raymond could fall head first.

'I—' Raymond stumbled. 'I-I-I-I...'

'I?'

'I don't know fuck all about the kid, I'm not some fucking nonce, right! Right?'

'And?'

'We shagged Dominika in Otterspool Park, but she was fuck-ing up for it all the way, the fucking foreign slag. I shagged her with pure hate in my heart.'

'We?' asked Hendricks. 'You shouldn't be doing this on your own, Raymond. Would CJ and Buster save your skin? Hmm? Give us their names. That could be a big game-changer for you.'

'Raymond,' said Mr Robson.

Raymond looked at his solicitor as if he'd just entered the room.

'Listen to me.' Mr Robson used his hands to create a shield

between Clay and Hendricks's eyes and the motion of his lips. His voice dropped and he whispered into Raymond's ear.

When the solicitor finished speaking, Raymond looked directly at Clay. 'You're asking me to give up the only people that I love in this world. He's asking me to do the same. You want their real names?'

'Yes,' replied Hendricks.

Raymond smiled. 'CJ's real name is *no*, and Buster's real name is *comment*.'

Chapter 91

11.11 am

Detective Sergeant Gina Riley sat next to Edward Storey, Alder Hey's head of security. They faced a bank of screens showing live-time CCTV footage from across the hospital.

'I've got something to show you, Detective Sergeant Riley. Based on the time-frame you gave me relating to Marta Ondřej's visitor, I've worked backwards from the arrival of the priest and traced his journey to the moment he stepped through the front door of Alder Hey. I've edited it together onto one continuous piece of film. Are you ready to watch?'

'Yes. I'll then need to take this film away, Mr Storey.'

He smiled at Riley. 'If it's what you're looking for, I'll send it directly to your phone after you've OKed it.' He pressed play.

Riley saw the revolving doors at the front of the hospital. The time on the screen was 12:51. Within moments, a woman with a baby in a carrycot entered and then, seconds later, a man dressed as a priest followed.

'That him?' asked Edward Storey.

'That's definitely him. Do you know him, Mr Storey?'

'He's definitely not a member of Alder Hey's chaplaincy team.'

There was a cut. Then she saw the man walking across the large reception, past the fast-food concessions and pausing at the information desk to ask a question. Cut. The man started walking up the staircase. Cut. He walked past the first floor and the second floor before the CCTV caught him walking onto the third floor in the direction of Marta Ondřej's hospital room.

Edward Storey paused the film. 'He's on the ward for under two minutes, then it's the same story over again but in reverse.'

'Thank you very much. I'm sure this'll prove helpful to us.'

'Do you know him?'

'Me, personally? No. But I'm hoping we'll be able to ID him soon.'

Edward Storey unlocked his phone and sent the footage to Riley's phone. In silence, she watched it again, double-checking that everything she'd seen on the security monitor was in place. Then she dialled Clay.

'Eve, I've got Alder Hey's CCTV footage of the priest.'

'Send it to me. I'll look at it and then pass it on to the team. Thanks, Gina.'

Chapter 92

11.36 am

In the incident room at Trinity Road Police Station, Detective Constable Barney Cole looked up from his laptop and let out a long thin whistle.

'What's happening?' asked Clay, walking into the room along-side Hendricks, as an incoming message arrived from Riley.

'I'm doing some digging on the Dare family. Carmel, the mother, is squeaky clean. Raymond has had several close encounters with Merseyside Constabulary but he's like a criminal cat with nine lives. Never been charged.'

'You're going to tell me something about Jesus-On-A-Stick, aren't you? What's he been done for?'

'Grievous bodily harm. Racially motivated. He battered the lights out of three Asian teenagers, all by himself, on the waterfront outside the Echo Arena. He claims they tried to mug him, and that there was no racial abuse at all from him. They said he tried to rob them but that he called them all the names under the sun before, during and after a sustained and vicious assault.'

'What did he get?'

'Two years in Altcar.'

'So, he'll have served one?'

'I don't know, but I'll find out for you.'

'Anything since he was released?'

'Not a thing. He's been a good lad, a sunbeam for Jesus it seems. Maybe he converted in Altcar.'

'Thank you, Barney.' She weighed up the news. 'Bill, you've got Jack Dare's contact details.'

'I have.'

'We need to talk to him as soon as possible.'

The phone on Cole's desk rang out and he picked up the receiver.

'Do you know where he's staying, Bill?'

'Last I knew, over the road from his home with a neighbour.'

'Give Jack a ring, tell him you want to have a chat about Raymond. Tell him you'll pick him up and bring him in to Trinity Road. Bring Carmel as well to soften the impact.'

'I'll get on to it straight away.'

Clay played the footage she'd just received from Riley. As the film unfolded, she whispered, 'Jesus... What were *you* doing around Marta Ondřej?'

Chapter 93

11.35 am

Lucy Bell stood facing Kate Thorpe in the old woman's parlour. In the fireplace, flames licked round the birch log recently placed on the hot bed of coals.

As she glanced at the large sheets of poster papers placed face down on the table to the left of the bay window, she took the consecrated host from the black box that housed it, held the wafer up towards heaven between the thumbs and index fingers of both hands and looked Kate in the eye.

'Behold the Lamb of God

Behold him who takes away the sins of the world

Blessed are those called to the supper of the Lamb.'

Lucy's eyes were fixed on Kate as she extended the host towards her.

'The Body of Christ,' said Lucy.

'Amen,' mouthed Kate, as Lucy placed the host on her left palm.

Kate went to pick up the host with her right index finger and thumb, but the wafer slipped out of her hold and fell to the carpet.

In silence, the women looked at each other, neither one moving.

'That was very clumsy of you, Kate. Pick up the Body of Christ.'

She pointed at the floor and, as Kate stooped to pick up the host, Lucy turned and walked to the table. She flicked through the paintings, glancing over her shoulder as Kate advanced with the host between her right thumb and index finger.

'Don't! Don't, Kate! Don't come near me...'

Kate stopped and placed the host on her tongue, her eyes fixed on Lucy.

Lucy picked out one of the sheets.

'When you saw me on your doorstep, you turned these pages over. Like you didn't want me to see them. Why? I come here to share the Body of Christ. Why hide things from me? What is this, Kate? Is this a vision you had? Because if it is a vision, you are the only one who saw it. And the only one who believes it.'

Lucy showed Kate another of her own paintings. 'A vision.' She held up a third picture. 'Another vision.'

Lucy started rolling the three paintings into a tube, watching Kate intensely.

'Are you smiling, Kate? You are happy. That is good. My father says he fears for you. He fears for your sanity. This is a private conversation he has had with me. I too fear for your sanity.'

Lucy's hands tightened around the pile of papers as the fire danced up the chimney.

'I used to visit a man in Broad Oak. He had paranoia and schizophrenia. He also had religious visions but they weren't good ones like yours. I was his only visitor, except for the devils and hobgoblins who visited him in visions. One Tuesday I turned up for my visit and his nurse told me that he had killed himself. It was most sad. His nurse and I were the only ones at his funeral. When he was alive, when he had the power of speech, he used to talk about his visions, and words being words, they used to drift into the air and disappear. All gone. But you express your visions...' Lucy pointed at the pictures. 'Like this.'

Lucy's face puckered into a grimace. 'I have never seen you laugh before, Kate.' Lucy smiled. 'What is so funny?'

Kate lifted her right hand and pointed at Lucy.

'That is hurtful to my feelings but I too have laughed at you behind your back. We must forgive each other. And as for these pictures? People will laugh in your face. Don't you understand?'

Kate lifted the fireguard away from the fire and pointed at the flames.

'Thank you for listening to my advice. Let us pray.' Lucy threw the paintings into the flames and watched as the fire consumed them. 'For Kate. May the world not laugh at an old lady who has religious visions. Lord, help me to protect her from the derision of mankind. Amen.'

Lucy collected her communion box and headed for the door.

'Don't worry about seeing me out. You stay here and enjoy the fire.'

Kate heard the front door open and close, then sat and watched her paintings turning to ash.

Chapter 94

12.01 pm

DCI Eve Clay stood on the step of the vestry next door to St Luke's Roman Catholic Church as Detective Sergeant Karl Stone tried the front door of the church.

'Locked back and front,' said Stone, walking down the church steps.

Clay rang the bell a second time and banged on the door.

'I'm coming, I'm coming, hold your horses.' Father Aaron's voice was light as he made his way towards the front door.

She looked at the spy hole and felt the weight of Father Aaron's presence behind the door. It opened, and Father Aaron Bell smiled at Clay.

'Come in, come in. Have you come to ask news of Sister Ruth?'

'No.'

'It's just that I haven't heard back yet. But do come in. I'll get the kettle on.'

'No, thank you. Father Aaron, I need to talk to you but it isn't going to happen here. It's going to be at Trinity Road Police Station.'

'Whatever's wrong?' The lightness left his voice and his face creased into concern and surprise.

'I'm not obliged to tell you. Please come with us.'

'Can't you give me an inkling?'

'No.'

'Is it about Lucy?'

'No, it's about you. Go and get your coat, and be as quick as you can.'

Stone crossed the threshold and headed towards the back of the house.

'Where are you going?' asked Father Aaron.

'He's going to secure the back.'

'I'm not going to run away. I've done nothing wrong.'

'Your coat. Now please, Father Aaron.'

As he headed back inside, Clay looked down the line of houses on Grant Avenue and into the Mystery. She saw a familiar figure walking up the road, dressed from head to foot in black, shuffling awkwardly across the snow and ice.

Lucy Bell stopped for a moment then picked up her pace when she saw Clay standing on her doorstep.

'What is happening, DCI Clay?'

'I can't discuss it with you on the street, Lucy.'

She came closer, her face deadpan.

'Where have you been?' asked Clay.

'I've been administering the consecrated host to the sick and elderly. Why are you here?'

Father Aaron Bell appeared in the doorway.

'Where are you going, Dad?'

'To have a chat with DCI Clay. Listen. Get into the house. Stay at home until I return. There's nothing to worry about.'

Stone followed Father Aaron as he walked out of the house and Lucy asked, 'Who is this man?'

'Lucy, in the house, now.'

She stood on the threshold. Clay felt her eyes in her back as they walked towards Clay's car.

Father Aaron turned and looked back. 'Don't be disobedient, Lucy.' There was a deep-seated anger in his voice. Clay heard the front door slam shut and wondered how long it would take the duty magistrate to issue the search warrant for Father Aaron's house and church.

Chapter 95

1.10 pm

'We've already had your fingerprints and DNA, Jack,' said Detective Sergeant Bill Hendricks. 'Thank you for cooperating and letting Sergeant Harris take an up-to-date photograph of you.'

'Why are we here, Detective Sergeant Hendricks?' asked Carmel Dare, quietly.

'Basically you're here because Raymond's here.'

'I don't understand,' said Jack.

'Raymond's here because he's up to his eyes in it. He's committed three racially motivated murders. CCTV tells us that there were two other people involved.'

'Do we need a solicitor?' asked Carmel.

'I can suspend the interview until you choose one from the list, and we can start again.'

They looked at each other.

'I'm happy to go on,' said Jack.

'Me too,' agreed his mother. 'So to speak.' A fresh wave of sadness washed through her eyes.

'It's standard procedure to investigate the family and friends of a person in custody who's about to be charged with an extremely serious crime, and we've done just that. Carmel, nothing came up about you. But Jack, you served time for committing a hate crime.'

Hendricks observed Jack forcing himself not to fall into a thousand pieces.

'Do you want to tell me about it? And if so, do you still not want legal representation?'

'The legal system from top to bottom hasn't been a friend to me,' replied Jack. 'No, I don't want a solicitor. I just want a massive miscarriage of justice to be overturned and to get my good name back. But that's not going to happen, is it?'

Carmel put her hand on his arm and said, 'Just tell it to DS Hendricks as it happened.'

Hendricks watched Jack as he poured himself a glass of water, and noticed a slight tremor in his hands.

'I went out for a run. It was seven o'clock-ish and twilight. I dipped down onto the promenade from the Dingle and headed towards the Albert Dock. When I turned back to run the other way, I saw these three figures walking towards me. I looked over my shoulder and saw that there was no one behind me and there was no one behind them. The closer I came to them and them to me, I saw they weren't as tall or as big as me, but I was outnumbered.'

Jack stopped and downed the water in one.

'I was a few metres away from them when they fanned out, blocking the space on the path. I stopped so I could move through the narrow gaps between them without barging into them. I walked to the gap that was riverside, and they closed it down. I said, *All right, lads, joke over, let me past.*

The smallest of the three said, *Who said we're joking, you fucking white piece of shit? Give us your fucking money, or we'll kick the shit out of you!*

Money? I've got no money. Why should I have money when I'm out running?

No money? another one said. *Then we'll just have to kick the shit out of your white arse anyway.*

In one moment, I had to make a decision. Fight or flight? I could feel a pull in my right ankle from an old injury. Flight wasn't going to save me. I grabbed the hair of the lad in front of me and smashed the side of his head into the lad next to him. I grabbed the other lad's head and smashed their skulls against each other. As they dropped to the ground, I saw the third lad kicking away at me. He was aiming for my groin. I caught his foot before it landed and threw him to the ground. As he got there, I kicked him in the head. I worked it out. The whole incident lasted between three and seven seconds. I looked at them on the ground, bleeding and pathetic, begging for mercy and offering me money to go away. *I'd rather starve than touch your money, you racist bastards,* I told them. I continued with my run, thought nothing more of it and then two days later there was a knock on our door, and the police took me in for questioning.

'They said I'd racially abused them and made threats and demands for money. When they refused to give in to me, they claimed I went into a racist tirade, calling them all the fucking Paki cunts, bastards, arseholes and pricks under the sun. They then asserted in their witness statements to police and under oath in court that I'd told them I was going to follow them home and rape their mothers and sisters.

'No one believed my side of the story. From the uniformed coppers who took me in and the DCs who interviewed me, over and over and over again, through to the jury and the judge who sentenced me. No one believed me.

'But here's the thing, Mr Hendricks. One of the lad's fathers was a doctor. Another one's father had his own highly successful business, and the third lad's father was an investment banker. They all lived in Woolton.'

Jack pointed to himself and indicated his mother. 'I was out of work at the time through no fault of my own. I lived in the Dingle with my mother who works in a fish and chip shop and my younger, vulnerable brother.

'At the end of the court case the predominantly white jury found me unanimously guilty. I suppose they didn't want to appear racist. I was given two years by the judge, and when I was being taken down to the cells, I looked up at the three of them in the public gallery. They were smirking at me. That was the last time I ever saw them.'

Jack moved the bottom of the glass against the surface of the table and then stopped. 'Are you going to question me some, Detective Sergeant Hendricks?'

'Your brother's here because he's a prime suspect on three

counts of murder. We know he didn't act alone. Were you one of his accomplices, Jack?'

'No. Absolutely not. If I was going to murder anyone, surely it would have been the lying Pakistanis who took my liberty and wrecked my life. Think about it, Detective Sergeant Hendricks.'

'You deny any involvement in the murders of Karl Adamczak, Václav Adamczak and Dominika Zima?'

'I categorically deny any involvement in these murders. One of the greatest of the Ten Commandments says, *You shall not kill*. I've changed my mind.' Jack turned to his mother. 'I don't want a solicitor. I don't trust them. But I need one, Mum.'

'I'll give you the list, Jack,' said Hendricks.

'With respect, I'm not going to answer any more of your questions until I have legal representation. Who's representing Raymond?

'John Robson.'

'Is he good?'

'I'd employ him if I was in police custody.'

'Then I'd like Mr Robson to represent me too.'

Chapter 96

1.30 pm

'This is very different to the last time we were together in a room such as this, don't you agree?' said Father Aaron Bell, sitting across the table from Clay. 'Do you have to say those words every time you interview someone?'

'Yes.'

Father Aaron looked at the brown bag on the table between them.

'What's this?' he asked.

'It's an evidence bag.'

'What's inside it?'

'Evidence. We'll come to that later.'

He looked back over his shoulder and up at the video camera high in the corner of the room. Father Aaron smiled as he looked directly at Clay. 'Is that—'

'It's filming the interview and recording the sound. The box on the desk is making an audio recording.'

He nodded. 'How can I help you?'

'I want to show you a film that I've transferred from my iPhone to this laptop so that you can get a better view.'

'And what is the film about?'

'It's about you, Father Aaron. Watch this, please.' She turned the laptop round and, pressing play, scrutinised his face.

Father Aaron watched the sequence without any facial expression, not a trace of surprise. 'It's all very *1984*, all these surveillance cameras.'

'Keep watching, Father Aaron.'

He leaned in closer to the screen and a smile drifted over his eyes. 'I've just walked onto the ward at Alder Hey. And now I'm leaving the ward.'

A glaze came over his eyes as if something was shutting down in his brain. He blinked slowly, twice, and life came back. 'It's finished now, DCI Clay, and I have to say it was rather dull.'

'Want to see it again?'

'No, I don't like looking at pictures of myself, certainly not moving ones.'

'Would you like to explain to me what was going on in the film?'

'It's perfectly clear what was going on. I went to the hospital to give a gift to an extremely unfortunate child. End of story. Don't you agree?'

'No, I don't agree.'

'What's the problem?'

'A child goes missing for over a week. By the laws of statistics, she should be dead. But then her captor, or captors, release her. That never happens. Child abductors don't set the key witness to their crimes free. We know the abductor has extreme fascist and pro-Nazi views. Your daughter Lucy discovers her in a public park close to your home and church, and promptly abandons her before we can get there. You go to Alder Hey to give my colleague DS Riley a gift to pass on to the child – a set of rosary beads. These are connections, Father Aaron. Connections I'd like to explore with you.'

'All right, DCI Clay. Let me explain something to you. I'm only telling you this because you're clearly suspicious about my motives in giving Marta Ondřej a set of rosary beads. I visit Alder Hey on a regular basis to give small gifts to children I read about in the media, children who have been hurt or harmed either accidentally or through the malice of others. Three weeks ago, I went to Alder Hey to see Eden Hart, the little boy with 50 per cent burns and the only surviving member of his family following a colossal house fire. In both cases, I left a set of rosary beads and prayed for them, for their recovery, for their acceptance of what had happened to them, that they would grow strong and move on. Why don't you check back further and see the CCTV of me visiting the burns unit, when I did exactly the same for little Eden Hart?'

'Did your daughter call 999 when Eden Hart's family home went up in flames?'

'No, she didn't.'

'Then, for the purposes of what I'm investigating at the moment, I'm not really interested in your visit to Eden Hart. If Lucy *had* called 999 and you had then shown up at the burns unit, I *would* have wanted to talk to you, just as I am doing now. Crimes are solved by either closing down connections or dismissing them as coincidences.'

'He's not the only one. There are dozens of children I've tried to extend a little hope to. And adults as well, DCI Clay. Both Lucy and I try to do our best to live by the church's corporal works of mercy, and that includes visiting the sick and the imprisoned. I never imagined in all my years that I would be taken in to a police station for visiting a child in hospital.'

In the silence that followed, Clay and Father Aaron stared each other down.

'She didn't like the rosary beads. In fact she became quite agitated when she had them in her hands,' said Clay, quietly.

She held back the rest of Riley's email report: how Marta had grown agitated when looking at the corridor outside her room where the priest had recently stood, and the child's words: *Catch the Devil. I want my hair.*

'Are you seriously thinking of charging me with visiting a sick, distressed child and leaving her a gift?'

Behind his bushy grey-black beard, Clay imagined a victorious smile forming.

'What you've done isn't against the law. But it has forced me to ask a set of questions that only you can answer.'

'And have I answered these questions to your satisfaction, DCI Clay?'

'For now.'

'Can I also tell you, given the sensitivity of Marta's situation, I tried to do this visit through Father James Dwyer, the senior Catholic priest in Alder Hey's chaplaincy, but he's been incommunicado for three days and nights. I believe he's been at the bedside of a dying infant. James and I have been friends for many years.'

'Is that how you knew which ward she was on?' asked Clay.

'Yes, through the chaplaincy. Sister Agnes gave me the information.'

'So, in short, Father Aaron, this hospital visiting is regular practice for you?'

'It's a corporal work of mercy.'

'You asked Detective Sergeant Riley if Marta had spoken since she'd been admitted to hospital. Why did you ask that?'

'Lucy told me that she thought the child was mute. I wanted

to find out if that was the case. It was like a thorn in my heart to think that the poor child was unable to communicate. Are we done now?'

'This isn't the only matter I want to speak to you about.'

Clay reached into the evidence bag on the table and produced an address book.

She opened it at the C page and showed it to Father Aaron.

'Do you recognise the handwriting?'

'No.'

'Do you recognise the language that the names and addresses are written in?'

He looked and thought about it. 'Polish.'

'Do you know any Polish people?'

'Yes. I know Karl and Václav Adamczak.'

Clay turned the page back to the B section of the address book, then turned the open address book towards him, and pointed to his name and contact details.

'Why do you have their address book, DCI Clay?'

'Because they were murdered in their flat on Picton Road.'

He frowned and a look of confusion was overtaken by shock. 'Say that again please, DCI Clay?'

'Karl and Václav Adamczak were murdered in their flat on Picton Road. You didn't hear about it through the media?' He shook his head. 'Their address book was found in their flat. The names and addresses are mostly based in Poland, but you're one of three people in England who they saw fit to detail in their address book. One of them is a mate from the building sites. Do you know Mickey Nolan?'

'No.'

'The other is a female friend from back home who lives in Liverpool. Do you know Aneta Kaloza?'

'I know of her, but I've never met her.'

'How do you know them?'

'I know Václav better than I know Karl. Václav shares the same devotion to the Virgin Mary that I do. We met in the Lady

Chapel in the Metropolitan Cathedral, beneath the giant statue of Mary holding the upraised arms of the infant Jesus. I take confession there each week. Václav was so strong in his devotion to the Virgin Mary, it was awe-inspiring. How did they die?'

'It's an ongoing investigation. I can't divulge the details to you.'

Father Aaron's eyes filled with tears that rolled silently into the jungle of his beard.

'Did Václav tell you about his feelings towards the Virgin Mary?'

'No. He had very little English and I have no Polish.'

'Father Aaron, if he had little English and you had no Polish, how do you know about his devotion to Mary?'

'Two ways. Faith of Václav's kind needs no language to communicate its strength and power. I could see it, I could feel it emanating from him as we prayed together in silence. There were times when he was in a state of rapture.'

'You prayed together?'

'Many, many times. In the Lady Chapel in the cathedral. Sundays mainly, because he was a working man. The first time I saw him he was on his knees, praying in silence, and the air around him was alive with electrical spiritual fervour. There were times when... when, I don't admire myself for this but there were times we prayed together when I felt his closeness to the Virgin Mary was such that I envied him. I actually envied another man's spiritual gift. What kind of a priest does that make me?'

He fell into the kind of silence borne of profound shame.

'You said there were two ways you understood about Václav's faith? What was the second?'

'The second? Mr Zięba, their landlord and the owner of the Polish delicatessen, talked to me about Václav's lengthy outpourings about his faith in general and the Virgin Mary in particular. Every time I went into Mr Zięba's shop, he used to update me. I used to go back to buy things I didn't need just to hear the latest instalment.'

'So, Václav Adamczak loved the Virgin Mary?'

'His love was the finest I ever witnessed.'

'You really had no idea about them being murdered?'

'I've had a lot on my mind lately, with Lucy finding the missing child and then leaving her on her own. The thought of her being abandoned by my daughter keeps coming back to me, and each time I feel a fresh sense of horror. And guilt. What could I have done in raising Lucy that made her act in this manner? She committed a sin of omission but the cause of it was mine. I've not watched television for weeks. And the only radio I listen to is Radio Three. They don't report regional murders.'

'Then I'm sorry to have broken the news to you, Father Aaron. Is there anything you wish to add?'

'I can't think of anything.'

'So Václav Adamczak truly loved the Virgin Mary?'

'Truly, he loved her with all his heart and soul.'

Father Aaron shook his head and looked down at the table as Clay formally closed the interview.

'Thank you for your time, Father Aaron. I appreciate it. You're free to go now.'

He stood and shook her hand across the table. As she opened the door for him, Clay asked, 'How old was the Virgin Mary when she conceived Jesus through the power of the Holy Spirit?'

'Her age isn't stated in the Gospels, but it's widely accepted, given cultural norms of the place and time she lived in, that she was thirteen years of age.'

'How times change,' said Clay, as Father Aaron headed for the doors leading into reception. 'Oh, Father Aaron, just for your information, I met two of your parishioners.'

He turned. 'Who?'

'Kate Thorpe and Mr Rotherham.'

Father Aaron looked perplexed but, fixing his face, asked, 'How did you meet them?'

'Miss Thorpe visited Trinity Road Police Station briefly, but couldn't recall what she came in for. Then Mr Rotherham phoned on her behalf and we arranged to meet in her home in Grant Avenue.'

'And you have had this meeting?'

'Yes, we have.'

'Why did they want to meet you?'

'He acts as her voice and she's an incredible artist. For some reason they wanted to show me her paintings. I got the feeling it was a pretext and that there's more to come. Can you think why they wanted to meet me?'

'I have no idea at all.'

'Her pictures, her religious visions? They seem so real. They're so… vivid. Kate Thorpe and Mr Rotherham, they're a remarkable pair, don't you agree?'

Chapter 97

2.33 pm

Poppy Waters placed two small evidence bags on DC Barney Cole's desk, one bag marked 'Raymond Dare' and one marked Václav Adamczak'.

'What's come off their phones, Poppy?' asked Clay.

'Robert Baliński, the Polish translator, worked right through Václav's phone with me technically assisting. Two things stood out on it. One were the pictures of young girls – nothing lurid, just lots of them, and a raft of flirty messages to and from Václav on Messenger. There are hundreds of pictures of teenage girls and a lot of them have clearly been taken without the children's knowledge or consent.'

'How do you mean?' asked Cole.

'There are pictures taken on the streets and in restaurants, public places in which the girls are going about their daily business, completely unaware that they were being photographed. Some of them were posed, but the majority were taken as life rolled on.'

'Definitely no pornography?'

'I couldn't find anything sinister, nothing from the deep or dark web.'

'Did he pretend to be a teenage boy to the girls he communicated with on Messenger?'

'No, he was upfront about his age and identity.'

'What was the other notable thing on Václav's phone?'

'There were hundreds of images of young girls, but there were thousands of the Virgin Mary.'

'Was there anything racist or political? Anything to suggest he had far-right views?'

'Absolutely not. According to Robert his politics were minimal, but if you had to give him a political label, it would be green. He was mildly into the environment. There was the odd moan about multinational companies and the harm they were doing to the planet, but that was it. It came across like a haphazard sixth-form rant.'

'Based on what Robert told you, how would you sum him up in a few words?'

'Religious donkey. Simpleton. Arrested development.'

'Can the same be said for Raymond Dare?' asked Cole.

'Raymond Dare makes Hitler look like Ghandi. He's into the English Defence League but he hates the BNP because they're too soft. I shouldn't be laughing, but it was the way you kind of compared Raymond Dare's politics with Václav Adamczak's hit-and-miss woolly liberalism.' Poppy took a deep breath as the lightness evaporated from her. 'He's in the process of writing a manifesto for the political party he's setting up with his lieutenants CJ and Buster, the English Truth and Justice Party. I found it on his phone. Once he's seized power, with the help of the generals, the RAF and the Royal Navy, and the English Truth and Justice Party are firmly lodged in 10 Downing Street, there will be no more elections, nationally or locally. All foreign nationals and those with foreign ancestry will be rounded up by the army and militias and herded into football stadiums. The young women will be separated out to serve as sex slaves in state-sponsored brothels to reward *good* citizens. The men, boys and women deemed too old or unattractive will be executed on a live television entertainment programme called *Killing Time Is Here Embrace It*. The ones who are fit and healthy will be organised into slave-labour units. Babies will be bred in laboratories and young people harvested for their bodily organs, to be sold on the global health market, creating a vast economic base for the UK economy. It just goes on and on and on. His views on Hitler are astonishing. According to Raymond and his whacked-out friends, Hitler just didn't go far enough.'

As she processed Poppy's account, Clay felt despair for the human condition that could envisage such misery.

'Black Sun – anything about that?'

'Yes. According to Raymond, Black Sun is the foundation stone for the fascist revolution. He was the captain of his Black Sun organisation and his plan was this: race war. Kidnap, murder, rape, mutilation. Crimes committed by Raymond's group would be set up to look like, say, the work of Pakistanis targeting Indians. Revenge attacks would follow. Each time the stakes get higher. Blacks against Asians, Jews against Arabs, Chinese against Southeast Asian nations. Etcetera. Get the ethnics to cleanse each other.'

'Have you got a paper copy of the English Truth and Justice Party manifesto, Poppy?' asked Clay.

Poppy reached into her bag and handed Clay a two-centimetre thick wad of white A4 paper. She opened it at a random page and marvelled at the writing.

Nigus, tha fynil selushun

'*Niggers, the final solution*,' Clay read out loud before skimming and scanning other pages of phonically plausible insanity. 'The spelling's Chaucerian, real old English.' She stopped and burst out laughing.

'Does he really believe that Ryanair and easyJet will fly every black British national to the Democratic Republic of Congo in exchange for a 10 per cent cut of all the deportees' assets?'

The fabric of Raymond Dare's logic played out swiftly in her mind and the nonsense that had just made her laugh was replaced by sombre questions she kept to herself.

Can I really, she asked herself, *believe a single word that comes out of his mouth?*

The door of the incident room opened and Hendricks walked in with a smile on his face that promised good news.

'The DNA report on Dominika Zima's skirt has come back. Raymond Dare was definitely with her on the night she was murdered. It's his semen.'

Chapter 98

2.59 pm

On her way to Interview Suite 1, Clay made a call to Sergeant Harris on the front desk.

'Can you please pull Raymond Dare from his cell and bring him to suite 1.'

'No problem, Eve. Hang on...'

In the background, she heard the voice of an elderly man that she recognised immediately.

'I'm talking to her right now. Eve, Mr Rotherham has just rolled up at reception and he's most insistent. He's got something for you and he wants to hand it to you personally.'

'I'm coming right now.'

As she came through the swing doors into reception, Clay noticed that Mr Rotherham was sitting on the same seat used by Father Aaron Bell on his first visit to Trinity Road Police Station.

He stood up with a blue cardboard tube in his hand, which he extended to Clay.

'She made two copies of three separate paintings. She wrote down what they are and asked me to explain the pictures to you. It's to do with Marta Ondřej.'

Clay withheld the words *Waste of my time,* and in spite of wondering what possible use the contents of the tube could be, said, 'Sergeant Harris, hold back on Raymond Dare. I'll see him after I've spoken with Mr Rotherham.'

In Interview Suite 1, Mr Rotherham sat next to Clay as she took the papers from the tube. She unrolled the three sheets and flattened them on the table.

Clay recognised the first picture as a representation of the Wavertree Mystery on the morning Marta was discovered, a view from Kate Thorpe's parlour window. Behind the black railings, fog and mist sat on top of the grass and in the distance beyond the railings a small figure – a vertical dash – stood on the spot where Clay had first seen Marta. A larger dash closer to the railings, which Kate Thorpe had managed through great artistic technique to energise – was moving away from Marta and out of the Mystery.

'What did Miss Thorpe tell you about this painting?'

'It's what she saw when the little girl was discovered. She saw two figures enter the park. They weren't clear. This is the point at which the person who abandoned Marta was heading in the direction of Kate's house and the houses of dozens of other potential witnesses, and then turned around suddenly and headed away from the houses on Grant Avenue. She said, *It was as if the person suddenly realised that other people could have seen them.* She said, *They were acting like they were panic-stricken.*

'Is there anything else you need to draw my attention to in this picture?' asked Clay.

'No. We can move on to the next now.'

Clay moved the image across the table and came to a second picture, which at first glance was a replica of the first. She looked at it closely and saw the railings of the Wavertree Mystery and the mist that swamped it. Looking at the background, she was relieved to find that the Virgin Mary and the infant Jesus had not suddenly made a guest appearance. Instead she saw two blurred lines around the spot where she had first seen Marta standing.

'Mr Rotherham, can you tell me about this painting?'

'Kate didn't know who the people in the painting were when she witnessed this. But now she does. This is the moment when Lucy Bell was with Marta Ondřej and Lucy called the emergency services.'

Clay focused on the blurred figures of Lucy and Marta and wished with all her heart for an epiphany, that the picture would somehow yield some profound hidden detail. It took moments for her to realise that she was guilty of wishful thinking.

'Can we move on, Mr Rotherham?'

'We can.'

Clay slid the second painting onto the first and felt the force of a hammer smack into the centre of her forehead as she turned her attention to the third picture.

She started from the top and worked her way down, left to right, through Kate Thorpe's picture of the heart of St Luke's Church. Clay noticed the details of the church's interior: paint hanging in scrolls from the plasterwork above the altar and the statue of Jesus dying on the cross that overlooked the whole scene.

Father Aaron Bell stood behind the altar, the blessed sacrament between his upraised fingers and hands, his eyes closed as he showed the transformed Body of Christ to the congregation.

She looked at the pews in front of Kate Thorpe's vantage point and saw the backs of two heads: Mr Rotherham and another elderly worshipper, a woman.

'Jesus,' she said under her breath, as her eyes fanned to the right of the altar and pinpointed the detail that had drawn her initial attention. She checked, checked again, and felt her blood turn thick in her veins as her heart rushed to pump it round her body.

In the doorway of the vestry, a teenage girl with a shaven head and dressed in striped pyjamas stood looking out, lost and confused, her hands raised in surrender to nothing.

'I couldn't see her from where I was sitting. Nor could Iris from where she was sitting. The only one who could see her was Kate.'

'What happened next, Mr Rotherham?'

'Father Aaron opened his eyes and saw Kate walking down the aisle towards her. She – Marta? Marta took fright and walked back into the vestry. At the time, I thought Kate was going up to the altar for communion. Then Father Aaron commanded Kate to go and sit down; it wasn't time for communion yet. I saw that. I heard that. I did. I was amazed at the tone of Father Aaron's voice. He said, *Your visions must never get in the way of the consecration of the bread and wine into the body and blood of Christ. This is sacrilege, Kate. Are your visions the work of the Lord or Satan, perhaps?*'

'What happened next?'

'Communion. And silence. After the blessing at the end of mass, he told us to go home and pray for Kate, for the balance of her mind, and to speak to no one of what happens in the house of the Lord. Amen? Amen.'

Heading for the door of the interview suite, Clay dialled Riley on her iPhone and said, 'Gina, show the footage of Father Aaron Bell to Marta Ondřej. Please stay on the line as you do so.'

She directed her attention to Mr Rotherham. 'Thank you for your help, sir, but I'm going to have to ask you to leave.'

As Mr Rotherham shuffled to the open door of the interview suite, Clay heard Riley instruct Kate to tell Marta that she was about to see a film of the man who brought her rosary beads.

'If you go through the swing doors, Mr Rotherham, Sergeant Harris will show you out. Thanks again for your help.'

The sounds of an alien language filtered into Clay's ear.

'Mr Rotherham, have you spoken with or seen Miss Thorpe today?'

'No. No, I haven't. Father Aaron was so rude to Kate. It was unthinkable. The three of us have decided to worship at St Paul's instead.'

'I am sorry for your upset, Mr Rotherham.'

Clay closed the door and waited.

More impenetrable language flooded Clay's senses, followed by a dense silence.

Marta spoke and Kate translated.

'He is the devil who cut my hair. He is the devil who locked me up.'

The talking stopped and the screaming began.

'Gina, I'm going to instruct a family liaison officer to watch over Marta. I need you back in the fold.'

Marta's screams grew louder, their intensity deepening with each outpouring of terror.

'I know you'll want to stay with her...'

Clay heard Riley leave the room and close the door.

'I don't think I can take much more. We have what we need.'

Riley's footsteps echoed down the corridor as she walked out of Marta Ondřej's life.

'I've done all I can here. I'll be much more use to everyone back at Trinity Road.'

Chapter 99

3.08 pm

In the incident room of Trinity Road Police Station, the ringing of the phone on Cole's desk roused him from the first sleep he had enjoyed in nearly twenty hours. He gave himself a mental shakedown in the two rings he counted before picking up the receiver. In the micro-beat of silence before he spoke, Cole detected that the call was long distance.

'Detective Constable Barney Cole, Merseyside Constabulary.'

In the background, there was old-time Country and Western music and the chatter of a bar: a slice of middle America in a snippet of sound.

'Mr Cole, I'm the author Dwayne Hare, returning your call, sir.'

'Thank you, Mr Hare, and can I begin by saying how much I enjoyed your book *White Supremacists*.'

'Well, I guess they're just one reason why we have the death penalty in the States. Tony Blair and New Labour really have a lot to answer for, closing down that option on your side of the pond.'

As Dwayne Hare spoke, Cole listened to him making his way from the interior of a bar to the outdoors, with cars zipping past in the distance in both directions.

'To put it mildly, Mr Hare, we're having a little local difficulty with a far-right group aping Black Sun. When we searched our prime suspect's residence, we found a copy of your book and related paraphernalia.'

'Timing's almost perfect.' Dwayne Hare laughed.

'How do you mean, Mr Hare?'

'After all these years of silence, one of the Black Sun bitches is set to meet her maker. Kelly-Ann Carter. Death by lethal injection next month. She took great delight in breaking into the homes of Afro-American families, lying the children down on their fronts and shooting them in the back. All in the name of Jesus and his heavenly father.'

'How did she justify the killings?' asked Cole.

'Obedience to the will of the Lord. Deuteronomy, Chapter Seven. Driving out the nations. *When the Lord your God brings you into the land you are entering to possess and drives out before you many nations – the Hittites, Girgashites, Amorites, Canaanites, blah, blah, blah, seven nations larger and stronger than you – and when the Lord your God has delivered them over to you and you have defeated them, then you must destroy them. Make no treaty with them, and show them no mercy.* Ethnic cleansing, rubber-stamped from on high. What the Canaanites were to the Israelites, blacks and ethnic minorities were to white Americans. White Americans who had the ears to hear and the sense to understand God's will were God's new chosen people. Bang, bang, bang, just doing the will of the Lord: you must destroy them. How many dead so far?'

'Three.'

'Not good but could be worse. You have the dudes behind bars?'

'One, yes. The others, no.'

'Shit. How can I help you, Barney?'

'In your chapter about Black Sun, you mention one or two names of the ringleaders but none of them have any relevance to what we know about the situation we have here. Then there are all the Isaac Isaac pseudonyms, again no relevance to what's going on here. What happened to the other members of Black Sun after it was infiltrated by the FBI?'

'They either died in a shootout with the National Guard and the South Carolina SWAT team at the headquarters in Columbia, or were arrested and sentenced to death. Two of the assholes got away. Kelly-Ann Carter and, oh shit, what was the guy's name? Kelly-Ann was picked up three days after the shootout in a McDonald's drivethrough. The guy got clean away and was never heard of again.'

'What was his name?'

'It's on the tip of my tongue.'

Cole picked through the bones of what Dwayne Hare had told him. 'What do you think happened to him?'

'A. He was from a moneyed family. B. The other fuckers were poor white trash. Aristotelian logic at its harshest. They're fucked, he's alive, free, watching the sunrise and pretending it was all a bad dream.'

'What was Kelly-Ann Carter's Black Sun name?'

'Sarah Sarah.'

'Can you think what his name was?' prompted Cole.

'Yeah. His Black Sun name was Abraham Abraham.'

A jagged icicle travelled through Cole's heart.

'You've gone very quiet all of a sudden. Are you OK, sir?'

'Can you recall his real name?'

'Got it! Got it... yeah... Christopher Darwin.'

'Did he have a religious denomination outside of Black Sun?' asked Cole.

'Wealthy family, the Darwins. Big Roman Catholic clan. Made their initial fortune in the seventeen hundreds up to 1865 out of the slave trade, and lost a shitload of it fighting litigation from the descendants of slaves.'

'Did they have to pay out a lot of compensation?'

'No. The American justice system backed the descendants of slave owners and traders. Surprise, sur-fucking-prise.'

'Dwayne, thank you so much. You don't know how helpful you've been. Could you do me a massive favour. My boss is called Detective Chief Inspector Eve Clay. Her mobile number is +44 7700 900204.'

'Again, please, Barney. I'll write it in my notebook.'

The click of a pen and Cole reeled off the digits.

'What do you want me to do?'

'Can you go into your filing cabinet and computer and dig out anything and everything you've got on Christopher Darwin and fill Eve Clay in on it.'

'Is he in Liverpool?' Dwayne Hare sounded somewhere between bewildered and excited.

'Possibly. Probably, even.'

'Be my pleasure to help you nail the bastard. Call me if you need any other information, or I'll call your boss Eve Clay when I come up with some information on Darwin. *Ciao*, Barney.'

Cole heard the door of the bar opening and Hank Williams coming from a jukebox as Dwayne Hare closed down the call.

Christopher Darwin, thought Cole, *the only surviving member of Black Sun not behind bars.* White supremacist. Roman Catholic...

He picked up the receiver to talk to Clay.

Chapter 100

4.01 pm

As Detective Constable Clive Winters entered Interview Suite 2, Raymond Dare said, 'Nigger.'

'Excuse me!' said Mr Robson, next to Raymond. 'Cut that talk out right now.'

Winters shrugged as he sat down, placing evidence bags and an envelope down on the table.

'I wasn't calling you names, I was thinking out loud. I mean, you're a copper and you're black? I just don't get it.'

'I'm getting déjà vu here. Don't worry about the colour of my skin. Worry instead about yourself and where you'll probably be spending at least the next twenty-five years of your life.'

Winters looked at Mr Robson who said, 'I can only apologise for my client's outburst.'

He smiled back at the solicitor, then honed in on Raymond Dare. 'I've listened to the recordings of the interviews you've been involved in with DCI Clay and DS Hendricks. We'll start with the good news. You were half-right about one thing. You did burn out the stolen white Fiat Uno. But you didn't do it in Sefton Park, as you claimed. You did it in the Festival Gardens.'

Raymond's face twisted. *Did I?*

'You didn't make a very good job of it, though. You abandoned Dominika Zima's T-shirt, jacket and skirt at the gateway into Otterspool Park.'

'I didn't take the bitch's clothes. She was wearing them when I left.'

'OK.' Winters slid a set of photographs out of the envelope and showed the top picture to Raymond. 'What's this?'

'It's the car I burned out and, yeah, yeah, I was getting confused but it was in the Festival Gardens.'

Winters showed him a second picture.

'That's the boot of the Fiat Uno, but I didn't leave it open.'

'We opened it, and guess what we found in the boot?'

'I don't know because I didn't go in the boot at all.'

Winters showed him the third of five pictures.

'In the picture you're looking at, what's in the boot, Raymond?'

'There's a bra and a pair of women's flat shoes. And a petrol can.'

'The clothing belongs to Dominika Zima. You took five items of clothing from her dead body. You ditched three but I'm putting it to you, Raymond, when it came to throwing away the shoes and underwear you just couldn't bring yourself to get rid of them. Right?'

'Wrong, wrong, wrong.'

'They were too intimate to throw away. You didn't want to get caught but you wanted something of hers that was very, very personal.'

'I didn't take any of her clothes.'

'You took her shoes and bra and you used some of the petrol to set her on fire near the railway bridge in Otterspool Park. As you drove away down Jericho Lane, reality head-butted you, and you realised that if you were in possession of her shoes and underwear, it was going to link you directly to her murder.'

'I didn't take her fucking clothes away. I didn't.'

'I'm saving the best for last here, Raymond, but look at this picture.'

Raymond looked at the fourth picture.

'It's a hand, so what?'

'It's not just a hand. It's her hand, and if you look closely at the palm you'll see something that we believe you inadvertently left behind. Can you see anything?'

'It's a hair.'

Winters looked at Raymond's hair. 'Same colour, same length as your hair, Raymond.'

'Maybe it is mine, because she pulled my hair when I was shagging her. That doesn't mean I fucking killed her and set her on fire because I didn't.'

'It's being tested in the lab. Just as we had Dominika's skirt fast-tracked for the semen that was on it.'

Winters showed him the last picture of Dominika's white denim mini-skirt. 'The result's come in,' he said, catching Mr Robson's eye. Raymond looked away. 'It's your semen. It's your DNA.'

Raymond looked at Mr Robson. 'Did I deny being with her? Did I deny shagging her? Don't just sit there, say something to help me, dickhead!'

'There were several semen stains but they all came from you. There was no sign at all of a second or third source of semen. It seems you were telling the truth – you were there on your own with Dominika.'

'Just as I'm telling it to you now – the truth.'

'Or, for CJ and Buster, it turned out to be a spectator sport because they were too whacked out and couldn't perform.'

'They weren't there.'

'You must have been in a lot better shape than them because you drove a car from the Dingle to Aigburth Vale. And guess what, Raymond? Well done, all the evidence points to the fact that you drove safely. You didn't weave in and out of the lanes. It looks like you had your wits about you. Would you say that was a fair comment?'

'No comment.'

'Do you think, with hindsight, you should have put her shoes and underwear on the front seat, so they'd have been more damaged by the fire?'

'No comment.'

'Do you think it was a mistake to leave them in the boot, which was left largely untouched?'

'No comment.'

'DCI Clay is unavailable at the moment, but when she returns she intends to charge you with rape and murder. What do you think, Raymond?'

'No comment.'

'If you cooperate with us, the judge will take it into account when sentencing.'

Winters closed the interview and called for Sergeant Harris.

'Mr Robson, I suggest you advise your client of the process that is about to follow, and how cooperating really is his best way to make his life slightly better in the long run.'

As Sergeant Harris opened the door, Raymond looked as if he were listening to an invisible man towering over him, and only he could hear his voice. He nodded slowly, as if in agreement.

Winters hit the record button.

'I didn't rape her. She wanted sex. It was afterwards. She hit me and I got angry and she threatened to cry rape and I panicked and I pushed her to the ground and she started to scream and I told her to shut the fuck up, but she wouldn't so I got on top of her and put my hands around her throat and I squeezed as hard as I could and it was like her eyes were going to pop out of her head and then and then and then she started to get weaker and weaker and it was like she couldn't struggle anymore and she went like a dead dog like Jasmine because I slit her throat the bitch the white bitch two dead bitch dogs...'

'Did you set her on fire, did you pour petrol on Dominika's face and head?'

'I must have done because I remember when I realised she was dead but she was still warm and I had a massive hard-on so I shagged her again and that was the best one because she was there but she wasn't there, y'know what I mean? I went to the car and got the petrol can from the boot.'

Winters formally opened the interview.

'Can you tell us that all over again, Raymond?'

'Yeah, I can. Because I'm fucked now, aren't I?'

'Did you rape Dominika Zima?'

'I didn't rape her. She wanted sex. It was afterwards.'

As Raymond Dare took a deep breath in through his nostrils, Winters wondered if it had occurred to the seventeen year old that the next joint he smoked or pill he popped would be behind bars on a segregated wing for sex offenders.

'Tell me again, Raymond, about your encounter with Dominika Zima?'

'She hit me and I got angry and she threatened to cry rape and I panicked…'

Chapter 101

4.34 pm

Clay sat on the back pew of St Luke's Roman Catholic Church, in the place Kate Thorpe usually occupied, looking at the church from the old lady's point of view. She eyed the unrolled painting on her lap and drank in the details before looking up at the church and replaying what had happened during the consecration at mass.

On the altar, Father Aaron Bell had held up the chalice, his eyes closed and his mouth open to say the ritual words. She imagined those words echoing in the vast spaces of the church where only three old people attended mass. Oblivious to everything other than the rite he was performing, Father Aaron failed to notice the young girl with a shaven head and wearing striped pyjamas who appeared in the open doorway of the vestry. The girl, Marta Ondřej, stayed in the doorway for up to ten seconds, making eye contact with the old lady on the back pew, before disappearing back into the vestry as quickly and quietly as she had appeared as Kate made her way towards her.

All the detail was in Kate Thorpe's painting.

Clay stood up and walked down the aisle towards the vestry to put together the pieces in her own mind.

She leaped forward in time by five minutes to the end of the mass.

She imagined Father Aaron walking down the step from the altar, and she walked into the empty vestry, projecting the priest ahead of herself and his reaction when the locked door to the small room, where he usually placed his rail of colourful vestments, was open and Marta Ondřej stood facing him in silence. She wondered how Father Aaron had managed to force her to be so quiet, what terror he had exposed her to.

Clay opened the door to the small room and turned on the bare light bulb. She took out her iPhone and, standing in the space, played back the eight pieces of film taken of Marta when she was in captivity. She checked the walls around her against the walls on the film, and noted the texture of the plasterwork beneath the yellowing white of the paintwork. They were a perfect match.

She paused the footage just before the light came on, and turned off the light in the room in which she stood. Clay turned the light back on and listened for the crackle of old electrical cables. The light flickered before it settled into life. She stepped out of the confined space and watched the light turning on in the film. The effect and density of the light was the same, as was the crackle and flicker.

She imagined the priest pushing Marta back inside the room, glancing over his shoulder as he did so, to make sure none of his flock had arrived to visit him over some insignificant troubles. None of them had. Good. He locked the door once the child was inside, changed quickly out of his robes and went back inside the church.

Clay pictured his relief when he saw Iris and Mr Rotherham heading out through the main door. He looked around and saw Kate Thorpe praying in the Chapel to the Virgin Mary at the left-hand side of the altar.

She walked in front of the altar rail towards the chapel and knelt before the statue of the Virgin Mary as Kate would have done, as she did after every mass.

On the floor beneath the Virgin Mary's feet, Clay saw a colour picture of a woman in an American court room, handcuffed and foot-chained, being led away by armed guards. She read the caption out loud. '*Serial killer Kelly-Ann Carter: her final appeal against the death penalty has failed.*'

Clay picked up the press cutting and read about the fate of the female white supremacist and what Barney Cole had said about her.

She took the picture of the seven core American Black Sun activists from her pocket and a feeling overwhelmed her as she looked at their faces: that she was staring at something that was at once clear and yet hidden. She picked out Kelly-Ann Carter's face in the group, folded the picture and put it back in her pocket.

Looking at the altar, she pictured Father Aaron weighing up that she was the only person in the congregation who could have seen the child. The relief he must have felt that it was her who had the chance to potentially see the girl was enormous.

The old woman? Clay imagined the priest considering the last picture she may have shown him. The Virgin Mary, hair in large rollers, wearing slippers and pink pyjamas, and looking a little depressed as she pushed Jesus as a toddler past the drinks aisle in Asda on Smithdown Road. No one, no one would believe such a scatty old woman.

Clay got up from the kneeler and headed back to the vestry.

She heard Hendricks's footsteps coming through the recently rammed back door of the church and into the vestry.

'How are things in the house, Bill?' asked Clay.

'There are gaps in his wardrobe. I think he's packed a bag.
He's left his car but I went into the desk drawer in his office. His
passport's not there, his wallet's not shown up. I've posted his
image to all ports and airports.'

'Thank you, Bill.'

'Terry Mason and Paul Price want to know when you want
them to pull the vestry to pieces?'

'Whatever they're doing in the house, please ask them to stop,
and start inside the cupboard built in the wall of the vestry.'

'What are you doing now, Eve?'

'I'm walking down Grant Avenue to check on Kate Thorpe.'

Chapter 102

4.38 pm

'Jack, your brother has admitted to a series of extremely serious offences.' Winters dead-eyed Jack across the desk. 'He's
denied rape but frankly, we don't believe him, and Dr Lamb,
the pathologist who conducted the post-mortem on Dominika
Zima's body, isn't supporting his series of events on that matter.'

Jack looked at the digits turning on the audio recorder to the
side of the table.

'Do you know Dominika Zima?' asked Winters.

'I know of her. She sent Raymond pornographic pictures of
herself over social media. I tried to warn him. He didn't listen to
me. He never does.'

'He's admitted strangling Dominika.'

'Where was she from?'

' Czech Republic. Why?'

'I was just wondering.'

'He's admitted murder, Jack. He's also admitted setting her
body on fire post-mortem. But he's also admitted that before he

did that, he committing an act of necrophilia on the woman's body. What are your thoughts on that, Jack?'

Jack looked Winters in the eye. 'I am disgusted with him. I am ashamed of him. I wish I'd never clapped eyes on him, let alone be his brother. But just because we have the same mother, that doesn't make *me* a party to *his* crimes.' He sighed from the core of his being and looked briefly at Mr Robson before finishing, 'I categorically and completely deny involvement in this abominable criminal behaviour.'

'Excuse me, Detective Constable Winters,' said Mr Robson. 'Jack and Raymond have the same mother but are from different fathers. The DNA's back from Dominika Zima's skirt. The only secretions on the skirt were from Raymond. There is no forensic evidence to suggest that my client had any involvement in this crime.'

'You're absolutely right, Mr Robson. But it's early days yet, and this isn't the only crime we're investigating. We have far to go with both Jack and Raymond.' Winters held Jack's gaze. 'You've done time for a hate crime. Your little brother admits to a hate crime but won't give up his friends, CJ and Buster. Are you CJ?'

'No.'

'Are you Buster?'

'No.'

'Then who are they?'

'Ask him. Ask Raymond. I've never met them and never wish to. I have barred them from my mother's house because of the bad influence they have had on my brother, my *half*-brother who as of this moment I disown.'

There was a knock at the door. When Sergeant Harris opened it, screams from deep inside the building filtered into the interview suite.

'DC Winters, you're needed immediately,' said Sergeant Harris.

Winters concluded the interview swiftly and followed Harris onto the corridor outside. The screams from the cells rose higher as they headed in their direction.

Sergeant Harris filled Winters in. 'It's Raymond Dare. He's having a massive episode. Medics are on their way, including a shrink, and he's being restrained by five officers but it's like he's possessed by the devil.'

'What's happening?'

'Broad Oak have got a bed for him.'

'What's your take on it?'

'I've seen it before, Clive. On top of his psychosis, he's suffering an extreme episode of hypermania.'

'I'll travel with him to Broad Oak when he's been spiked. Is Eve in the loop?'

'Of course.'

Winters opened the door to the corridor housing the holding cells and drew in a sharp breath as he realised the true scale of the storm.

'Jesus, the noise out of him. Out of all of them. It's like bedlam.'

'Ja! Ja! Jajajajajajajaja!'

Winters headed for the cell door behind which the loudest voice raged and raged. He looked in through the observation slot and saw five huge police officers on his arms and legs, with one lying sideways across Raymond Dare's thighs. Raymond banged his head against the blanket between his skull and the floor, and froth that formed around his mouth rolled down his red-raw cheeks.

He writhed and thrashed, screaming out bursts of incomprehensible language, his eyes wild with the ultimate rage of a blighted life. The alien language slowly morphed into a recognisable sound, and when the sound became clear, it was screamed out at the loudest and most enraged pitch.

'Ja! Ja! Ja! Ja! Ja! Ja! Ja!'

Footsteps hurried down the corridor. 'Paramedics!' came the voice with them.

Sergeant Harris unlocked the cell door.

'Jaaaaaaaaaaaaaccccccccccccckkkkkkkkk!'

Chapter 103

5.32 pm

From Kate Thorpe's front door, Clay could see Hendricks under the streetlights on the pavement outside St Luke's vestry, connecting her call on his iPhone.

'Bill, can you bring the ram down to Kate Thorpe's house.'

'Eve, what's the matter?'

'It's not good. I've called an ambulance. Hurry please, Bill.'

As she closed the call down, she saw Hendricks running at full speed towards his car.

Clay turned back to the living-room window. The inside of the glass was darkened with smoke, and the clean white net curtains were now a dozen shades of black.

She tried to look through the chinks in the curtains, but there was a dense band of smoke hanging in the air in the parlour.

Returning to the front door, Clay lifted the letterbox but then remembered that shouting out to Kate Thorpe was completely futile. As she raised the brass, her senses of smell and taste were overwhelmed and, for a moment, she was back in the Adamczak brothers' flat for the first time, smelling the horror of freshly burned human flesh.

She heard Hendricks's car powering the short distance down Grant Avenue; it screeched to a halt on the grass verge opposite her. He jumped out and crossed the road with the ram in his hand. In the distance, the edge of an ambulance siren approached.

'Shit!' he said, looking at the bay window and curtains.

He rammed the door, and it sprang back; the hall behind it was swimming in wreaths of smoke.

Clay hurried through the smoke-filled hall to the partially open parlour door, heat pulsing through its wooden panels. She opened the door wider with the sole of her right foot and trapped smoke poured from the room.

She reached in and found a light switch. She pressed it down but the light didn't come on.

Inside the parlour, smoke rose from the old 1960s three-piece suite and the carpet. Holding her breath, and blinking against the stinging air, Clay moved deeper into the room. On the wall to her left, she saw that the surfaces of Kate Thorpe's visionary paintings were all distorted, their vivid details hidden behind a haze of grime.

Hendricks appeared at her back and handed her a torch.

'Bill, can you check the rest of the house for me.'

She explored the space in front of her with the torch, the light picking out the heaving, polluted air. Through the smog, she found the wooden fire surround and what remained of the fireplace itself.

'Jesus,' said Clay, focusing on Kate Thorpe's corpse, as the smell of cooked flesh bit down on her nose, tongue and throat.

Kate Thorpe was on her hands and knees in front of the fire-place, all her clothing charred to ashes and her back and buttocks blackened and blistered, the leather of her shoes melted into the surface fabric of her feet.

The fire in the grate was out and full of ashes. What was left of Kate Thorpe's head was resting on the metal basket.

She shone the torchlight on the space where the back of her head should have been but all Clay could make out were chunks of blackened skull in the fireplace and the charred top of her spinal column.

Clay looked at the old lady's hands pressed down against the hearth, the backs of her hands and her feet duck-taped to the tiles; her hands were weighed down by a heavy poker, her palms melted into the surface of the hearth.

Each in-breath became increasingly painful, the smoke Clay was inhaling rapidly stripping the moisture from her throat and nose. She made her way to the bay window, turned the latch on the largest middle window and lifted the sash. She stepped quickly out of the room and into the hallway, and contacted Mason on her iPhone.

Opening the front door, she stayed on the step and drank in cold air, tears streaming from her stinging eyes.

'Terry, I need you to drop what you're doing in the church and the priest's house and put Paul Price in charge of those scenes. You'll both need back-up Scientific Support officers. Ring Admiral Street, see who they've got.' The stinging in her throat was creeping into the top halves of her lungs.

'You're splitting up a winning team, Eve. Are you sure?'

'You've both got extremely high levels of forensic knowledge of this shit-fest and we've now got three A1 priority sites. A church and two houses within spitting distance of each other. If I keep you both in the priest's house and the church and I put a fresh untried team here, things are going to get missed.'

'What's this other house?'

'131 Grant Avenue. One of our witnesses, Kate Thorpe, has been murdered in her front room.' She coughed and felt like her lungs were banging against her ribcage. 'Anything to report from the house and the church, Terry?'

'We've found the rest of Marta Ondřej's hair, Eve.'

A light went on inside the darkest place in her mind and she took the picture of the American Black Sun activists from her coat pocket. 'Under the boards in the room attached to the vestry in the church.'

'Spot on.'

'Anything else under there?'

'Yes. We found an early 1980s Smith & Wesson four-inch 686.371 mag revolver and a box of shells for it. We also found an empty box of shells for a Magnum Desert Eagle. The semi-automatic that uses those shells wasn't there but the empty box was. Again, it's an early 1980s American handgun.'

She unfolded the picture and looked at the men's faces. 'So the priest's on the run and he's armed with a heavy-duty firearm.' Clay tried to stop the sinking of her heart from creeping into her tone of voice. 'How long will you be?'

'Five to ten minutes.'

'I'll wait for you.'

Squinting and with a handkerchief over her nose and mouth, Clay walked back into the parlour to the bay window, where the ruined net curtains flapped in the raised sash, smoke pouring out onto Grant Avenue. She looked through the blackened pattern at the Mystery Park and reversed back to the last time she had stood in the same spot, when she had parted the curtains and had spoken to Lucy Bell on her iPhone as she made her way into the park.

Clay recalled the eye contact she had made with Father Aaron Bell's daughter, and the threat she had hurled at her about a reconstruction of her almost miraculous discovery of a child who should have been dead.

Hendricks's footsteps hurried down the stairs. 'Everything appears to be normal upstairs. I'll look downstairs now.'

'Thank you. As a matter of priority, Bill, I want Lucy Bell arrested under the Child Abduction Act of 1984. That is, if she hasn't sloped off with her father. We'll start small and work our way up with her.'

She handed the photocopied picture to Hendricks.

'What do you make of this, Bill?'

He took the picture from her and looked at it.

As Clay moved towards Kate Thorpe's body, the smoke in the parlour danced in the light from the torch in her hand. She got down on her hands and knees, and feeling her hand into the place where the old lady's head should have been, reached up into the lowest section of the chimney.

Her fingers hit a hard metal plate that had been wedged into the cement.

'Premeditated. Whoever did this to you, Kate, and I'm pretty sure I know who it was, planned it in advance and wanted to contaminate evidence with smoke by blocking the chimney.'

As Clay stood up, Hendricks looked up from the picture. 'What am I looking at, Eve?'

'Young man at the centre of the group of seven. Father Aaron

Bell. Or as he was known in the old country, Christopher Darwin, guiding light of Black Sun USA.'

Chapter 104

6.13 pm

Lucy Bell stood with her back against the railings of the Wavertree Mystery and looked at the policemen and women in white protective suits coming in and out of her house and her father's church. She rang him for the fourteenth time.

'The number you have called is currently unavailable. Please leave a message after the tone.'

Thirteen messages later, she'd said the same thing over and over. *Dad, where are you and what are you doing? Ring me back.* This time, she left a brand new piece of information for him.

'Dad, the police are crawling all over the house and the church. What's happening? Why aren't you returning my calls? I need to know what's going on. Dad, you're not being fair. Talk to me, Dad. Dad, I feel like my head's a pressure cooker. Dad, dad, dad...' Lucy wept as she closed the call down.

'I don't think your Dad's going to return your call, Lucy.' Clay stepped out of the shadows and into the edge of the streetlight on the pavement over the road.

'Have you been—' Tears streamed down Lucy's face.

'Waiting for you, Lucy? I certainly have. 6.13 pm home, same time every night.'

'I want my Dad. Where's my Dad?'

'You tell me where he is, Lucy. You know much better than me where he goes when he's upset or in trouble.'

'He's not in trouble at all, he's not done anything wrong, all he ever does is obey the will of the Lord and pray to Him through the intercession of the Virgin Mary.'

'It depends what the will of the Lord is, doesn't it, Lucy? Suppose the Lord were a historical character. Suppose he were like Stalin. Would you let him off the hook for even one second if he was ordering bad things to happen?'

Lucy's face twisted and, under the streetlight, she looked twice as old as usual.

'We need to talk, Lucy.'

'We can go into my house and talk. Just send your police officers home.'

'We're going to Trinity Road Police Station.'

'Again?'

'Are you putting this on, Lucy?'

'Putting what on?'

'Lucy, you've got a mind like a razor. My colleague Bill Hendricks is an incredibly intelligent man and he was dazzled by your lecture. You're classically autistic but you know what's going on, down to the last detail. The will of the Lord, Lucy? Or the will of Dad? Who is the Lord, Lucy? Who is in command? The Lord? Or what your Dad says the Lord is saying? Who told you to kill Kate Thorpe? The Lord? Or Dad? Who told you to bring Marta Ondřej to the park and call the emergency services? Who told you to join in with killing the Adamczak brothers?'

Lucy turned her back on Clay, squeezed her head between two narrow railings and twisted her neck, right to left over and over, trying her best to compress her skull and what lay within it.

'Don't do that, Lucy.' Clay lay a hand on her shoulder and the tender touch ignited a storm.

Lucy pulled her head away from the gap in the railings and banged her head at full force against the iron bars, once, twice, three times in rapid succession.

Clay dragged her backwards and cuffed her left wrist. She took her right wrist and locked it into the other cuff.

'Listen, Lucy. Listen to the people running towards you. Listen to what I'm saying. You cannot avoid what has happened. You cannot avoid what you have done. You cannot avoid what is coming next. Historical forces, Lucy. Broad ideas that motivate change in history.'

'Such as the genocide of the Canaanites at the hands of the Israelites following the will of the Lord, just after the beginning of time as we know it. Yes. Historical forces. Don't try it with me on historical forces, DCI Clay, because you won't win.'

Clay looked into Lucy's dazed eyes as the growing lump on her forehead swelled and turned a deeper shade of scarlet.

'An ambulance is on its way, Eve,' said Detective Sergeant Bill Hendricks.

Above the swelling on Lucy Bell's forehead, the skin broke and a bead of blood rolled into her left eye.

'All you have to do is tell the truth, Lucy.'

'Lucy?' she echoed back. Lucy dropped to the floor and Clay caught her, supporting her weight against the railings. On the pavement, Clay made a pillow of her knees and watched the lights going on and off in Lucy's eyes.

Chapter 105

6.32 pm

On Brownlow Hill, Father Aaron Bell digested the message his daughter had just left on his phone. He walked towards the side of the Metropolitan Cathedral and called Desmond Corrigan, the security guard.

'Desmond, I'm sorry to trouble you, but I've left some very important papers in my locker. Could you please open up and let me back inside. I'm at the door of the crypt.'

'No, problem, Father Aaron. I'm on my way right now.'

'Thank you, Desmond.'

'I won't keep you waiting, Father. It's a cold night.'

'Oh, Desmond...'

'Yes, Father?'

'I heard you've been working the night shift by yourself these past few nights?'

'Steve's not a bit well. Yeah, I'm all alone.'

'Solitude's not such a bad thing. Jesus himself sought it out.' He waited, listening to Desmond's footsteps approaching the door at speed, then the unbolting of a lock behind the heavy wooden door.

'Won't be a moment, Father Aaron.'

'No problem, Desmond.'

Father Aaron looked up at the multicoloured glass spire of the Roman Catholic cathedral and it produced the effect it always had on him. He felt how small he was in the scheme of things, and how from an early age his whole life had been a series of disasters.

A key turned inside the door to the crypt and as Desmond opened it, Father Aaron saw a patch of torchlight in the depths of the darkness beyond. Desmond Corrigan, a small man and the unlikeliest of security guards looked up at Father Aaron and into the priest's eyes. He hooked the ring of keys onto his belt and took his torch from his waistband.

'Come in, Father Aaron.' He shone his torch into the crypt and the light picked up the arches of the vaulted red-brick ceiling. 'I always feel like I've entered a different time and space when I come here,' he said. 'And I always feel that Jesus is close at hand and I am closer to Jesus.'

'You're closer to Christ than you think, Desmond.'

Father Aaron closed the crypt door.

'Do you think so, Father?'

'Yes, I'm sure of it.'

As Desmond turned his back on the priest to lock the crypt door, the security guard sniffed the air. 'Petrol?'

'You know me, Desmond.' Father Aaron shook the three-gallon

petrol can and the fuel sloshed against the metal. 'Head in the clouds. I had to fill my car up just now because the needle was well into red and I was almost out of juice. I forgot to put the can back in the boot – I was that keen to get my papers, I walked away with it in my hand. *Head in the clouds.*'

'Step this way, Father.' Desmond pointed his torch ahead of himself and walked into the light.

'We can get into the main section of the cathedral by the lift. I know a way of getting to the staff lockers that doesn't involve a load of messing around with the alarm system. I'll get you there safe and sound so you can pick up your papers, don't you worry, Father.'

'Thank you, Desmond.' They walked side by side deeper into the crypt. 'How are your children getting on?'

'Six, four and eighteen months. Never a dull moment. Here.' He reached inside his fleece, took out his wallet and showed Father Aaron a photograph of two older girls and a young boy.

'My,' said Father Aaron, taking in the children's facial similarities to their father, the black skin that made the whites of their eyes stand out; the girls smiled broadly, their teeth gleaming white, both with their hair in dozens of beaded plaits.

'How's your daughter Lucy, Father Aaron?'

'Nearly thirty years of age and, still, never a dull moment.'

Desmond stopped as they entered the central part of the crypt chapel and shone his torch in the direction of the altar, picking up the brick arches above their heads and the pews on either side of the aisle.

'Do you ever feel sealed off from the world out there when you're in the crypt?' asked Father Aaron.

'I guess that's why I feel closer to Our Lord when I'm down here.'

Desmond shone his light at the pillars, at one of the three-dimensional wooden relief images of the Stations of the Cross: Jesus standing before Pontius Pilate, the prefect of Judea, as he condemned him to death.

'I know what makes me feel closer to Christ,' said Father Aaron. 'Come on, Desmond, let's go to the devotional candles at the side of the altar.'

Outside the edges of the security guard's torchlight, shadows shifted in the silent pews and darkness pressed down from the curves of the perfectly constructed arches of the ceiling.

Father Aaron stopped by the three-tiered metal frame hosting the candles.

'Praying by candlelight, in the darkness, in the place where the dead *could* be housed as their souls fly to heaven. I think we should pray together, Desmond.'

'That would be a great honour for me, Father Aaron.'

Father Aaron pointed to the kneeler.

'You go there. I'll stand over you. My knees aren't as good as they used to be, so you'll be doing me a favour if you kneel. We will pray in silence, but first of all we must light some candles.'

Aaron produced a box of matches from his coat pocket. 'Desmond, keep your torch trained on the candles as I light them, please. Good man. Thank you.'

The tip of the match rasped as Father Aaron dragged it down the emery board and it hissed into life. He applied the flame of the first match to six candles, dropping the dying match to the ground. He struck again and, within moments, seven more candles were alight.

'One more for the Holy Trinity,' said Father Aaron, as he brought the last of the candles to life, filling the darkness with an oasis of warm light. 'Turn off your torch please, Desmond. You don't need it now.'

'What shall we pray for, Father Aaron?'

'Pray for your wife and children, and that God the Father will have mercy on you for your sins.'

The security guard nodded and said, 'Thank you for this, Father Aaron.'

Father Aaron stood over the kneeling security guard and counted to one hundred. He unscrewed the cap of the petrol tin and, stepping silently towards the guard, trickled petrol on the fleece on his back. He waited, saw the stillness of the man beneath him and made a trail of petrol either side of the first application.

As Desmond's head ascended slowly, Father Aaron guessed that he now had an inkling that something was not quite right.

'Father Aaron?'

'Yes, Desmond.' He lifted a lit candle and stepped back.

'Can you smell strong—'

Father Aaron touched Desmond's fleece with the flame of the candle and fire chased up the back of his jacket and into his neck and hair. The guard looked over his shoulder and his eyes widened in shock and terror as flames filled the darkness between him and the priest.

He tried to get to his feet. Father Aaron smiled back at him and flapped the fingers of his right hand up and down. Desmond's screams grew louder as each moment passed, and echoed back at him under the arches.

He fell onto his back and Father Aaron splashed petrol onto his chest and abdomen, using the candle to light the front of his fleece. Then he looked deeply into Desmond's eyes.

'I can see that you're wondering why.' There was work to be done in the crypt but there were words that demanded to be said out loud. He shook his head. 'Why?' He pictured Kelly-Ann sitting in a cell and waiting to die at the hands of the state. 'An eye for an eye. And I want you to get used to it. There'll be plenty more fires where you're heading.'

Chapter 106

6.35 pm

Carmel Dare stuck Raymond Dare's right leg into the right leg of his pyjamas, then did the same with the left.

'You'll have to stand up from the bed, Raymond.'

Slowly, he stood up, and she pulled the waistband to his hips.

'Hold your arms out.' As he followed the instruction, there was a knock on the door and Carmel said, 'Come in.'

She threaded the pyjama top over his arms as Doctor Ellington, the young female psychiatrist who had attended to Raymond since his admission to Broad Oak, entered. Carmel shuddered at the sight of the armed police officer at the door of her son's hospital room.

The smile on Doctor Ellington's face dropped.

'Get into bed, Raymond,' said Carmel, as the brutal weight of truth assaulted her: one son in police custody, the other on a psychiatric ward.

Carmel sat on the edge of the bed. 'What's happening, Doctor Ellington?'

'Raymond's seriously ill. It's not a decision that I've taken lightly but I'm afraid I'm going to section him under the Mental Health Act.'

'Thus taking away all his rights and choices,' said Carmel, evenly. 'Don't be sorry. He doesn't deserve to have rights, given the rotten choices he's been making, over and over.'

'Mum?'

Both women turned to Raymond.

'Did you get the message to CJ and Buster to come and see me in hospital?'

'You'll have to give me their contact details. But to be honest with you, Raymond, you don't need them around you, especially not now.'

'Mrs Dare.' Doctor Ellington leaned towards her. 'I'll put a message on the nurses' station. No visitors for Raymond other than the ones you allow. Particularly no boys of his own age. I suggest he has no visitors until we can assess him fully.'

Raymond turned on his side, away from the wall.

Doctor Ellington looked at him. 'That's right, Raymond, get some shut-eye. It'll make you feel a whole lot better.'

'Ja-Ja-Ja-Ja-smine… Come here, girl…'

'How long's he been taking illegal drugs, Mrs Dare?'

'Two years, but it wasn't always as intense as it has been lately. I know what you're going to say next, I've looked it up. His brain isn't fully grown yet, and there could be long-term damage.'

'Ja-Ja-Ja-Ja-ck, ck, ck, ck…. You fu-fu-fu-fucker…'

Raymond opened his eyes and, with great effort, levered himself up by his elbows. Doctor Ellington and Carmel Dare watched him closely as he made it to a sitting position, blinking hard, as if he had something urgent to attend to.

'Raymond, lie down. There's nothing you need to do.'

'Can I have pencils, coloured pencils?' he asked.

'No. You could harm yourself with them,' said Doctor Ellington.

'Feed me, feed me art. Then can I have felt tips, thick felt tips?'

'I suppose you could,' replied the psychiatrist.

Carmel looked out of the window at Broadgreen Hospital, overshadowing Broad Oak. 'I'll get them for you from the shop in the hospital.'

'Lots and lots, Mummy.' He turned his attention away from the women and stared hard for many moments at the silent door. 'Come in,' said Raymond. Silence. 'I said, *come in*!'

The door remained closed.

Although his eyes were dulled by medication, a light came on as he tracked the space between the door and the bottom of the bed.

'Nice one, lads.' He smiled at the empty space at the bottom of his bed. 'Come here, come here.' He turned his attention to the side of the bed and spoke into thin air. 'Thanks for coming to see me, lads.' He dropped his voice. 'Have you got any weed for me?' He reached out and took a slice of air, dropping it into the breast pocket of his pyjama top. 'Mum. Don't be sad. Don't cry. I've got visitors. Mum.' He pointed at the wall. 'This is CJ. And this is Buster.'

Carmel looked at Doctor Ellington.

'They're as real to him as you are to me and I am to you.'

Raymond started laughing. 'That's the best one yet, CJ.' He got the words out in fits and starts of laughter. He laughed and he laughed, tears rolling down his cheeks, and then fell into a puzzled silence. 'I can hear him. I can hear him coming. Jack's on his way here, right now. You'd better go. I'll call you when he's gone.'

Chapter 107

6.31 pm

Father Aaron Bell drew the shape of a cross with his eyes down the central aisle of the crypt chapel of the Metropolitan Cathedral and uncapped the petrol can in his right hand. He turned to the altar, genuflected and then raised the petrol can towards the Lord with his right arm and the Magnum Research Eagle semi-automatic with his left.

'By my right red hand, by my left, Lord, by my straight and narrow left!'

He turned and, walking down the aisle, splashed a continuous line of petrol onto the wooden flooring, fuel kicking up from the ground. Past pew after pew he headed for the top of the chapel, the weight of the can decreasing with each step forward.

Beneath the candles, he heard Desmond's inarticulate moan of pain and despair.

'Don't complain, Desmond. It was your grandparents who decided to leave Jamaica way back when. If they'd stayed where God placed them you wouldn't be in the position you're in now. This isn't *my* fault.'

Father Aaron stopped at the last aisle and looked back at what he had just done.

'Almost perfect,' he whispered. 'One more line.' He estimated how many steps it would take to reach a third of the vertical lines, and took four strides. He moved to the wall at the end of the left pew and released petrol onto the floor, moving in a straight line to the wall beyond the right-hand pew.

Behind him, Desmond wept and chattered on the floor.

'I am not in the mood for this. Shut up!'

Desmond's noise grew louder.

In the borrowed light of a host of candles, Father Aaron made out the shape of a petroleum cross down the central aisle and across a pair of neighbouring pews. He walked to the left of it, to the wooden relief Stations of the Cross, and focused on Jesus dying on the cross.

He moved towards Desmond and stood over him near the devotional candles. 'Obedient! Obedient! Obedient to the will of God, and such is the obedience of those who act as his hands and feet.'

Father Aaron placed the sole of his right foot on Desmond's chest and pressed down, extracting a weak but definitive cry of pain that announced the sudden escalation of his victim's suffering.

'How could this pain become more agonising? Is that what you're thinking?' Father Aaron knelt down and pressed his face close to Desmond's, drank in the astonishment in his traumatised eyes. 'You're worth more to me alive than dead at the moment, so let's find out just how good things are for you right now, and just how bad things could get?'

Father Aaron stood up and called Detective Chief Inspector Eve Clay on his mobile phone. She connected the call but said nothing for a moment.

'Clay?'

'Where are you, Aaron?'

'We need to talk, Clay.'

'Tell me where you are.'

'Listen.' He stomped on Desmond's abdomen. 'Can you hear those cries of pain?'

'Who have you got with you?'

'A hostage.'

'A man or a woman?'

'Does it matter?'

'I want you to release them right now.'

'They're unable to move.'

'Tell me where you are so I can get medical assistance to them immediately.'

'That won't be necessary. I'll call you back.'

'Where are you?'

'Guess. If you want the hostage to have any chance of surviving you come alone and, let me stress, you come unarmed.'

'Even though *you've* got a loaded gun, Aaron?'

'I have nothing to lose, Clay. Nothing. I am liberated. Tonight I will sit at the Lord's table.' He ended the call.

Desmond's sobbing was filled with fresh despair and, for a moment, it was sweeter than music to Father Aaron's ears, but then it sparked a memory of Kelly-Ann Carter that turned the noise sour.

Father Aaron took a pair of linen handkerchiefs from his pocket and stuffed them into Desmond's mouth. 'How close to Jesus do you feel right now?'

Chapter 108

6.35 pm

When the landline phone on Barney Cole's desk rang out and he saw the +1 prefix on the display, he guessed the call was from Quantico, Virginia, USA.

'Eve? It's the FBI.' Clay walked towards Cole's desk as he picked up the receiver and hit speakerphone. 'Detective Constable Barney Cole, Merseyside Constabulary.'

There was a series of clicks and then the voice of a young woman.

'Hello, Barney, my name's Cara Davis, FBI, and your request for information was passed on to me.'

'I'm handing you over to DCI Eve Clay. Thank you for getting back to us.'

'Hello, Cara. Christopher Darwin, leader of South Carolina's Black Sun group. Can we talk about him?'

'Do you have him in custody?'

'I'm sorry, no.'

'We have an extradition order for him. He's wanted in connection with multiple murders in South Carolina dating back to the 1980s. How's he on your radar?'

'I'm convinced he's reinvented himself as Aaron Bell. We've had a string of racially motivated murders in Liverpool. He's on the run and armed.'

'What do you want to know about Christopher Darwin?'

'Do you know how he got out of America?'

'No one's certain, but it's believed he made it over the Mexican border and bought his way out from there. He was a spoiled rich kid with a Messianic complex, and a pure hatred for anyone who wasn't white. He also hated white people who didn't share his religious fundamental ideals and political views. When Black Sun hit destruct, he had enough personal wealth to make sure that he could go anywhere and become anything he wanted to be. What's he doing in Liverpool, Eve?'

'He's a Roman Catholic priest.'

For a few moments, there was a puzzled silence, and the line crackled. 'Why should that surprise me? It's a perfect disguise.'

'Can you tell me how Black Sun operated?'

'Sure can. There was a lot of rotation in the organisation, but the constant factor was Christopher Darwin, Aaron Bell, whatever he's called. When they went out to murder people from ethnic groups, Darwin went every time to control the killings. To begin with he took two disciples with him, different disciples every time in the first three instances.'

'Disciples?'

'Black Sun revolved around Christopher Darwin and everyone else in the organisation was a disciple. It took us a long time to put this picture together, but Darwin truly believed he was on a level with Jesus. When the Black Sun disciples were first pulled in, they said nothing about him. Two or three years in they realised they'd been left to rot while Darwin walked free, so they started talking. The instructions he was giving out – from what was for breakfast to which house and family they were going to target that night – was the voice of God in his head telling him to tell them what to do. It was a fascist cult that behaved with impunity, because it was acting out the will of God. Those who didn't kill turned down plea bargains to protect Christopher Darwin, such was their loyalty to him.'

'What was the Black Sun MO when it came to murder?' asked Clay.

'Towards the end, we had two agents infiltrate Black Sun, but the murders had dried up. In the initial instances, they'd wait outside a house and when the family went out, they'd break in through the back and wait for them to return, help themselves to food, money, jewellery. Sometimes, they'd wait for hours. They'd spray their graffiti on the walls—'

'What was the graffiti of?'

'*Killing Time Is Here Embrace It*, and a weird occult Nazi globe, the Black Sun. When the families returned, they'd order them to lie face down in a line, and shoot them in the back of their heads at point-blank range. Then they'd set their heads and faces on fire.

'Kelly-Ann Carter claims she changed the MO. After the time-wasting waiting around of the first murder sprees, she started talking her way into the targets' homes. Once inside, she'd let Aaron and the third person in and the killings would happen.

'From then on Darwin took Kelly-Ann on every spree, her and another Black Sun disciple. Get this, Darwin never fired a shot. He just reeled out the order of death. Then the method changed again. It was just Darwin and Kelly-Ann in the end.

He called the shots. She fired them. When she was first arrested, she completely denied Darwin's involvement in any of the murders or other criminal activity. It was her work and the work of other renegade members of Black Sun.

'They'd mixed and matched their biblical justification for the way they carried on. Sexually, the men rotated the women because biblical big hitters didn't practise monogamy. The women had no choice who they slept with. Obedience was all. But there was one exception. Kelly-Ann Carter. She was exclusively for Darwin's bed. And it so happened that she turned out to be the brains behind him.'

'That really adds up, Cara. Did they target specific ethnic groups?'

'A lot of their victims were new to the country, but they weren't fussy. Anyone not American, anyone not white. Where are you up to with him?'

'I'm waiting for Aaron Bell to call me. He wants me to meet up with him,' said Clay, something dark turning at the centre of her brain.

'Be careful, Eve. He drew out two law enforcement officers on the pretext that he was going to surrender. Neither of them came back alive.'

Chapter 109

6.59 pm

Lucy Bell sat next to her solicitor Louise Jackson facing Clay and Hendricks. On the table between them was Kate Thorpe's artwork, face down, and a set of photographs in a card file. The bruising on Lucy's forehead crept beyond the gauze bandage that covered the wound.

Clay showed her the photocopied picture of the seven core American Black Sun activists.

'The man in the middle of the group is your father, Lucy. He's clean-shaven and a lot younger, and his real name is Christopher Darwin.'

'You're insane.'

'Did you know your father was going to do a runner, Lucy?' asked Clay. 'Do you know where he might be?'

Lucy played with the ends of her hair and looked in between Clay and Hendricks.

'You and your father are part of an organisation called Black Sun, Lucy, operating right here in Liverpool. What do you say to that? Are you going to reply?'

'You're talking nonsense and asking nonsensical questions. Why should I answer nonsensical questions posed by a nonsensical detective?'

'You should answer my questions because it's a chance for you to defend yourself. Maybe when your twenty-four hours in custody is up, maybe if you've given a convincing account of yourself, I can release you uncharged. But if you can't or won't help me to help you, then I doubt that's going to happen. You're looking at serious charges here, Lucy. The kidnap of a child. Murder.' She turned to Hendricks. 'DS Hendricks, show Lucy Kate Thorpe's paintings.'

'Kate Thorpe was a deluded old lady who thought she saw Jesus and the Virgin Mary every day. You can't possibly think of her as a reliable witness on any level.'

'Just look at her paintings and let me be the judge of her state of mind.'

'Between the head wound that my client has sustained, the large amounts of painkillers she has taken and the stress caused by the disappearance of her father,' said Lucy's solicitor, 'I want to go on record and state that her answers are prone to be unreliable to say the least.'

'Thank you, that's on record.'

'Lucy, I'm advising you again to go *no comment.*'

Hendricks turned over the first painting, of Marta Ondřej and Lucy Bell in the Wavertree Mystery from Kate Thorpe's parlour window.

'This is you running away from Marta Ondřej, Lucy.'

Lucy mouthed a four-word question.

'For the sake of the audio recording, when DS Hendricks showed Lucy this painting, she mouthed the words, *How can this be?* Miss Thorpe must have known she was in danger, Lucy. She made two copies of the same painting and gave one set to Mr Rotherham to give to me. That's the forward thinking of a lucid old lady, not the ramblings of an old woman who has difficulty differentiating between what is real and what isn't. Back to the painting. You walked Marta into the Mystery, then you panicked and ran away, but you ran away towards Grant Avenue, where there were dozens of potential witnesses including Kate Thorpe. What do you say to that, Lucy?'

Lucy's solicitor whispered in her ear.

'No comment.'

'This second picture that Kate Thorpe painted is of when you returned to Marta Ondřej and, probably, put in the call to the emergency services. Was it your idea or your father's to cover your tracks?'

'No comment.'

'This picture of Kate Thorpe's is of the moment in church when Marta Ondřej made a fleeting appearance at the door of the vestry. Look at the picture, Lucy. Do you recognise your father's church, your father on the altar, Marta?'

'No comment.'

'We're going to show you some photographs now, Lucy,' said Hendricks, opening the card file.

'Do you recognise this house? 131 Grant Avenue?' asked Clay.

'No comment.'

Hendricks turned the second photograph towards Lucy.

'The dead person in the photograph is Kate Thorpe. You

mightn't be able to recognise her because her head and face have been incinerated, but do you recognise her parlour?'

'No comment.'

'Did you go to her house to give her Holy Communion?'

'No comment.'

'Did you kill her after you'd given her Holy Communion?'

'No comment.'

'Did you kill her because she knew too much?'

'No comment.'

'Did you see the copies of the paintings that Miss Thorpe kept in her parlour?'

'No comment.'

'Did the pictures make you panic?'

'No comment.'

'Did you burn Miss Thorpe's paintings?'

'No comment.'

'Did you strangle Miss Thorpe?'

'No comment.'

'Did you stick Miss Thorpe's head in the fire?'

'No comment.'

Clay sustained silence, staring deeply into Lucy's eyes.

'What?' asked Lucy.

'Here you are in police custody, Lucy, and yet your father, who demands obedience from you, is nowhere to be seen. It follows a pattern, doesn't it?'

'No comment.'

'When you first came in for questioning, he was nowhere to be seen even though you begged him to come here. That's right, isn't it?'

'No comment.'

'He gave you no warning that he was going to run away and leave you, did he?'

'No comment.'

'If it's any consolation, Lucy, you're not the only woman he's done this to. Have you ever heard of Kelly-Ann Carter?'

'No comment.'

'She was your father's right-hand woman back in the old country in the South Carolina Black Sun. Did you know that?'

'No comment.'

'Your father abandoned her and ran away. Did you know she's on death row and is due to be executed in just over four weeks' time?'

'My father...'

'Your father?'

'No comment.'

Clay's iPhone rang out. She looked at the display screen and showed it to Lucy. She connected the call and hit speakerphone.

'Hello, Darwin. I've got your daughter here.'

'You're a liar, Clay, a godless, goddamned liar.'

'Say hello to your father, Lucy.'

'Dad, she's saying things about you...'

'Calm down, Lucy!' ordered her father.

'Don't say another word, Miss Bell,' said her solicitor.

'That you're abandoning me. Don't leave me here on my own, Dad.'

'You're not on your own. Don't tell me they haven't got Jack...? Make sure you trigger the pact. Don't answer the Devil's questions.'

'Don't worry, Christopher,' said Clay. 'On legal advice, she's said nothing so far.' In the background she heard the moaning and sobbing of a man who seemed to be on the verge of death. 'Did you set fire to him?'

'I want to see you face to face, Clay.'

She turned off speakerphone and covered the mouthpiece.

'Before I go to meet your father, Lucy, I'm going to remind you that we have your laptop and your phone. Our IT specialist has them open and is exploring them. Think on that for the next interview. If there's anything you want to confess to before we show you more evidence, I'd do it now.'

Clay got to her feet and headed out of the interview suite towards reception.

'Clay?' asked the priest. 'Are you still there, Clay?'

'I'm still here but I'm already on my way to you. You did this in the States, didn't you? Two law enforcement officers. Both came back in body bags. I'm not scared of you. Tell me where you are and I'll be down there as quickly as I can.'

As she passed the desk, she showed the phone to Sergeant Harris.

'Do not bring a firearm.'

'I wouldn't dream of bringing a Glock 17 pistol with me.'

Harris picked up the landline and dialled the weapons store.

'You come alone or I'll kill my hostage and then I'll kill you.'

'Cut out the threats and tell me where you are.'

'The Metropolitan Cathedral, in Lutyens Crypt. Brownlow Hill. At the side of the cathedral itself. The door is unlocked for you.'

'I know the door you mean. I know the crypt very well. Like the lines on the palms of my hands. That well.'

'Those other law enforcement officers. In America. How did you know?'

'How do I know? I know a lot about you. More than you'd like me to know. Kelly-Ann Carter, I know all about her. I'll be there before you know it.'

A ball of sickness twisted in her stomach and her mouth felt as dry as a brick.

'I look forward to seeing you.'

Chapter 110

7.03 am

As Clay drove down Grove Street towards Brownlow Hill, she saw a pair of constables ahead of her, stopping a car on the corner of Abercromby Square. The driver did a neat three-point turn and drove away in the opposite direction.

She listened to Hendricks on her iPhone.

'All the roads leading into and around the cathedral have been sealed off. The only vehicles in the vicinity are ours and the streets have been evacuated of pedestrians,' he said. 'Every available body is on the ground and there are guns on their way over to surround the cathedral as we speak.'

Clay pulled up in front of the constables and showed them her warrant card, feeling the coldest of comforts that no civilians were in the area. The constables waved her through and, as she turned onto Abercromby Square heading for Oxford Street and Brownlow Hill, she pictured Thomas putting Philip to bed and wished she was there.

During the entire journey from Trinity Road Police Station to the Metropolitan Cathedral, her mind was split in two. One half was adrenaline-fuelled, preparing for the battle ahead, while the other was filled with thoughts of her husband and son.

Mile after speedy mile, the conflict sharpened. *I'll call home before I go into the crypt. I'll call them if I come out alive.* Picturing their bewilderment, in the worst-case scenario, that she had gone in without speaking to them, she pulled up on Oxford Road and called home. Within moments, she heard Philip's voice.

'Hello?'

'You sound tired, love.'

'Mummy? Dad, it's Mum.'

'You don't sound as tired now, Philip.'

'I've been playing with Dixie.'

'Dixie?' In the background she heard Thomas skipping down the stairs to the phone in their hall. The light went on inside her. 'That's what you've called your cricket.'

The irony of Darwin's gift was bitter: that the armed killer she was about to face had given a gift to her son and that it was in her home turned her cold.

'I've been looking at him in the box. He doesn't do much but he does make noises. It sounds like teeth grinding against each other.'

'Listen, Philip. How much do I love you? I need to know.'

'More than the stars and the moon and all the planets. I love you the same.'

'That's right. I'm going to do my best to get home at some point before you leave for school in the morning. How does that sound?'

'Great, Mum.'

'Oh Philip, one thing. You mustn't have Dixie in your bedroom when you're sleeping. His chirruping might keep you awake. Promise me.'

'OK, I promise. I'll leave him downstairs.'

'Go to bed now, Philip. You know I love you.'

'I love you back, Mum.'

'Goodnight, Philip.'

'Night, Mum.'

She listened to her son run up the stairs and after a few seconds of silence, Thomas asked, 'Hello, Eve, what's happening?'

'I'm picking up a suspect for questioning.'

'A dangerous suspect?'

'They're all dangerous. But he's a priest. It should be a piece of cake. I called because I wanted to say goodnight to Philip.'

'You know what I mean.'

'I've got great back-up.'

'Should I be worried? I mean, I worry anyway, but should I be especially worried?'

'No, don't worry. Take it easy. I wish I was there, with you and Philip. I love you both very much and I *will* see you very soon. I've got to go.' She glanced at her watch.

'What can I say, Eve? We love you back just as much.'

As Thomas spoke the last syllable, he closed down the call, and the half of her brain that belonged to home closed down too. Her whole focus was now on the job in hand.

She headed to the corner of Oxford Road and Brownlow Hill and, looking up at the huge glass spire of the Metropolitan Cathedral, heard Gina Riley's voice on the wind.

'Eve?' Riley walked quickly towards her.

'Gina, I know the inside of the crypt really well. I'm guessing he's going to be on or around the altar, in the central part of the chapel. I've got areas to the right where I can observe him from when I go in. If he raises his gun, I've got a pillar of brickwork to hide behind. The door is really close to where I intend to place myself when I make a risk assessment.'

'What about the hostage?'

'If I can save him, of course I will. But I heard the poor man when Bell called me. First time I heard him I figured he was critical. Second time, it sounded like his condition had deteriorated. I'm sorry.'

Riley pointed at Stone on the University of Liverpool's side of the pavement opposite, standing with a sergeant carrying a black case and a thin sheaf of papers.

'Karl's going to ask you if he can go in behind you as back-up.'

'Nice idea but absolutely not.'

'The sergeant from firearms has got the Glock you asked for.'

'Glock the Old Trusty.'

As Clay walked across the road, she heard Riley call, 'Be safe, be quick and be back out here asap.'

A black unmarked van pulled up a little way down Brownlow Hill and, as the driver jumped out and opened the side door, a stream of firearms officers emerged carrying Heckler and Koch rifles, fanning out quickly in the surrounding space.

She walked towards Stone and the firearms sergeant, glancing at the steps leading down to the crypt chapel, and wondered if she was about to experience a premature burial.

The sergeant handed her a flak jacket.

'DCI Clay, put this on under your coat and please sign for the firearm you requested.'

Chapter 111

7.13 pm

As Clay approached the door to the crypt chapel, a prayer of sorts ran through her brain. *Please, please don't creak or make a noise as I open you.* She turned the black circle that was the latch and felt the cold metal in her hand. Holding her breath as she lifted it, she pushed the door open with her shoulder.

As soon as the door was open wide enough for her to squeeze through, she heard two distinct noises: the sound of a man in agony, and another voice speaking in a robotic monotone. The natural aroma of the crypt – wax, wood and second-hand incense – was drowned by petrol fumes.

Clay pulled the door shut and focused on the speaking voice. She recognised it as Father Aaron Bell, and estimated that he was around the corner at the far end of the chapel on the altar. His voice travelled through the air at head height but it sounded like the man in agony was on the ground.

There was some light in the chapel, but it was weak and unstable; Clay guessed it was from a multitude of candles somewhere near the altar.

She kicked off her shoes and walked three paces to the edge of an arched pillar and listened.

Aaron was saying the Hail Mary and reaching the final line, 'Pray for us sinners now and at the hour of our death. Amen.' He launched into the opening words of the next prayer. 'Hail Mary, full of grace...'

Clay looked at the shadows swathing the space beneath the wide vaulted arch at the back of the central aisle, and knew she had the advantage of darkness. She walked to the edge of the arch and took a fleeting look at the wider scene.

He was standing in front of the altar, facing her.

'And blessed is the fruit of thy womb Jesus...' He prayed on with a gun in his joined hands as the man on the ground, whom she couldn't see, wept and groaned.

She listened to him praying, heard him repeat the last line of the Hail Mary, and, as he sealed it with *Amen*, Clay joined in: 'Hail Mary, full of grace.' She spoke softly at first but her voice rose in volume with each line.

'Our Lord is with you. Blessed art thou among women, And blessed is the fruit of thy womb, Jesus!' She crunched down on the name of Mary's son and silenced Aaron Bell, her voice rising from the darkness at the back of the chapel.

'Holy Mary, Mother of God,' Clay continued. 'Pray for us sinners, now and at the hour of our death. Amen. Hail Mary, full of grace—'

'Stop!' said Aaron, his prayerful hands unfolding and his right hand clasping the semi-automatic Magnum Desert Eagle.

Clay took in the lethal handgun in candlelight and whispered, 'Jesus...' under her breath.

'The Lord is with thee,' she continued.

'Stop!'

'Blessed art thou among women.' She stepped deeper into the shadows and fell silent. His figure was ghostlike in the candlelight. His head appeared to be almost floating independently in mid-air, the optical illusion created by the black clothes he wore from the neck down.

'Where are you, Clay?'

She stepped to the centre of the aisle leading away from the back row of the pews and felt something damp at the edge of her right toes. Clay stooped, touched the dampness on the floor and smelled it. Petrol. She stayed down, the shadows running deeper on the ground, and touched the wetness of petrol running down the aisle in a vertical line.

'I said, *Where are you?*'

Standing, she moved to the arch to her right.

'Where... are... you? If you don't tell me, I'll shoot my hostage immediately.'

'Why waste a single bullet when there are dozens and dozens of police officers outside. You can walk out of this and face the consequences of your actions. If you kill him, the next body bag's got your name on it, Aaron. Or is it, Christopher? He's going to die anyway.'

'How do you know that, Clay?'

'Because I've been listening to him suffering. He's gone down-hill in the brief time since I first heard him. I've seen and heard many people dying. I am on close terms with death in all its guises. I've been at death's door myself on more than one occasion. Let me see. You poured petrol on him and set him alight. He was no more than a sound effect for you, a bit of background noise to raise the stakes and force my hand to come here and face you.'

'Come to the altar. Show yourself to me.'

'No. You step into the darkness. You, show yourself to me.'

'I am an ordained priest and this is the Lord's house. I am obedient to him at all times and *you* must be obedient to *me* now.'

The dying man's inarticulate, guttural noises stopped as if he no longer had the strength to make them. His breathing became hoarse, ragged and with no discernible rhythm.

'I know that sound,' said Clay. 'He's got minutes to live. He's drowning in thin air. The fumes in here and the severity of his injuries are working against him. His internal organs are damaged, his lungs for sure.'

'He's not the only one with minutes to live.'

'We've got Lucy in custody. We've got Jack Dare as well.'

'But you haven't got me, have you, Clay?'

'I've got something even better than that.'

'What?'

'I've got Marta Ondřej's hair from the vestry of your church. You left it under the boards in the room you imprisoned her in. You left the other half in the Adamczak brothers' flat on Picton Road to put us off your scent, to discredit them when they had no voices to defend themselves and to cause terror between different groups of immigrants. You cleaned that space with bleach but you couldn't bear to part with the second half of her hair.'

With his Magnum pointed in Clay's direction, Aaron moved sideways off the altar towards the candles. He blew the flames and, within seconds, the whole chapel was plunged into darkness, save for the votive light on the wall above the altar.

That's all the light I need, thought Clay.

She stepped into the central aisle to the right-hand side of the line of petrol, which she estimated went all the way to the communion rail, and took three steps forward.

'I did it because God told me to do it. I was being obedient to the will of the Lord.'

Clay estimated he was in front of the altar rail, closer to her than she wanted him to be but, after a lifetime's practice, her eyes were quick to adjust to darkness.

'Are you carrying a firearm, Clay?'

'Of course not. I was obedient to you.'

'Liar.'

'No, you're the liar.' She took a deep breath and said, 'You weren't being obedient to the will of God in taking that child hostage. Listen to what Jesus Christ said on the matter—'

'Don't you dare quote Holy Scripture at me!'

'*But if anyone causes these little ones to sin, it would be—*'

'Shut up, heathen!'

'Is this a little too close to home, maybe? *Better for him to have a large millstone tied around his neck and be drowned in the depths of the sea.*'

'How can you quote the word of the Lord when you don't even acknowledge his existence?'

'Listen. Can you hear that?'

'Hear what?'

'Exactly. Silence. I believe your hostage is now dead. It's just me and you, and you walked into the darkness into which I invited you.'

'The light gave you an unfair advantage, Clay. I wasn't following your instruction. I was making this fair for me.'

She heard him coming closer, slowly, and could make out a human form in the darkness. Moving forward, her toes came to another wet line. She explored it. This time the line was horizontal and, as Clay stepped back from it, she worked out that it had been poured in the shape of a cross.

'Where are you, you godless bitch?'

'Better to be a godless bitch than a God-fearing paedophile.'

'What did you just say?'

'You heard me, paedophile.'

Clay blinked hard, felt the weight of her eyelids as she gazed into the void, his figure becoming clearer. She could see the entire shape of him, the blackened bulk of his head and body and the lightest patch of his forehead.

She felt the weight of his moral outrage at the slur against his character, and she laughed at him in the darkness.

'How's your little boy?'

The question made the skin along her spine go cold and she felt as though a bunch of sharp hooks had embedded themselves into her scalp. She could feel his mounting rage hammering in her direction through the shadows.

'Why are you asking, paedophile?'

'Does he like his present from Uncle Aaron? And did you know, Clay, it's not just one new pet he's got. You think you're clever, Clay, but you're not. You think you're a good mother, but you're not. You let me into your child's life with two living creatures disguised as one.'

She stared at his form as it edged closer, saw his arms rise from his side and join together in front of him. 'I didn't give it to him. I took it out of the box and placed it on the floor. Then I stood on it, and ground it down into nothing.' She strained her eyes to get a better view of the man facing her.

'That doesn't surprise me, Clay. You know, the worst of Satan's children aren't the niggers or the other ethnic subspecies. It's the godless whites like you. Your sort makes me sick, Clay. You are more of an abomination than the blacks who crawl all over America and the Jews who crucified Jesus and run America from their banks and law firms. I brought you here to tell you, Clay... Where are you, you white trash bitch?'

'Here.'

She ran away to the right, and watched him swing the semi-automatic and aim at the place from which she had just spoken.

'But you're not there now, are you?'

She moved three metres to the right and behind the brickwork of an arch.

'I want you to talk to Kelly-Ann Carter's lawyer in America. I want you to talk to Kelly-Ann if you can.' She heard the unravel-ling of reason in his voice. 'Tell her I love her. Only you won't be able to speak to her, you won't be able to speak to her lawyer, you're going to die. What am I thinking of?'

'Let me go and I'll pass on your message.'

She hid behind the pillar of the arch as his voice advanced towards her. 'Why don't you walk out of here in one piece? Tell her yourself. Tell the whole world about the way, the truth and the life?' She moved inside the arch, heard his slow, laboured breath-ing, and made her way to the other side of the brick structure.

'I knew you'd do this or something like it, Clay.'

She saw the sudden beam of a torch stabbing the shadows and felt a weight of sudden fear drop to her core.

'You won't be able to move now because I'll easily find you. You won't be able to speak and run. See, I know how your mind works.'

His torch hit the brickwork nearest her head. She shrank deeper into the arch and, as the petrol hit the back of her throat, Clay stifled the urge to cough.

'I'm coming for you, you white pig...'

She felt the weight of the Glock 17 pistol in her right hand, saw his torchlight exploring the floor and walls around her at the front of the arch.

As Clay moved from the centre to the back of the arch, his

breath loomed closer and the smell of his wet clothes rose like tragic memories.

She held her breath. He moved along the brickwork at the front of the arch. He stopped, as if alerted by animal instinct that Clay was closer to him now.

'If only you could tell Kelly-Ann that I loved her with all my heart. And that it was impossible to visit her. Impossible for me to go back to America. America? Riddled with the black parasite that ate it from the inside out. Where are you, Clay?'

His torchlight stroked the back pews, within touching distance of her.

She watched him turning slowly in her direction and felt a bead of sweat trickle from her neck down her spine.

'Have you said goodbye to your husband and child, Clay?' His voice was soft but his breathing was heavy. 'Don't worry. Your husband will be fucking some other woman before you're cold in the grave. And your kid? Your kid's going to forget what you looked like or who you were before Christmas. He'll have a brand new mum, prettier than you, younger than you, at home to meet his needs rather than chasing after criminals because your ego says you must. You were the worst kind of mother imaginable and an absentee wife. You deserve to be forgotten. But you did do one thing right. I don't believe you killed the cricket. You obeyed me and gave your son a parasitic cricket. How does that make you feel? Pretty good?'

She heard the fabric of his clothes rubbing against the brick-work on the outside of the arched pillar in which she stood, felt it like an alien vibration.

'I can smell you. I can smell… fear, and the perfume on your skin.'

He reached the back of the arched pillar.

She moved silently, walking backwards, gun at the ready, to the front and behind him. She sidestepped past the brickwork to the right until she was directly behind him. She took out her iPhone, pressed record.

'I'm armed with a Glock 17 pistol. It is pointed directly at the back of your head,' said Clay.

'So pull the goddamned trigger. Shoot me in the back of the head and live with the consequences. Go on, shoot me dead. I'm not going to drop my gun. I don't follow orders from the likes of you, Clay. I only follow orders from God.' Outside the crypt chapel, in the sky overhead, the blades of a helicopter sliced the frozen sky. 'That's not going to help you any.'

She could hear the smile in his voice and the contempt within it.

On the floor near the altar, there came a sound of rasping. It moved slowly and it moved with care away from the altar.

'None of us are going to survive, none of us,' said Aaron. 'I wish I could have visited her, I wish I could have called her, told her how much I loved her.'

The noise on the ground came closer. 'Kelly-Ann, how much I loved her with all my heart and soul.'

'What about Lucy?' asked Clay, keeping Aaron distracted with his own thoughts.

'What about her?' replied Aaron. 'She was a human albatross from the day she was born. I loathe and despise Lucy. Lucy? The fat, useless bitch. She was God's punishment for what happened to Kelly-Ann.'

Rasp.

'I can see you now, Desmond,' said Aaron.

He walked towards the dying man from the arched pillar in the torchlight ahead of him.

'I see you...'

Clay raised her gun and, as she followed Aaron, she aimed at him, his shape in the darkness like the bogeyman from a child's worst nightmare.

Chapter 112

7.23 pm

Sergeant Harris walked quickly to Lucy Bell's cell, as other women in custody shouted and banged on their doors.

'Shut the fuck up, bitch!'

'I want my dad! I want my dad! I want my dad!'

It had started ten minutes earlier and Harris had watched it escalate on the monitor at the front desk. At first it had been a quiet protest but, within the last minute, when there was no response, Lucy had started shouting, her face contorting with anger and confusion. 'I want my daaaaad! Daaaaaaad! Daaaaaaaaad!'

Harris opened the door of her cell and called, 'Lucy! Be quiet!'

She fell silent.

'Sit down and be quiet.'

'Keep it fucking like that, you bitch!' called the woman in the next cell.

'I want my dad...' she whispered from the bed. 'Where's my dad? I want him.'

'He's not coming for you, Lucy, please accept that.'

Her face was blotchy and her eyes red raw, the wound beneath the gauze throbbing. 'I don't believe you. I don't believe what Clay said. He would never abandon me, never. There hasn't been a day in my life when I haven't been with him. I am always with him and he is always with me.'

'Lucy, I believe you're going to have to try to accept that that situation's going to change completely, and soon.'

She sat on her hands and looked up at Sergeant Harris with the eyes of a bewildered child. 'Can you get me my phone and laptop?'

'No, Lucy, I most certainly can't do that.'

'But they're mine, they're my property.'

'And the search warrant that we used when going through

your house gave us the right to seize anything that we deemed as evidence in this investigation. That includes your phone and laptop.'

'I don't like it.'

'Lucy, you're an intelligent woman, and I believe you understand just how serious these crimes are. What did DCI Clay question you about?'

'The child who went missing for over a week, and the old lady in Grant Avenue who fell face- and head-first into her own fireplace.'

'Kidnapping and murder. It doesn't get much more serious than that, does it?'

'My dad didn't do anything wrong. He wouldn't. He's a good man. He's obedient to God. He's a priest.'

'You look troubled, Lucy. What's the matter?'

'My phone and laptop. They're personal. They're mine.'

'Is there anything on there that you think *might* get you into trouble?'

'Yes. No. No comment.'

'Do you want to tell me about it?'

She didn't answer.

'Is the evidence incriminating?'

'There's nothing to tell.' She sat tighter on her hands. 'It's all a big fix anyway.'

'What do you mean by that?'

'If you want to say *I'm guilty*, you'll do what you always do, what you've done for years and years. You'll plant the evidence. That's how it works, isn't it?'

'No, that most certainly isn't how it works.'

She stared at Harris's feet and a fresh round of silent tears started.

'Be quiet now, Lucy. Don't upset the women around you. You're stressed out. So are they. It's not fair. OK? If you pull a stunt like this in prison…'

'Prison?'

'... You'll be torn from limb to limb.'

But as he closed the cell door, she started up again, each word louder than the last. 'I want my dad! I want my dad! I want my dad! I want my daaaaaaad!'

Chapter 113

7.39 pm

'Put the gun down,' Clay said, calmly. 'He's going to die of his injuries.'

'You got it wrong, Clay. You said he was already dead. You're not the authority on death that you think you are.'

She felt mounting sickness at the seemingly inevitable prospect of firing a bullet into another human being for the first time in her life.

'If you don't drop your gun, I'm going to have to shoot you. Do you understand?'

'Oh, I understand...'

'I'm going to give you to the count of three. If your gun's not on the floor, I will shoot you on three. One, two...'

She saw a blast of fire and heat from his Magnum, studded with sparks and aimed down at the victim. In the half-moment that followed the gunshot, the vertical line of petrol that divided the central aisle turned into a river of flame, a river that veered to the left and right as the petroleum cross caught fire.

Clay moved backwards and away from the horizontal arms of the burning cross that lit up Father Aaron Bell's still figure. He walked onto the right arm of the cross, the hem of his trousers bursting into a fire that licked up his legs and chased up his body.

She heard a noise like a stereo explosion, saw that the cross had connected with the perimeters of the room, and that it was framed by a rectangle of fire that locked her into the building.

She saw that the flames were already up to waist height and felt a wave of sweat break from under her clothes.

As she stood in the middle of symmetrical lines of fire, she watched Aaron's burning form turn in her direction and the crypt chapel was filled with fire and light.

She picked out the font at the back, a metre away from the perimeter of fire and, marching towards it, slipped out of her coat.

Aaron's rising screams drew her to look back at a burning man, his arms outstretched like Christ on the cross. Fire danced from his head, leaped from his arms and torso.

'My God!' he screamed, as Clay made it to the font. 'My God!'

She pulled the wooden lid from the font and eyed a section on the perimeter of fire, a way out to the wings of the chapel and back through the door she had entered.

'Why...' His voice was long, and turning from the thing he was into the thing he was becoming.

She sank her coat into the water of the font, picking it up and drowning it rapidly, repeating the action once, twice, three times.

'Have you...'

Through the cackle of the flames, his voice grew louder.

'Forsaken...'

She picked her spot on the burning perimeter, felt the water pouring through her hands as she made her way there. She heard the rapid discharge of bullets heading in her direction, dipped down, tasting blood in her mouth as she bit her tongue.

She reached into the fire with her coat, dropped it to the ground as she felt a series of explosions on her torso and smelled the corruption of burning fabric directly under her nose. A sensation of fists battering her body hit her chest and abdomen; bullets hit her flak jacket and she felt the blood draining from her extremities to her vital organs.

Clay stood up and saw a gap forming in the wall of fire where she'd thrown down her wet coat, the flames falling to centimetres above the ground.

'Mmmeeeeeeeeeeeeeee?'

The heat from his body and the cry from his core were behind her.

She turned. The flames that consumed him danced in her face, a metre away.

'Mmmmeeeeeeeeeeee?'

She saw the Magnum behind the wall of fire, pointed at her head.

Clay raised her Glock 17, pointed it at his face, a man completely on fire, his face melting before her eyes. She glimpsed into his eyes as she prepared to pull back the trigger, and saw the furthest corner of hell where profound madness ruled.

His arm withered, his hand dispensed bullets into the ground.

He swayed and his head drooped as he dropped the Magnum.

Clay looked down at him, the skin and muscle around his face dissolving into his skull, his weapon skidding across the wooden floor. He raised his burning gun hand towards Clay and made a noise as he fired the last delusional bullet in her direction.

As Aaron Bell died at her feet, she looked at the hostage through the arches and hurried to him, hoping to find a sign of life. She held his wrist and looked for a pulse, opened his mouth for signs of breathing, but none were there.

Clay looked at his face, torn by agony in the closure of his life, and hoped that when he was in the chapel of rest, his widow would somehow not see the torment that she had witnessed at first hand.

She walked back to the burning body of the man who had just tried to kill her and stared at him, watched and listened as the last breath left his body.

'Kelly... Ann...'

The overwhelming smell of roast pork rose from his fallen flesh, and Clay pushed down her gag reflex.

She picked up the aluminium bowl at the centre of the font and carried it to the space where she had dampened down the cage of flame. She turned the bowl upside down and the fire died before her eyes.

As she walked through the gap over her waterlogged coat, her body ached in every place and her throat felt lined with barbed wire.

'Lucy,' she said to herself, heading for the door, imagining the scene in an interview suite in Trinity Road Police Station. 'I've got some very bad news for you about your father.'

Chapter 114

7.51 pm

Outside the Metropolitan Cathedral, Detective Sergeant Bill Hendricks felt the pulse of his iPhone and connected the call.

'Hello, Poppy.'

'How's Eve?'

'We don't know. What's happening?'

'I've cracked open Lucy Bell's phone and laptop.'

He watched the door leading into the crypt and sensed great excitement beneath the anxiety in her voice.

'What have you found on them?'

The door opened and Clay emerged. She appeared to be in a world of her own, looking into the space in front of her.

'Eve?' He heard Riley's voice as she hurried down the stone steps towards Clay. She paused, pulled at the straps of her flak jacket as Riley reached her.

'What's happening?' asked Poppy.

'Eve's just walked out of the crypt. She's come out alive but I don't know if she's been injured. Paramedics are heading to her right now'

'I'm all right,' Clay called out. 'We need to call Scientific Support and the mortuary. We've got two dead bodies in there. Father Aaron Bell and, I'm guessing, supposing, someone connected with the Metropolitan Cathedral, a black male, mid-thirties, who probably died because of the colour of his skin.'

Clay handed her flak jacket and Glock 17 to Riley. At the top of the steps, she looked around and picked out Hendricks.

'Who are you on to, Bill?'

'Poppy Waters.' He listened to the civilian IT expert, and smiled. 'Thanks for that, Poppy,' he said, as Clay walked towards him. 'Sooner rather than later if you don't mind.'

'What's she come up with, Bill?'

He handed Clay his phone, smelled burned hair and saw the bullet marks on the flak jacket in Riley's hands. 'Shit!' he muttered.

'Poppy? What's happening?'

'Lucy Bell, Eve. She's an out-and-out monster, a monster without a proverbial leg to stand on.'

Chapter 115

8.59 pm

When Lucy Bell stopped howling and had taken many deep breaths, Clay made eye contact with her.

'Lucy, I'm sorry your father's dead but that doesn't mean that we can let you go,' said Clay. 'Please look at the items on the desk in front of you and identify them.'

'I don't know what they are. I've never seen them before in my life.'

'We took them from your house, Lucy.'

'That doesn't mean they belong to me.'

'If the laptop doesn't belong to you, why has it got thirteen drafts of your PhD dissertation, your lecture notes going back three years, your research notes going back even further, notes relating to your training and role as a Eucharistic minister in the Roman Catholic Church, the photographs you took of Jack Dare when he wasn't aware you were doing so and your secret diary outlining your graphic sexual fantasies about him?'

'This is such an invasion of my privacy, and at a time like this when I'm distraught because my father has just died.'

'No, it's not an invasion of your privacy, it's a serious criminal investigation and you are right at the dead centre of it.'

Lucy looked at her solicitor. 'Tell her to go away.'

'Miss Bell, I'd advise you to answer DCI Clay's questions.'

'How did my dad die?' asked Lucy.

'I'll testify to the coroner's court that it was probably suicide,' replied Clay.

'Liar! He would never do such a thing...'

'I was there, Lucy. I saw it. He must have doused himself in petrol, knowing he was going to catch fire.'

'Where is he?'

'At the mortuary.'

'I want to go to him.'

'That's not going to happen. Lucy?'

'What?'

Hendricks picked up the large brown envelope in front of him and shuffled out a wedge of A4 pages.

'What's that?' she asked.

'Over to you, DS Hendricks.'

'You keep two diaries, Lucy. The one you showed to Detective Constable Winters.'

'What's that nigger had to say for himself?'

'Pardon?' said Hendricks.

'I didn't say a word,' Lucy replied.

'You did say a word,' said Hendricks. 'A very bad word, and I don't want you to disrespect my friend and colleague like that again.'

Lucy looked at her solicitor.

'That was racist and completely unnecessary, Miss Bell. Please don't use that language in my presence.'

'Whose side are you on?'

'Lucy, we have a full account of your life during the past two weeks and stretching back before. In your very own words.' Hendricks pushed the pages towards Lucy. 'We have multiple copies of the same document printed off from your laptop. Have a look through it.'

She thumbed the pages, taking random stabs at the writing with her eyes.

'It's a fantasy. That's all. I was bored. I didn't know it would come true – how could I? If you think I'm going to sit here and implicate my father or Jack Dare in crimes that they didn't commit, you can think again.'

'Lucy, I'm going to remind you of a good piece of advice that you gave to your students at the end of your lecture on Joseph Stalin. A piece of advice that DCI Clay and I are going to follow really closely. *Never let your subject off the hook*,' said Hendricks.

'I'm going *no comment*.'

'Which you have the right to do, absolutely,' said Clay.

'My father loved me. I will not allow you to sully his memory. He loved me above and beyond all other human beings.'

Clay took out her iPhone. 'Do you want to hear some of his final words, Lucy?'

Lucy looked at Clay with the eyes of a woman seeing a ghost. 'Yes.'

'You'll hear my voice and the voice you'll hear in the background is the man who your father burned alive and later went on to shoot in the head at point-blank range. Who's Kelly-Ann?'

'I've never heard of anyone called Kelly-Ann.'

Clay pressed play. '*I'm armed with a Glock 17 pistol.*' Clay heard the iron in her own voice but, beneath this, the colossal tension she had sensed in those moments. '*It is pointed directly at your head.*'

'*So pull the goddamned trigger. Shoot me in the back of the head and live with the consequences. Go on, shoot me dead.*'

Lucy spat at Clay across the table and a ball of phlegm hit her on the cheekbone. Hendricks handed her a tissue from the box on the table and Clay wiped away Lucy Bell's spit.

'*I'm not going to drop my gun. I don't follow orders from the likes of you, Clay. I only follow orders from God.*'

'That's right, Dad! That's right… Go to hell, Clay,' said Lucy.

'*That's not going to help you any,*' said Father Aaron Bell.

'What's not going to help you any?' asked Lucy.

'The police helicopter was overhead at that time. Underneath the bravado, your father was really panicking at this point. That, Lucy, is the sound in the background of his victim begging to be finished off. Your father now…'

'*None of us are going to survive, none of us. I wish I could have visited her, I wish I could have called her, told her…*'

'Dad, you could have visited me…'

'*… how much I loved her…*'

'Even though you never said it, Dad, I knew you loved me all along…'

'*Kelly-Ann, how much I loved her with all my heart and soul.*'

As the sound of Father Aaron Bell's final victim crawling and moaning on the ground drifted from Clay's iPhone, she watched the blood drain from Lucy's face and the horror registering in her eyes.

'Turn! Turn it off!'

'*What about Lucy?*'

'*What about her? She was a human albatross from the day she was born. I loathe and despise Lucy. Lucy? The fat, useless bitch. She was God's punishment for what happened to Kelly-Ann.*'

Clay pressed pause.

'His final thoughts on you and Kelly-Ann, Lucy. I'm going to give you half an hour to think about what you've heard, to talk to your solicitor, and then I'm going to bring you back for interview.'

'We have so much evidence against you, evidence from your own writing, evidence from your phone, evidence about how you and Jack plotted to frame his brother for your joint racially motivated hate crimes,' said Hendricks. 'Cooperating with us is your only option.' He turned to Lucy Bell's solicitor. 'Can you please advise your client accordingly.'

'No, I'm afraid I'm walking on this one,' said the solicitor.

'I'll need a new solicitor,' said Lucy.

'I suggest,' said Clay, 'that you behave yourself when your next solicitor shows. Otherwise they'll walk. Stop acting like a petulant five year old, and get some grown-up manners.'

Chapter 116

9.28 pm

Clay looked at the blinking red 2 on her answer machine and, pressing play, looked out of the window of the incident room on the top floor of Trinity Road Police Station.

The first message was silent; the receiver was quickly replaced by the caller.

The second message began with a tentative, 'Hello...'

The voice was elderly and frail, and Clay wondered in the uncertain silence if it was going to be one of Father Aaron Bell's congregation coming forward with information about the priest, or springing blindly to his defence.

'Hello, Eve, Eve Clay. It's Sister Ruth – remember me from St Claire's? I was with you when you were a small girl, me and Sister Philomena. My number is 496 0688. I go to bed at seven in the evening but if you ask for the duty manager, Jane McGregor, you can arrange to come and see me. Any time is good for me except nine in the morning when I attend mass. It would be lovely to see you. Goodbye for now and God bless you, Eve.'

She rang back immediately and within a few seconds the person at the other end connected.

'Bethlehem House, Jane McGregor speaking.'

'Hello, Jane, my name's Eve Clay...'

'I've heard so much about you, Eve. Is this concerning a visit to Sister Ruth?'

'It is.'

'She had another visitor recently. Father Aaron Bell. He said you wanted to see her and that he was acting as the go-between.'

'Was he a friend of hers?'

'No,' replied Jane McGregor. Clay felt a modicum of relief. 'Sister Ruth told him she'd contact you, but Father Aaron said you didn't want her to get directly in touch with you.'

'That's simply not true. I'm more than happy to speak to Sister Ruth. I don't need anyone acting as my go-between.'

'He told Sister Ruth you'd contact her when you had the time. In the end, Sister Ruth grew tired of waiting. She contacted you directly in spite of what Father Aaron had said.'

'I'm so glad she did. He lied to Sister Ruth and he lied to me.'

'To be honest with you, DCI Clay,' Jane's voice dropped a few notches. 'No one here really likes him. He comes here to distribute the Holy Sacrament with his daughter. I don't know what it is about them...'

You're about to find out, thought Clay. 'I'd like to come and see Sister Ruth at some point tomorrow, if that's possible.'

'Ring before you're leaving and I'll make sure she's available. She doesn't receive many visitors so it will be a nice change for her to see a face from the old days.'

Clay saw Riley approaching quickly, her face lined with worry, and made a gesture acknowledging that they would speak immediately.

'I've got to go, Jane. I will call before I leave. Thank you for your help.'

As Clay hung up, Riley said, 'I've just had a call from Hendricks. Lucy Bell wants to talk with you. It seems she and Jack Dare have got some sort of pact going on. She's going to do all the talking for both of them.'

'I'll be down there in five minutes.' Clay picked up the receiver and called home.

'Eve?' Thomas sounded perplexed and stressed-out. 'I'm seeing all kinds of reports of a fire in the cathedral. Social media's buzzing. Were you involved?'

'I'm fine, stop giving yourself an ulcer. Pour yourself a drink and relax, I'll explain everything when I see you. How's Philip?'

'Loving his new pet, Dixie.'

The weight on her heart grew heavier. 'Do me a favour, handsome?'

'No problem.'

'Let the cricket go. Get rid of the box it came in, but get it out of the house asap.'

'Why?'

'It's got a parasite living inside it. And I've just watched the priest who gave it to Philip shoot a man in cold blood and set himself alight.'

'Another quiet day in the office. I'll release it then. Any place in particular?'

'Away from Philip. Away from our home.'

'I'll do that as soon as we hang up. What about the book he gave him?'

'I've just had a thought about that. Will you check it and see if there's a dedication?'

'One second.'

She listened to him leave and return, talking to himself, 'Dedicated to? Dedicated to? Eve, I've got it right here. It's dedicated to a Kelly-Ann Carter. Is that helpful to you?'

'Very. I'll send a constable around for it. I may well need it in the next few hours.'

'Are you all right, Eve?'

'Hopefully I'll be home at some point in the next few hours.'

'I'm off from the surgery tomorrow.'

'I'll join you.'

'Call me when you're on your way home and I'll run the bath for you. He's going to be disappointed when his cricket's gone.'

'Tell him... tell him we'll buy him a dog.'

'Really?'

'Really. We'll figure things out as we go along.'

'He won't be that disappointed then,' laughed Thomas.

'The sooner I go, the sooner I'm home.'

'I love you.'

'Ditto.'

'People around?' he asked.

'Yes. But that was a very big, loud ditto, Thomas.' Her voice became little more than a whisper. 'Loaded with a promise you'd be a fool to turn down.'

She replaced the receiver, straightened up into professional mode and picked up the printout of Lucy Bell's secret diary from her desk.

Chapter 117

9.48 pm

At the front desk of Trinity Road Police Station, Jack Dare stared into nothing and was as silent as he was vacant.

'Jack,' said Clay. 'You've just been charged with murder.'

The door leading into the station opened.

'And I've just responded. I understand...'

'But do you understand how serious this is for you?'

His eyes turned in her direction but he looked right through her. Footsteps approached and Clay turned to see Carmel Dare walking towards them.

'You're a liar, Jack!'

Jack faced his mother. 'What are you doing here?'

Clay weighed Carmel up, and saw a woman on the verge of collapse, whose world had turned inside out in a matter of days.

'I said, what are you doing here, mother?'

'I've come to see you.'

She folded her arms and glared at Jack. 'I went to see Doctor Salah, to get some medication for my nerves. I thanked him for helping Raymond, for having him back, for issuing him with a new prescription, for putting him back on track with Broad Oak. I sat there and praised you to the sky, said what a wonderful son and brother you are. He looked at me as if I wasn't right in the head. Why was that, Jack?' Carmel Dare stepped forward and held her son's gaze. The corners of his mouth cracked into the merest smile. 'Doctor Salah looked on his laptop, checked the medical centre's records. *Jack didn't make an appointment on his brother's behalf.* That's what he said, Jack. And me like a prize idiot said, *Are you sure, Doctor Salah?* He told me straight. *Jack didn't bring his brother in to see me and I didn't issue a prescription for Raymond's drugs.* I asked him to double-check with the reception desk. I could see in his eyes he was getting brassed off at this point, but I wanted so badly to believe that it was all a terrible mistake. Do you know what the receptionists had to say for themselves? *Jack definitely didn't make an appointment for Raymond.* All three of them, Jack. What do you say to that? What are you smirking at?'

'You.'

'Cheeky bastard.'

'Cheeky bitch. I've just been charged with murder, and you blow in here worrying about Raymond and what I have and haven't done for him. I'm more important than Raymond, and that's a fact you've never understood.'

'He was weak but you were strong. I had to protect him.'

'You're like a stuck record and I'm sick of listening to the jarring noise of your voice.'

Carmel hung onto the edges of the desk with both hands.

'Why did you promise me you'd help him and why did you lie to me?'

Jack looked away from his mother and at the clock on the wall.

'Look at me, Jack. Why did you lie to me?'

'Less than two minutes to go,' he replied.

'What does that mean?' asked Carmel.

'So I told a lie, Mum. What do you want me to say about Raymond? Why did you sleep with a man with nigger blood in him and bring his runt into this world?'

The blood flew from her extremities and her face turned chalk-white. Fury left her speechless.

'Do you want to know what else I lied about?'

He looked back at the clock as the minute hand edged closer to ten to ten.

'Go on.'

'I wasn't protecting him from the police when I burned his clothes. I made a pig's ear of it, so the police'd think it was him covering his tracks and destroying the evidence. I was setting him up. I planted evidence in his bedroom. I planted a template of the Black Sun symbol and black paint, the things I used to leave graffiti at the Picton Road scene. I wrote most of his manifesto and planted the words *Killing Time Is Here Embrace It* inside it. I planted ideas in his head. I flushed his medication down the toilet and convinced him he'd done it. We even set him up with some foreign slag called Dominika.'

'We?' Carmel looked as if she was about to explode with anger.

'Lucy and me.'

'Why?'

'Lots of reasons. But me, personally? Because I hate him, I always have done and I always will.' He looked at the clock, smiled broadly and said, 'Nearly there. But I don't hate him as much as I hate you.' He sniffed loudly. 'You stink. You stink of cooking oil and failure.'

As Carmel lurched towards him, Clay grabbed her and held on.

'Get him out of here!' said Clay. 'Carmel, please don't make us restrain you.'

Sergeant Harris took Jack by the arm and marched him in the direction of the cells. 'Have you got anything else to say, Jack?'

He looked back over his shoulder. 'Yes. His non-existent

friends, CJ and Buster. I put them inside his head. It's ten to ten, so these are the very last words that will proceed from my mouth. Such is the will of the Lord. The end. The vow of silence. Everlasting silence. Amen.'

As the door closed and Jack was gone, Clay felt the merest reduction of tension in Carmel's body.

'Let me go, DCI Clay.'

Clay released her arms.

Carmel looked at Clay, eyes brimming with tears. 'What's going on?'

'I'm about to find out, Carmel.'

'How can you find out if he won't speak, for God's sake?'

'I'm going to speak to Lucy Bell.'

'Her and her father. They've messed with his head. This isn't Jack. It just isn't him at all.'

'I'm sorry, Carmel. I really am sorry.' *But I believe it is.*

Chapter 118

10.03 pm

Clay sat down next to Hendricks, across from Lucy Bell and her new solicitor Mr Jones. Looking at the young woman, Clay could see a pronounced improvement in her demeanour. She glanced at Hendricks and saw the glimmer of a smile in his eyes.

'You know what, Lucy,' said Hendricks. 'You look like you did when I watched you give your lecture on Joseph Stalin.'

Lucy said nothing as Hendricks went on to formally open the interview.

Clay pushed the printout of the diary across the table. 'Would you like to say anything to Detective Sergeant Hendricks's observation about you?'

'Yes. Things that have happened in the past are classed as

history. I'm going to talk history to both of you. In this I have every confidence. I am not a useless bitch. I am not God's punishment for anything that happened or is going to happen to Kelly-Ann Carter, whoever she is. That is nothing to do with me. Aaron Bell has incensed me greatly.'

Lucy turned over a few pages of her diary.

'We've got everything in writing, Lucy, but we want to hear it from your mouth. We want to hear you tell your side of things for the benefit of the audio tape on the table beside you and the camera up in the corner pointing at you. The printed page is one thing. Hearing it directly from the central player is altogether different, and much more positive from my point of view. There might be things you have omitted from your written account that come to mind as you speak.' She turned to Mr Jones. 'Do you have anything to say on behalf of your client, Mr Jones?'

'She would like to apologise for her behaviour earlier.'

'I'm sorry for spitting at you, DCI Clay.'

'Miss Bell and I have had a long and serious discussion, and she now accepts that the voice on your iPhone was her father, and that you didn't manufacture it to undermine her. She is naturally upset at his death but she has been even more upset by the things he said about her. She became quite angry with him at one point and would be grateful if you could refer to him as Aaron or Aaron Bell as you question her.'

'Not a problem,' said Clay. 'Let's start with something I know nothing about, Lucy. You have a pact with Jack Dare.'

'We made a pact. In the event that we got caught, he would take a vow of silence. He would honour the Lord by speaking only to God, in prayerfulness in his heart, in his soul, in his head. I will do the talking and when I have finished I will join him in that silent act of lifelong worship.'

Clay put herself in Carmel Dare's position, imagined Philip squandering his future and taking a ridiculous vow to gag himself indefinitely. 'You do realise that this pact may be unworkable when you go to court?'

'We will seek guidance from the Holy Spirit when the time comes.'

'Tell me what you know about the abduction of Marta Ondřej,' said Clay.

'This was nothing to do with me. I advised against it. I told them crimes against children have terrible consequences. They did not listen to my advice.'

'They?'

'Aaron Bell and Jack Dare.'

'Did they target Marta?'

'Yes.'

'Why?'

'Karl Adamczak told my father about the girl. He was sorry that England had allowed Czech Roma into the country.'

'Who picked her up?'

'Jack, in Aaron Bell's car. I was with my academic tutor at the time. Aaron Bell was in his house or church. As I stressed in my diary, I was not there, so I cannot be sure of the details.'

'Jack could tell us?'

'Jack could but he won't.'

'What did he tell you?'

'The Adamczak brothers told Aaron Bell about the multiple tenancy that Marta lived in with her mother and other people. They told him that the people in the house were giving other migrants a bad name. Jack, who was obedient at all times to Aaron. Jack, who knew everything about Aaron's crimes in America. Jack, who knew everything about the crimes in England, and joined in willingly.'

'Stop!' said Clay. 'Your diary stretches back over years, detailing your visits to Jack when he was in prison. You brainwashed him when he was inside, and when he came out Aaron Bell finished the process off. Between you, you reset his moral compass and made him believe that evil was good and good was evil, and that everything you did was God's will. And when you're caught, how convenient for you – Jack closes down.'

'Are you saying I'm lying about Jack's involvement in the abduction and murders?'

'What I'm saying is this. Jack's going to have a lot of time to think between now and going to court. Don't bank on him keeping up the vow of silence forever. According to Jack, he's already been burned by other people's lies about him. I don't believe he'll allow it to happen a second time. His dog was killed by his brother. His faith's been rocked. It's only a matter of time before he stands up for himself.' Clay smiled. 'Tell me what you know about the abduction of Marta Ondřej.'

'Jack Dare waited on the corner of Smithdown Lane in Aaron's car. When Marta walked down the road on her own, he opened the door of the car and she got in meekly, like a lamb to the slaughter.

'He had been observing Marta and her mother for days, on Aaron's instruction, which was therefore the will of the Lord. She always wandered out by herself to the end of the road and back to the house at roughly the same time each day. Jack waited for her. And instead of allowing her to turn and walk back home, he opened the door of the car.

'Aaron Bell's next plan was to murder the Adamczak brothers. This was brought forward when Marta got out of the cupboard in the vestry. She showed herself to Kate Thorpe in the doorway between the vestry and the church. On Aaron's instruction, on the morning after the murder of the Polish parasites, I released Marta in the Mystery. I thought the weather was good for such a thing because of the fog and poor visibility. When I took her there, I looked back through the haze at all the houses on Grant Avenue, and 131 in particular. Kate Thorpe's house. Busybody. Eyes everywhere. Calmness deserted me and chaos filled my head. *I told them not to involve children, and I'm the one delivering her back into the world.* I ran away and then went back to her, figuring I'd call the emergency services to stop them suspecting me.'

'What happened when she was in captivity?'

'I do not know. I did not involve myself.'

'That chimes with your diary entries,' said Clay. 'What did Aaron hope to achieve by abducting a child?'

'Black Sun logic. The stirring up of hatred between the sub-humans. Poles will hate Roma with a violent passion. Roma will hate Poles with an equally violent passion. Hate will breed hate. Violence will escalate violence. The ill-treatment of children quickens the blood for such hatred. It was a deterrent, also. *Don't come to this land. This is what will happen to your children.*'

'How did Kate Thorpe let Aaron Bell know that she'd seen Marta emerge from the vestry?'

'She wrote it down. He burned it after he'd tried to convince her that she'd had another of her visions, but he knew he hadn't convinced her one little bit. He knew that Marta had escaped from the cupboard – when mass finished, she was standing still as a statue in the vestry with the door to the cupboard wide open. He believed with each passing second that Kate was becoming more and more of a danger. That she would tell someone what she had seen. This is why I was instructed to release her.'

'How did Marta get out of the cupboard?'

'I let her out.'

'Wasn't that an act of disobedience?'

'I was being obedient to God, who has more authority than Aaron Bell. I did not want to be a part of Black Sun. I did not want to be party to the kidnapping of a child. I did not want to kill or hurt the Adamczak brothers. I did not want any of it. This is why God told me to release her. So others could see. So that Aaron Bell's plans would be overturned.'

'When she was in captivity, who made the eight films of her?'

'Jack filmed the abuse. Aaron Bell committed it. He told me he was following the will of the Lord. I believe he lost contact with the Lord years ago, and the only will he was following was his own.'

'You used the word *abuse* just now. Did Aaron Bell ever abuse you when you were a girl?'

Lucy held her hands out, palms upwards and prayerful.

'We're trying to get a wider picture of who you are and why you're the way you are,' said Hendricks.

'Abuse me as a girl?' asked Lucy, dropping her hands and looking back and forth between Clay and Hendricks.

'What form did Aaron's abuse take?'

'Imprisonment in my room. Imprisonment under the floorboards. For days on end when I was disobedient. With very little or no food. Hardly any water. It made me think of the wisdom of obedience. My spirit was broken piece by piece. Once, under the floorboards, I lost the will to be me.'

'What else did he do?'

'Once he cut my hair off, though I didn't want it to be so.'

'Do you know he did these things to Marta?'

'I was sorry for her.'

'Why did you kill Kate Thorpe?'

'There was really no choice in killing Kate Thorpe. I did it because I was scared. I believed I was following the will of the Lord in releasing Marta into the vestry, but it was the voice of the Devil. All it did was make matters much, much worse. I shouldn't have done it.'

'Did Aaron ask you if you'd released her?'

'He did. I lied. I said *No*.'

'Were you directly involved in the murder of the Adamczak brothers?'

'Yes, I was. We all were. The whole of Black Sun was directly involved.'

'Did Black Sun include Raymond Dare?'

'No. He's a clown. He's racially inferior.'

'In what way was he racially inferior?'

'His paternal grandfather was half-caste.'

'Did Raymond know this?'

'Raymond knew this. His mother told him. There were photographs of him when he was a baby with his father. His father had the facial features of a negro and was clearly not white. His mother knew his grandfather. His grandfather had a white mother and a Jamaican father. His father left before he could remember him. Raymond was not eligible to be part of Black Sun. But he could be our scapegoat.'

'Tell me about Dominika Zima.'

'I confess now to the murder of Dominika Zima. I knew her from Levene House where I volunteer. I took pictures of Dominika on her phone. I told her about Raymond. I told her he was a rich young man and looking for a girlfriend, an older woman. I gave her his number. I knew about her date with Raymond from Jack. I tailed her in Aaron's car and when Raymond picked her up, I followed them to Otterspool Park.'

'Stop. You said in an earlier interview that you couldn't drive. You took one lesson and hated it.'

'Well, I lied. Doesn't everybody lie? What is the truth?'

'What happened after they'd had sex?'

'When they argued after sex and he left, she was still alive. I set up a Black Sun murder: the Black Sun graffiti and the words *Killing Time Is Here Embrace It* on the inside of the railway bridge. It would link Raymond to her death and to the deaths of the Adamczak brothers. He has the misfortune of being openly racist, a drug user and mentally ill. He was the ideal candidate to suffer the consequences of our actions.'

'Are you really a religious woman, Lucy?' asked Clay.

'I am a human being. I am religious. As were the saints, Peter and Paul. Saint Peter was an inveterate liar and Saint Paul was a mass murderer. I am in good company, am I not?'

'What happened when the Adamczak brothers died, Lucy?'

'After I'd murdered Dominika, I spoke to Aaron and Jack and told them what I'd done. Aaron said, *Let's not let our bloods grow cool. We'll kill the brothers and wreak havoc, leave Marta's hair at the scene, transfer the films of Marta onto Václav's phone. We will laugh at the police as they hurry down a blind alley where Raymond Dare will be waiting for them, wiped out on drugs, psychotic, unaware of what day of the week it is.*

'Aaron went to their flat and drank with them, telling them of the old lady in his congregation and her visions of the Virgin Mary and Jesus. Karl understood but was unmoved; Karl translated and Václav cried like a baby. When Karl and Václav were drunk, their doorbell rang. It was me and Jack. We had come to walk Aaron home on account of his old age and the dangers on the streets. Karl left the kitchen for the bedroom, wanting to sleep, very drunk indeed. Jack followed Karl and strangled him. Aaron prayed with Václav before he died in the kitchen at Jack's hands. Jack carried him to the bedroom, stone dead. We did the graffiti, planted the evidence then set them on fire.'

'Who set their heads on fire?' asked Clay.

'I did. But they were already dead. So that doesn't matter. Jack walked towards the nearest CCTV camera in Raymond's clothes, walking like Raymond, walking like an ape, a vain and empty ape. Aaron and I walked the other way. Out of sight and out of mind.'

'Why did Raymond stop taking his anti-psychotic medication?'

'Jack ordered him to.'

'How did you kill Kate Thorpe?'

'Strangulation. I am a fast learner and I saw how Jack did it. After I'd given her communion and burned her images of me and Marta, I blocked the chimney, set up more coal and firelighters and left Kate face down in the flames. No longer a threat. How is Jack?'

'Obedient to your pact. Silent now. You won't be able to retract this confession, Lucy,' said Clay. 'It's all in your diary.'

'Nothing I have said or written will be retracted.'

Clay reached into her bag and placed Aaron Bell's book on the table. She turned it around for Lucy to see and showed her the dedication page.

'Who was Kelly-Ann Carter and what was she to Aaron Bell?' asked Clay.

'She was no one. What else can I say? No one. I've never heard of her.' Lucy sat back on the chair and let out a long sigh of relief. 'Confession is good for the soul. Will I be able to see Jack?'

'You'll see him at the Crown Court, Preston probably, when you're both being tried for murder. He for the murder of Karl and Václav Adamczak. You for Dominika Zima and Kate Thorpe.'

'Did you have more killings planned?' asked Hendricks.

'Three young Pakistani men. But there would have been more. *When one man dies, it's a tragedy. When a million die, it's a statistic.* Joseph Stalin.'

An idea that had irritated Clay since Aaron Bell had asked her about the cricket he had given to Philip came to the front of her mind. 'Aaron mentioned something to me about a cricket. A cricket with another creature inside it. What was he talking about?'

'The cricket he gave to your son, like many crickets and grasshoppers, was like a Russian doll. Inside the cricket he gave to Philip is a black hair worm. It caught the parasite from the vegetation it's been eating. The cricket is an ideal environment for a parasite. It's wet, it's warm and it's full of nutrients. The black parasite eats the cricket from the inside out, feasting on the host's sexual organs. It can force the host to commit suicide by throwing itself into the water. It interferes with the host's neurotransmitters, making it depressed. The black parasite exits the host's body from the back passage; it wriggles its way out and lives on. This is science as a perfect metaphor.'

'A metaphor for what?'

'The cricket is God's earth, the world of the white Christian men and women. The black parasite is anyone and everyone who isn't a white Christian. They are Satan's children, placed here on earth to test their superiors. I now join Jack in the vow of silence, and that silence will join us together wherever we happen to be, however far apart we are. Tell him I'm sorry I won't be able to visit him this time round. Tell him I love him. Tell him Aaron Bell is dead and gone and the only thing that can come between us now is time and space. And what is time but a counting game? And what is space but the distance between one divided body and another, our body, Jack and me!'

Chapter 119

11.47 pm

'Simon Wheatley speaking. How can I help you?'

Clay was surprised not to hear an American voice and pinned the lawyer's accent down to South Wales. 'Hello, Mr Wheatley. My name is Detective Chief Inspector Eve Clay. I'm from the Merseyside Constabulary. I believe you represent Kelly-Ann Carter?'

'I have done for the past ten years.'

'I'm sorry to hear Kelly-Ann's last appeal has failed.'

Wheatley was quiet for a while, and Clay sensed a bitter disappointment that went beyond professional pride. 'So am I. She's my friend. I'm very fond of her.'

'Does it work both ways?'

'Certainly. I've been her only visitor for the last ten years. We rub along well.'

'Does she share personal information with you?'

'Yes. Where's this going, DCI Clay?'

'I've got some news to deliver. Father Aaron Bell is dead.'

'Kelly-Ann will be devastated. He's been her pen pal for years. How did he die?'

'It was a fire but it was self-inflicted. Before he died, he asked me to speak to you and pass on the message that he loved Kelly-Ann.'

'I'll tell her, of course I will.'

'Mr Wheatley, I know your priority is to defend your client, but I'm not going to hold back. There was a lot more to Father Aaron Bell than appeared on the surface. Would you agree with that?'

'I would if I'd ever met him.'

'Aaron Bell was not his real name. His real name was Christopher Darwin, and he was the leader of a group called Black Sun of which Kelly-Ann was a member. Mr Wheatley, I think you know all of this already, but I'm not going to tell anyone. I know the consequences would be devastating for you.'

'I really don't know what you're talking about. I know nothing about Christopher Darwin, other than what's in the media and common knowledge Father Aaron Bell was Kelly-Ann's pen pal, end of story. On my mother's life.'

'Okay. But I need some information. Who is Kelly-Ann Carter?'

There was a pause. Then Wheatley said, 'She's Christopher Darwin's daughter by a relationship he had when he was in his late teens, early twenties. His family paid the mother off with a monthly allowance and a gagging order. The Darwins were wealthy Catholics and Suzie-Mae Carter was poor white trash. Aaron Bell loved Suzie-Mae and he was devastated, but they threatened to cut him off completely if he went anywhere near her.

'When Darwin started out as leader of Black Sun, Kelly-Ann tracked him down and joined. Suzie-Mae was dead by then, so he was her only parent.'

'Were they close?'

'Yes, too close if you ask me.'

'In what way?'

'They shared a bed. No one else in Black Sun knew the real nature of their relationship. Kelly-Ann was smart. When the FBI infiltrated the group, it took her half a day to smell a rat and she advised her father to stop ordering killings. When she was certain they were Feds, she warned her father. He split, and Kelly-Ann went out alone for one last spree. She knew she'd be caught, but she took the rap for Darwin and got the treatment he deserved.'

'Thank you, Mr Wheatley. It's all falling into place now.'

'When Kelly-Ann dies, I'm stopping this work to spend more time with my family. I need a new start.'

'I wish you well in that.'

As soon as Clay hung up, the phone rang out again and she wondered what bombshell was coming next.

'DCI Clay speaking.'

'It's Doctor Ellington, Broad Oak. We have a patient on the wards who I'm told is still in your custody. I think you ought to come over and see what he's done.'

'I'll be there as soon as I can.'

Day Four

Thursday, 4th December

Chapter 120

1.01 am

'Many psychiatric patients have strong artistic leanings,' said Doctor Ellington as she took Clay to Raymond Dare's door. 'I've met hundreds, some of a very high standard, some only able to paint like children, but this...'

Clay saw the armed officer at the door of Raymond's room and said, 'Evening, PC Rodgers.'

'Evening, DCI Clay.'

They stopped at the door and PC Rodgers moved aside. Doctor Ellington knocked lightly, waited for a few moments and opened it. Clay stepped into the open doorway and saw Raymond Dare's back; his face was turned to the wall behind his bed. His pyjama top was wet with sweat and clung to his back. He squatted on the bed with his elbows jutting out and his hands pressed down on the pillow.

'I called you here, DCI Clay, because I thought this could be relevant to your investigation. Raymond?'

The silence in the room seemed to drift from the walls, floor and ceiling and for a moment, Clay wondered if Raymond had drifted into suspended animation.

Clay walked deeper into the room, her eyes drawn to the floor where dozens of fat felt-tip pens littered the floor, their caps discarded randomly.

'Look behind you, DCI Clay, at the wall beside the door.'

Clay turned and wondered if she was hallucinating through sheer exhaustion and stress. On the wall was a huge image made up of thousands of points of colour, felt-tipped dots and dashes, intricate and stunning in its detail. She took out her iPhone and captured images of the whole painting, then close-up pictures of the sections.

'Is this relevant to your investigation, DCI Clay?'

'It's early days. It could be.'

Clay stepped back and drank in the large image of a pair of young men, both wearing designer jackets with their hoods up, casting their faces into shadow. They each wore tracksuit bottoms and designer trainers. The youth to the left carried a Kalashnikov in one hand and a massive smoking joint in the other. The teenager beside him had an outstretched arm and open hand in which there were many tablets – ecstasy and speed. His other hand pointed up in the air, the middle finger of his clenched fist raised in stark defiance.

'Who are they?' asked Doctor Ellington.

'I'm going to answer your question because I believe you'll need to know for clinical reasons. It's his imaginary friends, CJ and Buster. Please don't convey that information to anyone unless you have to for clinical reasons.'

'Raymond, you have a visitor,' said Doctor Ellington. 'Are you going to turn around and say hello?'

He didn't move a muscle.

Above their heads there was writing.

RIP Raymond Dare 2003–2020.

Clay noticed details in the shadowy space where their faces should have been. As she moved closer, a shiver ran through her as she recognised two halves of a face painted in the darkness, framed by their two hoods. In the hood to the left was the left side of Raymond's face, and in the hood to the right was the right-hand side of his face.

She looked at the writing across their hearts. 'CJ.' And then she read the next name. 'Buster.'

Clay took a picture of their names and their single face, then turned to face the bed.

'CJ and Buster,' said Clay.

Staying in the same posture, Raymond Dare started to turn around.

'CJ and Buster,' repeated Clay, two names that accelerated his turning until he faced her, still squatting on the bed.

Raymond's face was alive with multicoloured felt-tip dots that turned from one thing into another along a dead vertical centre from his hairline down the centre of his nose and to his chin. The surface of his face was no longer his own. He had used pointillism to make the left-hand side of his face that of Jasmine and the right-hand side that of Jack.

Raymond pointed at the left-hand side and said, 'Jasmine.' He pointed at the right and said, 'Jack.'

Clay looked around the room and saw there were no mirrors.

'We've moved back in,' said Raymond, in a voice that sounded like it had fallen from Jack's mouth. 'We're all together again, a small but happy family. Raymond's soul has left to join CJ and Buster in the underworld. Do you get it, Clay?'

'I get it.'

'Where do you get it?'

She pointed at her right temple, but Raymond shook his head.

'Where do you get it?'

'Tell me. Tell me, where I should get it?' The closeness of his voice to Jack's made her scalp crawl. She looked into the glaze of his half-closed eyes, a doorway into a bizarre inner world and wondered if he would ever truly return to the real world around him.

He whispered, and she walked closer to him. 'Did you get that?' he asked. 'The answer to a question you once asked me. I am Jasmine and I am Jack and we live in the body that Raymond Dare left behind. You'd better get that into your soul.'

Epilogue

It was five past four. Looking at the clock above the reception desk, Eve saw she had been waiting for ten minutes for Sister Ruth to appear.

She sat between Thomas and Philip, who was still in his school uniform and growing increasingly restless.

'It's been ages we've been waiting,' whispered Philip. 'And it's so quiet in here.'

'Be patient, Philip,' said Thomas. 'This is important for your mum.'

Clay saw Jane McGregor, the home's duty manager, walking down the stairs towards them. Clay looked around the reception of the modern purpose-built care facility and wondered if she was sitting on a seat once occupied by Aaron or Lucy Bell.

'She's ready to see you now. She was napping when you arrived and she's a little slow to wake up. She is getting old.' Jane eyed up Thomas and Philip. 'Sister Ruth has said she wants to have a private chat with you, Eve.'

'Are you OK with that, boys?' asked Eve.

'We've got a games room with a snooker table,' said Jane. Philip brightened up immediately. 'You two come with me then. Eve, when you get to the top of the stairs, take a left and her room's the third door along.'

As she walked up the stairs, Eve felt the onset of nerves. She hoped that the private conversation would be positive, though she knew that whatever emerged, it was all in the past and beyond repair.

She knocked on Sister Ruth's door and heard her say, 'Come in, Eve.'

The elderly nun was sitting up in bed and the smile on her face when Eve entered told her that her nerves had been misplaced.

'Have a seat.'

Eve pulled up a chair and faced Sister Ruth. 'Thank you for agreeing to see me.'

'No, thank *you* for coming to see *me*, Eve.' Sister Ruth held her hand out and Clay held onto it, felt the thinness of her skin and the bird-like frailty of the bones beneath it.

'It's strange to think that you live here in Dundonald Road and I live five minutes away in Mersey Road. How long have you lived here?' Clay asked.

'Six years.'

'I had no idea you were so close.'

'Well, we know now,' Sister Ruth smiled. 'I can still see the little girl in your eyes, the little girl who lived at St Claire's all those years ago.'

Her eyes closed slowly and Clay thought she was going to drift off to sleep. She opened her eyes and said, 'I have two things to give you and a piece of information that I hope will gladden your heart. If you open the locker beside my bed, the things I have for you are there. I say they're from me but they're from Sister Philomena really, God rest her soul.'

Clay opened the locker door but the only thing on the shelf inside was a very old black leather Bible.

'Take it out, Eve.'

As she did so, Eve saw there was something stuck between the first few pages of the Old Testament.

'Open it near the front, the very first page in.'

Underneath the words *The Holy Bible* was cursive writing, blue words formed from a fountain pen.

Clay turned hot at the centre of her being and the heat spread to her entire skin. 'This is Sister Philomena's handwriting, isn't it, Sister Ruth?'

'She surely was neat. What does it say?'

'It says, Ruth Chapter 1, Verse 16.'

'You'll easily find it – there's a book mark of sorts at the opening of Ruth.' As Clay opened the Bible, Sister Ruth said, 'Naomi was left without a husband or sons, the husbands of Orpah and Ruth. She told her widowed daughters-in-law to go back to their own land, their own people, their own gods. After many tears and much protesting, Orpah left, but Ruth stayed with Naomi. Read what Ruth said to Naomi, Eve. Chapter 1, Verse 16.'

'*But Ruth replied,*' Clay read, '*Do not urge me to leave thee or turn back from thee. Where thou goest, I will go and where thou stayest, I will stay. Thy people will be my people and thy God will be my God.*'

'When I left St Claire's,' said Sister Ruth, 'Sister Philomena gave me two Bibles. One was for me; the other one, which is in your hands, was for you. She asked me to mind it for you, to give it to you before I died.'

As Clay reread the verse, she lost all sense of time. In her mind, seconds became minutes and minutes hours. She watched Sister Ruth drifting in and out of sleep and remembered what she was like as a young nun, constantly cheerful as she followed Sister Philomena's instructions.

Her eyes flicked open and Clay asked, 'What did you do after you left St Claire's, Sister Ruth?'

'I spent the rest of my working life in children's homes. Sister Philomena was an excellent teacher. When I acted on her advice down the years, something good always came of it.'

'It was a shame, in one way,' replied Clay. 'That she didn't have children of her own.'

'Well… there's a thing. I don't know if it's true, but a story did get out that before she took Holy Orders, she was married with a daughter. The story went that her husband and daughter died in the Blitz. I never spoke to her about it directly. Some people

believed it. Some dismissed it as the work of gossips. But let's talk
of something we know is definitely true. Sister Philomena knew
in her heart you'd never leave her, and she wants you to know in
your heart that the same is true for her. She loves you very much,
Eve, and death and the gathering years can do nothing to stop
that love. I'm glad we met. I'm happy to pass this on to you.'

Sister Ruth held out her hand. As Clay held onto it, she closed
her eyes briefly, and a buried memory from St Claire's played
out inside her head as if it were happening now. Looking over
her shoulder, Eve shrieked with delight as Sister Ruth chased her
down the back garden and Sister Philomena laughed in the
kitchen doorway.

Clay opened her eyes and watched Sister Ruth's eyes close
over, heard the thickening of her breathing as she drifted off to
sleep. She watched her sinking further away, then flicked through
the pages of the Bible.

Face down against the final verses of Judges was a photograph.
Clay turned it over.

It was a black and white image of Sister Ruth standing over
Sister Philomena, who was sitting in a chair with a little girl aged
four or five on her knee. The little girl was Eve.

Sister Philomena looked down on Eve with a smile as broad
as the one Eve wore looking up at her. It was a portrait of two
women and one little girl – but more than this, to Eve Clay's eyes
it was a picture of unconditional love.

Eve Clay withdrew her hand from Sister Ruth's and made a
silent promise to come again soon and visit her. Quietly, she stood
up and left the room, walking down the stairs with the Bible
and photograph in her hand. She followed the sound of snooker
balls cannoning off each other and arrived at the entrance of the
games room.

Thomas looked across and said, 'Shall we wind up now, Philip?'

'You're only saying that because I'm beating you,' replied
Philip, standing on a box and aiming the white ball at the last
pair of balls on the table.

'No, take your time, boys, finish your game.'

Thomas grinned, 'Yes, but you're not allowed to use your hands to guide the balls into the pockets.' He smiled at Eve. 'How did it go?'

She opened the Bible and showed him Sister Philomena's handwriting, then the Bible itself and the photograph.

'That's it. I've won.' Philip left the cue on the snooker table and wandered over to his parents.

'Have you seen this, Philip?' asked Eve. She showed him the photograph.

'Is that you?'

'Yes, it is, with Sister Philomena.'

'And, is that other nun the one you've been to visit?'

'That's right.'

Philip took the photograph from his mother and looked at it. After much scrutiny, he said, 'Obviously you're a girl and I'm a boy… but… we look really like each other, Mum.'

'Have you told him yet?' Eve asked Thomas.

'Told me what yet?'

'You know how your cricket got out of its box and escaped from the house?' said Thomas.

'That was bad, that.'

'Well…' said Thomas, 'your mum thought we could get a dog.'

Philip's eyes filled with light and he looked at them with astonishment and joy. He threw his arms around both of them and said, 'I love you both so much.'

Clay smiled back at her son as he looked up at her and took a picture with her mind, a picture that echoed the love and happiness in the black and white photograph that Sister Ruth had just given her.

'Who are you two looking at?' she asked.

'You, Mum,' laughed Philip.

'*And just who am I*?' She thought for a second. 'I am the luckiest woman in the world.'